HEART'S ORDERS

By the Author

Basic Training of the Heart

Heart's Orders

HEART'S ORDERS

by
Jaycie Morrison

2017

HEART'S ORDERS

ISBN 13: 978-1-63555-073-3

This Trade Paperback Original Is Published By
Bold Strokes Books, Inc.
P.O. Box 249
Valley Falls, NY 12185

First Edition: October 2017

CREDITS
EDITOR: RUTH STERNGLANTZ
PRODUCTION DESIGN: STACIA SEAMAN
COVER DESIGN BY JENNA ALBRIGHT

Acknowledgments

With the publication of this, my second novel, I have a new group that I'd like to acknowledge—my readers. I'm deeply grateful for the support of those of you who already knew me, appreciative of those folks with whom I've exchanged a few words in person or online, and beholden to the ones who took a chance on a new, unknown author. And my special thanks to everyone who took the time to write and post a review. Any author will tell you how highly your responses are valued.

Parts of this story make reference to a journey that all of us take at some point, although the duration of our travels will vary, and we may arrive at profoundly different destinations. Wherever you may find yourself before, during, or after your passage, I hope each of you finds comfort and peace along the way.

I'd also like to express my gratitude to the brain trust of Bold Strokes Books, who continue to produce outstanding LGBT literature, and my fellow authors who have provided friendship, laughs, and inspiration. Again, I send a special nod to Ruth S., editor extraordinaire. I truly appreciate the time you take pushing, teaching, and occasionally indulging me, and I freely admit how much I need every bit of it.

Charles Dickens wrote, "A loving heart is the truest wisdom." This is for my friends and family and for that God- (or goddess)-shaped piece of my heart, all of whom have made me more loving...and hopefully wiser.

And to my most beloved wife, with whom I have been better and worse, richer and poorer, healthy and sick, but always having and holding. Happy anniversary, my love.

CHAPTER ONE

Golden Pond, Kentucky
September 10, 1931

Helen squatted beside the road with her head down. Her mama had been sad again this morning, and sometimes that sadness seemed to trickle right through into her own heart. She knew it had to do with the new little brother or little sister that Mama was supposed to be having. Four times now, and each time there was that scary quiet in the house before her mama would start to wailing and shedding tears, which would then go on for days and days and days. The first two times, when she was too little to help with most of the chores, her daddy had told her that being a good girl was the best thing she could do. Now she was big enough to light the fire in the mornings and sweep the floors and help her brother fetch the water. But no matter how good she was or how much she tried to help, her mama's morning hugs and good-night kisses had turned into nothing but a scarce pat on the head now and then. More frequently what she got was a swat on the behind for something she hadn't done good enough or didn't even know she was supposed to be doing. When her brother Sinclair tried to stand up for her, Mama would start screaming and they'd learned it was better to just leave. They'd stay gone until their bellies were growling with hunger and then they'd creep back, only to find the house empty. Or sometimes, if Mama was still around, she'd act like nothing had happened for a while and then the whole business would start over again. Just thinking about it made the prick of tears start up in her eyes, until the approaching sound of a whining engine made her head come up. *There he is. Run!*

The dry dirt of the road came up in little puffs from under her bare feet. She tugged at her worn, shapeless shift when it rose up her thighs as her pace increased. If she didn't catch Mr. Hall before his truck shifted gears again, it would be moving faster than she could go. Then she wouldn't get to ride with him and she'd have to go to school instead. The very thought made her pump her arms a little faster. The kids at school had started teasing her about the way her mama fixed herself up when she went into town these days. She didn't quite understand it all, but she knew it was bad because of the way the older kids laughed. It was something about Mama getting money from the payroll man at the Pearcy Coal Mine. But that didn't make no sense, because while her daddy and just about every other man in town worked for Pearcy, her mama didn't. Her brother Sinclair told her it weren't nobody's business since Mama always had dinner ready for them when her daddy got off shift, and that right there proved she was a good wife and mother. But Sinclair was older, bigger, and good with his fists, so no one never said nothing to him anyway.

Now that she could see herself in Mr. Hall's side mirror, she hollered out his name and waved. When the truck slowed and Mr. Hall's arm motioned her forward, the weight of sadness lifted off her like the way dynamite could blow a big stone clean off the mountain. She saw him slip that small bottle into his pocket as she came around the passenger side and hopped up on the running board. "Doncha need some help today, Mr. Hall?" she asked, a little breathless.

She knew he did, even if he didn't want to say so. They'd both seen how folks a little farther away from town tended to be more skittish when an older man in uniform came to their door. But a friendly little girl like her could hop out, put the mail on their porch with a wave, and be back in the truck before anyone got disturbed.

The postman cocked his head a little. "Ain't you supposed to be in school, Helen?"

Her gut tightened but she made sure to keep her best smile in place. "Nah. I'm doing so good the teacher give me the day off."

She figured he knew it was a lie, but he'd been the one to teach her about how that was sometimes necessary. Like how she couldn't never, ever tell anyone that she helped him with his Postal Service deliveries or say anything about the little bottle that he pulled on from time to time when he thought she didn't see him. The most important thing to her was that he not be lying about his promise to teach her to drive when she got tall enough to reach the pedals and the steering wheel both. That and those special occasions when her daddy would take her and her brother to visit with her Aunt Darcy and Mrs. Murrell in their tidy little house in town were the things she most looked forward to in life.

❖

Fort Des Moines, Iowa
September 10, 1944

The way it was with Helen Tucker had happened so gradually that Tee wasn't sure how to explain it. Not like she would even try. To anyone, ever. 'Cause what scared her the most was how right it felt. Like natural, almost. But of course it wasn't. It was wrong and evil and sinful as anything. You couldn't live your whole life as a good Baptist girl and not know that. Now, Helen didn't care what the Bible said. Tee remembered how shocked she'd been when Helen declared that she wasn't a believer, that she'd never given her life to Jesus or hardly even been inside a church at all. But even knowing that, Tee had secretly found Helen's bold, daring manner inspiring and almost... exciting, in a way. As far as she could tell, the rest of the girls in her squad liked Helen, too, and were willing to allow for her occasional heated outbursts. In fact, they seemed to respect her disposition to say or do exactly what was on her mind, especially since she had so far managed to stay just this side of insubordination. No one like that had ever wanted to be her friend before, and Tee had been proud that Helen had saved her the next bunk over when they first got to the barracks and almost always sat by her in the mess hall and in classes. When the gradual thing first started happening, Tee had thought it was just part of becoming someone's best friend. Lots of girls held hands at some time, didn't they? And when they'd both passed their first test, that long, tight hug of celebration had felt just wonderful. But she hadn't thought there was anything unusual about that either.

She remembered Helen from her first moments at Fort Des Moines. Thinking back about their arrival, she shuddered, remembering how the drill instructor who first greeted them was so mean, screaming at her because she wasn't answering fast enough. The stocky Sergeant Moore had made a very unkind remark about Helen, too, just because she was thin and, well, the coal dust under her fingernails did make her look a little dirty. Luckily for them all, Sergeant Rains had come along and taken over and Tee had been able to get enough words out to answer what was being asked of her. Sergeant Rains was just as intimidating in her own way, with her piercing black eyes and black hair and serious command presence, but they soon learned that she was firm but fair, and genuinely interested in helping each of them succeed in the Women's Army Corps. After Helen introduced herself, she'd looked straight at Tee and said that maybe being in the Army would help them not always be depending on someone else, even if they were girls. Tee hadn't had the nerve to answer her, but she'd managed a slight smile.

That day, even before they got settled in and started learning the routines of the camp and about being soldiers, Sergeant Rains had told them that they would become like a family. Tee hadn't been sure if that would be a good thing or not, but so far, it had been. For one thing, they ate a lot more regularly than her family had lately. The food was real good and there was plenty of it with no sign of anything being rationed. Tee also liked the way their days were arranged for them, so that they knew exactly where they were supposed to be and no one would get mad at them as long as they followed the rules. Some evenings they even had a little time for themselves, and most of her squad mates were already finding other things to do, like going to one of the bars or the movies, or joining a club or an organization that interested them. Tee hadn't ever joined anything other than the church, so she just wrote letters home as she listened to the chatter around her, until her new friend Helen had struck up a conversation. They seemed to have a lot in common, and pretty soon she and Helen were talking about any and everything, Helen waiting with surprising patience as she stammered over her words. Tee had pretty much decided she was going to enjoy being a soldier, in spite of what some of the folks back home had said about women being in the Army.

But when their classes started, Tee was afraid that she might not get to stay in the WAC after all, because she couldn't seem to keep up. Not doing very well at their assignments and tests was one more thing that she and Helen shared. Luckily, Sergeant Rains assigned Bett Smythe, the smart college girl, to help them both with their studies. Bett was nice and patient and better at explaining their lessons than a lot of the instructors. Once Tee began to catch on better and was able to stop feeling so anxious all the time, she began to notice that Helen always brushed her teeth or put on a clean shirt or made sure to comb her hair back out of her eyes when it was time for them to meet with Bett for tutoring. Tee started wondering if Helen would rather have Bett as her best friend, and it gave her an awful ache inside. Bett was beautiful and smart, whereas Tee was slow in lots of ways and nothing special to look at. She'd been told both of those things plenty of times. When that thought about Helen and Bett got settled in her head, she couldn't stop feeling down and the lump in her throat made it even harder to talk, so she didn't.

After two days, Helen pulled her aside one night as they were walking back from dinner.

"What's the matter with you?" she'd demanded impatiently.

Tee had turned away, shaking her head. She didn't like it when Helen got mad. It made her think of her daddy and the way he'd yell when it hadn't rained enough or it rained too much or there was too much wind to plant or the mule went lame or any one of three dozen other things that would upset him. But Helen didn't get madder this time. Without another word, she'd taken Tee's hand and pulled her along until they got to the bleachers at the deserted parade grounds. There, she'd pointed insistently, so Tee sat.

Helen straddled the bench and faced her, her voice forceful. "Tell me what's wrong."

When Tee only looked down, Helen put her hand on Tee's cheek, very carefully raising her face. Her voice had changed to match the touch. The anger was completely absent, and only sweetness remained. "Please, Tee. I hate it when you're unhappy. You gotta let me know what I did so I can try to fix it."

The thought of explaining it all in words was exhausting, so she simply stammered out Bett's name.

Helen stood up, her fists clenched. "What about her? Was she mean? Did Bett say something that upset you?"

Tee put her hand on Helen's arm to pull her back down, almost smiling. "Nuh-uh. She—she's just so…pretty." Her head lowered again and her voice was softer, even through the sputtering sounds of her words. "I know you like her better than me."

Helen's mouth opened a little and she sat back a bit, as if she was surprised. Tee risked a quick glance, hoping that reaction wouldn't change to irritation. To her relief, Helen's mouth stretched into a grin.

"Look, Tee. Bett's a doll, all right? And yeah, maybe I put on the dog for her a little bit, okay? But it don't mean nothin'." She took Tee's hand again. "You were brave to tell me that. So I'm gonna be brave, too. I'm gonna tell you something that you might not like to hear. But I'm gonna hope that maybe, just maybe, it'll be all right."

Tee wanted to close her eyes. Her mama always closed her eyes when her daddy was telling her bad news. But then Helen had taken her other hand, too, and that alone made the moment suddenly feel too important not to watch.

"You're not only my best friend, Tee." Helen took in a long breath. "You're the person I most want to see, the one I most want to be with. You're special to me." She let the rest of her breath out. "I have those kinds of feelings for you. Is that all right?"

For a moment, Tee thought she might cry. She didn't think Helen was the type to say such nice things to someone. And here she'd said it to plain, stuttering Teresa Owens from Haskett, Oklahoma. Helen was looking at her really hard, like she was trying to see what Tee was thinking.

"Please, say somethin', Tee."

Tee swallowed hard, trying to choke back the stream of emotions—relief, excitement, joy. *Helen still likes me best.* She put her hands on Helen's face, the way her mama did to her when she was trying to soothe a hurt. "Okay," was all she could manage, but Helen's smile let her know it was enough.

After that, it seemed like one thing just led to another. They'd started sitting a little closer, touching a little more often, and then those touches turned into soft petting strokes. Sometimes Helen's touch made her want to curl up in her lap and purr like a cat. But recently, more and more, she felt a wanting for something else, something beyond Helen's fingers on her arm or hand on her thigh. She'd liked it when they'd started hugging for no real reason at all, although when her body got close with Helen's, it made her feel both settled in and wound up at the same time. It was during one of those hugs that Helen first kissed her. It was just a little brush of lips, almost like an accident. They were close to the same height but when they hugged, Tee liked to rest her head on Helen's shoulder, facing into her neck. They seemed to fit that way, and she never thought another thing about it until Helen's mouth had turned into hers for that quick instant. Tee would have been upset—*should have been upset*, she corrected herself—but Helen's lips were so soft and it had only lasted a second. There hadn't been much kissing in her home, but she'd kissed each of her three older sisters on their wedding days, so she tried putting that in her mind. Yes, Helen was her best friend and her WAC sister, so it was okay to think of Helen as family.

Until the next time. On a Saturday night when they both declined another offer to join some of the girls and their escorts at the NCO club and had taken a walk around the base together instead. Tee's insides got real stiff when she realized where Helen was leading her. Everyone said that corner of the base they called the grove was a make-out place after dark, and good girls would never let someone take them there. Why would Helen be headed in that direction, unless…? She let Helen's words from before come back into her mind. *I have those kinds of feelings for you.* Was she suggesting something more than friend feelings? Suddenly Tee wasn't sure what anything meant, and her heart began pounding like the way it did when she was fearful.

Her mind flashed to the time when she'd been most frightened in her life. They were still calling her Teresa then, and that was the name that her daddy hollered out that time that he'd come into the barn and found their hired man working his zipper down as he pushed her face toward the bulge in his pants. The look on her daddy's face still hurt her when she thought about it, and her daddy didn't even know this wasn't the first time.

About six months before, she'd been putting the chicken feed bucket away in the little tack room when Morris Gallagher had come in behind her and shut the door. The room was small and he was close. Real close. Too close. She told him she wanted out and he'd nodded, putting his hand on the door like he was fixin' to open it. Then he'd clenched his teeth, wincing like he was in pain. Teresa hated to see any kind of suffering, and Mr. Gallagher knew it. He knew she was the one who found homes for the two kittens that their barn cat had so her daddy wouldn't get rid of them in the creek. He'd seen her mothering those baby chicks and petting the new calf that their milk cow had birthed. When he'd seen her crying over the paralyzed little rabbit that had gotten its hindquarters caught in the thresher, Mr. Gallagher was the one who'd offered to put it out of its misery for her. The rabbit had been screaming as it writhed helplessly and when Teresa began to cry, he'd pulled her to him, patting her awkwardly and telling her she was just too tenderhearted.

After that, he'd always been real nice to her, telling her how she was comely or kind or had a beautiful singing voice. Now he said, "I just need you to do something to stop me from hurtin', pretty girl. And I know you'll want to help, 'cause you're sweet that way."

She'd stopped moving toward the door and asked him what it was he wanted. "You know how your mama will knead your daddy's shoulders when he's tired, and sometimes he'll massage her feet after she's been on them all day?" Teresa didn't really remember either of these things actually happening, but she could imagine them, the way Mr. Gallagher described it, so she'd nodded. "Well, I got this muscle here that's swollen bad." He'd run his hand over the front of his pants. "And I think if you'd just rub on it a little for me, it would get all better."

Everything in her had gone real still, and she could feel a tug-of-war going on inside her. She'd been around animals all her life, and even though she didn't have any brothers, she was pretty sure this was a private place on a man. But then he'd taken her hand and kissed it gently before putting it there on his body where she would feel something hard under his jeans. "Uh-huh," he'd grunted, leaning back against the door, his eyes closed. "That's helping me a lot." Teresa wasn't so sure that was true, because the hard place didn't seem to be getting any softer. When he made a groaning sound, she tried to move her hand away, but he'd covered it with his, showing her how he wanted it done. "Just a little harder, pretty girl," he told her, his voice hoarse. "That's it. A little faster now. Good…good…good. Yeah." After a bit he'd let out a long kinda grunting sound and breathed a few shaky breaths. "That's my girl," he said after a minute. As she was noticing how there was some wet on his pants now and a strange new scent was drifting around the tack room, he'd stroked her hair. "You did good." Then he held the door and said, "You go on out now, and remember—you're my special doctor. You can't tell nobody else, hear?"

About two weeks later it had happened again. Even though she'd secretly liked the idea of being a doctor, Teresa wasn't so sure that Mr. Gallagher was truly hurting. Actually, whenever she thought about what had happened, she felt kinda sickly herself. So she'd been real careful not to be alone with him, but he'd snuck in behind her that next time. She'd tried to tell him no, but that was the time when her words first started sticking in her throat and wouldn't come out even and smooth like normal people. Not even that one word. *No.* She'd started shaking her head, but then Mr. Gallagher had looked so hurt and disappointed. He'd begged her, telling her how much it hurt and how she was the only one who had ever helped him that way. When he took her hand and put it there, like he'd done before, she felt powerless, like an animal caught in a trap.

Another time, he'd tried to reach for her as she rubbed him, but she'd stopped, backed away as much as possible, and managed to say no. He'd cornered her then, and that begging look he'd had before changed to something threatening. "If you don't want me to touch you, that's fine. But you'll finish what you started, pretty girl, if you know what's good for you." After that, she'd tried to avoid going into the tack room at all, but then her daddy yelled at her for not putting things back where they belonged, adding if it weren't for their hired man, their whole place would fall apart. That night she wondered if it was possible for a person to fall apart if they got things inside them that didn't belong.

Each occurrence with Mr. Gallagher made her feel worse and worse, but she didn't know what to do to make it stop. The next time, when he'd unzipped his pants, she'd hidden her face in her hands and started to cry. He'd stormed out, but later he'd made sure she saw him holding up Lula Belle, the puppy she'd gotten for her birthday, while his hands twisted around like he was going to wring her neck. So there had been twice more where she closed her eyes and tried to think of anything else. Once she'd been able to sing hymns in her own head loudly enough to cover up his noises, but the second time he'd gotten closer and she could feel his body bumping up against her, but she couldn't move away 'cause he'd grabbed her shoulders, while he groaned bad words right next to her ear. When they were done, he'd said, "I think next time you might need to kiss it to make it all better. What do you think about that, pretty girl?"

She thought she'd never been so fretful. It seemed like her stomach hurt all the time, and even her mama had noticed there was something wrong with her speaking voice. They'd prayed about it at church but it didn't help. Teresa wondered if it was because she couldn't find the words to confess her terrible secret that nothing else would come out right neither. She felt like that little paralyzed rabbit, thrashing about helplessly, unable to run or hide—and she couldn't even scream. Desperate to give herself a way out the next time, she had pried a nail out of a board in their plow horse's stall and hammered it in crooked on the tack room door frame, leaving a bend in it so the door wouldn't close all the way. But Mr. Gallagher was so pleased with himself for having caught her in the tack room again so soon that he didn't even notice about the door. Maybe her daddy just happened by and saw that door not closing right or maybe he heard something that he knew didn't belong there, but sometimes Teresa pretended that the Lord chose to look down right then and decided to help her. And even though Lonnie Owens had run Mr. Gallagher off that very minute, he'd made it clear that Teresa had done something terrible, too, something that had made their hired man treat her that way, as if she'd encouraged him to put his big rough hands on her or had wanted to hear his wheedling voice that would sound so encouraging at first and then listen to him grunting like some animal in heat at the end of it. "It would break your mama's heart if she knew about this," was the last thing her daddy told her before he walked away in disgust. So that was where the secret stayed. And when her talking never really got any better, the family started calling her Tee, meaning it as a joke at first, but then it stuck.

She didn't really blame her daddy for being mad at her. She'd heard often enough how hard it was trying to run a farm with nothing but four worthless daughters to help him, even though they'd all tried to do their part. She'd just turned sixteen when Mr. Gallagher left. Her older sisters had all gotten married off already, but none of their men were interested in helping on the Owenses' land. Teresa didn't know if Mr. Gallagher had told the men in the town about their times in the tack room, but when she was at school, none of the boys her age seemed to want anything to do with her, with her sticking words and her shy ways. Even at church, boys would just barely acknowledge her and then keep walking. And if truth be told, she was just as glad. It upset her terribly if she even thought about a boy wanting her to do the same things that Mr. Gallagher had. About the time her mama had started fussing in earnest about her needing to get wed, the war had come and then there weren't many men around anyway. Tee hadn't minded the idea of being her mama's baby a little longer, but once they'd lost the farm and moved into town, it was obvious she was going to have to do something more to help out.

There'd been a lot of discouraging talk about her joining the WAC at home and in town, but she really hadn't had much trouble adjusting. It was probably because she'd been raised mostly in the company of women and had always felt more comfortable with them than around men. Which led her to thinking about why her feelings for Helen had seemed so familiar at first. Good. Safe. Happy. Nothing about their being together had ever worried her until recently, when she'd begun to realize that those feelings had gradually gotten much stronger than anything she'd ever felt for one of her real sisters. Sometimes, like now, it worried her, how important it was. It wasn't just nice to be with Helen, or fun. It had become something almost…necessary.

As they got closer and closer to the tall trees that made up the grove, Helen must have felt her starting to draw back, 'cause she said, "Look, Tee. I just want us to be somewhere that we won't keep gettin' interrupted. We'll just sit here on the outside edge of this place, put our backs to these nice trees, and talk for a while, okay?"

Tee had nodded with relief, except then Helen led her another few steps before turning to face her. Even in the dusky light, Tee could see something unusual in Helen's eyes. Part fear and part…she wasn't sure what. But she knew she didn't like seeing Helen scared, so she'd stepped closer and put her arms around Helen's shoulders, patting her back lightly.

"S'okay," she whispered, liking the little sigh that Helen made as her arms came around Tee's waist.

They stood like that for a minute, their bodies molding to each other. The bad memories that had been in her mind faded away and Tee relaxed into the closeness that had become so familiar. Warm and soft and sweet. Easy. Then Helen's hands stroked slowly up and down her sides, making her want to wiggle with pleasure. Her insides felt tickly and she pressed closer in response.

"Tee." Helen's voice was a little bit breathless. "Tell me if this doesn't feel as good to you as it does to me."

But when Tee opened her mouth to speak, only a shaky little *ah* sound came out. Helen's head turned into her and Helen's lips pressed onto her neck. Helen's warm breath mixed with the slight wetness of her mouth to create the most incredible sensation that Tee had ever known. The pressure of Helen's motions streaked into her belly and somehow made its way down between her thighs. As if reading Tee's mind, Helen shifted slightly so her leg was there to meet that feeling. When Helen's body began moving slightly against hers, Tee's arms tightened and she heard herself make that sound again.

Then Helen's mouth was at her ear and she whispered, "Sometimes I stare at your mouth all day, just wondering what it would be like to really kiss you. Would you let me find out, Tee? Could I kiss you right now?"

Tee had lifted her face to say no, but Helen was already leaning toward her and that friction that was happening even through their clothes had made Tee's lips part just a bit, and Helen must have seen that because she didn't stop. Their lips met and it was soft like before but not quick. No, not quick at all. It was slow and deep, and for a minute, Tee only knew that she didn't want it to end. She didn't know anything about kissing, really, so she just imitated Helen's movements and when Helen made her own sound of pleasure, she felt so pleased with herself that she let it go on and on. Dimly, she was aware they were both breathing faster, but then she didn't think about that anymore because a little flick of Helen's tongue had played across her lips and that same streak of warmth shot through her, all the way down to her feet. A wild vision danced behind her eyes as one of Helen's hands stroked slowly down her back, pulling her closer—the two of them naked, lying together while doing these same things to each other. She pulled back with a gasp.

"I want—" Tee stopped the words because the rest of the thought was too outlandish to speak out loud. But she couldn't stop picturing Helen's nakedness, her body's lean, tight lines and small, firm breasts. There was no such thing as privacy living in a barracks with so many other women on the same schedule from morning till night, so of course they'd seen each other's bodies. During the very first week she'd felt embarrassed when she'd caught Helen admiring her full bosoms, until Helen had grinned and told her she looked like a woman was supposed to. Now, arching under Helen's touch, she brought her hand to Helen's chest, amazed as a hard, tight peak rose right through the material and pressed against her palm. Curious, Tee tried the same thing with the other breast, but the nipple there was already hard. Helen groaned and

Tee felt a strange sense of power. She imagined herself strong enough to rip Helen's shirt open and bold enough to put her mouth there, sucking on her small breasts until Helen begged her—

"God, Tee," Helen said hoarsely, cupping her bottom as they both moved in time to her rhythmic massage.

The tempo matched something building deep inside Tee, until Helen's utterance penetrated her reeling mind.

God. What would God think of what they were doing? Tee pressed both hands against Helen's shoulders and pushed lightly. Shuddering at the loss of contact, she managed just one word. "Wait."

Helen gripped Tee's waist and held her at arm's length as she steadied herself, head down. They were both still breathing roughly. "I'm sorry. I'm so sorry, Tee. I never meant to take you that far. You just—you feel so good to me." She looked up into Tee's eyes. "Forgive me?"

Tee's insides deflated like the skin of a balloon when all the air had been let out. Part of her wanted to blow it back up, to keep on blowing until the thing popped, but the sound of a popping balloon had never failed to startle her, so that must not be a good idea. She shook her head, trying to bring some sense back to her swirling thoughts.

Helen let her hands drop from Tee's waist, clenching them at her sides. "Please, Tee. I know I must have scared you, but I really didn't mean to. I just—I let myself go crazy." She blew out a breath and Tee thought she might have seen the glint of tears in her eyes. "I'm really sorry if I upset you," she repeated softly.

Tee wasn't sure what to say, but she couldn't let Helen take all the blame. She'd let Helen do the things she'd done, and if she was honest, she knew she'd even encouraged her. But the main thing, what mattered most, was that Helen had stopped when Tee asked her to. She wouldn't force her to do something she didn't want to do. Helen wasn't like Mr. Gallagher.

"Okay," she said. "But you m-mustn't…" She couldn't finish and resorted to making a gesture between them.

To her surprise, Helen smiled that roguish grin, the one that usually meant she was up to no good. She stepped back in a little closer and took Tee's hands. "Honestly, Tee, I can't say I won't try again sometime."

As if in response, Tee's rebellious heart began beating more quickly again.

Helen's eyes met hers and her smile widened. "Because I didn't hear you say *no*. I heard you say *wait*. So I will promise to do that."

Tee couldn't answer. Even if her words could have flowed as smooth as honey, she had no idea what to say. Helen seemed to know something about her that she hadn't even known herself. She remembered her mama's words when they'd dropped her at the train station to come here. *You remember who you are, Teresa Owens. Don't let them Army folks make you into something you ain't.* Were these new feelings about Helen part of what she already was, or were they something she wasn't? She shivered a bit and Helen's expression turned sympathetic.

Helen rubbed Tee's shoulders, as if she was trying to warm her during a cold spell. "Don't worry, Tee. Everything's gonna be all right, hear?"

After a few seconds, she turned, and Tee automatically followed as they started back toward the barracks. Tee could hear the smile in Helen's voice as she said, "If you don't distract me next time, I wanna tell you about my Aunt Darcy."

CHAPTER TWO

Private Tucker?" The voice was quiet but she still jumped. Helen had been wallowing pretty deep in her own misery for the last two days, the image of Tee's stiff back moving quickly away after she had not only told her *no*, but added *never again*, playing over and over in her thoughts. Now she didn't have to look up to know who was speaking. Over the last few weeks she'd gotten to know that voice really well. She'd even come to respect Sergeant Rains, if not actually like her, so she sure didn't want to think about how their drill instructor must see her now. Pervert. Queer. Dyke. Lesbo.

Dreading what was coming, she stood quickly at attention, keeping her eyes focused in the distance as she'd been taught. "Yes, ma'am." She hadn't talked to their drill instructor privately since Sergeant Rains had done her the biggest favor of her life. Or so it had seemed at the time. Now that things were definitely over between her and Tee, she sometimes wondered if it would have been better if they'd both gotten kicked out of the WAC. Maybe they'd still be together. At the thought, her insides about seized up again and she clenched her fists, trying to make the pain go away. She surely hadn't found the answer in the drinking she'd done last night. Liquor only made her head hurt almost as much as her heart. At least she'd passed out right after CQ and hadn't had to toss and turn like she'd done the night before. The night everything changed between her and Tee.

"I'd like to speak with you about an opportunity that's come up. Would you walk with me?"

That was a surprise, but Helen stood, nodding, and they started off, falling into a comfortable rhythm. Another thing she'd always liked about her sergeant was that the woman seemed to understand that sometimes you just needed to move. Some people wanted to spend every available moment on their backsides, but Sergeant Rains wasn't like that. Neither was she. They'd run laps together a few times when one of the officers had made her mad or when she'd been about to get into a fight with Barb, who bunked on the other side of her, because Barb was always on her case about her messy footlocker. The sergeant didn't seem to be in any hurry, so it wasn't hard for her to keep up with the taller woman's stride. "It's my understanding," Rains continued after they'd been walking for a bit, "that you're interested in the motor transport school."

Helen didn't bother to wonder how her drill instructor knew this. "Yes, ma'am," she said again, feeling compelled to make her case. "I've had a little experience with that kind of driving and it suits me." She hoped the sergeant wouldn't ask for details since she couldn't very well tell about her unofficial Postal Service duties. But Rains merely nodded as if she already knew this also.

"There's a vacancy in the school at Fort Oglethorpe in Georgia that begins on Monday," she resumed in the same level tone. "A WAC who was scheduled to attend has taken ill. I'd be willing to recommend you for the opening"—she hesitated briefly and let her eyes slide to Helen's face—"if you are up to it." Helen supposed that the sergeant was referring to her drinking episode the previous night. She suspected that if Sergeant Rains had found her drunk again tonight, she wouldn't have made the offer. "If you'd prefer to wait another week, you will still have the opportunity to participate here at Fort Des Moines on our regular schedule. This offer is somewhat irregular but I thought—"

"Yes, ma'am. I'd be very interested in going now." Helen jumped in, not wanting to hear any more. Even if Rains could find a delicate way to put it, they both knew what she meant. Things weren't going to get any better until she had some distance from this situation. She couldn't begin to voice how much she'd been dreading the coming week. Listening to Tee's breathing in the bunk right next to hers, trying to avoid her in the shower, finding someone else to sit next to in class and in the mess hall—it all seemed too much to bear. They'd spent every day of the last five weeks growing close, and the pain of Tee breaking it off between them was too raw. "But I guess I'd be back here for graduation. Right?" Tee might have said it, but Helen wasn't ready for *never again* to be the way it really was. Not quite.

"Yes. In fact, you and the rest of your squad will have seven class days left of basic training when you return. You'll pick up with them for the remainder of that week and then they'll be in their individual training classes during the following week, so you can finish up your general studies with another squad."

Perfect. It dawned on her that Rains had probably done something extraordinary to make this happen. Helen felt her throat tighten with gratitude and her voice came out thickly as a result. "Thank you, Sergeant Rains. I really appreciate—"

Rains stopped walking and cut her off with a wave of her hand. "No thanks necessary, Private. Just make the best of this new opportunity. That's all any of us will ask." She started away and turned back. "Your train is at noon tomorrow, so I'd recommend that you gather your things after breakfast."

Helen swallowed. After breakfast, Tee and a lot of the other girls would be in church. Since it was their one completely free day, everyone else would probably be shopping at the PX or doing some other kind of errand. She wouldn't have to answer a lot of questions or deal with any strained good-byes. Even if it was only good-bye for now. "Yes, ma'am," she said firmly. "I'll do that."

Tee slipped into the chapel and took a seat in the second row from the back. She hadn't been completely faithful about attending services at the WAC camp, but it wasn't her first time there either. Right now she was just grateful that this was one place where there was no chance of her running into Helen. There was quite a bit of space between her and the next person, but she nodded automatically at the form down the pew and then put her bag and her hat beside her, hoping to discourage anyone else from sitting near her. Settling in, she began reading over the bulletin. Even though she had no hope of any real solace, it would be wonderful to sing just one or two of her favorite hymns. "Abide with Me: Fast Falls the Eventide" or "What a Friend We Have in Jesus" would go a long way to ease her troubled heart. Tee loved to sing and she used to be a bit proud of her high, clear voice. Now she thought that the best thing about her singing was that she didn't stammer when she did it. There was one song listed that she didn't recognize and then "All Hail the Power of Jesus' Name." That was a good one, too.

She lifted her own King James Bible and marked the passages that were to be read with the two ribbons her mama had sewn into the binding—blue for the Old Testament and gold for the New. Staring at the book in her hand, she remembered standing in front of the whole church, along with one other girl and three boys close to her age, and professing Jesus Christ to be her Lord and Savior. Then everyone had driven almost an hour to the Arkansas River and all the teens had been baptized and received their Bibles. It was a wonderful time. But sometimes she wondered if she'd done something wrong that day, if maybe her heart hadn't actually been right or she'd been false in her promises somehow, because Mr. Gallagher had come to the farm that very spring, and that had led to so many bad things. The organ began to play and Tee forced her thoughts back to the present. She noted the pastor's name—Dr. Harold Landover—and below that it said Guest Preacher. There had been a guest preacher the last few times she'd been here, too. She supposed with so many men gone to the war it was hard to find someone full-time at a place like Fort Des Moines.

The service was satisfying in its familiar routine. The all-women's choir did a beautiful job with the musical offerings, and even the unfamiliar hymn was easy to sing. Tee knew she couldn't read the Confession aloud without stuttering, so she just moved her mouth even as she repeated the words from 1 John 1:8–9 to herself with as much fervor as she could muster. "If we say that we have no sin, we deceive ourselves, and the truth is not in us. If we confess our sins, He is faithful and just to forgive us our sins, and to cleanse us from all unrighteousness." *God, you know my sin as well as I. I pray you'll cleanse me from my iniquities*, she prayed silently.

Afterward, the pastor stepped up to the pulpit where he read the Gospel lesson with great zeal. He was a beefy man with a florid face, and even as far back as she was sitting, Tee could see that the fingers that came together as he offered his opening prayer looked thick and insensitive. Not like Helen's hands. She had the sweetest touch, one that never failed to—*Stop it!* Tee scolded herself. Those kind of thoughts were bad enough by themselves, but they were surely heresy in the house of the Lord.

The preacher began by reminding the congregation that this was his last Sunday with them, and as such, he was finishing his series on What Happens When You Die? Tee swallowed, hoping for a message of hope and comfort, given that so many men were fighting and dying even as they spoke. She wondered if the other women present were thinking of husbands or cousins or uncles who might have already made the ultimate sacrifice for their country. For a fleeting second, she allowed herself to think of Helen again and her stories about her brother. Apparently, they were as close as two siblings could be, and up until the day he was drafted, Sinclair Tucker had made it his personal mission to care for his sister as best he could, given that their daddy worked all day in the mine and their mama just didn't seem up to the job after she'd lost those four babies. She was glad that Helen had someone like him, and offered up a quick personal prayer for his safety. Then she brought her attention back to the pastor's words.

"Hell is real," he was saying, "and it is a place for people who do not make amends for their sins by asking for God's mercy. Entrance into heaven or hell is not based on whether you're good or bad, for the Bible says there is none righteous. *All have sinned and fallen short of the glory of God.*"

Yes, Tee thought, feeling some relief despite the seriousness of the message. *I'm not the only sinner here. Everyone has done things they're not proud of.* Landover shifted his comments to emphasize what the Bible said regarding the reality of damnation, delving into the story of the rich man and Lazarus, found in Luke 16. Tee turned in her Bible to follow along. She worked the meaning of the old wording out in her head, the way Bett had taught her to do with lessons from the WAC courses, and understood that those souls who were sent to hell wouldn't get a second chance to make it to heaven, and likewise, no one in heaven could even visit hell for a minute.

Tee couldn't help thinking about Helen again and the fact that she was going to hell because she didn't believe. Was she herself now going there, too? The very thought made her shiver. Once, when their preacher at home had done a sermon about hell, he'd painted such a frightening picture that one woman actually fainted. For a solid year after that horrible time with Mr. Gallagher, Tee had prayed and prayed, desperately afraid that she was going to be punished for her part in it. Then one night, she'd been awakened from her sleep by the faint honking sound of migrating geese flying over. She opened the window to look out and the sight took her breath away. It was a small flock, less than twenty or so, high up in the sky. The full moon was out and the light on their wings made them look white. *Like angels*, Tee had thought, and in that moment she was filled with a profound sense of peace. "Thank you, Jesus," she'd whispered, incredibly grateful to know the grace of His forgiveness.

The pastor's voice intruded on her memory, quoting Jesus, who threatened of a place where "sin is punished and God's wrath is poured out." Landover continued, "It makes sense that hell exists. If it didn't, why would Jesus have urged his followers to follow God and repent? Be warned that your good deeds alone won't get you into heaven. Trust Jesus, and pray for forgiveness. Because without repentance, you will not enter the kingdom of heaven. Amen."

As the preacher stepped away from the pulpit, Tee's heart contracted inside her chest. *Repent.* Had she? Was she truly repentant for what she and Helen had done? She knew she wasn't. Deep inside her she was still feeling the warmth of Helen's mouth and the sweetness of her embrace and finding it good. No wonder she hadn't found a moment's peace for the last three days, ever since Sergeant Rains stepped out of the shadows and stopped her and Helen after they'd been together in the equipment room.

That Thursday night, as she'd followed Helen into the small room, Tee could tell that Helen had been in there earlier to set everything up, because some of the equipment was pushed to the sides and a mat was laid out on the floor. Instead of feeling ashamed, as she should have, she'd felt that tingling excitement in her belly, the urgent pulsing she only felt when she was with Helen. But when Helen went to shut the door, she'd almost panicked. Without meaning to she made a little whimper, and after one look at her face, Helen left the door open just a crack. For a minute they just looked at each other, and then Helen had taken her face in her hands and kissed her softly. Just like that, the fear was gone and everything inside her leaned toward Helen like she was a flower and Helen was the sun. Talking sweetly to her between kisses, Helen was so charmingly patient, never making her feel rushed or pressured. But soon, their kisses got harder and more insistent and her knees felt so weak that she'd willingly lain down on the mat. "Can you imagine if we had our own place, Tee?" Helen had asked as she gathered Tee into her arms. "It would be like this every night when we went to sleep." Having Helen hold her and feeling the warmth of her all the way down her body was like having some kind of spell cast where everything in her had just wanted more, more, more.

Tee wasn't sure which of them was more surprised when she was the one who moved first, unbuttoning Helen's shirt and parting the fabric with her hand to give her mouth access. Touching Helen's breast with her tongue and then taking it into her mouth was every bit as wondrous as she'd imagined that night in the grove, and hearing Helen's soft groaning only made it better still. She'd felt so free, so immodest, as Helen's caresses had hiked her skirt up so she could straddle Helen's body as she fumbled with the buttons on her own blouse. They'd giggled at the way Helen was equally shaky when she tried to help, but once her shirt and bra were off, the laughter died away.

"Oh, Tee. You're so incredibly beautiful." Helen's voice was almost reverent as she looked her way up Tee's body until their eyes met.

Tee's breasts were aching for the feel of Helen's hands. "Please," she whispered, her voice surprisingly sure. "Touch me."

Helen's hands cupped her and they moaned together. When Helen's thumbs moved lightly onto her nipples, it was so enjoyable that Tee had to close her eyes. Without really knowing what she was doing, she pressed herself into Helen's body as Helen gently rolled the hard tips between her fingers, over and over. Short panting sounds were coming from her mouth and Helen said her name again, almost in a growl. Tee could feel Helen thrusting up against her and she suddenly realized that her panties were very damp, almost soaked. What had happened? Had she somehow wet herself without knowing it? "Helen, wait," she said earnestly, and something of her distress must have penetrated Helen's awareness, because her fingers stilled, her hands simply holding Tee's breasts, and she sat up just a bit.

"What is it, baby? Did I hurt you?"

Tee shook her head, blushing at the endearment but also because of what she'd apparently done. Helen sat up the rest of the way and pulled Tee onto her lap as she held her against her chest. Their breasts brushing together made Tee whimper just a bit as Helen stroked her back, her voice soothing. "Tell me. Let me make it okay."

It had taken Tee almost a full minute to get enough words out to make herself understood. When she finally did, Tee could tell that Helen was trying very hard not to laugh. "It's not funny," Tee insisted, but she wasn't really mad.

"No, it's not, baby, but it is perfectly natural. That's what women do when they're...excited."

"You, too?"

Helen breathed out a little sound of certainty. "Oh yeah. I'd show you, but if you touch me there, I don't think I'd let you stop." She kissed Tee very gently again and then held her face, looking into her eyes. "And I want us to be somewhere special when we get to that part, because you're so very special to me. I want it to be the best time of your life."

Tee didn't want to think about what *that part* was. She'd only wanted to believe that Helen would take care of her, and that everything between them would be good. She trembled a bit, thinking about being all the way naked with Helen, the way she'd also imagined before, lying on a big bed in a place where they were safely alone together. She nodded and then hugged Helen close, wishing she could say in words all that she was feeling. They'd stayed that way for a time and then dressed quietly, stopping for quick kisses along the way. Then Helen had taken her hand and they'd walked out into the evening, closing the door behind them. After just a few steps, Sergeant Rains had appeared as if from nowhere, and in the span of a few seconds, she'd gone from feeling amazingly wonderful to totally distraught. She'd known immediately that their being caught was punishment from God, so when the sergeant strode away after ordering them to report to her the next morning, she'd told Helen that she didn't want anything more to do with her. Imagining what was going to happen next, she'd agonized over how she could possibly explain a blue discharge to her parents and the people of their small town. Even when Sergeant Rains had somehow found the mercy to let them stay on, she'd felt stained, damaged, and humiliated.

❖

The organ music started up and Tee jerked back to the present, recognizing they were singing the Hymn of Response. By the time she'd found it, the song was almost over. She folded her hands and bowed her head, praying to find her way back to God's good graces. *Forgive me, Jesus. Please forgive me*, she repeated over and over. Then someone near her cleared their throat and she startled to see the usher extending the offering from the aisle. Quickly she fumbled in her purse and dropped a few coins from her wallet into the plate. She was shaking so badly that the shallow platter almost tipped as she moved across the pew to hand it to the next girl, who thankfully caught it before the money spilled onto the ground. Her face hot, she moved back to her seat without looking, but then the pastor announced the Passing of the Peace and she had to stand again. This time, the girl down the pew moved to her, and after they'd exchanged a handshake and Tee had just managed to mumble enough of the words that it sounded like she'd actually said something, the girl lingered. "I'd like to invite you to our Bible study tomorrow night. It's here in the chapel just after dinner. Our regular pastor will be back." She seemed to be smothering a giggle and Tee looked up. The face was friendly, the expression genuine. "It's a little different from this service," she whispered with a quick glance at the ushers making their way back to the front. "For one thing, we always sit in the first row instead of at the back." Smiling, she added, "I hope we'll see you there." Tee could only nod and the girl seemed pleased as she made her way back to her seat.

When Tee returned to the barracks, the little comfort she'd found at church vanished like mist in the morning sun. Helen's mattress was rolled up and her footlocker stood empty. Tee's heart began stuttering as badly as her speech at the thought that Helen was gone from her forever. She felt a hot flush of guilt as she realized she'd been so focused on her own suffering and shame that she hadn't even stopped to consider that Helen might be hurting, too. What kind of Christian was she to act that way? She stood there staring, unable to even formulate a prayer, because she couldn't work out what it was she should ask for. A slow rise of murmurs around her indicated the shared bewilderment that someone like Helen would wash out so late in their training. Then Jo's voice called them to attention as Sergeant Rains entered the room. She strode midway into the long room of bunks and stopped, announcing to the group that Helen had volunteered to take someone else's place at the driving school at Fort Oglethorpe in Georgia. As the agonizing tightness in Tee's chest began to ease, the sergeant added, "She'll be back in a little over a week." She was speaking to the group, but Tee felt every eye on her. She nodded slightly, relieved when Rains departed so she could sit on her bed before her shaking legs gave out on her.

Around the barracks, everyone seemed determined to be extra cheery, but Tee didn't feel much like talking. At each meal, she only picked at her food. When Monday evening came around she excused herself, collected her Bible, and walked slowly to the chapel. She knew she had almost an hour to wait and had expected to just sit on the steps and think, but she arrived at the same time as an older woman who came from the opposite direction. The simple facts that the woman was hatless and wearing a light-colored flowered dress instead of a uniform would have made her stand out, but her relaxed manner was also quite unmilitary.

Smiling warmly at Tee as she pulled open the unlocked door, she asked, "Is there something I can do for you, dear?"

Tee held out her Bible, dreading, as she always did, the prospect of talking to a stranger. Bett had told her to try talking very slowly, so she did. "I'm…here…f-for…" Suddenly her throat was so dry she couldn't continue.

"For the Bible study?" the woman asked gently.

Tee nodded gratefully. She never minded when people helped her finish her sentences, even though they sometimes guessed wrong.

"Come on in." The woman gestured. "You're a little early, which is great. You can help me set up and we can get acquainted." Tee followed her inside, wondering if she was the pastor's wife. The woman made her way to the front of the church. "I'm right that you're new to our group, aren't I?" She looked a little anxious until Tee nodded. "Good. I've been gone for several weeks, but I didn't think we'd met. When did you arrive at camp?"

She asked a series of easy-to-answer questions, and Tee gradually relaxed. They cleared the altar and the woman put out some cookies, encouraging Tee to take one. It was delicious.

"Mm." Tee held her hand over her full mouth, but she wanted the woman to know that she thought the cookie was good.

"They're my mother's recipe. She's the reason I was gone. She'd taken ill. Pneumonia. By the time I got there, she was in the hospital."

"Is s-she okay now?"

The woman stopped what she was doing, a contemplative expression on her face. "I believe she is, yes. She had a long life and was a person of great light. She suffered very little. I believe the love that she showed every day will live on forever."

Tee tried to replay the words in her head, but she wasn't absolutely sure what the woman meant. "Do you mean she...p-passed on?"

The woman nodded. "Yes. Quietly. In her sleep. Surrounded by her family and loved ones."

"Oh!" Tee felt terrible for asking. "I'm so, so sorry."

"Please, don't be." She came around the altar and sat on the front pew, gesturing for Tee to do the same. Now that they were closer, Tee could see that the woman's dark brown hair contrasted with light brown, almost amber eyes. Fine lines at the corners of her mouth and laugh lines along the outside of her eyes made her oval face appear kind. The woman put her arm along the top of the pew, not touching Tee but almost as if she were reaching in her direction. "I see you've brought your own Bible, which tells me you have some religious background." Tee nodded vigorously and the woman smiled softly, deepening the lines that Tee had noticed. "Let's see if we can find some common ground. I believe elements of God's Spirit and divine energy have been instilled in every human soul. You've read that we were made in God's image, haven't you? So that means that God's light—or the seed of Christ, if you prefer—is present in you and in me and in every human being who ever has existed or ever will exist." Tee's brow furrowed slightly as she considered this. "All right so far?" the woman asked. Tee nodded again, but much more slowly. "So, I was taught that having a life after death is not an exchange for righteous living, nor is it a reimbursement for suffering or difficulties we may endure in our lives. And I don't believe that we become better people by living under a threat of punishment. If you want to see the real indicator of what life is intended to be, look at the love and care that people show for one another, even in frightening times like these." Tee frowned and the woman touched her Bible with her other hand. Her voice softer, she added, "In worship, we see proof that Jesus's death did not lessen the impact of his life, nor did his trust in God's love become undone. But it's not necessary to be in church to know that. You can be in the presence of God anywhere you feel that quickening of your spirit."

For the second time in as many days, Tee thought about the geese-angels and the peace they'd brought her. She'd always believed that God had revealed His forgiveness to her in that moment, but she'd never spoken of it to anyone, because it seemed blasphemous to assume that the Lord God Almighty would take the time to speak to Teresa Owens.

The woman was watching her closely. "You've had such an experience, haven't you?"

"I don't know. Maybe."

Smiling again, the woman took her hand off Tee's Bible and touched her own heart. "You know in here. And that's what matters."

Unexpectedly, Tee felt tears very near the surface. She looked down, a wash of emotions swirling through her. "Just listen to me go on," the woman said, her tone lighter as she patted Tee's leg briefly. "I know you didn't come tonight for another sermon. I just didn't want you to feel bad because you asked about my mother's passing. Talking to me carries a certain occupational hazard, I'm afraid."

Tee raised her head and blurted out her question so quickly that she didn't stutter at all. "Who are you?"

The woman blinked once and then began laughing. The rich, genuine sound was contagious, somehow, and Tee found herself joining in. Finally, as they were both wiping tears from their eyes, the woman said, "I can't believe I didn't introduce myself. I'm the minister, Reverend Emily Culberson. Who did you think I was?"

Tee's mouth opened a bit. "You're the minister? I-I thought you might be the minister's wife, or just…just someone helping."

The woman nodded, still smiling faintly. "I get that a lot."

Tee wanted to ask a dozen more questions. How could a woman be a minister? What faith did she practice? What did her husband think about her having this job? But the door to the chapel opened and the reverend stood and waved. "Hi, Casey. We're up here."

A stocky, masculine-looking woman in a corporal's uniform strode up the aisle.

"Casey, this is Tee. She's joining us for the first time tonight.

Tee, this is Casey." She lowered her voice as if telling a secret, but not so much that Casey couldn't hear. "Casey's real name is Clara, but if you'd ever seen her play baseball, you'd know why we call her Casey."

"Hey, now." Casey acted offended. "I don't strike out that much." Then she smiled, and her face gentled from tough to almost pleasant as she offered her hand and Tee took it. "Nice to meet you, Tee. Welcome."

That had been the key word for the evening, Tee thought later. *Welcome.* No one went by rank, only by first names. Everyone was so nice, and they'd all gone out of their way to talk with her and to listen patiently to her responses. They were also very good about making sure she understood how their Bible study worked, which was a good thing since it wasn't like any other church program she'd ever been to. Reverend Culberson had brought in some chairs and arranged them so they were facing those sitting in the first pew. Another girl named Janet explained that this was to help them be aware they were together in community. Tee was greatly relieved when two other girls brought friends for the first time, so she wasn't singled out as the only new girl. Everyone was taking their seats after a few minutes of socializing when the girl who had invited Tee burst in the door. "Brenda!" several voices called, and she was brought into the group with hugs from a few of the other girls.

"I'm so sorry I'm late," she began, looking like she had much more to say. Reverend Culberson put her hand on Brenda's shoulder and murmured a few words. Brenda took a seat and the room quieted again. The reverend explained that they would start their meeting in silence, with what was called attentive waiting. She said the purpose was to let go of worry and seek a peace of mind and heart that would enable them to find joy and purpose in God's creation and acceptance of their place in it.

Then it was quiet. Tee looked at the faces around her. Many had their eyes closed, but some looked up toward heaven or down, as if praying. She closed her eyes. She appreciated the reverend's words, but she knew she couldn't accept herself as she was. Even though she'd tried all her life to be good, for some reason she'd been punished by that awful experience with Mr. Gallagher, and now being with Helen seemed like it had unlocked some other bad thing in her. She was a lost soul, a dreadful sinner. But as the silence drew on, she found herself recalling what the minister had said about the true nature of life being revealed in the love people had for one another. She knew it said in the Bible that God was love, even though she hadn't heard many sermons on that idea. Probably because so few people really knew what love was, any more than anyone could actually know what God was. She knew her mama and her sisters loved her, but was it only because they were family, and that was what family was supposed to do? Her daddy loved her, too, in his gruff way. She also knew what Mr. Gallagher felt for her wasn't love at all, but some kind of sickness. And that brought her mind back to Helen.

In the safety of the hushed church, surrounded by people who had been only kind to her, Tee let herself feel again what it was like to be with Helen. She left out the physical part, because she didn't want to be guilty of thinking about that again in God's house. But from their first day in this place, Helen had watched out for her and made her laugh, even as they shared the difficulties of their studies and the strangeness of being so far from home. They'd told each other stories of their childhood and listened to each other's dreams. She'd come to believe that Helen genuinely cared about her, but was it more than that? *Helen loves me.* Tee tried on the idea as if it were a new dress. *That's why she thinks it's okay for us to kiss and touch each other the way we do.* It fit. Tee felt like she was on the verge of something really important. And how did she feel about Helen? Why had she allowed Helen's warm caresses and enjoyed the soft touch of her lips? She'd even touched and kissed Helen back. Was it that she was lonely? Was she just afraid of losing her best friend? Or was it something more? She gave the thought a chance because she simply had to know if it was true. *I love Helen.* The perfection of it struck her heart like the clear tone of a bell being rung, and for just a moment, she wanted to stand and shout it with joy. *Helen loves me and I love Helen!*

"Does anyone have anything they'd like to share?" The lady minister's voice startled her back to reality.

Tee would have laughed if she hadn't been so flustered. How could she be joyful about being in love with another woman? That was a sin, and certainly not part of God's plan. A voice spoke up and she thought she recognized Brenda, the girl who had come late. "Anger and frustration make the silence hard. For about half the time tonight I just wanted to scream. But then I tried to seek God's will in this, and I got real calm. So I guess that's what God wants me to do right now, is to just stay calm."

One person said, "Amen," and there were some other quiet sounds of agreement. Tee realized she still had her eyes closed. When she opened them, she saw the reverend was looking at her. The woman raised an eyebrow slightly and Tee looked away quickly, not wanting to be asked to share anything. Several other girls spoke about different things that they'd experienced or situations that had happened during the week. One girl even talked about a falling star she'd seen and how she'd felt guilty about praying that it didn't mean that her uncle had died. Casey, who was sitting next to her, patted her shoulder, but generally no one made any comments or corrected anyone about the righteousness of anything they said.

Then Reverend Culberson read a Bible verse, from 1 John 4. "No man hath seen God at any time. If we love one another, God dwelleth in us, and his love is perfected in us. Hereby know we that we dwell in him, and he in us, because he hath given us of his Spirit." Another long moment of silence followed this, but Tee was too agitated to even think about what had been spoken. After a time the reverend said, "I have a feeling we need to talk some about prayer next time. Would you all give some thought to praying and how and why we do that?"

Nodding and general sounds of assent followed this and then everyone stood up. Brenda came over and took one of Tee's hands. "I'm so glad you came." She gave the hand a little shake and grinned. "Told you it was different."

Tee bent to pick up her Bible, so Brenda let go of her hand. "Yes," Tee managed. "Nice."

"I hope you'll come back," Brenda said. "There are meetings on Wednesdays and Fridays, too. Not everyone comes every time, but just so you know."

Part of her wanted to get away as fast as she could before someone asked her anything more about herself, but Tee was curious about something that Brenda had said. "What were you upset about?" she stammered.

Brenda sniffed. "Oh, my drill instructor…again. She makes me so crazy. I honestly think she's mean enough to keep me late these days on purpose, just 'cause she knows that coming here is something I want to do."

Tee wasn't sure what made her ask, but she had to know. "Who?"

"Sergeant Moore. Just my luck I got here the week she got back from vacation." Brenda brought her hands together like she was praying. "But I'm going to stay calm." They both laughed. "Who's yours?"

"Sergeant Rains."

"You like her?" Tee nodded. "Yeah, I've heard good things about her." Brenda glanced at her watch. "I'd better get going. Word is, we're having a surprise inspection tonight." She made a face and they both laughed again. Starting toward the door, Brenda looked back over her shoulder. "I hope to see you here again."

"Okay." Tee hoped she sounded more positive than she felt. When she looked around, she realized that everyone else had left and she was alone with Reverend Culberson again.

"Are you all right, Tee?"

The question took her by surprise and the casual answer she should have given refused to come to her lips. *Fine, thanks.* She couldn't even bring herself to nod. After several seconds of silence, the reverend said, "If you ever want someone to talk to, my door is always open." She gestured at the back of the church. "I have a little office where we can have some privacy. And nothing you say to me will ever go any further." She held up the Bible that she'd read from. "I give you my word."

When Tee finally forced her mouth to open, she couldn't believe the rush of words that came out. "A man who worked for us made me… made me touch him. I didn't want to but…but he told me that it would help him…so…so I did." Not once did she stutter.

"Oh, honey," Reverend Culberson said. Something in her tone, in her tender expression, made Tee's tears become a flood in only a few seconds. The reverend took her in her arms and held her like a mother soothing her child. After a little while, the reverend said, "You've never let anyone else know about this before, have you?" Tee shook her head, sniffing as she tried to compose herself. The reverend kept an arm around her as they walked together to her office and they talked and talked until it occurred to her to look at the clock.

The small measure of calm that she'd found vanished as she jumped to her feet, almost frantic, her stutter returning as she spoke.

"Oh no! I'll be late for CQ. Sergeant Rains will put me in the stockade or something."

"Sergeant Rains won't do any such thing. I'll walk back to the barracks with you and explain the situation." She must have seen Tee's alarm, because she added, "That you and I were talking and the time just got away from us."

Amazingly, she did just that. The sergeant's usually stern expression softened somewhat at the reverend's appearance. "Go get yourself ready for the sack, Private Owens," she ordered and Tee scurried off.

The two women stepped out onto the barracks porch. "She's terrified of you, you know?" Culberson said.

"Which is as it should be," Rains agreed solemnly, and the reverend laughed. Before she could turn to go, Rains touched her arm briefly. "If it won't violate a confidence, may I ask if you feel that Private Owens is doing all right?"

Emily Culberson hesitated. "I think she has a lot on her mind and on her heart right now. More than even I know at the present time." She looked up and Rains met the gaze of the reverend with whom she had enjoyed more than one interesting discussion on the nature of God and the purpose of religion, back when Colonel Issacson had assigned her to counsel with a younger, somewhat recalcitrant Private Rains. The reverend had surprised Rains by never proselytizing or ever suggesting that she come to church, and with her willingness to accept what little Rains shared about her own beliefs as valid. Rains had gradually come to trust her, as much as she trusted anyone on the base, and on rare occasions would even speak with her about a particularly difficult recruit or troublesome situation.

"Does she have any good friends in the squad? Is there someone she can talk to, just be herself with?"

Rains looked away. "There's no one here now with whom she's particularly close, but she's well liked. I can think of several in her squad that I could ask to keep an eye on her if you think it's necessary."

"I'll certainly let you know if I sense she's in trouble. For now, maybe just give her a little extra positive attention here and there." She nudged Rains familiarly with her shoulder. "And you might ease up on her just a tiny bit."

"Hmm. Is that just your advice, or is there some commandment in your Bible saying it's best to ease up on someone when they're in some distress?"

"What makes you think my advice and the Bible aren't one and the same?" the reverend asked, her eyes dancing.

The sergeant touched the brim of her hat. "Good night, Reverend."

"Good night, Sergeant."

CHAPTER THREE

Tee was having even more trouble than usual keeping her mind on the morning lessons. She'd hardly been able to keep pace during the exercise period earlier, and after all these weeks that part was practically automatic now. Even though her brain had known that Helen wasn't there for the past week, her heart couldn't seem to remember. She'd never stopped looking for Helen's face in their group, had repeatedly caught herself waiting to start her evening studies as if Helen was about to join her, and found herself longing for the comforting sound of Helen's now-familiar voice saying good night as the last thing she heard. Finally, it was the day that Helen was due back, and she couldn't seem to keep her heart from jumping every time she thought about it. More than once, she'd caught herself wondering if this was what love felt like. Then she would pray that she wouldn't have those reactions anymore, or try to pretend that everything she was feeling simply applied to any normal friendship.

She knew Helen's train would arrive just before dinner and Sergeant Rains would go to pick her up. Tee couldn't bring herself to wait in the mess hall, even though that's where all of Helen's other friends would be. She went back to the barracks and unrolled Helen's mattress, leaving the final version of the note that had taken her most of the week and innumerable sheets of paper to write on Helen's bunk.

Dear Helen,

I just had to write this down because it would take me too long to say it, even though you've always been real patient about waiting for my words to make their way out, and you know how much I appreciate that. Anyways, I wanted to say I understand about why you left the way you did. Oh, I was sad at first and even a little bit mad, but then Bett said that you had a opportunity to do something you love and you were right to take it. It got me to thinking I might have did the same in your position. On the other hand, I'm sorta glad you went to Georgia, because it give me some time to think, and I guess that's something else you probably wanted, too.

I been spending more time at the church here, including going to a Bible study group that meets three nights a week. Did you know their real preacher here is a lady? She ain't a Baptist, of course, 'cause Baptists don't believe in women teaching men, although there ain't no men that come to the Bible meetings, so I guess it would be all right. But the point I wanted to make is this lady preacher give me some new ideas about how to look at God, and I'm trying them out to see if they fit me. People back home would wonder why would I do such a thing, and weren't the things I got taught to believe in our little church good enough anymore? They'd tell me the Bible hasn't changed and the truth doesn't change and God doesn't change, so if anything's different, it must be me. And you know what I'd say? I'd tell them they're right. I have changed. And you know what else? It's you that's changed me, Helen.

Knowing you and thinking back over the time we spent together, well there's no doubt that I'm a different girl than I was six weeks ago. I'm still not sure if I'm good different or bad different, but I just know it's like when you pull a real big piece of material out of a box when the material's all been folded up real tight and once it gets exposed to air and shook out a bit, it ain't never likely to fit back into that same box in the same way again. I could say you shook me out, Helen. And I guess I didn't quite know what to do about being out of that box I've been stuffed into all of my life. Tell the truth, I got scared for a lot of reasons, but you know that, too.

So I reckon what I've been building up to saying is I really missed you and I'm so glad you're back. There's parts of me that wants to tell you more than that, but then other

*parts don't think I should and so the rest just don't know what
to do. All I can hope is you'll get that and you'll maybe even
be willing to wait until I figure myself out. See, I'm scared to
even guess how you might feel about me anymore. All I know
is I just want to give you a big hug and ask you not to go
away again. I hope you'll let me do that. But if you can't, I'll
understand. Just know that no one else has ever meant to me
what you have, and I can't imagine anyone who ever would.*
    Your friend 4-Ever,
    Tee

Then she went to the parade grounds and sat on the bleachers,
waiting.

Conversation at the squad's mess hall table had abruptly gotten
quiet and the girls sitting opposite her were smiling. Bett was about to
turn and look behind her when hands covered her eyes and a soft twang
asked, "Guess who?"

Bett considered answering *Kitty Brunell*, naming a famous female
British race car driver, but she knew such a response wouldn't be
understood. Instead she said, "Mrs. Roosevelt, is that you?" which
caused uproarious laughter all around.

Helen plopped into the seat beside her, sighing deeply. "How
quickly they forget."

Bett hugged her, whispering, "You were missed, my dear."

Helen blushed and then everyone else joined in the hugs and
greetings. Tanned and looking relaxed, she sat easily with the group,
declining anything to eat. "I'm full of that fabulous train food." Soon
she was talking about her motor transport training classes, answering
questions about Fort Oglethorpe, and keeping everyone laughing with
her stories of run-ins with various officers, most of which were clearly
exaggerated. Finally, as most of the squad rose to put up their trays and
head back to the barracks, Helen turned back to Bett. "Where's Tee?"

"I don't know, Helen. She was in class earlier but I guess she
wasn't hungry. Why don't you check in the barracks? I'm sure she's
anxious to see you."

Helen's eyes scanned the area quickly but no one else was nearby. Even so, she lowered her voice. "Do you really think so, Bett? We had a little scrape before I left."

Bett nodded. The abrupt chill between Helen and Tee had been apparent to everyone, especially because they'd been so close before. While most speculation had the falling-out to be over a man—one of the officers or even an MP—Bett didn't think Tee's behavior since Helen's departure fit that theory. "Tee doesn't strike me as the type to hold a grudge, Helen. In fact, she's been spending a lot more time at the base chapel lately. To me, that's someone who's looking for help to find their way through a problem of some kind."

"Great," Helen said, without any enthusiasm.

"What about you?" Bett asked.

"What about me?"

"Are you the type to hold a grudge?"

Helen looked away as she spoke. "Yeah. I am. I have a really hard time forgiving someone who's done me wrong or hurt me. I don't like giving people second chances."

Bett considered her response carefully. She'd been guilty of feeling the same way on more than one occasion. Unexpectedly, it had been Sergeant Rains who had taught her many lessons in forgiveness, giving her chance after chance in the WAC and—unintentionally, perhaps—with her. "Has anyone ever given you a second chance?" she asked, finally.

Helen turned back to her, eyes narrowing, looking almost suspicious. After a few seconds she took a steadying breath. "Yeah," she said softly. "Once."

"And how did that make you feel?" Bett prodded.

"Kinda surprised. And really grateful."

Bett smiled and inclined her head as if her point had been made. Helen recognized the gesture. Bett used to do that a lot when she'd led them to an answer in their studies but wanted them to make that final step of discovery by themselves.

Helen stood. "Excuse me, Bett, but I need to go find my best friend."

❖

She was nervous about seeing Tee again, but Helen was also distracted by what Bett had said about second chances. For a second, she'd reacted to the question with anger, spurred by the notion that Sergeant Rains had told the squad about her and Tee. But once she'd thought it through, she'd dismissed the idea, partly because she really didn't think Rains was likely to do that, and also because everyone had so readily welcomed her back. *If they knew, they might not even speak to me.* Encouraged by the greetings from squad members she hadn't already seen, she made her way to her bunk. As surprised as she was to find her mattress already rolled out, it was the envelope with Tee's handwriting on it that made her heart jump. Of course nosy Barb was watching, so she just casually picked the note up and put it in her jacket pocket. No way was she reading it in front of anyone else. She forced herself to take the time to make her bed and unpack a few things, even making sure that her footlocker was back in order after the trip. Then she checked the clock and saw she had two hours before CQ. "I think I'll take a walk," she said to no one in particular, being sure to keep her pace unhurried. Once she was clear of the barracks she made her way to a quiet spot near the administration building and read the note under a light. Then she read it again. Finally she folded it back into the envelope and stared at it, thinking.

She'd had a good time at Fort Oglethorpe, considering her state of mind when she'd left Iowa. On the trip out, she'd pulled herself together, generally managing to push Tee from her thoughts so she could make the most of this new situation, as Sergeant Rains had suggested. Her motor transport school instructor in Georgia, Sergeant Washburn, was as tough as Rains when it came to the skills she expected her drivers to have, but she also had a sense of humor, and if you could make her laugh, you were in. She'd liked Helen right off. Maybe because Helen already had some skills or because Helen's brother Sinclair had taught her all kinds of jokes. None of the instructors at Fort Des Moines seemed to care much for Helen's jokes, but she was always looking for an opportunity to tell one. It was windy on the day she chose to test the waters at her new posting. As Sergeant Washburn was showing them the fine points of the converted cattle trucks that were used to transport the new recruits to base, everyone was holding either their hat or their skirt or both.

"Hey, Sarge," Helen called as one of the other girls was raising the hood. "Did you know that an observant man claims to have discovered the color of the wind?" Washburn looked at her as if she was crazy until Helen added, "He says he went out and found it blew."

After a beat, the whole group erupted in laughter and Helen felt about ten feet tall. She quickly became one of Washburn's favorites, and sometimes she sensed that they had something in common besides a liking for motor vehicles. After the fourth day's class, when she'd been the first one to finish and gotten the highest scores on the arduous driving test for the Willys MB, better known as a Jeep, her new sergeant had pulled her aside and murmured, "I'm having a little get-together at my house tonight. Interested?"

Helen tried to act casual. "Sure, Sergeant. That would be nice."

Washburn looked at her closely. "It's all women. You understand?"

Helen grinned. "Even better."

So she'd had an introduction to the world of house parties, where women like her got a chance to meet and mingle. Many were already paired up, but there were several singles, and Helen's company and conversation were very much in demand. She'd declined any serious offers, explaining that she was only there for the week. But by the end of the evening, after multiple beers had turned one casual flirtation into a very close dance in a secluded corner, she'd decided to put in a request to transfer to Fort Oglethorpe after basic training was over. After all, Tee had said *Never again*. If Baptists had nuns, Tee would probably become one. This was when she should be enjoying life, Helen told herself, not pining away for someone who wouldn't ever be able to come to terms with how they felt about each other.

Helen had experienced her first serious crush in sixth grade, and she'd been looking for the right girl ever since. At that time it was Louise Farmer, a beautiful girl whose partial deafness had caused her to be placed in the group with other slow learners or those with poor attendance, like Helen. Helen's increasingly short temper had cooled when she sat next to Louise, and she discovered that she didn't mind repeating things or even writing them out for her as long as she got one of Louise's grateful smiles in return. When she'd confided to her brother that she intended to live with Louise when she grew up, the way her Aunt Darcy lived with Mrs. Murrell, Sinclair had looked off in the distance for a moment. "Yeah, I kinda figured that about you," he'd said. His expression suggested that she might have said something bad, but nothing more came of it except that Helen's attendance improved, as did her grades, until she came in one day to find she'd been moved to a different group and dull-witted Teddy Herschel was sitting next to Louise, who was smiling up at him with that same special smile. Heartbroken, Helen had taken another break from school and gone back to helping her friend Mr. Hall with his Postal Service deliveries. But she'd gotten the image in her head of her perfect girl—sweet, caring, not overly talkative, and pretty.

It was true that Tee had fit the bill on all of those qualities, but Helen had been drawn to her determined, steady manner, and to the courage with which Tee faced her adversities. Someone who didn't know her well might think that Tee was timid or unsure because she was quiet. And yeah, sometimes Tee seemed to be a thousand miles away. But Helen knew that Tee took pride in herself and her work and she had some steel in her gut. Perhaps that was why Tee's unwillingness to fight for what they had had hurt Helen to the core. She herself would have quit the WAC or challenged Sergeant Rains to prove that anything immoral or even against regulations had actually happened, but Tee had given up on them just like that. Or that's how it had seemed.

This note seemed to indicate that Tee was having second thoughts about cutting off their relationship. Even as Helen's heart swelled happily at the idea, her head told her to take it easy. Talk was cheap. She knew she couldn't expect Tee to go back to the grove or the equipment room tonight. But she'd need to lay down the law about how long she'd let this *figuring myself out* business go on. She had other options, after all. But when she came upon Tee, sitting slumped over on the bleachers with her elbows on her knees and head in her hands, her heart took control. She knew she wasn't going anywhere as long as there was any chance for the two of them. Tee was the one she wanted and needed, and while she didn't actually believe in this love business, she was willing to give it a try if Tee would.

Tee was drifting, almost asleep sitting up, when she heard Helen's voice. "Hey, Tee." For just a second, she thought she was back in the barracks. She hadn't been sleeping well at all and when she did finally doze, Helen was often in her dreams. She'd talked with Reverend Culberson almost every evening, either after Bible study or just on her own. The reverend had made her feel a lot better about her encounter with Mr. Gallagher, but she hadn't told her about Helen. Well, not exactly. The reverend seemed to know there was something else on her mind, but she never pushed. Finally Tee had found the courage to ask, "Do you think I'll ever have a n-normal relationship?"

The reverend cocked her head slightly. "Do you mean an intimate relationship with a man?" Tee nodded. "Is that what you want?"

Tee blinked. "Isn't that what I'm s-supposed to want?"

Smiling her gentle smile, the reverend had answered, "I think you need to listen to what your heart tells you about what you want, and not worry too much about *should* or *supposed to*."

Then Sunday, Reverend Culberson's sermon had been about love. She first talked about friendship, and how an easy and pleasant conversation could turn to something new as two or more people listened avidly to each other. How often interesting or eye-opening discoveries were made and you came away from the conversation lighter and happier, as if God had been with you.

Tee couldn't help thinking of Helen. There had never been another person in her life with whom she had shared so much of herself—sometimes just in the day-to-day moments and sometimes in those deep conversations that went on for hours. Maybe it was God's presence she was feeling, rather than love.

As if reading her mind, the reverend went on to give her definition of love. "Love is what cultivates growth and development in any relationship, enriching us both separately and together. As love magnifies perfect individuality, freeing each to be their truest, most complete self, it also binds us to all that lives. So what makes such a unique connection flourish? Tenderness in safekeeping, a shared responsibility of needs, and the mutual commitment to care. When these are present between two of us, surely God is, too."

Tee realized she was holding her breath. There had been no specific mention of a man and a woman in Reverend Culberson's description. Was the pastor actually suggesting that a relationship such as hers and Helen's might be acceptable to the Lord Almighty? "Why would we be created with this ability if not to implicitly acknowledge the God in us each time we speak of love for another? Doesn't love—this generous, open offering of one's self to another—offer us a reflection of what God has so freely given to each of us?" she heard the reverend say. Tee's mind was reeling. Was that the reason she felt the way she did about Helen? Would loving her somehow help her understand more about God's love?

"For those who believe that God is working in everyone, we know it is because God loves and cherishes everyone. Are we not commanded to do the same? Anyone can know God and anyone can be a part of God's plan. What Jesus showed us of God's love is that it was not given because certain persons had been exceptionally good or had achieved some special status here on Earth. Rather, we are to find our worth in the knowledge that God loves us unconditionally. This is the example we follow. Because we trust that God loves and values all people, so do we love and value all people."

Tee wished she'd found a way to ask Reverend Culberson what kind of Christian she was. The minister had a way of always keeping their talks focused on Tee instead of about herself. She had managed to ask the reverend if she ever worried about going to hell. The reverend's smile was a bit sad as she said, "The problem with striving only to avoid hell is that it makes people concern themselves more with the future instead of focusing on the here and now. When you use Jesus as your standard for compassion, and you work to grow the love you have inside you, you are living life as you are meant to do. We mustn't be so intimidated by avoiding punishment in hell that we miss the joy of the present."

During one of their conversations, Reverend Culberson had told her that she judged herself much too harshly. Tee answered that she thought judging was how you gauged where you were not measuring up to what God expected of you. Then the reverend suggested that judgment was God's job. "You don't want to be playing God, do you, Tee?" Tee couldn't even count how many sermons she'd heard about damnation, but that idea didn't seem to be in the reverend's vocabulary. One thing was certain—the lady reverend didn't talk like any preacher she'd ever known when they were in private, and this sermon hadn't sounded a bit like the ones she was accustomed to, either.

When the reverend came out from behind the pulpit and stood between the two aisles, holding out her arms as if embracing the entire congregation, Tee could sense the connection of community that was always emphasized during Bible study. It was almost like they were all humming the same note, and the oneness of it made her feel whole. "God's strength is centered in creation and love, capacities which I believe are also found in all of us. There are stories of this power in many other traditions and cultures, and yet God is greater than all of them. But even God's being cannot exist in a vacuum. God needs us to respond, to give back, so that we can be redeemed by the spirit that we share. Only then can we be freed from the heaven and hell we have created for ourselves and be truly open to the terrifying vulnerability of love."

The terrifying vulnerability of love. The notion was so painfully beautiful that Tee had to wipe tears off her cheeks, but she tried to act like she just had a cold or something and hoped no one noticed. At the door she saw Casey, whose eyes looked a little red also, and they simply nodded to each other. She hadn't lingered as she might have otherwise but had gone back to the barracks and rewritten her note to Helen one last time.

Now, opening her eyes without lifting her head, she could tell it was getting late. Suddenly she remembered that Helen was coming back today, so the voice she'd heard might really be her. *And here I am, practically drooling, probably with those red sleep marks on my face.* She raised her head slowly. Silhouetted in the last of the evening light, Helen appeared to be almost glowing. "Helen? Is that really you?" Was it possible that Helen was an angel, too? Could she have been sent like the geese, not to show Tee forgiveness, but to show her love?

Tee's question sounded so hopeful that it made Helen's heart beat a little faster. *Play it cool*, she told herself. "Yeah, kiddo, it's me. Back from beautiful Fort Oglethorpe." Then she noticed that Tee looked a little dazed, with dark circles under her eyes. Helen squatted, bringing her face even with Tee's. "Are you okay? You look kinda...lost."

Tee stood, wobbling a bit. Helen straightened, too, wanting to put out a hand to help her but not sure if she should, considering how they'd left things. When Tee steadied, she raised her gaze and Helen let herself just look at her. From the beginning she'd been drawn in by the softness of Tee's brown eyes, and now it was like coming home. She saw welcome and worry, profound sorrow, and something deeper that she didn't know how to name. Tee blinked and her lips parted, but she made no sound for a few seconds. "I—I am lost," she said faintly, and stopped. Helen didn't answer because Tee's throat worked as if she planned on saying more. It had never bothered her, Tee's stutter and the way she sometimes struggled with getting out everything she was thinking. No sharp-tongued, quick-thinking woman could match Tee's heart. Helen would have stood there all night, looking at her sweet face, even as she waited for whatever judgment might come. After a shaky breath, Tee added, "I'm lost without you." Still, Helen didn't move until Tee stepped closer and put her arms around Helen's neck. "I can't fight this anymore. I don't...I don't want to."

Then nothing on this earth, not even President Roosevelt himself, could have kept Helen from pulling Tee as close to her as she could. "I'm lost without you, too. So there's not going to be any more fighting, okay? We're gonna figure out a way to make this work, Tee. You and me. Together. That's how it's gonna be, okay?" Tee's face was pressed into her neck, and in another second, Helen could feel the wetness of tears. "No, baby, no," she shushed her. "Don't cry. Please don't cry."

Tee lifted her face enough to ask, "But what about Sergeant Rains?"

Helen hated to let her go, but she took hold of Tee's hands, moving carefully so they could both sit back down on the bleachers. "I done some thinking about that on the train when I was leaving here. When she told us we could stay, she didn't say we couldn't be together. She didn't even quote regulations. She mostly said she was going to give us another chance because we'd both improved so much and she thought we were going to make good soldiers. I think she cares more about that than about, you know, the other."

As she thought back to that afternoon in Rains's office, Helen didn't think she'd ever felt as alone as she had while waiting to hear her fate. Tee hadn't spoken to her all day, and no one else in the squad seemed to know how to act toward either of them, so they'd pretty much acted like neither of them were there. Even Bett, who could usually be counted on for a friendly smile, seemed preoccupied. At least Rains hadn't dragged it out like she could have, torturing them with waiting to hear her decision like some creep who tested how well a grasshopper could hop each time he pulled a leg off. As soon as they'd closed the door and come to attention in front of her, she'd said, "I'm not going to remove either of you from the service at this time." Tee had made a little choking sound, and Helen was so relieved that she'd slumped slightly as her eyes drifted to Rains's face. For just a second, she thought she saw something like sympathy there. Just as quickly, the sergeant had resumed her usual firm expression and had gone on to stress her expectations, which really weren't anything more than what she'd always asked of each of them—to give their very best effort and always strive for excellence as they did their duty with honor and pride. Tee was out the door the moment *dismissed* came from the sergeant's mouth. Helen had the presence of mind to say, "Thank you, ma'am." Then she'd gone and spent the evening with Maria and Charlotte and a few other squad members at the NCO club, drinking hard liquor until they'd stumbled back to the barracks just before CQ. Luckily, Sergeant Weber had done their walk-through that night, and she wasn't nearly as observant as Rains.

"Besides," Helen went on, pushing back the memories, "we've only got a little more than a week till graduation. After that, we're not her responsibility anymore."

"Won't she tell our next command?" Tee had stopped crying but she still looked a little wobbly.

"Nah. She's not blabby like that. Besides, we'll be working in different places, so she'll probably think things will cool down between us when we're apart. But they won't, will they, Tee?"

Tee shook her head, saying, "Apparently not," with a tone that sounded so much like the way Bett Smythe said it that they both smiled at each other.

Thinking of her experience at Fort Oglethorpe, Helen added, "And you know what else? I bet there are more people like us here than we know." It was dark enough that she felt safe to give a quick kiss to Tee's forehead. "We've just gotta stay out of trouble for two more weeks." She could just make out Tee's indignant look, so she amended, "Okay, *I've* gotta stay out of trouble. But I can. And I will. Because you're worth it."

"We're worth it," Tee answered as she squeezed Helen's hands, and Helen's heart soared as she tried to remember if anything else had ever felt so good.

❖

The next morning, Sergeant Rains pulled Helen aside after their exercise period. "Sergeant Washburn at Fort Oglethorpe has given me a very favorable report of your performance."

Relieved that her drill instructor didn't want to discuss something more personal, Helen let her breath out carefully. She knew Tee was probably watching from somewhere, so she nodded, somewhat enthusiastically. "Thank you, ma'am."

"She's also under the impression that you would like a transfer to that base when you're finished here. Is that correct?"

Helen swallowed. In her delight at patching things up with Tee, she'd forgotten about her plan to return to Fort Oglethorpe after basic training was over. "Oh. Well, I..." Helen realized she was sounding more like Tee than herself. Clearing her throat, she started over. "I've changed my mind about that posting, ma'am." She and Tee hadn't really discussed their plans for the future beyond the fact that Tee had become accustomed to Fort Des Moines and hoped to be posted at the post exchange on base. "I believe I'd prefer to stay on here, if a position as a driver is available."

The sergeant cocked her head slightly, and Helen could feel her gaze sharpening. Grateful that she wasn't supposed to be looking at Rains, Helen tried to keep her face expressionless. She was quite certain that Rains was assessing this information in light of everything else she knew about her. But when the sergeant spoke, her voice was surprisingly gentle. "Are you certain that's the best choice for your career, Private Tucker?"

Rigid now, and very still, Helen answered promptly. "Yes, ma'am."

"And is this also the best choice for Private Owens?" Rains asked, her voice hardening slightly. "Or should I ask her?"

There was no doubt in her mind that Tee would be terrified if the sergeant called her over. "You don't have to do that, ma'am," Helen answered promptly. "I believe I can speak for Private Owens on this matter. She wishes to remain at Fort Des Moines as well." She hadn't exactly answered the question, but perhaps it would do.

After what seemed like a long pause, the sergeant spoke again. "Very well, Private. You are dismissed."

"Thank you, Sergeant." Helen took one step back and turned to go. With her back to Rains, she couldn't be certain whether she'd actually heard the sergeant whisper, "Be careful," or if it was just the wind. The strangest thing was that it sounded more like a blessing than a warning.

❖

Sergeant Gale Rains had known without looking that Teresa Owens was nearby. She could practically feel her anxiety flowing past her and Helen Tucker in waves. While Reverend Culberson had indicated that she thought Tee was doing better with each of their sessions, she wondered what effect Tucker's return would have on her condition. Deciding not to worry Owens beyond what she already had, Rains had dismissed Tucker, thinking to let the situation with the two women work itself out without interfering any further. She'd already played her part by not dismissing them from the WAC, and apparently the time away from each other hadn't put a permanent end to their relationship. Perhaps this, too, was something that was meant to be.

She sighed as she watched Private Tucker walk away. Although she'd surprised herself with her last words, she recognized they might well be directed inward as well. For a little more than six weeks, she'd been clinging to the duty she'd accepted years ago, while fighting a rising desire that had been banished for an even longer time. She knew her counsel to Tucker skirted the line between the professional and the personal, but she'd been living in that middle place since she'd taken on this last session of recruits and begun dealing with her new squad leader, Private Bett Smythe.

The woman in question was actually Elizabeth Frances Pratt Carlton, daughter of the forty-second richest man in America. The striking blonde, who was known by her nickname Bett, had registered under the surname of Smythe after her manipulative father tried to change her mind about enlisting by convincing her that being identified as a Carlton among the riffraff of the volunteer Women's Army Corps would put her in danger of kidnapping. Bett herself would now be the first one to admit that idea was complete and utter rubbish, as she would say in that fascinating British accent of hers. Shaking away the image, Rains brought herself back to the point, which was that her relationship with Smythe had already ventured beyond the absolute limits that she would normally set between herself and a squad member. Bett had a way of pushing past her boundaries, and something in her warmly winning manner, combined with a strong will and an equally fierce focus on what she wanted, had combined to lower Sergeant Rains's defenses on more than one occasion. Perhaps they could have been friends, a very rare commodity in Rains's life, except for the uncrossable divide of their roles in the WAC. Drill instructors did not fraternize with their recruits. Period.

But no matter how firmly Rains repeated to herself the need to back away from Smythe, things between them only seemed to intensify. Even as she fought to keep their association within the bounds of what she considered acceptable, there was no denying that in the two and a half years that Rains had been in the WAAC and then the WAC, she'd never found herself so attracted to someone. That Bett had made it clear on more than one occasion that the feelings were mutual didn't make things any easier.

And now, in this matter of finding Tucker and Owens in a compromising situation, she wasn't very far into her thinking before admitting that if she and Bett had been two different people, it could just as easily have been them. From an early age, she'd seen that her natural way of being was different from others, but she'd been readily accepted by her Lakota people and, more importantly, by her family. She pitied the Whites for their fear and their hateful attitudes toward those who were like her, but she was also aware that it was a completely different matter when someone in authority preyed on the weak and the helpless in this way. Such was not the case with the two young women in her squad and, she had to admit, neither was it so with her and Bett. Still, as a drill instructor, it was her job to find the path between a very clear violation of regulations and two who were, without question, the most improved members of her squad. She had spent many hours examining very carefully what her decision should be and why.

Even with Bett's face and her voice and the feel of her skin in her heart as she'd fallen asleep, upon waking, the sweet sensations were quickly dislodged by a harder truth: Bett's time here was almost over. Soon she would graduate and start her new life with the cryptography group after making the choice to work in Washington DC or possibly in New York. And Sergeant Rains would remain, in this solitary world without attachment, spending each day doing her duty and waiting for the small hours of the morning to wonder about what could have been.

CHAPTER FOUR

Helen found Tee waiting just beyond the parade grounds where they did their exercises. Tee's face was a picture of worry, so Helen assured her that their sergeant had simply asked some routine questions about her experience at Fort Oglethorpe. There was no reason for Tee to know about the plan she'd made to go back there. They parted for the rest of the day, attending different classes and drills, but after dinner they had time to take a long walk and catch up. Tee told Helen that she wasn't going to be attending the Bible study group for now, because she didn't like spending that much time away from her. She added that she did want to continue speaking with Reverend Culberson for an hour or so on Tuesday and Thursday evenings.

"She's helping you, isn't she?" Helen asked. It seemed to her that even Tee's stutter was getting better, and for a brief moment, she wondered if she should be jealous.

Tee nodded. Then she took a deep breath. "Why don't you come to church with me on Sunday? You could meet her." They'd been very careful not to touch or even stand too close whenever there was a chance that anyone might see, but she risked taking Helen's arm for just a second. "There's no hellfire and damnation there. I promise."

It was probably the combination of Tee's physical gesture and the imploring look in her eyes that made Helen reluctantly agree. She would go to the dang church, just this once, and then Tee wouldn't be able to say she hadn't tried.

❖

The next afternoon was the class about leadership training, which was for potential officer candidates, and the drill instructors presentation for non-coms. Sergeant Rains was sitting onstage with the presenters, wearing her dress uniform. Helen had seen her sergeant's eyes sweep briefly over the squad before the speakers began, and she was relieved to note there was no special attention given to the fact that she and Tee were sitting together again. She would have felt really bad if the sergeant had given them that look—the one Helen remembered getting from the church ladies when she was with her Aunt Darcy and Mrs. Murrell in public.

She'd seen it as they were going to or from the general store or any such errand, when the faces coming toward them reflected disgust, as if they were smelly dirty. She couldn't understand it at first, because her aunt's house was the cleanest she'd ever seen, to the point that it made Helen willing to have a wash whenever she visited, so she wouldn't mess anything up. Oh, her aunt still hugged and kissed her the minute she came through the door and so did Mrs. Murrell, though she didn't hug or kiss her daddy the way Aunt Darcy did, since he was grown and she wasn't no kin to him. Somehow, she knew not to say nothing to either of them about the look, so she asked her daddy one time when they were going back to their own home. His face had gotten sad, then thoughtful, like he was wondering how to explain it to her.

"Well, Hat"—he called her Hat when they weren't around her mother because her middle name was Abigail, so her initials spelled out *H-A-T*, which they both thought was funny, though Mama didn't approve—"some people don't like it that Mrs. Murrell has kept on running the saloon after her husband died even though she pretty much ran it when he was alive. Some people don't like it that your Aunt Darcy used to have herself a job, too, and that she never did get married at all though she got asked plenty when she was younger. And some people don't like it that they're living together now." He sighed and didn't say another thing. The more Helen thought about it, the more it seemed to her like there was always gonna be something that somebody somewhere didn't like. When she told her daddy that, he'd just laughed and swung her around, something he didn't hardly do anymore 'cause she was getting bigger and his back hurt a lot.

The sound of polite applause brought her back to the present. The officers had finished and the non-coms were about to take their turn. Helen looked around, finding her squad members interspersed in the larger platoon. Bett was in the front row, as usual, taking notes and paying real good attention the way she always did. Jo, too, was practically on the edge of her seat, eager and focused on every word. By now everyone knew that their sergeant had loaned her a drill instructor's manual for a couple of days, and Jo had made it obvious that she was interested in getting into the non-com school. Helen knew the other girls were making their plans as well—Maria wanted to be a pharmacy technician and Barb was going into the cooking school. Helen couldn't imagine anyone wanting to work in a kitchen all day, but she supposed that someone needed to keep them fed. Phyllis was getting a tryout as a radio operator, while Tee—Helen didn't turn her head but she let her eyes slide to the sweet face beside her—well, Tee didn't want a job where she had to talk to people, for obvious reasons, she supposed.

She recalled how Tee had been almost panicky about finding her place in the WAC until one Saturday afternoon when they were about halfway through their basic training. Sergeant Rains had appeared as if she'd been summoned, given a quick *as you were* to her startled squad members, and then spent almost an hour going through some options with Tee and a couple of the other girls who were still undecided about their area of specialization. Helen had noticed before that while Rains could bark out commands like any other officer, at other times she had a calming, easy way about her. She imagined that gentle voice that she used with Tee was how she talked at home, when she didn't have to be a sergeant. Finally, Tee had chosen to try for the stock and supply area of the quartermasters and said that she wanted to stay at Fort Des Moines, working in the PX. The sergeant had simply nodded, but Helen had every confidence that she would make it happen. After all, Rains had taken care of her, too. Even if she'd intended for Helen's week in Georgia to be the end of what was going on between her and Tee, which it might have been if Tee hadn't had a change of heart, the fact was everyone could tell that Sergeant Rains wanted each of them to be the best soldier they could be. What was different about her was she accomplished that not by bullying or trying to scare them, but by caring enough about them to understand who they really were. Helen spent another moment examining her sergeant's profile. You'd never call her pretty, but Sergeant Rains was well put together and could even be considered attractive, though Helen doubted if anyone ever got past her serious and generally unapproachable manner. *Too bad*, she thought, and this time she did turn her head slightly to smile at Tee. *Everybody deserves someone.*

When the non-coms finished, they had Sergeant Rains stand and Colonel Issacson, the base commander, presented her with another ribbon. Helen could tell that her sergeant wasn't the least bit intimidated by the colonel and it made her proud of Rains to see that she actually looked rather comfortable with someone as important as Colonel Issacson. Helen was thinking how she hoped her time in the Army would give her that calm certainty that Rains seemed to have, that conviction that she really did belong here, when someone yelled out for Rains to make a speech. So the sergeant started talking about what she'd gotten from the Army and about the war and about women and their roles in the world. As Helen listened, she found herself reflecting on a new idea—the notion that she was a part of something bigger than just herself. A little glow of pride started up inside her as she considered how what they were doing there might, as Sergeant Rains had suggested, actually change the world. Helen wondered if the inspiration she was feeling now was what Tee felt in church, and perhaps that was what prompted her, when Sergeant Rains had finished, to say into the awed silence, "Amen, Sister."

Then everyone was applauding, the officers onstage and even the colonel, until a voice started yelling from the back. "Traitor! She's advocating treason!"

Helen looked around from her seat on the aisle and saw Sergeant Moore pushing her way to the front. Just seeing the ruddy-faced woman made Helen's lip curl in disgust, remembering Moore's meanness to her squad before Sergeant Rains had taken over. "That bitch better hold her tongue unless she wants more trouble than she can handle," she muttered, clenching her fists.

The applause was dying down and Moore's voice was rising above the din. Helen saw the colonel turn in her direction, head cocked slightly as if listening, just as the sergeant repeated her accusations. Clearly she'd found objection to Rains's comments about the ruling men of their day. When Moore reached Helen's row, Helen moved before anyone else could react. She put all the hurt and disappointment and anger she'd ever felt into the first punch, and it knocked Moore back against people sitting in the seats on the other side and shut her up, but good. *Well, that one was for me*, Helen thought, launching herself onto Moore's staggering form with her fists still pummeling her target, the way her brother had taught her. *These are for Sergeant Rains.*

The rest was a blur. It wasn't until the door of the stockade swung shut that her breathing began to slow. Alone, she swallowed back the last of her anger and felt a sense of regret growing in its place. It was probably stupid—no, definitely stupid—for her to fight with a superior, even if she was a downright evil person like Sergeant Moore. Fight was not the right word for it, actually, since Moore hadn't even swung at her, only scratched her arm a bit when she'd tried to deflect one of her last blows. Remembering how the smug expression on Moore's face had quickly turned to fear, she felt a grin tugging at the corner of her mouth, but it disappeared at the next thought. *They won't kick me out for this, will they?* Her sudden worry echoed in the silence until she was about to panic. She couldn't say how long it had been before the light shifted and a moving shadow became Sergeant Rains. Helen had been standing at the bars, looking out, but she still hadn't seen or heard Rains approach. Startled, she jumped back but quickly covered her movement by coming to attention.

The sergeant stood without speaking for what felt like minutes. Helen kept her eyes focused elsewhere until she had the notion that she might have imagined Rains being there. When her eyes shifted to Rains's face, the sergeant spoke. "Are you injured? Hurt anywhere?"

"No, ma'am." Helen's snappy reply echoed loudly in the empty space, so she quieted her voice. "A little scratch on my right arm, but that's it. No problem, ma'am."

Rains sighed. "Private Tucker…" she began, but Helen knew she had to have her say first.

"Ma'am, I'm sorry, but I just couldn't let that bit—uh, that rude woman keep talking about you that way. It wasn't right." She lowered her eyes to the ground, her voice carrying the weight of regret. "You're not gonna get hurt by this, are you?"

"That is not your concern, Private Tucker. What you need to worry about is whether or not you'll be out of here in time for graduation. Or if there will even be a graduation for you."

Helen's eyes moved back to Rains's face, only dimly aware that she was doing so. Her voice anxious, she asked, "They've gotta let me graduate, don't they, Sergeant? You know I did real good at the motor transport school, and I know they need drivers just about everywhere." Rains narrowed her gaze slightly and Helen looked away. "I'm sorry, ma'am."

"Sorry for hitting a drill instructor?"

"Uh…" Helen didn't want to lie to Rains, but she didn't want to sit out her graduation in a jail cell either.

She heard Sergeant Rains blow out a breath of air that almost sounded like a chuckle. The idea that she might have pleased her sergeant almost made Helen smile, too. Then Rains let her off the hook, the way she had before. "You might want to remember that sorry feeling when someone else questions you, Private Tucker. In the meantime, I'll see what I can do. But it won't be much less than a week, and that's cutting it pretty close to the end of your basic training." She paused, looking away for a moment in that way she did when she was thinking. When she looked back, her face was serious again. "Do I have your word that you won't cause any more trouble while you're in here?"

"Yes, ma'am, you sure do. And I appreciate it."

"As do I, Private Tucker," Rains said, turning to go. It was several minutes before Helen realized what she'd meant. Without actually saying so, Rains was thanking her for sticking up for her. Helen moved into the cell and sat on the bed, determined to do her time as quietly as possible. She was ridiculously pleased when Bett Smythe came with a dinner tray, and they talked for a few minutes while she ate. After Bett left, Helen was just beginning to worry about Tee when she heard her soft voice, talking to the MP. Helen stood and gripped the bars and Tee's fingers came around hers. Their faces were close. "Guess I won't be going to church with you this week after all." Helen tried to sound glum.

"I thought we had a d-deal about staying out of trouble," Tee replied, her anxiety bringing her stutter back.

Helen lowered her gaze. "I know, baby. I'm sorry. I just— something in me kinda snapped. Sergeant Rains doesn't deserve that crap. Think about it. She took pains to help out all of us, not just you and me." Helen grinned. "She even put up with Bett's smart mouth." Tee stifled a giggle. "So I just couldn't sit there and listen to it for another second."

Her face sobering, Tee asked, "What's going to h-happen to you?"

"The sergeant said it would be less than a week. I should be out in time for graduation." She put her hand through the bars and stroked Tee's face. "Besides, I sure can't get into any trouble in here."

Tee managed a small smile. "You'd better not."

Tee couldn't help thinking how these days and nights with Helen in the stockade passed much more quickly than the last time she was gone. She didn't think it was that she knew exactly where Helen was or that she knew pretty much what she was doing. It was because she felt so much better about what was between them than she had before. Since Helen was in for at least a few days, the MPs were now bringing her food, but over the weekend Tee brought her own dinner to the stockade so they could eat together and catch up. The first news she had to share was how well things had gone at their sergeant's hearing. It was obvious that, other than Sergeant Moore, no one had any intention of damaging Rains's reputation by letting the treason issue drag on. Since so many of them had missed their Friday class in order to testify on Sergeant Rains's behalf, a makeup class was scheduled for Saturday. Helen wouldn't be out in time for that, and Tee planned to ask Bett to loan Helen her notes. Surprisingly, Bett wasn't in class either, so Tee tried very hard to write down anything that might be important. When she was eating dinner with Helen that night, she handed over the twelve pages that she'd scribbled during the lecture on the signal corps.

Helen took one look at the handful of sheets and started laughing. "Well, I can see how my exciting Saturday night is shaping up."

Worry made Tee's voice stricter than she'd intended. "If you can pass the test, you won't have to make up the class. You can still graduate on time, but you have to work at it."

"You sounded almost like an officer just then." A slow smile came to Helen's face. "I might like it, you ordering me around sometime." She ran her eyes up and down Tee's body. "But first, come a little closer and I'll tell you what I really want to work at."

When Helen's grin widened, Tee felt color rise in her cheeks. She looked around for the MPs, but Helen had been such a model prisoner so far that they'd already relaxed their vigilance. Still, she lowered her voice, trying to deny the pulse that had begun beating in her throat—

and elsewhere. "Don't, Helen. You're supposed to stay out of trouble, remember?"

"You only trouble me in one way, baby." The roughness in Helen's tone sent a tingle up Tee's spine. Helen moved up close to the bars. "Come over here and let me put my hands on you for just a second."

Tee picked up her tray and moved toward the door, her voice a harsh whisper. "I said *don't* and I meant it. I don't like that kind of talk. You can spend tonight thinking about what you really want to say to me." She took a few steps away. "After you finish s-studying, that is."

She decided not to go back to see Helen again until after she got out of church the next day and had lunch with the squad members who were around. Everyone was excited to start learning more about their specializations, and Tee was trying not to feel anxious about being in her classes without being able to turn to Bett or Helen for help. She'd made a pretty good score in the signal corps class, though, and that made her feel a little better. She also felt pleased about how she'd stood up to Helen, something she wouldn't have done with anyone about anything before she started talking with Reverend Culberson.

Walking toward the stockade, she glanced up at the steeple in the distance, thinking that she might try seeing the reverend before she started the evening services that some girls called Vespers. Tee wasn't familiar with that practice and she'd stayed away, at least partly because it had become her squad's routine to use Sunday evening to finish their personal grooming and clean up their individual areas—especially Helen, who tended to let things get a little messy on the weekends—before Monday's inspection. In truth she hadn't enjoyed attending the evening service at home once she'd gotten to be a teenager. That's when she was supposed to start sitting with the other young people in the back pews, like her sisters had, where they would whisper among themselves and giggle until some adult turned around and gave them the eye. Then it would stop...for a while.

After her thirteenth birthday Tee had only gone twice and she'd felt terribly awkward and out of place, what with the girls acting all silly or pouty and the boys pulling their hair or teasing them with pokes or pinches. In spite of her older sisters' encouragement, she just didn't feel comfortable with any of that, so most Sunday evenings she had a bellyache or a headache or some kinda work that she absolutely had to get finished for school on Monday. Finally, one Sunday, her daddy had yelled, "Just let her stay home, Verna. I'll give her enough to do that she'll be beggin' you to go next week." But she hadn't. While she still loved Sunday morning church with its familiar arrangement of songs and prayers, she'd felt much closer to God being by herself with the animals, or in the fields with the crops, than among the rowdy teenagers on Sunday evening. Today, she was still trying to figure out how God felt about her and Helen. She'd been edging away from being 100 percent certain that they were both going to hell, and since lightning hadn't struck her yet, she took that as a sign that maybe she wasn't truly straying from her faith.

As Tee automatically took her shortcut between the buildings, she was so lost in her thoughts that she almost didn't notice Sergeant Moore standing on the steps of the guardhouse, talking to Sergeant Rains. Moore had positioned herself on a higher step, so she and Rains were about the same height. Tee ducked back into the shadows, not wanting to be seen or to interrupt. The angle of the light made her notice how, as Moore shouted, little flecks of spittle flew from her mouth. Tee wondered how Sergeant Rains could stop herself from flinching.

"I'm pressing charges." Moore's voice blared. "She struck an officer. That's insubordination, at least."

Rains's mild voice seemed even quieter by comparison. Tee had to lean as far out as she dared, and even so she missed the first couple of words. "...says the superior officer must be acting in the execution of her duty at the time of the assault in order for the action to be insubordinate. That was not the situation on Thursday."

"That little hillbilly assaulted me in front of an entire platoon. I have a clear case." *This time*, Tee added the unspoken end of Moore's last sentence, thinking of her unsuccessful attempt to accuse Sergeant Rains of treason, of all things. *How can Sergeant Rains even stand there and talk to her?*

When she saw her drill instructor tip her head as if listening to something in the distance, she shrank back against the building. After a few seconds, Rains continued, her voice firmer. "There is another matter. Regulations state that it is not insubordination if the superior officer acted in such a way that made the superior officer lose the right to be respected." Tee ventured another look, seeing Moore scowling as Rains continued. "For example, if a superior officer attacks a subordinate, another subordinate would be within her rights to strike the officer in defense."

"You can't think that will stick. I was giving my opinion. I didn't attack anyone."

Rains crossed her arms and leaned toward Moore, but her voice was so low that Tee practically had to read her lips. "You attacked me verbally, Agnes. She's a member of my squad. She was defending me."

Apparently the use of her first name made Sergeant Moore give up on her official stance. "She hurt me. I want her to hurt. I want her to pay." She touched the swollen side of her face, her tone petulant.

"What if someone else pays for her?"

"Like who?"

Sergeant Rains looked in her direction so quickly that Tee didn't have time to duck back. Discovered, there was nothing for her to do but act like she was just now walking toward them. Rains waited until she reached them before speaking. "Private Owens, please tell Private Tucker that I'll be in to see her later."

"Yes, ma'am." Tee didn't dare look up, lest Sergeant Moore see and remember her from that awful first day at Fort Des Moines. Thankfully, Rains was already leading Sergeant Moore away as they continued their conversation.

When Tee got to Helen's cell, Helen was standing with her back turned, looking at the wall. "Hey," Tee called softly. "You okay?"

She had to step closer to hear Helen's muffled reply. "Depends."

"On what?"

Helen turned and walked toward the front of the cell, her hands cupping two paper flowers. They were fashioned like roses, and one even had dark red on the top edge, while the other was all white, like the paper. "On if you'll ever forgive me. I never shoulda talked to you like that, Tee. I'm just going all kinds of crazy in here, and the biggest way is how I'm missing you. But that don't make it right, what I said. I know that." She extended the flowers. "I woulda got you some real ones but..." She looked around sadly.

As her fingers tightened on the delicate buds, Tee thought Helen's eyes might have teared up a little. Quickly, she reached between the bars and touched Helen's hands, drawing Helen's gaze back to her. "These are beautiful, Helen. How did you make them?"

Helen took another step toward her. "My Aunt Darcy taught me. She had a little glass bowl with these in it, only hers were all different colors. When I was little, I used to think they were the prettiest things in the world." Her last step brought her to the bars, close enough that Tee could see the shadows beneath her eyes. "'Course, that was before I'd seen you," she whispered.

"Oh, Helen." Tee's heart jumped. "I miss you. I hate it, too, you being in here." She looked at the flowers again. "How did you make that r-red one?"

Helen grinned and pushed back her sleeve to show the scrape that Sergeant Moore had given her. It looked red and puffy, a new scab forming. "Might as well get something good out of this cat scratch."

Tee gave a worried frown. "That needs iodine, Helen." She looked toward the MP, but Helen squeezed her hands.

"You can tell them that when you have to leave. Talk to me now. Tell me everything that's going on."

Tee knew she couldn't mention having seen Sergeant Moore, so she covered her delay by lowering herself to the floor, so they could sit close and talk. Her mind was still occupied by the conversation she'd overheard. She needed to get Helen talking until she decided what, if anything, to say. "Maybe you should tell me about your Aunt Darcy now."

By the time she'd had to leave Helen and return to the barracks, Tee had decided not to tell anyone anything about what she'd overheard. But at lunch that Monday, when their squad's celebration of Helen's return was cut short by the inexplicable sight of Sergeant Rains serving Sergeant Moore her meal, Tee had to come clean about what she now understood from the conversation between their sergeant and Sergeant Moore. She'd figured it out after one of the girls from her new class on stock and supply told her about seeing Sergeant Rains going into Sergeant Moore's room with cleaning supplies. Quickly, Bett came up with a clever way for the squad to show their support for Sergeant Rains, and Helen topped it off by quickly reworking the trophy that she'd gotten so it now had their sergeant's name and BSE on it, which Helen told the entire mess hall stood for *Best Sergeant Ever.*

When Helen joined Sergeant Webber's squad for the first of her makeup classes that afternoon, she was surprised to find herself something of a celebrity. Nothing got around the base faster than juicy gossip, and Helen's takedown of Sergeant Moore, combined with her display of loyalty for Sergeant Rains, made for a good story. Helen had come to the class fully intending to keep her head down and simply do the work, but it was hard to ignore the questions and notes and smiles that kept coming her way. The instructor had to stop twice and correct one of the girls who wouldn't stop talking to her, while Helen tried to look like she was paying attention to the lesson. Afterward, when she had finally finished all the conversations and was heading back toward the barracks, she heard her name called again. She looked around to see two girls who she'd noticed but hadn't spoken to previously coming toward her. Something about the way they walked and the way they stood a little too close together made her think they might be special friends, like her and Tee. They introduced themselves as Wilma and Pauline.

"We were just wondering if you might be in the mood for a little fun after graduation," Pauline said. Helen's attention sharpened. One of the girls at Fort Oglethorpe had told her that *in the mood* was a phrase women like her sometimes used to signal a certain kind of party.

"Maybe," Helen said, shifting her gaze from one to the other. "What kind of fun are we talking about?"

"Oh, just a few of us getting together at someone's house." Wilma's tone was light and she made a casual gesture with her hand as if to say it was nothing. "We usually have a gay time, though."

Helen grinned. The use of the word *gay* was a definite hint. "That might be just my style. Can I bring a friend?"

"Someone you know pretty well?" Pauline asked. There was just the slightest hint of nervousness in her question.

"Oh, yeah," Helen assured them. "And she knows me the same way."

They all laughed and the girls promised more details after lunch the next day.

❖

Aunt Darcy came for graduation, and after the ceremony, Helen proudly introduced her to anyone who was standing still for more than two seconds. During those meetings, Tee stayed nearby, trying to make a good impression. When Aunt Darcy turned her familiar green eyes on Tee and asked, "Are any of your people here today, Private Owens?" Tee shook her head and gathered herself to explain that there wouldn't have been money for a luxury like a trip to Iowa, but Aunt Darcy patted her arm as if she already knew why. "Well, I hope you'll consider me your family for today." She smiled and added, "Or for longer, if you'd like."

Tee blushed, not knowing exactly how to feel. She already knew that Helen's Aunt Darcy lived with another woman, and she'd gathered from Helen's story that they were…well, more than just roommates. But Aunt Darcy looked pretty much like anyone else's relatives who were there. There were still some darker streaks in her mostly gray hair and she wore a nice print dress. Although she was a little heavy by WAC standards, she carried herself easily and with almost military posture. When she smiled, though, her mouth had the same roguish twist to it that Helen's often had. When Helen pulled Aunt Darcy over to meet Sergeant Rains, Tee stayed where she was. She was still pondering the words that her sergeant had spoken to her when they'd shaken hands during the ceremony. "The Women's Army Corps is proud of you, Private Owens. Be proud of yourself, too." For Sergeant Rains to say that to her after everything that had happened, she'd just about started crying right there on the stage. But she'd managed to pull herself together enough to actually look her sergeant in the eye and say, "Thank you, Sergeant," like she'd heard the other girls saying. She thought she'd felt Rains's grip on her hand had tightened ever so slightly, and then they called the next girl's name.

Afterward, while Helen and her aunt were talking with their squad mate Maria's cousins, Tee saw Sergeant Rains talking to a man whose expression looked like he'd eaten something sour. Then Bett pushed by her, and when she made her way to their drill instructor, Tee thought she heard Bett say *Father* to the man before the rest of the conversation was lost in the noise. Tee couldn't see that his face got any happier, but then someone moved into her line of sight. A minute later, when Tee was able to see them again, their sergeant was walking away—alone— until Bett caught up to her after a few seconds. Anyone with eyes could tell that Bett's daddy was upset when he stalked off in the opposite direction, and for the first time, Tee wondered if Bett's life might be kinda hard, too. Just hard in a different way, maybe.

Aunt Darcy wanted to take them both out to dinner at the nice hotel where she was staying. Tee thought she shouldn't go to give Helen some private time to visit with her aunt, but Helen insisted. "I want you to see this place," she'd whispered, "'cause I want to take you there someday." They had freshened up back at the barracks and were sitting on their bunks, facing each other, as they'd done so many times over the past weeks. Tee had planned to just stay and write a couple of letters about graduation to her family. They were alone and Helen leaned to brush her fingers across Tee's cheek with a quick, soft touch. "Please come. I want to show off my girl."

Tee shook her head again when a question occurred to her. "Does your aunt know...about us?"

Helen shrugged. "She knows what she knows. She knows I like you and we're best friends." She moved over to Tee's bunk, sitting close. "Is there something more I should tell her?" She picked up Tee's hand from where it was resting on her lap. "Is there something more you want to tell me?"

The past week had been so busy. They hadn't been together at all during daylight hours, and sometimes not even at meals. Between pushing Helen to make sure she finished her general studies classes and her own nervousness about actually getting to graduate, Tee hadn't hardly had time to think, much less talk about any other feelings. After Helen's release from the stockade, they'd agreed to be extra careful for those last few days. Now she closed her eyes, trying not to show how much she'd missed Helen's touch. The relief that they were really done with basic training, along with her apprehension about what their future held, was almost overwhelming. More than anything, she wished for a quiet place where they could lie next to each other, alone. She wanted Helen to tell her that everything would be fine. She wanted to tell Helen how much she'd thought about them being together. When she opened her eyes, Helen was smiling at her and she smiled back. For just a second, she thought Helen might be going to kiss her again and she was astonished by how much she wanted it.

The barracks door banged shut and a voice that could only be Jo Archer called out, "Yo! Am I the last living cell in the body?"

With a slight squeeze Helen let go of Tee's hand and strode over to where Jo was surveying the nearly empty space. Tee heard them discussing when they'd get assigned to their new quarters, Jo's non-com classes, and Helen's strong dislike of Lieutenant Yarborough, the woman in charge of the Fort Des Moines Motor Pool. "Bet you're wishing you stayed in Georgia, huh?" Jo asked.

Tee's heart fluttered desperately at the thought. She rose and joined them, taking Helen's arm. Other girls did this sort of thing all the time, and Jo didn't give her a second look. "What t-time do we need to meet your aunt?"

CHAPTER FIVE

Sergeant Gale Rains woke at first light, as was her longtime habit. Almost always, her mind and her body came fully alert as soon as she opened her eyes, but this morning her being had a leisurely heaviness and consciousness dawned slowly. An intoxicating scent occupied her awareness. It wasn't just a memory or a faint trace from a piece of clothing or recently visited location. She was fully immersed in it as her nude form was in very close contact with an equally bare and distinctly feminine body. Her face was at the woman's back, her arm across and hand resting on her belly. *Bett.* She was in the home—in the bed—of her former squad leader, and the situation was as unusual for her as was the woman beside her. Nothing in her admittedly limited previous experiences of being with another person compared to the last days and nights with Bett. She couldn't stop a smile from making its way across her lips.

When she'd been confined to her quarters the night after her speech to the platoon, Bett had brought dinner, telling her that she was accepting a job at the cryptography center in Des Moines "for us." They were standing so close their bodies were touching and Rains knew much more would have happened had the MP not come by. Two days later, she'd thought herself back in control at their last squad leader meeting, until Bett had teased her to the point that she'd thrown her hat onto the table in frustration. When the devilish look in Bett's eyes was replaced by one of deep longing, Rains could only remain motionless. It seemed like there was so much to say, but nothing else registered after Bett's lips met hers in a light but lingering kiss. Once more she fought back the rise of desire, forcing out the words of obligation and why the duties of her rank had to come first, before anything between them. But when Bett asked what would happen after graduation, she'd answered by taking Bett in her arms and kissing her with every feeling she'd had about her since the day they'd met. Rains knew that by accepting Bett's invitation to visit her new home, she was giving them both permission to explore what might be between them, but by then it had seemed like something that was meant to be.

Private Smythe's report date had been pushed back a week due to the installation of some new cryptography equipment, and Sergeant Rains just happened to be at loose ends herself, due to a pending investigation of a clash she'd had with a corrupt MP who had tried to use Bett as a way of punishing Rains for having him transferred. On the day she'd arrived at Bett's house, as it became obvious that they wouldn't continue as merely *Sergeant* and *Private* to each other, they'd talked about names. Only to the Army was she Gale Rains. When an inattentive clerk had added an *s* on the English translation of her Lakota name, Wind and Rain, she'd let it stay. But if she was going to be her true self with Bett, she needed to use her real name, or be called the way her family knew her—as just Rain. So far, she had no Lakota name in her mind for Bett, but such things came in their own time, and she knew how to wait. At least, she had known how before these last five days.

Now as Rain breathed in, she savored the newness of laughing and talking and touching so freely with another person. Especially the touching. Rain felt so different physically, it was as if she inhabited a new body. In the places that had been empty, or occasionally yearning, she was now enjoying a fulfilling hum of satisfaction thanks to the experience, skills, and sexual appetite of one Elizabeth Smythe. After spending most of her childhood in a household with only her father and two brothers, and having lived most of her adult life alone, Rain would never have believed how perfectly natural it felt to lie like this with Bett, naked and close, completely relaxed and entirely open. But once she had surrendered to her feelings, the intimate dance of sleeping together was something she seemed to have always known, an innate understanding that had only been waiting to reveal itself at the right moment, as if she had picked up an untried musical instrument and been able to play it perfectly.

Everything about this new relationship seemed to bring her fulfillment. The giving and receiving of their most intense physical moments, certainly, but also the times when their closeness was emotional, personal, conversational...even spiritual. They had already learned to respond to each other's most obvious outward preferences and desires, but they had just scratched the surface of the rest. Rain thought she could spend the remainder of her life pursuing the nuances of Bett's more subtle or complex passions as well as coming to know all of her, the wholeness of her being. For the first time, she understood why people married—to reserve each other's time for this captivating process of discovery.

Bett's manner had changed, too, in some ways. She was still clever and quick, but the edge of anger or frustration that had often colored her tone during basic training was gone. Something about her had softened, opened, and Rain was finding the implicit invitation into a life with her increasingly irresistible. Sometimes in Bett's eyes she saw a reflection of the wonder she felt.

In reaction to these thoughts, her fingers flexed and stroked ever so softly on Bett's belly. Bett had just the slightest roundness there that Rain liked to feel. But then, there wasn't anywhere on Bett's body that Rain didn't like to feel. It had been easy for her to channel her long tradition of wandering and exploring to the terrain of Bett's body, and in a way that Rain had yet to fully understand, this physical closeness had made it possible, easier even, for them to become closer in other ways. Her hand moved slightly upward on Bett's body and Bett's hips pressed closer for a few seconds and then relaxed again, almost like a little stretch. Her breathing remained deep and even.

Rain considered how parts of her own past had begun appearing in her mind as she lay with Bett or sat across from her at the little breakfast table or watched the fire with her. Not the really bad things or even the occasional good things, just little recollections from a day or a moment. She had seen a perfect double rainbow stretching from one mountain peak to another; it had lasted almost a full minute and then a hawk appeared in the sky where it had been and flew to a tree not five feet away from her. Once when she and her younger brother Nikki had found scattered bones on one of their hikes and had spent part of an afternoon reassembling them until the form of a coyote was revealed. Another day when she had gotten stung at least twenty times getting some honeycomb from a bee tree and had been unable to eat for two days. Her older brother Thomas had saved her some of the honey, though, and then showed her how to move without angering the bees. An afternoon when she had spent hours thinking about something she had read, her mind swinging back and forth between agreeing completely and disbelieving entirely. She found she could simply open her mouth and these memories would come out as Bett was stroking her hair or her arm or lying up against her, holding her hand, and Bett would simply listen. Sometimes she would ask her a question that would lead to another story, or sometimes Bett would tell her a story of something in her life. This sharing of herself that Rain had never been comfortable doing with another person now seemed effortless. *Is it because I want her to know me that I am becoming better at knowing myself?* One thing she knew for certain—every moment she spent with Bett was making her life more meaningful and her heart richer.

Rain's hand moved up again; she was almost to Bett's breasts. Rain could freely admit to herself that as much as she enjoyed all the other parts of Bett's body, she absolutely adored her breasts. Their perfection held her in thrall and Bett seemed to know it; sometimes she would bring Rain's hands to them or push herself up to Rain's mouth, just to break the spell of Rain's enchanted stare. Bett wasn't above using them to get her way in little things, convincing Rain to go out when she didn't know if she really wanted to or making sure that Rain wasn't too upset about Bett not doing the dishes yet simply by brushing her breasts across Rain's face or pressing them into her back when she spoke. Because the vision of them was now permanently imprinted on her brain, it made only a little difference if Bett was clothed or unclothed when she did this. As Rain's hand moved nearer, she heard a distant sigh of encouragement from Bett's throat. Rain had gathered that Bett's experience with sex had almost always been at a much faster, almost frantic pace, while she—having delayed this gratification for much longer—liked to go as slowly as they could tolerate. Both ways were equally good; anything physical with Bett was good; anything with Bett was good; Bett was good. Rain's hand cupped the underside of Bett's breast and any logical thought departed. Bett's hips began moving again and the encouraging sound was much closer now. As Rain's fingers stretched to touch Bett's nipple, she brought her lips to the back of Bett's neck, kissing, then grazing with her teeth, then kissing again. Bett's breathing changed, shorter, shallower breaths with faint moans starting each exhale. Her nipple hardened under Rain's touch and Rain felt herself grow wet. Her hand closed and squeezed gently and she felt a tremor of excitement pass between them.

Bett turned slowly in her arms until she was facing her. Her voice was sleepy but her eyes were bright. "I had a sneaking suspicion that you were a morning person, Sergeant. I see you have figured that out as well."

Rain put her hand back on Bett's breast and opened her mouth to answer. *I think you have made me an anytime person*, she was going to say, but no sound came out. Bett was too beautiful, too perfect for words.

"So what can I do for my early riser?" Bett saw the desire in Rain's eyes and smiled. She ran her tongue across Rain's lips as she rested her hand on Rain's chest. Her other hand made its way between Rain's legs and an eyebrow went up. "Oh, I see. Someone had a nice dream, maybe?"

"No," Rain managed to moan as Bett's fingers began stroking lightly. "I had a nice waking. With you. Because of you."

Bett kissed one of Rain's breasts and then the other. "What a sweet thing to say." It was a very nice waking for her, too, but she decided to tease a little longer before letting Rain know that. Her hand was teasing, too, making sure to move in one of the ways she'd learned Rain liked, knowing from the slickness and the heat that swells of arousal were building inside her. Then she slowed...and stopped. "You woke me up, you know," she whispered in Rain's ear, pretending to scold.

"Yes, I—" Rain started to explain but Bett's fingers were moving again and she couldn't continue.

"Well, you're by far the most desirable alarm clock I've ever had, so I suppose that's all right." Bett's fingers pressed a little quicker and a little harder until Rain's breathing matched her tempo. Unintentionally, Bett's mind brought her memories of other times that she had been awakened for sex. Twice, maybe three times? In each of those cases, of course, alcohol was involved. She'd been on a date and had too much to drink and passed out before having sex. Which was, of course, the point of the dating and the drinking. Another time, she seemed to recall, she'd actually passed out during sex. In each case, her date had managed to rouse her and they'd reached some kind of finish before she'd staggered back to her room. *Was it only for sex that Rain awakened me?* Her fingers slowed again and stopped.

"Bett…" Rain groaned.

"I'm sorry, dearest. I guess I'm just not quite awake yet." She pulled Rain on top, centering Rain's wetness on her thigh. "Maybe you should take over for a while." In fact, Bett's mind was completely awake and she wanted to know something about this moment; she wanted to see if it was just the orgasm Rain wanted or if there was something more. She reached down to move Rain's hips, sliding Rain against her. She could tell by Rain's breathing and by how wet and swollen she was that it wouldn't take much for her to make herself come. Bett watched Rain's brows knit and thought perhaps she was concentrating on finding the right place to move, but then Rain rolled off and pulled Bett back on top of her.

"No. I didn't mean for it to be like that." Her voice was rough. "I want…I wanted you—" Her eyes were searching Bett's. "Don't you want to…?"

Bett didn't like seeing the question in Rain's eyes, doubt around the margins where there had been absolute certainty before. *Don't be stupid!* she told herself. *This is not like those other times. She's not like that.* She sat up on Rain's stomach, giving Rain the best view of her breasts by way of apology. "I'm so sorry." She leaned forward and gently kissed Rain's lips. "I shouldn't tease you like that, not first thing in the morning. Will you forgive me?"

She could feel her own slippery hardness as she slid back down Rain's body, intending to finish what she'd so unkindly left unfinished. But as she dipped down Rain's slightly concave stomach, she contacted the mound of Rain's pelvis, and her eyes closed with the sensation of touching herself there. Rain saw and pulled her closer, forcing that movement again. Bett breathed out a little moan, and when Rain moved beneath her, Bett's head went back. "Mm."

Rain rolled them both over and slid her narrow hips between Bett's legs. She thrust against Bett's wetness and Bett felt herself giving in to it, in spite of her best intentions. "Wait, Rain…oh yes, right there. No, I was going to…wait, I…oh God, yes."

Rain stopped moving. "While we are together, I will be the only one here in your bed, won't I? The only one you are with in this way?"

"Yes, Rain, yes, you will," Bett answered immediately, wanting to pour the words into Rain's heart and let it lift with the truth of what she'd said. She moved her center against Rain again. "Yes," Bett repeated, finding her rhythm, tightening her arms around Rain's back.

Rain stilled, another question in her eyes. "And I will be the only one in your heart?"

For a few seconds, Bett kept moving, enjoying the sensation too much to stop. But it wasn't the same as when Rain was moving with her, so she stopped again. Her answer was easy and she knew it was right. "You already are, Rain. You are and you will be." She closed her eyes as Rain thrust her hips forward again and Bett found the place she wanted. Her voice softened. "Oh yes, there…there, Rain."

As the pitch of Bett's voice shifted up, Rain stopped again. "Then could I also be the only one in your mind when we are together like this?"

Bett stopped moving again, too. She opened her eyes again and looked at Rain slanting over her, hair hanging loosely past her shoulders, the request in her eyes as real as the strength in her arms. *Can I be in the moment with just her and let those others go? Can I trust her to do the same?*

"Yes, Rain. I will try, I promise. You know how my mind is—it just gets too busy sometimes. But yes, I will put my thoughts on only you when we are together like this."

Rain rolled them over again so they were facing each other on their sides. She looked at Bett for a long moment and then kissed her. And kissed her. And kissed her. Mouth soft and gentle. Like kissing after sex, but deeper somehow. Bett let herself drift with it, so sweet and easy. Nothing else in the world but Rain's mouth, wet and warm. The one hand lightly caressing Bett's back, the other in her hair, the touch unhurried and loving. The pressure of tender lips. Bett's body felt like a vessel, filling slowly with pure, fresh goodness after every old and bitter thing had been poured out. After a time, when Rain started to pull away after finishing a kiss, Bett's mouth followed and her little sound of want brought Rain's lips back to hers, an answering hum of delight from her throat. It was so much more than simply physical contact. It was a conversation of possibilities, an exchange of promises. Bett wasn't sure when it stopped because she was still feeling it, the splendor flowing slower now, even though her head was on Rain's shoulder, and then Rain's voice in her ear, low and tender, "My beloved."

They were so close it felt like every part was touching. Bett couldn't raise her head, could barely tighten her arms around Rain for a second's embrace. She said, "Mine," but only a mumbled sigh came out. Rain's caresses had slowed and Bett could feel her own breathing getting deeper, more relaxed.

Rain was gone when she woke up, but Bett felt her presence nearby. As she stretched, she looked over and saw something on Rain's pillow. It was a small piece of milky quartz crystal, with just a bit of contrasting dark material of some kind at the top. Bett picked it up. It was warm in her hand. She could hear Rain making their tea, the familiar sounds measured and precise. She kissed the stone and put it in the drawer of her bedside table. Oddly, she didn't feel the least bit frustrated or unfinished, the way she had the few times that she'd been with someone and hadn't achieved an orgasm. *No,* she told herself, *I'm not thinking about those times anymore. It's now and it's Rain and that's all.*

As she dressed, her eye fell on the calendar hanging near her small writing desk in the corner of the bedroom where next Monday's date was circled. Now it was Rain, but what about next week when Rain would return to her duty at the Fort Des Moines WAC base and she would have to report to the cryptography center building in town? How would they arrange to see each other, to be together? It had taken almost the entirety of basic training for her to get Rain to let down her guard enough to acknowledge the extraordinary attraction that had been there almost since their first meeting. What would it take to ensure that this wonderful certainty that she felt between them wouldn't become obscured behind the wall that Rain would surely rebuild once she returned to her duty?

She went into the kitchen. Rain was at the stove in her jeans and flannel shirt, her hair still loose. Bett ran her hand across Rain's back and Rain turned, smiling shyly.

"I'm so glad you're here," Bett said, looking up at her. Seeing a brief distance come onto her lover's face, she imagined that Rain might be thinking of her home, of the base, or of other places she had been. But when she looked back at Bett, her smile grew.

"There is nowhere I would rather be than here with you."

Bett put her head against Rain's chest trying to push back the familiar feelings of panic. But this time, her worry wasn't about needing to leave. She wanted Rain to stay. *We'll figure out something. This can't be over so soon.*

❖

Sometime in a conversation, Rain had told Bett that most of the towns where her family had lived were too small to have their own movie theater and there wouldn't have been money for them to go anyway. And even since she had been in the WAC, living at Fort Des Moines where the on-base picture shows were free, Rain had never gone because it seemed a frivolous waste of time that she would prefer to spend away, outside, alone. So that Saturday afternoon, when she sensed that Rain was a little restless—they hadn't been out of the house and had barely been out of the bed for five days—Bett suggested they take in Rain's first movie at the theater in town. There were a few elderly couples and several other young women in the theater, but most of the WACs went to the movies on the base; they didn't see anyone they knew. To Bett's surprise, Rain said she was glad they were still in their civilian clothes, because she wasn't ready to think about saluting or other Army protocol just yet. They saw *To Have and Have Not*, even though Bett had already seen it, since Rain categorically refused to see the other feature that was playing, which was a Western. Bett tried not to be jealous when Rain's mouth opened at Lauren Bacall's first scene with Humphrey Bogart.

"Did you think she was pretty?" Bett inquired of Rain afterward.

"She's not as pretty as you—just bigger," Rain answered, and Bett giggled all the way to the grocery store. They were running low on tea and other essentials and Rain wanted to stock up before they went back to work.

Rain shopped very slowly, touching and smelling different fruits and vegetables before she made her selections, sometimes pausing for several moments to look at an area of the shelves where there were multiple choices, like the cereal aisle.

"Just get what you like best, Rain," Bett said, putting the basket on her arm, trying to hurry Rain along. "I'm sure I'll eat anything."

"I don't know what I like best," Rain answered. "I haven't tried them all."

Bett coughed into her hand, stifling a laugh. "Well, you could go through them all alphabetically, making notes, like in those travel guides. Then we could publish your findings in the paper."

Rain looked at her doubtfully. "Who would want to read that?"

"Busy housewives and cereal connoisseurs." Bett was starting to giggle again. "People who purchase large quantities—" She snapped her fingers. "The Army! They'd want to know which brand is the best according to Sergeant Gale Rains, our national cereal critic."

Rain's uncertain look had turned into a menacing squint. "You are teasing me."

"Then you could move on to breads"—Bett was giggling again as Rain came closer—"canned goods, paper products…"

Rain had gotten close enough to reach out and tickle Bett under the arms, getting a satisfying shriek in return as Bett tried to wiggle away. Just then, a man in a store apron came around the corner. "What's going on here?" He approached them quickly, focusing on Rain, taking in her coloring and her braid at a glance. Rain had already moved a step away from Bett, but the man gave her a shove, pushing her back another few feet. "What do you think you're doing? You keep your filthy red hands off her, you hear me? Now get out of here before I call the police."

Bett saw a flash of anger cross Rain's face, that same dangerous look she'd had when a woman in their squad had taken a swing at her when she'd been caught stealing. She stepped into the man's line of sight. "No, no, you misunderstood, sir." From the corner of her eye she saw Rain turn and walk back up the aisle toward the front of the store. "We're friends. We were just being silly."

Satisfied that Rain was leaving, the man turned his attention to Bett. He looked her over with an appreciative sneer. "You got no business being friends with the likes of that. They're all thieves and liars, you know. You should stick to your own kind."

Bett was so appalled that she almost didn't know how to respond. Handing the man her basket, she said, "She is my kind," and walked out.

Rain was nowhere in sight. Bett went home, hoping she would already be there, but she wasn't. Bett sat and thought about the friends she had made at Kent and Oxford, the girls she had been with in her past. Before her time in the WAC, almost everyone she'd ever known had been pretty much like herself—young, white, mostly rich or at least comfortably well-off—except for... An image that she'd deliberately kept away for some time swam into her thoughts: thick glasses, wild reddish hair, white oxford shirt misbuttoned so it hung unevenly, a slight gap between her front teeth that would make a faint whistling sound with certain words, the smell of cigarettes...*Lexi.*

❖

Kent, England
September 10, 1935

Bett had turned fourteen the year that the fall term started with everyone talking of a new girl—a townie—who had been admitted on a limited, trial basis. Even though she'd been boarding at the all-girl preparatory school since she was ten, Bett wondered if it was her American heritage that made the concept of some girl pulling herself up by her bootstraps less unseemly than it was to her privileged classmates. Of course, she didn't tell anyone else that. Especially Emma Prosser, her secret crush.

That morning Emma had sent Bett into the biology lab early, giving some excuse so she could make an entrance later. Even though it was against the rules, she ordered Bett to save her a place, fluttering her eyelashes and squeezing Bett's arm in a way that made her unable to refuse. Bett sat at one of the two seat tables up front, imagining late nights of study with Emma. She was so busy making plans that she didn't notice an unkempt-looking creature come around and take Emma's chair until she heard some giggling and chattering from the girls nearby. When Bett looked around and saw the girl, she startled. "You can't sit there," she stated firmly. "That seat is saved."

"Ya can't," a working class accent replied brusquely.

"I certainly can," Bett responded promptly. "My friend will be right in. She's just gone to the loo."

"Would that be her, then?" working class asked, tilting her head toward the door. Bett looked over just in time to see Emma slip in, give her an apologetic shrug, and take the seat next to Catherine Higgerton-Giles. Bett had always been intimidated by that hyphenated name, and now the vision of Emma and Catherine poring over their books together made her huff an antagonized breath. The new girl didn't seem to notice.

"I'm the townie, as you probably guessed. Name's Alexis Greene. Call me Lexi."

This is social suicide. Bett grimaced. Sometimes she thought it was only her willingness to do whatever it took to maintain a close relationship with Emma that kept her from hovering hopelessly on the fringes of this tightly woven collective of titled names and old money. That and her sharp wit and gift of mimicry that could get everyone laughing…except the unfortunate target of her parody, of course. But being lab partners with the most socially objectionable girl in the school might take a thousand jokes to spare Bett being painted with the same undesirable brush. Their instructor walked in and the room stilled. Bett's mind was working a mile a minute, but she couldn't think of any way out of this situation. It was absolutely intolerable but apparently unalterable.

"What's yours?" At least the girl had enough sense to drop the volume of her jarring accent.

"Be quiet," Bett ordered as sharply as it was possible to do in a whisper. The girl sighed dejectedly and fiddled with the worn nub of a pencil. Bett got out her fountain pen and began taking notes, mostly just to give herself something to do. The instructor was already using scientific terminology that was completely foreign to her. Lexi took out a ragged-edged notebook and found a blank page toward the back, but she wrote nothing. Normally, Bett wouldn't even notice, but she was so annoyed that she thought she'd at least put the girl in her place. "You're supposed to be taking notes," she murmured in her most condescending tone.

Indulgently, as if Bett were a three-year-old who needed these things explained, Lexi replied, "But only when you don't know somethin', right?"

The professor's voice rose into a question. "Who can tell me the concept that reduces the confirmation bias by formalizing the attempt to disprove hypotheses rather than prove them?" Bett rolled her eyes internally. *As if I had the faintest idea…*

"Falsification," Lexi whispered softly, but didn't raise her hand. There were several incorrect guesses. Lexi tilted her head from Bett to the professor as if to say *go on*. Bett frowned doubtfully. After two more incorrect guesses, Lexi drew a hand on her paper and tapped on it, clearing her throat very softly. Feeling she had nothing left to lose, Bett raised her hand.

"Falsification, sir?"

Professor Maxwell beamed. "Very good, Miss…?"

"Carlton, sir. Elizabeth Carlton."

"Lexi and Lizzie," the townie pronounced very quietly while the room buzzed. Emma looked over with eyebrows raised and Bett gave her a confident little smile to show her what she was missing.

That night Bett had everyone in stitches with her imitation of Lexi's accent and her description of the pathetic pencil and well-mauled notebook. But later, when she lay alone in her bed, Bett felt slightly sick to her stomach. *Had that mockery really been necessary?* She supposed not, if she didn't mind becoming an untouchable outcast practically overnight. In her heart of hearts, Bett detested this aspect of Kent—the snobbery, the hierarchy of social strata, the system that let family and money and looks win out over heart and mind. And she hated herself for taking part in it so willingly. Was this really who she wanted to be? Was this who she had to be for Emma?

Bett only saw Lexi in that one class, where she never wrote one thing down and answered every question correctly—or rather, she let Bett answer, should she choose to do so. After two weeks, Bett stalled while her friends left, pretending to be reorganizing her satchel. When everyone but Lexi was gone, she said, "Look, I can't keep taking credit for your knowledge. It's not right."

"I don't care about that. I've just gotta do my time here before I can go up to Oxford."

"What?"

Lexi explained, "Gotta have proof from some posh prep school, don't I? Not enough to make the grades at our good old local Highview School."

Bett was intrigued. "How is it that you're so good at this?"

"Done it already. Did this level years ago with my dad. He was a bleeding genius. Biology, chemistry, physics—he knew it all and loved it. But as the oldest of seven kids, he had no chance to go on in school. Had to support the family, didn't he? Even worked here on the grounds for a while, part time, and filched a textbook or two from the trash at the end of term. We'd read them evenings before he took his shift at the pub." As a slow smile spread across Lexi's face, Bett watched the fondness of memory transform her slightly uneven features into a warm comeliness. "I guess not many girls had bedtime stories about subjects like carbon and the molecular diversity of life, but I adored it. And not just because he did. Well, maybe that at first, but then I came to respect the perfection of structure, its exactness of function." She stopped, suddenly self-conscious, but Bett nodded encouragingly.

Lexi's tone became confidential. "I'm going to be a surgeon, Lizzie. The best ever. And then I'm coming right back here and help those that don't get a shot at decent care." She took a breath and looked down at the table. "Those that die when their appendix bursts and they have to wait six hours for the doc to show up from his country club bridge party and operate even though he's had a wee nip too much."

Bett was wondering at the bitterness that had entered Lexi's voice but then she put it together. "Your dad?" This time her impersonation wasn't meant to be cruel. She had been so caught up in Lexi's story that it had come out unintentionally.

Bett's sympathetic expression helped Lexi finish, even though just the one nod made her bite her lip and blink back tears before she straightened determinedly. "I was named after him anyway, and when I'm done with school and hang up my shingle, I'll take back Dad's rightful name. I'll be Alex Greene. Dr. Alex Greene."

Bett never imitated Lexi again. Emma clearly noticed the change, because she began spending more time with Bett, flopping down beside her in the common room and complaining about her nails or about Catherine's impossibly curly handwriting, even complimenting Bett on her most recent English paper, which was unusual because it was a subject in which they often competed. Then she would try to lure Bett into joking about Lexi's clothes or her hair, but Bett refused to take the bait. More than once, she caught Emma looking over at them during class.

Toward the end of the term, Lexi missed a week of classes. Bett felt unexpectedly bereft, and she knew it wasn't just the bonus points she was missing. Sitting with her unorthodox classmate was practically pressure-free, other than Lexi occasionally drilling her on the subject matter, and in many ways Bett was the most contented she'd ever been at Kent Prep. There was no one-upping, no worries that her family was too nouveau riche, no competing for advantage in style or substance, since Lexi didn't worry about either. Even their senses of humor meshed well, once Bett decided to quit playing the prig and started being herself. *And who is that, exactly?* she questioned on the night of Lexi's third absence. During last week's lab she'd given Lexi the giggles by narrating their assignment on circulation in a perfect rendition of Lawrence Gilliam, a popular BBC radio commentator. While Lexi snorted laughter into a fraying handkerchief, her unabashed joy made Bett feel good in a way that she never experienced when she was mocking someone. She and Lexi were a good team, Bett realized, so in less than fifteen minutes she managed to coax Lexi's address from the dean's office. She implied that she intended to write, but she was on her way in a taxi within the half hour. It was dusk by the time she reached the town and there was no light in Lexi's house. When she knocked, a neighbor's white head came out the window next door.

"Whatcha want?" he asked suspiciously.

"I'm looking for Alexis Greene," Bett answered. "We're in school together and I need to speak with her."

"At the pub, of course." The neighbor yawned, pointing down the block. "Where else?"

The sound of popular music and a thick layer of smoke threatened to drown out everything except the pungent smell of alcohol. The loudest table held four couples, buying what was obviously not their first round from a little waitress holding a large tray. When Bett stepped through the doorway, the level of conversation dropped so much that the waitress turned to see what was happening. It was Lexi. She was wearing a gray uniform with a stained white apron. Her mouth dropped open as Bett walked over to a vacant seat at the bar.

Lexi crossed the room and stood beside Bett, arms over her chest, tapping her foot impatiently. "Just what do you think you're doing here?"

"I'm looking for my lab partner," Bett answered innocently. "She missed another class today." She ordered a Shirley Temple from the curious bartender.

"Well, Mum's been sick, so I had to take her shifts, didn't I? If she can't work, we won't make our tuition payment and then no more Kent Prep for this girl. Then no Oxford and no medical school." Lexi's tone had been somewhat defensive, but she leaned forward with anticipation as she questioned, "Did you start on graphing?"

"Yes, and I'm completely lost already." Bett looked around. The pub was no place for a girl of Lexi's intelligence to be working. "How much does your mother make for a shift?"

Lexi's face reddened and her hands moved to her hips. "That's none of your damn business, is it?"

"No, it isn't, but I have a selfish reason for asking. I want to hire you as a tutor, and I'll pay you twice what your mother makes so you won't miss any more classes. Honestly, Lexi, it's the only thing that's going to get me through this course. Please?"

So Bett's new strategy for the term abandoned the idea of time with Emma in favor of actually learning biology and enjoying the screwball personality of Lexi Greene. Only once did the two plans intersect. The final was coming up and Emma begged to be allowed to stay and join Bett for her tutoring session with Lexi. It was disastrous. Once the classroom was empty of everyone else and Lexi took up the instructor's position, Emma began playing with Bett's hair, whispering in her ear, poking her under her arm with her pen, and generally distracting her in every way possible. Normally, Bett would have been in heaven to get so much of Emma's attention, but she felt oddly conflicted. When Lexi suggested that she had seen whores with better study habits, Emma responded that she had seen dogs with better haircuts and walked out in a huff. Bett apologized to Lexi and tried to hand her the agreed-upon fee as she gathered hers and Emma's things. She knew Emma would be waiting outside, sniffing impatiently. Lexi refused the money, saying she hadn't earned it.

Bett was reaching for the door when she heard Lexi's voice, as quiet as on the very first day of class. "She doesn't really love you, you know." Bett turned back very slowly and watched as Lexi drew the top half of a circle on the board. "Real love arcs away from oneself over all obstacles and toward the other"—she added the lower half, completing the circle—"with feelings much deeper than what shows on the surface. That's why we use rings when people marry." She then drew two parallel lines and added a slash through them both. "This is what you have with Emma, Lizzie. You'll never come together because both of you love the same person. Her."

Bett swallowed and closed her eyes. She couldn't stand thinking that Lexi knew this about her and she certainly didn't want to consider any possibility of the truth in what Lexi said. Breathing in, she put the money on the nearest desk. "Here's your severance pay. You're fired."

Lexi never returned to biology class, apparently having received special permission to take her exam early. Bett sincerely hoped she'd made it up to Oxford, but she was too embarrassed to visit the pub again to find out. Deciding to avoid other sciences, she focused her graduation plan on languages instead.

Three years later, during her own first year at Oxford, Bett happened to be walking along the campus toward the train station, ready for a wild weekend in London, when a young woman in front of her dropped a folded notice from her pocketbook. She picked it up and was about to call out when her eye fell on the announcement: "Reception For Doctoral Candidates." The third name on the list was Alexis Greene. Bett turned around and went back to her room to get dressed.

Lexi's gown didn't fit particularly well, but her hair looked nice. Bett waited, standing behind Lexi while she spoke with an earnest young man. When Lexi turned, it only took a few seconds for her mouth to drop open, just like it had in the pub.

"I wouldn't blame you if you haven't forgiven me," Bett said quickly, "but I just happened to see the announcement of this event with your name on it and I had to come to offer my sincerest congratulations. And I wanted to tell you that you were right. You were totally, one hundred percent correct about everything and I was a stupid, pitiful arse."

Lexi blinked and then threw her arms around Bett's shoulders and hugged her close. "I can't imagine a more wonderful surprise, Lizzie. Seeing you has made this night complete." Bett felt the sweet wash of grace—forgiveness that hadn't been earned but was so freely given that it simply must be accepted. "Come here." Lexi pulled Bett's arm excitedly. "There's someone I want you to meet."

The dark-haired woman turned from the punch bowl and smiled warmly as Lexi made introductions. She had a lovely face and a slightly plump figure. "This is Eleanor Ferguson, another of our doctoral candidates. Elea, this is Lizzie, my biology lab partner from Kent Prep."

Elea's smile faded. "You're Lizzie?" Her tone suggested some deception was taking place.

"Yes, but I go by Bett now. It's nice to meet you." Wondering why Elea seemed so upset, she watched as she slipped her arm somewhat possessively through Lexi's. Then she saw. They were wearing matching rings.

Lexi gestured at Bett as she looked at Elea. "I told you about that term, remember?"

"Of course I remember. I was at Edgefield," she added, almost as an aside to Bett, naming a rival girls' school. She turned back to Lexi. "But in all your reminiscing, you never bothered to mention that your fond lab partner was extraordinarily attractive."

Lexi searched the ceiling as if her recollection could be found there. "Didn't I? Are you sure?"

Elea swatted her arm. "Yes, I'm sure. Because any story with the words *gorgeous woman* in it automatically sticks in my first level recall."

"Memory," Lexi said to Bett by way of translation. "Elea's doctorate is in brain research."

They drank until the bartenders went off duty, scandalizing the remaining guests with ribald jokes and stories that often referenced anatomy. As they staggered into what remained of the evening, Bett leaned in and kissed Lexi on the cheek.

"Congratulations, Lexi. You deserve every happiness. I hope I'm not speaking out of turn when I say that your father would be very proud." Lexi's eyes moistened. Bett shook Elea's hand. "And congratulations to you too, Elea. You've got a good one here."

"Don't I know it," Elea said, and Bett watched them smile at each other in a way that made her feel very sad…for herself.

Years later, Lexi was among those killed in London in the first terrible round of V2 rocket attacks. Bett had grieved for a solid week at her father's Los Angeles home, not leaving the house, alternating between mourning and rage, running a thousand different scenarios in her head but not one of them brought Lexi back to life. In the end, the only way that any of it ever made sense to her was the day she saw the WAC recruiting office and went in to join up.

So yes, Rain was the first person she had really known who was a different race and from a different culture. And from what little Bett knew, Rain's family was much poorer and much less high functioning then Lexi's. Always before, whenever someone in her wealthy circle posed hypothetical questions about falling in love with someone poor, Bett had thought of Lexi, and how her incredible scientific mind had evened everything else out. But Lexi's real lesson for her had been about how to treat others, no matter their station in life. With Rain, it was the Army that had been the great equalizer, and through Rain, she'd learned even more about herself. Bett wondered what would have happened if she and Rain had met in some other way. Did it really matter, the differences between them? Wasn't it Rain's good heart and beautiful spirit that made Bett move beyond her initial physical attraction to wanting to know and be with her?

During the eight weeks of her basic training, Rain's determination to maintain the honor of her position as Bett's drill instructor had been an obstacle between them. As much as Bett had resented it initially, she'd come to respect that the sureness of Rain's unfailing sense of right and wrong was an essential part of her. And now, since the artificial barrier of rank had fallen, what was growing between them was so much more than Bett had ever expected. Although they hadn't talked about it, she knew she was in love with Rain, and that meant she loved her emotionally as well as physically. Previously, she would have thought the most frightening part of a relationship would be admitting those feelings, even believing—as Bett did—that Rain felt the same toward her. But today, for the first time, she truly understood that they would also face the obstructions of others' reactions to who Rain was. They'd already shared some of the bruises of their pasts. As she tried to decipher what this new awareness meant for their future, Bett glanced at the clock again. Her worry returned. Rain would come back, wouldn't she? Call for me with your heart, Rain had told her once, and I will hear you. *Rain, please come home*, Bett's heart implored. *I want you, and I need you.*

Chapter Six

Helen couldn't wait for her probation period in motor transport to be over. She shouldn't even have to be tested, but since she'd had her training at Fort Oglethorpe instead of here, Lieutenant Yarborough had insisted she get checked out again. But next Monday she'd get to do her first solo drive, and from then on she'd be on her own. Every day this past week she'd had some higher-up riding along, watching her every move and judging if she was worthy of being trusted with an Army vehicle. Or, more specifically, the vehicle's cargo. Lieutenant Yarborough's second in command, Sergeant Harris, told them that industrial production was finally catching up with demand, and new trucks were arriving more regularly than they had during the first years of the war. She added that the distraction of a passenger was a primary concern when they carried personnel, especially if the passenger was a flirtatious male. Helen held back her laugh on that one. But extra attention had to be paid when transporting munitions or foodstuffs or any of the dozens of other possible payloads. They would be given an invoice that would list the freight to be picked up at the train station, from a supplier, or, on rare occasions, at another base, and the shipment that was delivered had to match exactly. *Exactly.*

Each day after their trial runs they were given a different scenario: What would you have done if...? Helen thought these what-ifs were really a waste of time. How likely was it that there would be a blackout while she was on a night run or that her vehicle would need decontamination after a gas attack? *If there really was a gas attack the condition of the vehicle wouldn't be my problem anymore*, she thought, remembering the panic she'd felt when she'd had to put on that gas mask during basic training. She'd rather die than wear one of those contraptions again. What was more likely was that some careless grease monkey would forget to put the radiator cap back on or tighten the lug nuts properly. Today, one of the male non-coms was riding with her, and once they were on the road he teased her about being so conscientious about checking the maintenance before they'd departed.

"Are you that careful with everything, Private Tucker?" Corporal Newton asked. "Do you count every bar of Ivory soap in each box, just to make sure your invoice checks out?"

Helen knew he was kidding. The wiry, balding guy wasn't even in the motor transport department. She'd been told he was just doing a ride-along as a favor to Sergeant Harris, so she smarted off just a little.

"Well, Corporal, if we were talking beer bottles instead of soap, I could be tempted to run off with a couple. Or if Ivory sold for more than ten cents apiece, I might try to find that black market everyone always warns you about."

During the few seconds of silence that followed, Helen focused on the road again as she swallowed, thinking she might have gone too far. Then he laughed and said, "So booze or dough will do it for you, huh, Tucker?"

Relieved, she smiled back at him. "Nah. I do it all for love."

❖

"Very nice, Private Owens."

Tee tried hard not to blush. Such praise always embarrassed her but she kept her head down and said, "Thank you, sir." She'd been very nervous when she'd realized that her new commanding officer, Major Edley, was a man, but the head of the PX had often encouraged her during last week's intensive training class. After a few false starts, Tee had found she had an eye for setting up displays, and even the more complicated logistics of procurement and sales were beginning to make sense. Now the major stood smiling as he looked over her new arrangement of postcards. "Keep up the good work."

"Yes, sir." The major stepped away to look over the snack bar area, but Tee didn't move because she knew that the highest-ranking woman in the PX, Captain Madison, was still scrutinizing her work.

Madison was a member of the Quartermaster Corps and a very strict, by-the-book type of officer, a bit like her former sergeant. But unlike Sergeant Rains, Tee never got the sense that the captain actually cared whether people in her command succeeded or not. At first Tee thought that Captain Madison just didn't like her, but now at the end of her first week of work, she'd pretty much determined that Madison didn't like anyone.

So she was stunned when the captain remarked, "You have the potential to do really well here, Private Owens. Is that something that interests you, or are you one of those just-putting-in-your-time soldiers?"

"No, I…I am interested, ma'am." Tee was afraid her stutter would make her sound uncertain, so she tried to firm up her voice as she added, "I like working here."

"That's good to know, Owens." Captain Madison walked off without another word.

Once she'd calmed herself after the officers were gone, Tee returned to her work, and to one of her favorite flights of fancy. Often, when she was stocking new lipsticks or exchanging older issues of magazines for new ones, she'd begun imagining how it would feel to have her own store. In this daydream, Helen would be the driver who delivered her goods, and what would start as a casual flirtation between them would end up with Helen pressing against her while she reached to get something from a high shelf, and when Tee turned—always acting shocked—Helen would kiss her. Once the kisses heated up and the pretend shock was gone, Tee would have to pull herself away from her fantasy, partly because she was afraid her face would show a flush but also because she wasn't exactly sure how things were supposed to go next.

They'd moved to their new barracks, which were located nearer to the officers' quarters, and had managed to get bunks next to each other, just like before. And even though they weren't together during the days like they had been in basic training, knowing the evenings would be all theirs helped the time pass more quickly. Claiming that history wasn't so boring when you were a part of it, Helen had taken an interest in a club that was devoted to preserving the story of the Women's Army Corps in general, and the activities at Fort Des Moines in particular. Tee decided to continue her visits with Reverend Culberson when Helen went to her weekly meetings. She trusted the reverend, but she hadn't yet figured out how to talk to her about Helen.

All that week she and Helen had been taking long walks after dinner, catching up on the day's events and finding some space for private talk. When they reached the areas of the base that were unoccupied during the evening, they would move closer, their shoulders lightly touching as they went.

Tonight, as they passed by the grove, Helen pulled her in for a long embrace. "I miss being with you. I want time to be alone, like this. Lots of time."

Being in Helen's arms seemed like the most important thing in the world. Tee didn't even think, she just answered. "Me, too."

"At least we'll have some time at the party on Saturday night."

"Mm." Tee stepped back enough to look into Helen's face. When Helen had first brought up the party invitation, she didn't even want to consider going. First, she didn't like parties. Although her stutter was much less noticeable than it had been, she was shy and didn't like being around that many other people. Second, she was scared to think about going to a party like this one, where there would only be women. Helen had told her they could dance together and even kiss and no one would think anything about it, but she couldn't imagine such a thing. And third, even if all of that was true, wouldn't she be risking her job in the WAC by going to such a place? They'd already had one close call, and she still kept Sergeant Rains in her prayers every night because of it. What if the MPs came this time and arrested them all or simply put them all on the train for home, with a less than honorable discharge and no future?

Her worries must have shown in her expression, because Helen reached out and brushed her cheek, her fingers gentle. "If you don't like it, we can leave. I promise."

Something occurred to Tee that she hadn't thought about before. "Will you go, even if I don't?"

Helen shrugged. "Yeah, probably, for a little while. The girls who invited me took a big chance, and I wouldn't want to worry them by not showing up at all. Plus, it would be nice to make some new friends." She took Tee's hands in hers, squeezing lightly. "Especially friends that you could really be yourself around."

The image of Helen alone, entering a room full of welcoming

women, made Tee shake her head slowly. Helen had been drastically thin when she'd entered basic training but had filled out to a dynamically sinewy frame. Tee remembered watching her get ready to go out with some of the other girls from their squad once before, and how she used a gel to slick the sides and back of her brown hair into a style that resembled Frank Sinatra's. Tee was sure she wouldn't be the only one who found Helen's confident swagger and dangerous grin almost irresistible. The thought made something purposeful rise up inside. "Are we going to walk there?"

"Walk?" Helen scoffed, taking her arm as they started back toward the barracks. "Not my girl. I been putting a little money aside, just for something like this. We'll take the Curbliner bus. Wilma says the place is less than a block from the third stop."

The muted music swelled and light spilled out onto the porch as the door opened to Helen's knock. A large woman looked down at them, her white-blond hair almost as short as a crew cut. Although she was wearing a man's suit, Tee could tell she was a woman by her bustline. Her expression was not particularly friendly.

"Yes?"

Helen smiled. "Hi. Wilma invited us."

"Don't know anyone by that name." The woman moved as if to close the door.

"Wait," Helen said, and the nervousness in her voice made Tee feel even more worried. "We were told to come here if we were in the mood for a gay time."

As the woman looked them over again, Helen reached to take Tee's hand. Apparently that decided it. "It's three dollars for the both of you with an extra two dollars if you want a room for an hour." The white hair didn't move as she glanced at her watch. "And there's a forty-five minute wait right now."

Tee gasped, but Helen reached into her pocket and handed over a five dollar bill as if it was nothing. The woman stepped aside and Helen kept hold of Tee's hand as they walked through the door. The narrow entryway opened up to a room on either side and both were dimly lit. The room on the left contained a series of couches and divans, many of which were occupied by entwined couples. The only furniture in the other room was a small table against the wall, where a radio tuned to a music station played at a sensible volume. Four couples were moving slowly, holding each other close. Brighter light shone from the far end of the hall where there were sounds of conversation and the occasional clinking of glass.

"Drinks and singles mingle in the kitchen and breakfast area," the woman said.

"Thanks," Helen answered as Tee moved a little closer to her. "We're good here."

The woman nodded and pulled a little square of paper from her pocket and wrote the number twenty-three on it. "Give me your coats and hats."

Helen glanced around quickly. It looked like everyone else had checked that part of their uniform, so it was probably okay. She wasn't carrying a bag but Tee was. She held it out, questioning, "Will this be okay?"

The woman nodded. "Yeah, it will." Something in her certainty made Helen feel better. They handed over their things and the woman said, "I'll find you when your room is available." She shuffled toward the kitchen, calling back over her shoulder, "You can call me Neil. Have fun."

Tee didn't mean to stare at the women who were swaying together, but looking in the other room was out of the question. In a way, the dancers' movements seemed almost instinctive and quite graceful. It was hard to see faces in the shadowy lighting, but her impression was that everyone here—except for Neil, perhaps—seemed, well, normal. Several were in uniform, like the two of them, but quite a few weren't. But there were no freakish oddities, no fearsome demons waiting to initiate her into some bizarre ritual. In fact, after a quick glance when Neil closed the door, no one was paying them the slightest attention.

All week she'd been terribly anxious about being here, and by the time they caught the Curbliner just outside the base, she was nothing but a bundle of nerves. But Helen had sat close to her and talked like they were just on their way to market or something, telling stories about her work and the people she'd met. At one point she'd leaned in real close and murmured, "Everything's gonna be just fine, Tee. I promise." Tee couldn't even bring herself to nod. Then Helen's shoulder had brushed hers and she added, "Now smile like I just told you something funny." Tee had forced her lips up slightly while Helen patted her arm.

The music stopped briefly and an announcer's voice came on, introducing a number one hit from last year. When the opening strains of a more upbeat number, "Taking a Chance on Love," began to play, Helen squeezed her hand. "Come on, baby. Let's take a chance on a dance."

She looked into Helen's face for the first time since they'd arrived, and breathed out slowly at the sight of familiar green eyes over a playful smile. Tee had no idea how to dance, since it was against her religion. Of course, so was touching and kissing another woman, and she'd already done that. Dancing might not be so bad, comparatively. So she let Helen walk her into the room, not minding at all when Helen's arms came around her waist. "Put your arms around my shoulders," Helen directed. Then she began to lean side to side in time to the music, gently pulling Tee's body with her. "Now just shut your eyes and let me lead you," Helen whispered, stepping closer.

That should be easy enough, Tee thought. *She's been leading me since we met.* But when she felt the familiar warmth and tight lines of Helen's body, a sharp awareness of wanting to keep this contact filled her mind. Longing swelled in her, and her arms tightened, bringing Helen's chest into hers. Helen hummed a sound of pleasure and shifted so their lower bodies brushed as they rocked slightly. Thrilled at the sureness that Helen wanted to be touching her, too, Tee followed her movements unconsciously, willingly. For the first time since Helen had left for Georgia, Tee thought of the time they'd been together in the little exercise room and what it felt like when their skin made contact. Hot. Urgent. And yet so wonderfully sweet. She shuddered with the memory and Helen pulled back enough to look into her face.

"Are you okay, Tee? Is this all right?"

Tee blinked with a sudden understanding. Helen might be leading them at this moment, but in most other ways, she let Tee control what happened between them. If Tee said no, she wasn't all right, if she asked to go home, would Helen take her? Yes—she could tell by the way Helen waited, by the way she'd stopped dancing, that she was preparing herself for an unfavorable answer. When Tee smiled and nodded, whispering, "Okay," Helen relaxed and began moving them again.

The song ended and another number one from 1943 began to play. This was a slower, sweeter tune, "Sunday, Monday or Always." Resting her head on Helen's shoulder, Tee wondered whether it was also true that she could move them in the other direction. Could she hasten the excitement between them, add to that arousal that Helen had started inside her weeks ago? Curious, Tee let her breath out in a little stream, knowing it would tickle Helen's neck. She snuggled in and let the tip of her tongue graze over the same spot. One of Helen's hands drifted down and caressed her lower back, her fingers daringly close to Tee's rear. Tee kissed softly where her tongue had been and heard a rumble in Helen's throat. Helen's other hand eased around and she pulled Tee firmly against her.

"Do you have any idea what you do to me?" she muttered. Her voice was quiet but the tone was rough.

I do have control. I have power. Like some awakened animal, Tee let her teeth skate over the same spot, nibbling and biting softly. Moaning, Helen turned her head, reaching for Tee's mouth with hers. Tee leaned up to meet her, letting her tongue part Helen's lips. When Helen's mouth opened, that same primal drive led Tee to push her tongue inside. It was so unlike anything she'd ever done but so exactly what she wanted to do. When Helen sagged against her, Tee felt dominant, triumphant, and deeply stirred. Then Helen's tongue met hers, and a shock wave of desire streaked into her center. She pulled Helen tighter, as if their kiss could burn through any reason, any belief, anything that might ever stand between them. She wasn't aware that they had stopped moving until a hand tapped her shoulder.

"No making out on the dance floor."

They pulled away from each other, each breathing hard. A woman in a corporal's uniform pointed toward the other room. "Neil's rules. Dancing only in here. You can make use of one of the couches in there, though."

Helen managed a nod. "Okay. Sorry."

The woman grinned. "Figured you didn't know. Your first time here, right?"

Helen nodded again. "Yeah. It's nice." Tee was still close enough that she could feel Helen trembling slightly. She stepped back and felt the dampness in her panties again.

"I have to go to the bathroom," she said to Helen.

The soldier pointed to the hallway. "Last door on your left before the kitchen."

"Thanks." Helen gave a slight wave and the corporal turned back to her dance partner, a woman in civilian clothes. She put her hand on the small of Tee's back and guided her down the hall. "Take all the time you need," she said as Tee went into the small lavatory. "I'll be right here."

When Tee had freshened up as much as possible, given that she was still flushed and her underwear was still uncomfortable, she opened the door to find Helen leaning against the wall, sipping from a bottle of beer. When her eyebrows raised, Helen shrugged.

"One of the girls from the kitchen offered me a cold one, so I said yes." She pointed the bottle toward Tee. "You got me kinda overheated, you know."

Since she'd joined the WAC, Tee had had several occasions to wonder about the allure of drinking. At home, she'd been told that nice girls would never consume alcohol, but most of her squad mates seemed to enjoy going to the clubs on base, and they were all nice girls. And lots of the veterans talked about a bar downtown called Sweetie's, one of the few places in town that made the WACs feel truly welcome. She'd never had even a taste of anything alcoholic, but Maria had told her once that it wasn't really about the taste. "It's about how it makes you feel," she'd said. "You get a little looser, you know? You don't worry so much about what someone else thinks and you just have fun."

When Helen tipped the bottle toward her again, offering it, she shook her head. There probably wasn't enough alcohol in the world to make her stop worrying about what other people thought. More importantly, she'd already defied another of her childhood lessons by dancing tonight. Breaking one rule at a time was the best she could do.

Helen drained the bottle and tossed it into the trash in the restroom. They went into the other room and sat on the couch. "So what do you think about the party so far?"

"It isn't exactly what I thought a party would be," Tee remarked, focused again on the dancers.

"This is more of the private, couples area, I guess. If you want to meet some other people, we could go back into the kitchen," Helen offered.

Tee turned back to look at her. She'd never been around someone who cared so much about what she wanted. She ran her fingers across Helen's cheek and down to her jaw. "You're sweet to offer but I'd rather be with just you."

"I was hoping you'd say that." Helen leaned in and kissed her very gently. "'Cause I feel the same way."

She could hear the music playing faintly, but the rest of the room and everyone in it seemed to fade away. "Helen," she whispered, "why do you feel so good to me?"

"Maybe because you know how I feel about you." Helen was kissing her neck, and it made her body arch into her. They seemed to be molding into one being, even though they were still sitting side by side.

Tee ran her fingers through Helen's hair and put the other hand on her waist. She rubbed her cheek against Helen's, loving the soft fineness of it. "Tell me."

Helen brought her mouth back to Tee's. "I want to be with you, Tee. I want you to be my girl." She kissed her again. "And I want to be yours." Tee felt like she was falling, and only Helen's embrace was holding her up.

"All right, you two." A gruff voice made Tee startle. For a second she imagined Sergeant Rains had caught them again, but it was only Neil. "Your room should be ready in a few minutes. Let me walk you over there."

Tee was grateful for Helen's hand helping her up, because she was having a hard time catching her breath. The jolt of anxiety from the memory of being found out had awakened her apprehension, and she only followed for the promise of being alone with Helen, of being unseen and uninterrupted, even if only for an hour. Neil walked them to the far side of the dance room to a hallway Tee hadn't even noticed. When she got to the first door, she rapped loudly with her fist. "Time's up, ladies." A muffled acknowledgment of some kind came from inside and Neil seemed satisfied. "They'll be out in a few." She looked them both over and sneered. "Enjoy."

After she was gone, Helen leaned back against the wall and pulled Tee against her, turning her so they were both facing out. It should have felt nice, but her stomach lurched as she realized that it was the same way that she'd had to stand with Mr. Gallagher. "No," she said more forcefully than she'd intended, pulling Helen away from the wall. "I want to be in the back."

"Okay, baby." Helen's voice held a hint of surprise, but she went on quickly, "You can always tell me what you want, you know. Tell me what you like or what you don't. I want you to." She settled in against Tee's body, also facing away. "I want to please you. More than anything." She took Tee's hands from where they'd settled on her waist and brought them up to her breasts.

A sharp, forceful surge of pleasure filled Tee's belly and her worry fled. Helen nestled into her and the wetness flowed again. Wanting to ease the fullness between her legs, she thrust forward slightly, rubbing herself against Helen's slender hips. Helen's nipples hardened against her fingers and the fullness increased. Helen took Tee's right hand and directed it down her front, placing the flat of Tee's palm between her legs. She moved as Tee did, pressing and breathing a little harder each time. The rising heat between them was making her feel like she might burst into flames. When the music stopped for a few seconds, she heard herself making little grunting sounds, almost like Mr. Gallagher had. She forced herself to stop moving, and Helen groaned. Tee took a second to let her head clear. "Helen?"

"Uh-huh." Helen's voice was throaty and low, and it made Tee want to move against her again.

"Will there be a bed in that room?"

Helen puffed out a breath. "I sure as hell hope so."

Tee lowered her head until her mouth was close to Helen's ear. "While we're in there, will we…will we take our clothes off?"

Helen straightened a little and drew Tee's hand back to her waist. Something had changed. Why?

Helen turned in Tee's arms. Facing her now, she put her hands on the wall on either side of Tee's shoulders. She looked into Tee's eyes and spoke slowly. "I want to, Tee. I want to have you naked beside me. I want it real bad, right now. But when I really think about it, I don't want to only have an hour that way. And I don't want it to be in a house with other people around. I want it to be just us and to have all night. I want it to be perfect. Beautiful. Just right for you. For both of us."

Tee felt tears prick her eyes and she put her face into Helen's neck. Helen caressed up and down her sides, the way she liked, and Tee felt the words bubble up. *I love you.* Helen was good and sweet and kind to her. She was cute and funny and sure of herself. And she made Tee feel things, things she didn't think she'd ever feel, things she'd believed only love would make you feel, so it must be true. Tee knew if she opened her mouth, those words would come out. But maybe it wasn't the right time. Maybe she should wait until Helen said it first. Maybe—

The door to the room opened and Tee looked over, almost glad for the interruption. Helen turned slightly also, letting her hands drop to her sides. A bleached blonde came out first, closing the top button on a pink blouse that stretched tight across her breasts. A dark skirt clung to shapely hips and a thick white sweater was draped over her arm. "See you next week, sugar?" she asked.

"You know it, doll," came the reply as a uniformed figure followed her out the door.

Tee gasped. She couldn't help it. But the sound made both women turn toward her.

"Tee?" the uniformed woman asked, after a few seconds of silence. The surprise in her voice was genuine.

It was Clara—the one they called Casey—the woman Tee had first met in Bible study. Tee turned her head away even though it was too late. "N-no," she tried, hearing herself stutter again, knowing that would only give her away more surely.

"What's wrong, baby?" Helen asked, but Tee had no answer. There could be no explanation. That a person from church would see her in this place, waiting her turn for a room to do some disgraceful thing...there was only shame, stark and raw, coating her like a stain. Helen had moved away a bit when they'd heard the door open, leaving her unfettered. So she ran. Back down the hall, she dodged past the dancers and the small table and sprinted out the door. She heard Helen's voice just before a crash and the music stopped abruptly, replaced by the sound of cracking wood and glass breaking. Angry voices rose but she was already beyond them, the wind in her ears blunting the words. *No, no, no* pounded in her head, but it was too late. In Casey's eyes she saw herself exposed, her sin revealed to the world. She ran blindly, tears obscuring her surroundings, ran until her lungs felt like bursting, wishing they would, wishing she could just fall down and die where she landed.

❖

Almost two hours later, when it was fully dark, Bett heard a knock at the front door. Rain was there with a bag of groceries in each arm, her face expressionless, her body stiff. Bett threw her arms around Rain's neck, crumpling the sacks between them.

"I'm so very glad to see you, Rain. And I'm so sorry. That stupid, stupid man."

Rain said nothing. Bett let her go. She carried the bags into the kitchen and began putting things away. When the job was finished, she turned to Bett. "Being with you these days made me forget about that part of the world. But they haven't forgotten about me. So it's good that you should see, that you should know. Something like this could happen anytime you are with me in public, Bett. Maybe it will just be a look, sometimes more, like today. I should have warned you, but I just wasn't thinking. If you…if this preconception by others is something you don't want to deal with, I'll understand." She stood with her arms crossed, her jaw tight, her serious expression looking more like Bett's former sergeant than her current lover.

"Where have you been?" Bett asked, not answering the question yet.

"I ran over to another store I know, near Mel's. Then I walked back."

Mel's was the restaurant she'd followed Rain to during basic training. It was on the other side of town—at least five miles each way, Bett calculated. "I would have come with you, you know." She stepped closer.

Rain shook her head. "I wouldn't have been very good company."

"That doesn't matter. I want to be with you, Rain. More than anything. And you don't have to be anything but who you are. It doesn't matter to me one bit what those foolish people say. It only shows their ignorant prejudices." Bett pulled Rain's arms away from her body and drew them around her own shoulders. She put her arms around Rain's waist and looked up at her. "I may not be a warrior like you, but I want us to fight this battle together." She felt Rain lean toward her, heard her breathe out. When Rain's body had moved fully against hers, she added, "And we have already won because all they have is mindless hate, while we have each other."

When she got Rain back in the bedroom, Bett undressed her very slowly, kissing and caressing each part as the clothes came off.

In spite of Rain's stoic attitude, Bett was certain she had been hurt by the man's words, and she wanted to take away that pain and replace it with the happiness that Rain deserved. She unbraided Rain's hair and brushed it with her own engraved silver baby's brush that she kept on her dresser. She took off her own clothes as Rain lay quietly on her stomach. Slipping under the covers, Bett could feel that Rain was still holding back, reserving something of herself in a way that she hadn't done since they'd been with each other in this house.

By some measures, it was too soon for some of the things that she whispered in Rain's ear: how much she wanted Rain's body and how Rain's mouth and hands made her feel so incredibly good, how she admired Rain's heart and her spirit, that what they had meant everything, and what other people thought meant nothing. Then she said, "You asked me to put my mind only on you when we were together like this. Can I ask you to do the same? Can you put that moment aside and be here with me again?"

Rain looked into her eyes then, for the first time since she had come back to the house. "I wasn't prepared for how much worse it was to hear such words in front of you. For myself, I used to feel such rage. Then I learned to overcome the anger with a different understanding of the world. But today, I could only feel shame that you had to hear that kind of talk and that you would think you needed to defend me."

"The shame is his, not yours, Rain. And why shouldn't I defend you? You are my beloved and you would defend me if the situation was reversed." Rain looked away. Bett could still feel a distance between them. "All right, then," she said, pulling Rain on top of her, "here is another way of understanding for you. Who is in my bed right now? That ugly man, or you, Wind and Rain?"

Rain looked back at her, startled at Bett's use of her real name. A smile started in her eyes and then Bett heard a little chuckle. "That is an interesting way to measure the things of life."

Bett raised her chin, making a face of great confidence. "And why not?"

Rain's smile widened and Bett felt her eyes travel across her body. Feeling a new tenderness come into their embrace, Bett pressed herself closer, wanting Rain to feel the pleasure, the rightness between them. She hoped her lover would recognize that no one who was filled with this kind of goodness could act with the meanness and intolerance of that man. When their eyes met again, Rain nodded. "Why not, indeed?"

Relieved to see Rain's manner warming, Bett ran her hands over Rain's back and down the backs of her legs as far as she could reach before starting back up. Just as Rain shifted her body for a kiss, Bett's hand unintentionally brushed against a patch of raised flesh on her thigh. Rain stiffened and rolled off Bett and onto her side. "What is it?" Bett asked, hardly aware of what had happened. Rain said nothing, her expression uncertain. Bett could only think that Rain's vehement reaction to her touch must mean something important. She sat up. "Rain, what is that place on your leg?"

Rain sat up, too, and ran a hand quickly over her face. Only one other person in her life knew the truth of these marks. When she was a recruit, showering and dressing with her squad mates, to the few who had noticed and asked, Rain had simply said, "It's a scar." That was not a lie, but it wasn't the whole truth. What did it say about what was between them if she gave Bett that half answer? But did Bett truly want to know? She looked at the remarkable woman sitting next to her, waiting, her face showing concern and yet so open. *She just pledged to fight beside me and asked for me to be only with her. What other proof do I need?* The words were there and she was ready to speak them.

"It is a ceremonial mark that I made when I was younger," Rain began, turning in the bed to face Bett squarely.

Bett faced her, eyes troubled. "You did this to yourself?"

Rain ignored the worry in Bett's voice, believing that if she could only explain clearly, Bett would see. "The moment my mother died, I—I knew it. When I felt her spirit go from this world, I wanted to go with her. I didn't know how to be here without her. She was the one who could always explain things, who helped me understand this life. So without her I was…" Rain trailed off, her eyes closing as all of the terrible sorrow of that time reared up in her again.

"Lost," Bett filled in, stroking Rain's hair. "And very, very sad."

Rain opened her eyes, knowing that Bett would see the gathering tears. "Yes," she whispered.

Bett put both hands on Rain's heart, as if she wanted to push the sorrow away. Rain hesitated, thinking that perhaps this much was enough. Her feelings for Bett were already so far beyond anything she'd ever known as to defy description. But was it right to share her elemental grief, knowing it would also hurt this person she cared so deeply about?

As if seeing her thoughts, Bett took her hands and brushed them across each side of her cheeks. "Please, go on. I want to understand."

Decision made, Rain took a breath. "For a time after she went, I hid inside myself and let nothing of the world in. Eventually I began to see my grief had become selfish and my brothers needed me. But I needed help, too, something to clear a path back into life again. I can't really explain why, but I thought perhaps I could trade the unbearable pain in my heart for the manageable pain from a cut." She nodded slowly and covered Bett's hands with her own. "It helped. So each year, at the same last moon of September, I made another cut. It became a way for me to know things, and I used the time to honor my mother and to feel connected to my people."

She watched as Bett bit her lip, knowing that she was trying to keep her tears from coming. Unexpectedly, she realized that as Bett took in her hurt, she in turn shared the courage to face it. She squeezed Bett's hands with a very light pressure, letting herself feel the wonder of that discovery.

"When did you stop the cutting?" Bett asked, bringing her back to their conversation.

Moving her hands, Rain shifted her leg so Bett could see the scar more clearly. Bett dropped her hands from Rain's chest. "After six years. The same amount of time that I had with my *iná*." She gestured as if counting but did not touch the spot. Her voice dropped to a whisper again. "She came in a dream and told me to stop."

Bett hadn't heard Rain say that Lakota word before, but she gathered that it must mean *mother*. "Does it still hurt?" Bett asked evenly, relieved that this was not an ongoing thing.

"No, not of itself." Rain spoke slowly, struggling with her response. "But it is a place of loss and pain." Her fingers hovering, she added, "It is where I find my mother's spirit."

"I think you are wrong about that part," Bett said, her voice gentle but steady. "Your mother's true spirit is not in a place of pain and loss." She was worried that Rain might think her disrespectful to speak of this matter, so she rested her fingertips very lightly on the top of Rain's hand that still wavered above the scar, trying to feel her reaction. "Your mother is the one who taught you about love. She lives here"—Bett put her other hand back on Rain's chest—"in your heart." Rain's expression was one of genuine surprise. Bett went on, not knowing where the words were coming from but letting them flow. "Your mother is not in a place of suffering and she is not lost. And she would not want you to be in either of those places. She is with all those who loved her. You and your brothers and even your father." Rain blinked slowly but Bett pushed on. "She lives on in the beauty you see around you and in the goodness you do every day. I know your heart is so much bigger than this place of hurt." Bett traced the rectangle shape of the scar on the back of Rain's hand. "And as your mother's spirit is also greater, you mustn't confine her to that small space. Let her be in the place where she can feel your joys and your devotions."

Rain's hand shifted and she grasped Bett's palm tightly, as one needing rescue, but her eyes were downcast. "I don't know how to do this thing you speak of."

"What is it that binds all the good things in your life, Beloved? What is the common thread between past and present, between those who are no longer in your life and those who are here now? What is it that makes our hurts and pains heal over time, just as this scar is no longer a place that aches and bleeds? Why are we able to remember with great warmth the times of kindness and rightness in our lives?"

Rain closed her eyes, clearly trying to follow the words. Bett hoped she'd find images of the people who had helped shape her into the wonderful person she was. She knew some from their talks— Rain's brothers, Jessie, the local shopkeeper's wife—and she hoped there were others Rain had known. She hoped her lover would recall them clearly and see that they were united inside her, not by the pain of losing them but by something much greater. Rain opened her eyes, looking into Bett's face with a look of wonder. She whispered another word in Lakota, almost stumbling over the sounds as if it was both an answer and a question.

As a scholar, Bett had always put her trust in logic and proof, but she was in too deep not to take this leap of faith now. Whatever the word had meant, she could only hope that it would lead Rain in the direction she hoped for both of them. "You knew it, didn't you? As soon as you found the answer, you could feel it was true. You could feel it in your heart, couldn't you?"

"Yes," Rain whispered, and Bett saw the start of tears again.

"You've let me be with you, Rain. Now let me take away the sadness you hold here." Keeping her hand on top, she pressed Rain's hand onto the scar. Rain flinched. "Does that frighten you?" Bett asked carefully.

"Yes." Another whisper as Rain's eyes filled almost to overflowing.

"Can you tell me why? What are you afraid of?"

Rain swallowed hard, brushing at her eyes with her free hand. "I'm afraid to let go of what I know, even the part that is painful. I don't want to lose the power there. I'm afraid that nothing will ever be the same again. And if I become too different, how will my mother's spirit know me? How will I know myself?"

The anguish in Rain's voice was almost too much, and Bett had to hold her. They moved together, both letting go of the scar. Lying side by side, facing each other, Bett pulled Rain's head to her shoulder. "That hurt is only a small part of who you are," Bett explained, stroking Rain's hair. "You are so much more. You are brave and strong and beautiful and sweet. I know your mother saw all these wonderful qualities because they've always been in you. Those things have never changed and they never will. You will never lose your power. It will merely flow from goodness instead of pain. Letting go of the sorrow will make more room for the real you." Rain said nothing, but Bett knew she was listening, thinking. Bett rested her face on top of Rain's head and spoke softly. "Nothing has to happen today. Nothing has to happen ever, unless you decide it is right for you. You and I have just begun our journey together, Rain. We can make this part of our passage whenever you wish, or not at all."

They lay quietly for a time, Bett's hand tracing the lines and curves of Rain's back. How was it so easy, so good, just lying here together? Bett mused, thinking of nothing except Rain's steady heartbeat. Then she felt her lover take a long, slow breath.

Rain pulled back and looked into Bett's eyes. "All that you speak of is already true. Everything in me has changed since I met you. Being with you has shown me what real power is."

Bett kissed her lightly on the mouth. "Good, because there's something I need to tell you. I think I might have said it almost eight weeks ago, and I'm not terribly surprised that we're naked"—Bett smiled down at herself—"though I don't want you to think I'm only acting under the influence of your fabulous body when I tell you."

Rain looked troubled and Bett took her face in her hands. "I'm in love with you, Wind and Rain," she said slowly and clearly. "And not just because you taught me how to be a soldier and peel potatoes." She smiled, but Rain didn't, so she rushed on. "That, too, of course, but also because of everything else about you. Because of your cooking and because you smile for me now and because of the way you touch me and the way you look when you're making a fire. Because you are brave enough to show me your deepest self and strong enough to let me show you mine." Rain drew back slightly, her expression shifting to something entirely unexpected: fear. She swallowed. "Oh, I'm making a terrible mess of this, even though I've been thinking about it for so long." Her voice softened, and she traced Rain's cheeks and then let her hands drop. "And please, don't feel like you have to say anything back to me. I know I've sprung this on you. You can take all the time you need. I just thought you should know."

Rain turned away abruptly and sat up on the edge of the bed. Bett was stunned. She was quite certain she had seen Rain's eyes mirroring her deepest emotions on more than one occasion, and the way Rain touched her surely meant that she felt…Bett swallowed. How could she have misread this so badly? Maybe she'd just pushed her too fast and now she was—

"I don't know what love means," Rain said, almost inaudibly. "No one has ever said those words to me before and I've never said them to anyone."

"When you said that we were *Beloved* to each other, what did you think that meant?" Bett asked gently. Rain didn't answer. "The word you said just now, that which connects those moments of worth. What was that?"

"Those words are translations from something I understand. I don't understand about love."

"No one understands love, Rain. It just is. It can't be measured and it can't be proven. But the love I feel for you is what exists in the hearts of two people when there is something between them that is unique. It's what makes them fit together like pieces of a puzzle. It's something that makes them want to be with each other, no matter what. Something that makes their time apart almost unbearable and then their time back together so much sweeter."

She sat up on her knees and leaned against Rain's back, stroking her hair. "You could cut out my heart and look at every piece and you wouldn't be able to see it, but I love you more every time we wake up together and every time we sleep together and every minute in between. I know you feel it, too, Rain. I think you've felt it from the beginning, just like I did." She eased her arms around Rain's shoulders. Rain was trembling. "I know it's frightening to feel so much, especially when you're not used to it. And particularly when you believe that it's only going to cause you pain. And I can't promise you there won't be any pain, because we are human and humans hurt each other sometimes. But if you'll promise me you'll keep trying to forgive me if I do something thoughtless or stupid or selfish, then I promise you, if you'll let go, I'll catch you. And then we can fall together."

There was a moment where Bett felt Rain deciding, and the last of her stiffness, her self-control, fell away, like the shedding of a shell. Then Rain's mouth was on hers and her hands everywhere on Bett's body and she was kissing her and holding her, the words rushing out. "Yes, Bett, I do love you. I felt it from that first moment, when I watched you stand up to Sergeant Moore and every day since. I loved you when you won that race and when you waited for me at the hospital. Ever since I first breathed you, it's been in my heart, and then I would tell myself it wasn't because I thought it was wrong, that I was wrong, that I couldn't have you—I shouldn't have you. And now since I've touched you and you've touched me, I only want you, and I—"

Bett knew she had to get Rain's naked body next to hers right that moment. She pulled Rain to her as she fell onto her back, adoring the warmth of Rain's skin, pulling tightly with her arms until she felt the fullness of Rain's body pressing into her. It felt so good that she couldn't stop moaning with pleasure. In their brief time together, the only thing Rain had ever acted the least bit self-conscious about was that she was bigger—taller anyway—than Bett, and so she had always been careful when she was on top, supporting herself with her arms or hands, keeping most of her weight there. Now Bett felt like she had all of Rain for the first time, and she thought it might be impossible to ever let her go.

CHAPTER SEVEN

Rain awakened very early with a terrible heaviness growing inside her. Her heart had been so full when they'd fallen asleep in each other's arms that this sudden change took her completely by surprise. In her early childhood on the reservation, her mother had taught her to trust her intuition, and she'd since learned to read the messages that her emotions carried. *What is the source of this sudden concern?* She sent her mind out to her brothers, but she didn't feel anything special there. She could envision her artistic brother Nikki happily putting paint on a canvas somewhere she didn't recognize and Thomas, the soldier, was as safe as he could be, bedding down somewhere in Europe with his company. She thought then of Bird on the Wing and her family at Pine Ridge, but nothing unusual came to her.

A child's special clock struck in her memory. *Time.* Time had passed with such breathtaking sweetness this week, but it was Sunday now. Tomorrow she would have to go back to the base and resume her life as Sergeant Rains. Rain tried to recall the person she had been a week ago, eight weeks ago even, before she had laid eyes on the woman who would change her forever: Elizabeth Smythe. She tried to identify the emotions that had been inside her while she worked with the squads and ate Army food and slept on her single bed in the officers' quarters. Not the warmth of Bett's love and the joy of these days together. Where would that go when she left this house? And for Bett? Bett would start her career in the cryptography center on Monday, a very good and important job for her. And…? What changes would her new life bring? Would the distance between them uproot the delicate seeds they'd planted in each other's hearts?

Rain couldn't quite see the time ahead. Weekends? Would she just come back to this house, to that bed, and try to pretend like everything was the same for a day or two and then tear herself away again? She shook her head, unable to know how to be with Bett like that. Not now, after she'd been marked forever by all that had passed between them. So should she try to find it in her to end it now, to leave before Bett got up? Return to the base without awkward good-byes and forced pledges of another time and try instead to reclaim herself as the aloof, dedicated Sergeant Rains? Might it be better for them both to part only with the memories of these days together instead of trying to find their way through the strangeness of living apart? As she tried on the idea of moving in that direction, the thought was accompanied by a pain in her heart so sharp that she felt it in her core. As difficult as it was to know how to continue their relationship from here, not seeing Bett, not holding her, not talking, and not being together in the way that—even after only five days—seemed to fit her better than any other life she'd known, such a choice seemed impossible. She'd never before said *I love you* as she had last night, and she admitted to herself that she had no wish to walk away from the woman who had inspired those words and all they implied. Her search for a solution unsuccessful, she turned on her side, away from Bett, pondering if love had to end in the place where duty began.

"Rain?" She heard Bett's sleepy voice.

She had no resistance for the way Bett said her real name; she knew she never would. She rolled back, returning to the warmth and put her arms around Bett. "I'm here, Beloved," she whispered.

Bett snuggled against her, burrowing in close. "Good, 'cause I had a bad dream."

"Do you want to tell me about it?"

"No, just don't go." Bett was drifting away, her voice becoming vague. "Don't...ever...go."

Rain whispered *no* very softly and listened to Bett's slowing respiration, breathing in the aroma of her slumbering body, her breath and hair and skin. She felt herself falling asleep again, too, unable to summon her earlier resolve to be gone. *Coward!* she scolded herself, even as she wondered which was more cowardly, leaving or not leaving.

When she woke again, Bett was gone from the bed but Rain could hear sounds coming from the kitchen. A lot of sounds. Pots and pans banging, silverware clanking, and an occasional muffled word. At the smell of food—something burning?—she sat up and stretched. Just then, Bett came in with a tray.

"Oh, you're up. I wanted to surprise you with breakfast in bed," she said, smiling.

"You are surprising me," Rain replied. "I hope you're joining me, too," she added, patting the bed.

"Of course," Bett said, handing her the tray. "I'm not that noble." She jumped in beside Rain and pulled the covers up.

Dark toast and runny eggs sat on the plates, along with two cups of tea and an envelope. Rain reached for her tea and saw the note. On the outside Bett had written, *Don't Say No.* "What is this?"

Rain looked at Bett who only smiled mysteriously and said, "You can read it anytime today. Eat first, if you're hungry."

Rain put the note down and sipped her tea. "It's not about shopping, is it?" referring to an earlier topic that Bett had mentioned and one that she'd declined.

"No, and I'm not giving any more hints, so either read it or stop talking about it." Bett was not one for delayed gratification, as a rule. Rain tapped her fingers on the tray and stared at the note. When she looked over at Bett, Bett was looking away.

She took one more sip of tea, moved the tray aside, and opened the envelope.

My Beloved Rain,

I can't begin to tell you what an astounding week this has been. Becoming your lover has taken me to places I've never been, both physically and emotionally. And beyond that, I can't even describe what it has been like to get to know what an astonishing and incredible woman you are. More than I've ever wanted anything, I want both of those experiences to continue for as long as you are willing.

I'm not sure that I can say I've experienced <u>every</u> emotion with you, but I am writing now about the one that is foremost in my heart at this moment: sadness. I can't stand thinking that this lovely time is almost over, and I really can't tolerate the idea that next week you won't be beside me when I fall asleep and when I wake up. I know it's all been very *sudden in some ways (though I consider a mostly chaste seven weeks to be a decent enough courtship) but I want to ask if you'd consider moving in with me. I have to believe that your colonel would agree to your request to move off the base, even though she might not approve of you moving into my arms—but that part can be just between us, can't it?*

Wherever your heart might land on this matter, I can tell you that mine will still be with you, anywhere you might choose to live. That's why I asked you not to say no. If you must, say, Not yet. If it is not to be that we live together now, then I have faith we will make it work between us until such time as we are able to do so.

Yours,
Bett

Rain read the note three times. On the second reading, she felt Bett begin to fidget, but there were several words that she needed to see again. *Lover...continue...moving in...yours.*

After the third time, Rain brought her hands to her mouth and then covered her eyes. *Tell me what you want,* Bett had told her when they'd agreed to become *Beloved* to each other. *Don't ever be afraid to do that,* she'd said. But she had been afraid and had almost left in the weakest way possible. Had Bett known her struggle, or was this invitation just another part of the beautiful, instinctive connection that was forming between them?

Rain thought she had composed herself enough to speak, but when she opened her mouth, a choking breath came out. Bett turned back to her in time to see Rain put her face back in her hands. She felt Bett's face close to her ear. "Forgive me for being such a coward that I had to write it. I just didn't trust myself to ask you in the right way." She put her hands on Rain's shoulders and pulled her close, tightening her arms around Rain's back as her hands stroked gently. Rain felt Bett's touch resounding in the deepest chamber of her heart, the pain leaving as Bett's hand stroked her hair, her voice whispering soft, hushing sounds. The tears left and she felt like every old hurt had been washed away.

"You are in no way a coward. You are my conclusion. The answer to my question and the end of my journey."

Bett smiled, a little teary herself. "Does that mean yes?"

"Yes. Yes. Yes. Oh yes." Rain began kissing Bett everywhere she could reach. "Yes. Yes." She reached some more. "Oh yes. Yes." Rain moved lower in the bed until she could reach Bett's feet.

Bett was giggling and squirming. "Rain, if you kiss my toes I'll have to scream."

Rain did. And Bett did, just a little.

So it was Monday, the day for Helen's first solo drive, and instead of feeling eager and enthusiastic about it, Helen felt about as lousy as she ever had. She was tired, she was upset, she was angry, and she was sad. Nowhere could she find the state of mind she should have to do her job today. And wouldn't you know Lieutenant Yarborough had chosen today to show up early, unlike most days where she barely made it in time to see the first set of drivers out. Now Helen had to listen to her trying to act like she was in charge when everyone knew it was Sergeant Harris who ran things. Or tried to. In Helen's opinion, things just sorta drifted along in the motor pool. Repairs got done or didn't, schedules got posted…eventually, and the drivers and grease monkeys worked it out as best they could.

"Tucker!"

God, she hated that woman's voice. But she forced herself to attention and waited.

Lieutenant Yarborough waved the clipboard in her hand. "Are you planning on driving today or are you just going to stand there like you're posing for a WAC recruiting poster?"

Everyone knew Yarborough thought she was real clever with her sarcastic remarks and her it's-all-funny-until-it's-not attitude. But no one knew where the lines were because they could change at any time. So Helen tried to play it by the book. "I'm gonna drive, ma'am."

"Then you'd better get the hell over here and get in that truck."

"Yes, ma'am."

She worked to keep her face neutral, repeating to herself, *You've got the job you wanted, just ignore the jerk and get on the road.* Driving calmed her like nothing else, and she loved being behind the wheel with something meaningful to do. But when Yarborough's clipboard swatted her hard on the behind as she passed by, her reflexes took over, and she turned sharply with her fists clenched. A swell of reaction filled the garage bay as all the grease monkeys and other drivers hooted and yelled. Yarborough's expression turned vicious.

"Oh, are you going to do something, Private?" she taunted. "You think you can catch me off guard like you did with Sergeant Moore?"

Helen let her fists open and tried to relax her stance. Obviously, Lieutenant Yarborough was not someone who would find her scuffle with Sergeant Moore admirable. She should have expected that some officer was going to make a point of singling her out. *Why did it have to be today? And why this bitch?* However good it might feel for the moment, she told herself that slugging Yarborough would only make a bad day worse. She quickly straightened to attention and set her gaze off Yarborough's face while still keeping her in her peripheral vision. "Excuse me, ma'am. May I board my vehicle now?"

"Your vehicle?" Yarborough sneered and Helen knew immediately she'd made a mistake and was about to hear about it, but good. The onlookers were making approving noises like kids in a schoolyard when the biggest bully turned his eyes on someone other than them. "I don't suppose you have a receipt for this vehicle of yours? Or could you tell us exactly where and when you purchased this fine vehicle? Perhaps you remember the name of your salesman?" The lieutenant began a slow stroll around the truck, acting like she'd never seen it before. "This sure is an interesting paint job you have on *your* vehicle, Private. You know, this olive-green paint color and white star remind me of something I've seen before." She pretended to be thinking. Helen struggled to keep her temper in check, knowing they weren't done yet. Yarborough was enjoying herself too much. She came back around and stood directly in front of Helen, her face only inches away. Her voice was soft but menacing. "What do you suppose this truck looks like to me, Tucker?"

Just play your part and it'll be over, Helen told herself. "An Army truck, ma'am?"

"What? I don't think I heard you."

That singsong voice did it. Helen was ready to scream, *Fuck you and fuck the Army,* and launch her best punch into Yarborough's smug face, when for some reason, she thought about Sergeant Rains. When her drill instructor had shaken her hand at graduation, she'd said, "You've made exceptional progress here, Private Tucker. But from here on, the kind of soldier you will become will be up to you." The sergeant had looked like she wanted to say something more, but they'd called the next girl's name, so Helen thanked her and the moment passed. Really she knew with one more assault on an officer, she wouldn't be a soldier at all, so she swallowed the bitterness and shouted, just a bit louder than necessary, "An Army truck, ma'am!"

For half a second, Lieutenant Yarborough looked almost disappointed. Then she snarled, "That's right, you little shit. An Army truck. And don't you forget it, or I'll have you transferred to the mess and you'll be scrubbing pots for the rest of the war, you got that?"

"Yes, ma'am," Helen replied smartly, still seeing Yarborough's face from the corner of her eye. The lieutenant would only look like an ass if she went on anymore, so Helen decided this round was a tie. But there would be a reckoning of some kind, she vowed. No Yankee bitch was going to get the best of her. Not today or any other day. She remembered what her brother Sinclair used to tell her—don't get mad, get even.

Tee had gone into the PX that Monday morning, even though it was the last thing she wanted to do. Major Edley had taken one look at her and ordered her to the infirmary. "Come back as soon as you're feeling better," he'd said, stepping away a little as if she had some kind of flu. Would she ever feel better? Tee didn't think so. She'd never deliberately disobeyed an order before, but she wasn't going to the infirmary. They couldn't do anything for her there. Almost by habit she found herself walking toward the chapel, but stopped, undecided if she would ever set foot in there again either. This church probably wasn't the place for her. That had been made clear two nights ago when she'd run out of the house party without Helen and gotten so lost she couldn't begin to know which way was the base. When she couldn't run anymore, she walked. And when she couldn't walk anymore, she'd found a bench in a park and sat.

She remembered how she'd started shivering, once she'd caught her breath. The night was cooling and she'd left her coat and hat and even her bag at the party. The party. She'd shaken even harder then, telling herself she needed to put it all out of her mind. Helen. Neil.

Dancing. The way she'd felt just before Casey came out that door. She'd been swayed. Demons came in many forms, she'd been told that for years. But she'd let herself be tempted, let Reverend Culberson's kind face and easy words pull her from the truth. She'd let Helen…no, she wasn't going to think about that ever again. Those feelings were what had led her to this calamity. She was a terrible sinner with one foot in hell already. Such terrible thoughts and conflicting emotions were making her dizzy, and she raised her head. A sign across the street came into focus: Living Faith Bible Church. That was exactly what she needed—to live her faith, the Biblical teachings she'd been brought up with. Perhaps the Lord would give her one last chance.

The handle squeaked and then the door cracked open at her pull. When she had it just wide enough to squeeze through, she let it go and it banged loudly. In only a few seconds her eyes had adjusted enough that she could make her way to the back pew. She sat, intending to pray for all she was worth, but in only a minute or two a great weariness came over her. She knew it was the devil again, trying to keep her from forgiveness, and she started the Lord's Prayer.

When Tee felt something pushing at her shoulder, she opened her eyes and realized she was lying on the pew. She sat up quickly and a man's dark visage loomed over her. For a few seconds, she thought she might faint. Satan had come for her. She'd often heard the devil described as black, but she'd always assumed the description was from the sooty darkness of hell's fires. Now it seemed the Lord had given her over to eternal damnation.

"Are you all right, child?" a deep voice questioned. Tee was surprised by the compassionate tone. And she was still cold. Perhaps she hadn't been admitted to hell yet. Apparently the dark brown eyes had taken note of her uniform because the next question was, "Are you one of those Army girls? What are you doing out here this time of night?"

Tee put her face in her hands, trying desperately to push away her turmoil and confusion. She didn't want to look up yet but she knew she should answer, perhaps with confession and prayer? She couldn't control her stutter anymore and she mumbled into the floor, "I-I know I've been so…so lost. P-Please let me go b-back."

With obvious bewilderment the voice replied, "Of course you can go back. But if you're lost, you'll need someone to take you."

She risked a look into his face, and to her relief, she saw only very human concern on a tall somewhat stocky black man's face. Working to focus her vision as well as her mind, she nodded. "Okay," was the most she could get out.

"Wait right there," he said, holding out a palm to indicate *stay*, as if she might not understand what he was telling her. "I'll go get my wife."

As he walked away, Tee slumped back against the pew, wondering if one of the damnations of hell was that you never got enough rest.

She must have napped again because the next thing she was aware of was being helped into a car by a very thin, light-skinned black woman. She caught a few snippets of a conversation the woman seemed to be having with her husband.

A sniff. "Not drinking?" A few more steps. "Touched?" She'd heard people call her that before when they heard her stammering. It meant they thought she was not quite right in the head.

"I'm not," she blurted out and it grew silent around her.

Then she was sitting up and a car engine started. She roused herself enough to look over, just making out the woman's face. "Who are you?" she asked.

The woman gave her a long look before she put the car in gear. Finally she wet her lips and said, "I'm Vondra Washington, the pastor's wife."

Pastor? Tee frowned for a few seconds before remembering she'd sought refuge in a church.

The woman must have read the doubt in her expression because she muttered, "The one who got out of bed in the middle of the night to take some lost WAC back to her base."

The weariness she couldn't seem to shake made her feel more guilty for stealing this woman's slumber. "Why didn't he take me himself?"

They were at a stop sign. Mrs. Washington gave a sharp little laugh and then turned to look at Tee again. There were no fires in her eyes but there was anger. "Even a pastor got no business driving a white woman alone at this time of night. You oughtta know that."

Tee couldn't think of what to say. Blinking, she felt her thoughts begin to clear. Was anything she thought she understood real? Were her feelings? Her fears? Her beliefs? She only knew the truth right now was she'd gotten lost when she'd run from the party and this nice couple was helping her get back to base. Tears started down her cheeks as they drove, and she turned her face to look out the window. When she felt the car stop she wiped her face with her hands. "I don't know how to thank you," she stammered.

Mrs. Washington's expression softened. "You just stay out of trouble, honey, and everything will be all right."

As the car pulled away, a figure came out of the guardhouse. Tee thought it would be an MP, but it wasn't. It was Helen.

"God, Tee, I've been worried sick. Are you okay?"

God. Just stay out of trouble and everything will be all right. She'd been given a message. She almost laughed at herself for her first impression of the pastor's identity, when he and his wife were clearly just angels on earth. "I gotta stay out of trouble," Tee said, almost to herself.

"Come on," Helen said, reaching for her arm. "Let's get you to the barracks. You need a hot shower and some sack time."

Tee shrank back. "I gotta stay out of trouble," she said again, more firmly, stepping around Helen and walking away as quickly as she could.

She'd slept through breakfast that Sunday but Helen was there when she awoke, offering her some fruit and a roll. She'd known she had to turn it down. There couldn't be anything more between them, not even friendship. All that day, Helen had practically shadowed her every move, but Tee refused to speak to her. Or to anyone else, for that matter. When they had a private moment while walking to dinner, Helen tried to talk to her about what had happened at the party, but Tee simply turned and went back to the barracks.

Helen had raised her voice then. "Tee, please…"

But Tee had repeated to herself, *Just stay out of trouble and everything will be all right,* until the anguish in Helen's voice faded away.

Now she didn't know what to do with herself. Major Edley would likely go by the infirmary to check up on her. Maybe she should just leave. Go home. Maybe she wasn't cut out to be a soldier after all. The more she thought of it, the better that sounded. Her daddy might be mad that she'd come back without permission, but Mama would take her in. She went back to the barracks. Everyone else was at work. She started packing.

"Hey."

A husky voice made her turn abruptly. It was Casey. Tee shrank back against her bunk.

Casey didn't seem to notice. "Your friend is really worried about you."

"I gotta stay out of trouble." Surely the angels' words would keep her safe.

"You're not in trouble, Tee. Helen—your friend's name is Helen, right?" Tee nodded despite herself. "Helen told me how upset you were about…uh…running into me at the party." Tee nodded again. "Look, I was way more surprised than you were. I mean, I never would have guessed…about you."

Gotta stay out of trouble. Tee shook her head, stuffing her underwear into the duffel bag. "Please. I don't—"

Casey cut her off. "Can I sit for a minute? I work on the grounds crew and I'm pretty much on my feet all the time. I'm just on my lunch break." She indicated Helen's bunk. "Do you mind?"

Tee didn't want Casey to sit. She wanted her to go. She gestured toward her open footlocker. "I need to—"

But Casey was already lowering herself to the side of the bunk. "Thanks. So you're just out of basic, right?" Tee was still trying to think of what to say to make Casey leave, but she nodded. "Do you like working in the PX?" Tee blinked in surprise. "Helen told me to look for you there," Casey explained.

"Yes." Maybe if she kept her answers short and kept packing, Casey would get the hint. But she did like it, actually. That would be something she would miss. No store in town had wanted to hire her before and now there really wouldn't be a chance, her coming back AWOL…

Casey continued their conversation, interrupting her thoughts. "They're pretty good about matching people with what they like doing, don't you think? I really like working with plants." She smiled. "I don't exactly know why. Maybe because they're very nonjudgmental." Her smile faded as she gestured at herself. "I used to get a lot of knocks at home, as you can probably imagine."

Tee could imagine. Casey was tall and solid, with straight dark hair and a broad face. *Masculine looking*, Tee had thought when she'd first seen her, and she was sure that was the source of Casey's knocks. The people in her town would have said unkind things about Casey, she was sure. *Built like a football player* or *All the makeup in the world wouldn't help that one.*

Casey sighed. "But what was I supposed to do? I wasn't going to turn into a petite, curly haired blonde, no matter how much I wanted to. At times I thought I'd never find a place where I'd fit in, you know?" She looked away and her voice got so soft that Tee leaned toward her slightly to hear. "For years, I felt so all alone. And I got to believing that I...I must be some kind of mistake. So I decided that I should just, you know, end it. Because I didn't know how to live with being so different."

Tee sat on her bunk, her hand slightly outstretched in Casey's direction. She knew she should say something, offer some comfort, but she had no words.

Casey swallowed hard. "I got my dad's revolver and I sat with it for a long time, while I imagined living the rest of my life with nothing but those disapproving looks and hateful insults." She looked over and Tee saw tears pooling in her eyes. "I put that pistol to my head and I actually pulled the trigger. It just clicked. I sat there, shaking and listening to that empty sound echoing around the room." Casey took a breath and wiped at her eyes. "You've got to understand, my dad always kept his guns cleaned and fully loaded. Later, I remembered that he'd shot at a snake that had come up from the creek a couple of days before. But that shouldn't have mattered, 'cause he must have told me a hundred times that there was no point in having firearms in the house if they weren't primed." She sniffed and pushed her dark hair away from her face. "Anyway, something changed in me at that moment. I came to believe there was going to be a reason for me to live, so I just kept going.

"I tried, you know, dating—when I could find a guy who'd go out with me. But I never felt anything for them, and they always expected something I didn't want to give. Then I met a woman who lived outside of town. Her husband had died a while back but she'd stayed on. By then I was working at the feed store and I delivered some seed out there. She needed some help with the place and I worked for her a bit.

We got to be friends and then…more. Then I knew how it was supposed to feel when you wanted to be with someone. Looking back, I could see my feelings had always been for women." She looked back at Tee and shrugged. "Why? I don't know. I don't think anybody knows. But that's the way I am. And I've come to believe that's the way God made me."

Tee blinked. She felt terrible for Casey's pain, but she had to say what she knew. "But the Bible says it's wrong."

Casey nodded. "We didn't go to church when I was younger, and I never thought much about what the Bible said, to be honest. But I've heard that, and I'll tell you that the ones who were the worst to me were the church folks. I guess they thought they had a right to be that way." She rubbed her hands together, a slow smile returning to her face. "Janet got me to go with her to the chapel here. I had such a crush on her I would have walked through fire if she'd asked. But anyway, Reverend Culberson's message was so good that I kept going, even after Janet gave me the brush-off." Her eyes met Tee's. "I even talked to the reverend about, you know, about the way I feel about women."

Tee gasped. "You did?" Casey nodded. "What did she say?"

"She said a lot of things, 'cause we met several times. It would take me more than one lunch hour to tell you, and I pretty much got the impression that I wasn't the first person she'd talked to about it. But one thing she told me was how the Bible was written over so many years and it's been translated so many times, that you have to read it with your heart more than with your head. She said that—" Casey grinned sheepishly. "Look, Tee, I'm no preacher and this language, well, it's all new to me, okay?" When Tee nodded eagerly, she went on. "Well, what I think she said was since God's spirit is in each of us, we can listen for what God is trying to tell us personally instead of trying to fit ourselves into what might be in the Bible for someone else. She also said how our understanding of the world is so different from what theirs was, that if the Bible was written today, a lot of things might be expressed differently." Casey straightened slightly. "But what I most remember is her saying that God made me the same as everyone else—good and perfect. And that's true for all of us, Tee. For you, and for Helen, and for anyone else you know."

Tee's head ached. In some ways, the lines of this argument were so clearly drawn. What she'd been told her whole life about God and the Bible was not the way Reverend Culberson and her followers saw things. She wished she could know what was the right way. She wished she had someone that she could trust absolutely to ask.

Casey glanced at her watch and stood up. "I need to get back to work. Thanks for letting me talk to you." Tee stood, too, and Casey glanced at her open footlocker and the duffel on her bunk. "Look, I gotta say one more thing, and I'm sorry if you think I'm out of line. But that girl, Helen? She loves you." When Tee's eyes widened, Casey added, "No, she didn't say so, but I could tell. And believe me, having someone feel that way about you doesn't come around very often, Tee." She reached out hesitantly and touched Tee's arm. "Reverend Culberson says that love is God's language. So I hope you get the message that God wants you to hear."

Tee's throat was too thick with emotion to speak, but Casey had been brave to tell her story, and she wanted to acknowledge that. Taking a deep breath, she stretched her arms around Casey's broad shoulders and squeezed. The contact was surprisingly soothing, and after she let go, she managed to whisper, "Thank you."

Casey grinned. "Hope I see you in church." She winked. "Or wherever." She turned and strode out.

Once Helen was on the road, she rolled down her window and yelled out everything she'd wanted to say to Lieutenant Yarborough, cuss words and all. She had to make it kinda quick, since she was only going to the railroad station. She figured they wouldn't give her any longer routes until she'd proven herself, and that was fine. She needed to be around right now, to try and figure out what to do about Tee. After Tee had refused to have anything to do with her all day yesterday, she'd gotten the brilliant idea to have someone else talk to her. Problem was, she didn't know anyone else who was like them, except for that gal from the party whose appearance had made Tee run. Helen figured it had to be a church thing, since God made Tee panic like nothing else. So when Tee fell asleep after missing dinner, she went over to the chapel and waited. Sure enough, that girl—she learned she was called Casey—came out with some others, and Helen grabbed her. About two hours later, Casey had the whole story and they worked out a plan.

"I'll owe you," Helen told her. "I ain't got much, but you're welcome to it."

Casey shook her head. "I like Tee. And you, doing this for her… it's nice. If I can help, I'm glad to do it." She clapped a hand on Helen's shoulder. "It's us against the world, kiddo. We might as well stick together."

Helen's mind was only half on her job as she watched two men loading crates into her truck.

"Tucker, right?"

She turned. It was the corporal from her last ride-along. Nelson? Nichols? "Yeah. Hi. Are you doing a ride-along with someone else?"

He shook his head. "I got some other business to tend to." He pulled out a pack of cigarettes and offered her one. When she declined, he lit one for himself, blowing the smoke out the side of his mouth toward the outside. Watching him, Helen was debating with herself about taking up smoking. Lots of the men at home smoked, and the corporal—Newton, that was it—made it look almost cool. Catching her eye, he grinned. "So how's your love life?" Helen frowned. "You said you do it all for love, remember?"

"Oh yeah." She grimaced. "Don't ask."

He glanced inside the cab of her truck. "This your first solo?"

Helen turned her attention back to the crates. "Yeah. I'm supposed to be watching them load." With dismay, she realized the men had finished the job as one of them reached for her manifest and scribbled something on the bottom. She sighed and shot an annoyed glance at the corporal. "Since you distracted me, I'll have to go through and count everything."

"Sorry. Let me help you."

She held the clipboard while he counted. Everything checked out except for one stack of boxes toward the back. "Thirteen here."

Helen looked again at the paper. "This says twelve."

He came around and looked over her shoulder. "Sure does. Maybe I messed up. You count."

She did. Thirteen boxes. Unlucky. And of all the days to have something go wrong, never mind it was her first solo. They'd been warned repeatedly about shortages, who to talk to, what to say. She searched her memory for what they'd been told to do if the amount was over. *Report to your commanding officer* was all she could recall.

Probably it happened so rarely that no real process was in place. She wasn't sure if she'd even recognize the men who had done the loading, and there wasn't another soul in sight at the moment.

"What's in here anyway?" the corporal asked, hefting one of the boxes.

She looked at the invoice again. "Sugar."

The corporal put the box down and patted it reverently. "You might as well have said gold."

Helen nodded. "That's for sure." Sugar had been the first thing rationed when the war broke out and ration books had been issued to control the distribution of the supplies they did get. Every housewife had adjusted her recipes to allow for the lack of sugar. One of the great things about being in the Army was being exempt from those worries. "What do you suppose a box like this would bring on the black market?" The question had slipped out before she'd realized how it sounded. They'd joked about it before but she needed to cover herself. "Not that I—"

"About fifty dollars." His voice was soft, but very serious. "But then, everyone involved would have to get a cut. So no one would get that whole amount, see? Each person takes some risk, so each gets some reward. Makes sense, right?"

Her heart started beating the way it used to when she'd chase after Mr. Hall in his Postal Service truck. *Fifty dollars!* Then her mind took over. This was a setup. She was being tested. Lieutenant Yarborough wanted her gone, and this was the way she was going to do it. Might as well play along, though. "And how would you know about all that, Corporal?"

He laughed, but it didn't sound genuine. "You hear things. I got a buddy, he gets around."

"Sure. Or *she* gets around," Helen suggested, smacking her hand against the clipboard with resentment as she thought about Yarborough trying to get rid of her.

This time his reaction was real—and it was pure shock. "You know about that?" he whispered. Then his features hardened. "Is that why she shorted me last time? Are you moving in on this deal?"

Just that quickly, Helen knew she was in over her head. She had to be very, very careful. "Look, I'm just trying to do the job and get what's coming to me."

"What did she offer? Five?" He reached into his pocket and slid a sawbuck onto the clipboard. "I can work with you, Tucker. We can cut out the middleman." He sneered. "Or the middle woman." His face came close but she didn't flinch. "But if you think you're gonna double-cross me, you'd better think again. I know where you work. I know where you eat. I know where you live."

She stared at the money, a dozen thoughts competing in her head. *A few more of these and I could get my own place—or Tee and I could. Things would be a lot better then. No, this is wrong. And if I get caught, I'll be in that stockade for a lot longer than a week. Ten extra dollars every trip would add up to a lot of money. But am I stealing from the Army? Man, this would truly fuck Yarborough.* That last one turned the tide.

"Let's call this our test run, Corporal. Everything goes okay, we'll talk again. Otherwise, you go your way and I'll go mine. I never saw you and we never had this conversation. Agreed?"

He looked at her for a long moment, but she knew how to stand her ground. "Agreed," he said finally.

He hefted the box again and disappeared around the corner of the depot. She wondered if this had been his *business* all along. She put the ten dollars in her pocket.

Chapter Eight

Early Monday morning, Sergeant Rains checked in at the gates of the base and then went directly to her quarters. She changed into her uniform, which felt almost as unfamiliar as it had the first time she put one on. Shaking off the strangeness, she reported to the colonel's office.

"You're looking well, Sergeant," Colonel Janet Issacson said as they saluted each other. She regarded Rains carefully. "You seem… rested."

"Yes, ma'am," Rains replied, a twist of apprehension making her shift the slightest bit, despite the standard reply. She wondered if she really did look as different as she felt.

"Did you go home?" The question was almost routine. Issacson knew more than anyone else on the base about Rains's background. Once Rains had indicated that she'd leave the base rather than being confined to quarters during the inquiry about the incident with Corporal Crowley, the colonel had expected that she'd use the time to visit her people.

"No, ma'am."

Issacson's eyebrows rose. Clearly she was going to need more of an answer.

"I…I stayed with a friend here in town."

She felt the colonel's eyes on her for a few more seconds, and her throat went dry with anticipation of questions she didn't know how to answer. When the colonel looked back down at the paperwork on her desk, Rains swallowed with relief.

"Things went as expected in the hearing, Sergeant, but there's been a snafu with your promotion, somewhere up the line. I've had too much going on to look into it but now that you're back, I will. In the meantime, I want you to go ahead and assume your new duties as a master sergeant, and when the promotion comes through, I'll make sure your pay is adjusted, retroactively. Any questions?"

This was it. She took in a breath, fighting to keep the trepidation from her voice. "Uh, yes, ma'am. Since I won't be working directly with the squads anymore, I'd like permission to move off base."

Issacson got up from her desk and went to look out the window. There seemed to be some tension in the set of her shoulders. "Have you already found suitable housing?" the colonel asked.

Rains was certain her commander's mind was assessing the particulars of her request. "Yes, ma'am."

It had clicked. "With your…friend?" Issacson asked.

"Yes, ma'am," Rains replied, hearing the tightness in her own words.

Colonel Issacson turned back abruptly, but Rains didn't flinch. "Sergeant Rains, I'm sure I don't have to remind you of the conduct that is expected of you under the Army's Uniform Code of Military Justice. You have the makings of a good officer and I don't want to see you jeopardize your career."

Rains's eyes remained fixed on a spot on the wall behind her.

Issacson sighed, then gestured almost diffidently. "Look, Sergeant, you know I don't make it my business to meddle in the affairs of my staff. As long as they do their jobs and maintain Army discipline, I'm happy. You also know I'm committed to the work we are doing here. It's important for the war effort and it's important for the women of this country." Rains nodded stiffly. "So I'll ask you this just once, Sergeant Rains. Are you sure this is what you want?"

"Yes, ma'am. Absolutely positive." Rains couldn't believe her voice was so calm. Inside, she felt like jelly.

"Fine," Issacson said. "Fill out the address form and leave it with my secretary. Request granted."

Not trusting herself to speak further, Rains saluted and walked out. At Delores's desk, she filled out the card, her handwriting much worse than usual since she couldn't seem to stop shaking. She fumbled her way through the morning's introduction to her new job. Fortunately, there wasn't too much for her to do, since it was the first day. In the early afternoon, she went back to her room and packed her extra uniforms and few remaining personal items in her duffel bag. When she looked back, it was as if she had never been there.

She walked slowly toward the house on Hillcrest, wondering if it was a mistake to leave the base. Living there had been the most stable period of her life. What if she and Bett had a fight and Bett asked her to leave? *I guess I can always go back to the officers' quarters.* She opened the door and carried her gear through to the kitchen.

Bett was cooking, an apron covering her uniform. She had gotten flour everywhere, even in her hair. In the hours they had been apart, Bett had rarely been out of Rain's thoughts and yet it was as if she was seeing Bett's breathtaking loveliness for the first time. Rain dropped her duffel. The sound made Bett look up and then she saw the bag on the ground. She jumped into Rain's arms, covering her with flour and kisses. "I had this terrible thought that you weren't coming—that you would change your mind or that Issacson would say no." The kisses slowed and deepened. "Oh God, Rain, I'm so glad to see you. I'm so glad you're home." Rain felt all the tension drain out of her body, and it filled instead with unconditional certainty: *Home. So right.*

❖

"Maybe we should just bring your mattress out here," Bett suggested, sleepily. They were lying on their makeshift bedroll in front of a dying fire after dinner. "You know I'm not as comfortable on the floor as you are."

"Good idea. Since that bed is smaller than yours it will be easier for me to find you," Rain suggested.

"You don't seem to have any trouble doing that." Bett smiled. Rain had been stroking her arms and back in a way that made her more relaxed than aroused, although she knew that could change quickly. *God, I love her touch.*

"Tell me about your new job," Rain said quietly.

"Oh, I think it's going to be very interesting," Bett said, trying to wake up a bit. "I'll start with just general coding, checking the incoming and outgoing transmissions, but if I get good enough, I'll be working with just one of our soldiers in the field. That will be my goal, I think. What about you?"

"I don't know. I was too shaky from my conversation with Colonel Issacson to remember much of what they said. I can't even remember now why I wanted to be a quartermaster. It doesn't seem much like a thing I would want to do," Rain said. "But I guess I've changed since I went to the training. It feels like I've fundamentally changed in the week I've been here with you. Or maybe I'm not really different, I just see myself more clearly."

"Is it too late for you to switch, to get another job?" Bett asked, sitting up. "What would you do if you could do anything?"

Rain looked at her and smiled a very slow, suggestive smile. "Sergeant!" Bett said, acting shocked. "You know I was referring to your training choices."

"Hmm," Rain replied, pulling her closer, nuzzling her neck.

"You are not getting out of this conversation yet," Bett said, trying to keep her thoughts going. "Would you want to go back to working with recruits?"

"No," Rain said, touching Bett's cheek. "I've found the recruit I was looking for."

"All right then, if you're going to be so charming, we can change the subject. But I want to talk about this again in a few days, once you've had a better chance to try this job. Promise me?"

Rain nodded. Bett wrapped her arms around Rain's neck. "Good. Then take me to bed. We both have big days tomorrow."

Bett fell asleep almost immediately, spooning around Rain's relaxed form. Rain let her body rest, but her mind was working. *What job would I do if I could do anything?* She tried to remember her experiences in each of the introductory sessions during her basic training. It had been almost three years ago now, and that seemed like a long time past.

Nothing clerical. She had that job now. She knew she wasn't suited for scientific research work, or cryptography, like Bett. She wanted to do something with her hands, to do something concrete, not abstract. The motor pool! She remembered how much she had enjoyed putting the engine pieces together until…that lieutenant, the one in charge, had seen her braid when she took off her hat for just a quick moment to wipe her brow. It had been stifling hot in the bay where they were working and everyone was perspiring heavily. The girls in her squad were used to seeing her hair by then, but this officer came over to her and began making comments.

"Hey, Chief, how's it going?" Rains snapped to attention but didn't answer. "I asked you a question, Crazy Horse," the officer persisted.

By this time, Sergeant Moore had joined them. "Answer the officer, Private Rains."

"Yes, Sergeant. It's going fine, Lieutenant." Rains's sample piece was already put together. No one else was finished yet.

"Thought you might have a deaf and dumb Indian on your hands, Sergeant." The lieutenant laughed. "Like the ones out front of the cigar stores."

"Well, Private Rains doesn't talk much but it looks like she might be a good fit for your motor pool group," Sergeant Moore said, pointing out Rains's completed work. It was as much praise as Rains had ever gotten from her sergeant.

The lieutenant walked very slowly around Rains, who already had more sweat running down her face. Rains stayed at attention while the moisture dripped into a small pool on the table in front of her. "Oh, I don't think so," the officer said, finally. "No, I don't think she'd fit in here at all."

"As you were, Private," Sergeant Moore said, walking away with the lieutenant.

After they left the motor pool, Sergeant Moore had started in on Rains in full view of the rest of the squad. "Why didn't you answer that officer, Private?"

"I didn't know she was talking to me, Sergeant," Rains responded loudly, as Moore had trained them to do.

"She was looking right at you," her sergeant shouted back. "Who did you think she was talking to?"

"A chief named Crazy Horse, ma'am," Rains replied, and some of the other girls began giggling. She allowed her eyes to slide toward them and her volume lowered. "But I can't imagine why. He was from my tribe, so I happen to know he's been dead for about sixty years." The girls began to laugh more, which made Sergeant Moore furious.

"Shut up, Rains. I guess we're gonna have to try running that goddamn stubborn streak out of you again. Take ten laps, starting right

now." She turned to one of the laughing girls. "Cowan, you think this is so funny, you go with her and count 'em off."

As they walked over toward the parade grounds, Eileen Cowan offered to pad her total—two for one. "That wasn't right, what the lieutenant said," Cowan offered sympathetically. "And Moore had no reason to punish you either."

"It's okay, Cowan. I really could use a run." Rains started away and then came back. "But thanks," she added. When she got to ten laps, Cowan was waving and yelling for her to stop, but Rains ran two more, just for spite. Eileen told everyone at the barracks that Rains was definitely crazy, even if she wasn't Crazy Horse.

Rain turned over onto her back and sighed. After a few seconds, Bett made some complaining sounds, found Rain's arm, and brought it around her as she turned, bringing Rain willingly over beside her. Relaxing into the wonderful feeling of Bett's body, Rain decided to check and see if that same lieutenant was still around.

Rain had fallen asleep when she heard Bett say her name. She swam up into consciousness feeling Bett move her hand onto her breast. She listened again to the echo of sound in her head; Bett's voice was full of desire. She came fully awake then and caressed Bett's tightening nipple while she kissed the back of her neck.

"I was dreaming of you," Bett murmured, beginning to move in response to Rain's touch. "And then I decided I'd rather have the real thing."

"Good," Rain answered, moving closer. They both turned onto their backs. She reached her hand between Bett's legs and found her so wet that it made her moan. She felt her own body respond.

"See what you do to me?" Bett's voice was still soft, but rougher now. As her hand moved between Rain's thighs and felt that Rain was ready, too, Rain could only repeat, "See?"

Moaning louder, Bett turned her face toward Rain, moving her mouth toward the side of Bett's neck. Bett tilted her head, giving Rain access to her throat. Rain growled softly as she tasted the soft flesh, even as she could feel Bett's shoulder rubbing gently against her own breast. They were moving together, and touching Bett and being touched by her this way was electrifying every part of Rain's body. Sex with Bett was more arousing than anything she could have ever imagined. As the sensations gathered inside, Rain tried to keep her focus on stroking Bett, but then felt Bett moving against her, setting her own pace. Hearing Bett's breathing getting faster almost pushed Rain over the edge, and then she realized she was moving against Bett's fingers in the same way. When she felt herself approach the place where nothing else existed but her and Bett, she whispered, "Oh yes," in Bett's ear. She meant to only say it once, but then she couldn't stop and then the word changed to Bett's name until Bett's high descending call covered everything. They lay still, while their breathing ebbed. Then Bett turned over and embraced Rain tightly, her tone quivering with emotion. "I can't get close enough to you sometimes."

Rain nodded, not trusting herself to speak at first, just holding on as firmly as she could without hurting. "I know," she said at last. "I never knew anything could feel as good as being with you." She let her fingers trace over Bett's skin, storing the feeling where memories of Bett lived inside her.

"God, Rain, is there anything you can't do?" Bett asked after a bit, relaxing and snuggling in, her voice fading slightly.

"Yes," Rain said, turning Bett over so she was now on top. "I can't stop loving you more every minute. I can't stop wanting you, wanting to be with you, wanting to touch you, needing you to touch me—" Rain's voice caught. She had spent her whole life making sure she didn't need anyone and suddenly she recognized that Bett's presence seemed as essential as water. In that one second, she was so frightened she almost couldn't breathe.

"Beloved, don't stop. Please don't. Don't ever," Bett said. Then, feeling Rain's tautness, she added, "I'm scared, too, Rain. If I even for one moment imagine being without you, I think I'd go crazy somehow. So we just won't, okay? We won't let that happen, will we? We can promise that, can't we? I can. You can promise me that, too, can't you?"

Bett eased her hands up Rain's back and willed her warm breath to brush the fear away and replace it with a feeling new and tender.

Rain only nodded at first, and when she finally spoke, her voice was raw with emotion. "Yes, Bett," she said, looking into her beloved's eyes. "I can promise you that."

Coming back to each other after the first day that they had spent apart since becoming lovers, they both felt the solid core of their developing relationship. And there was a trust that encompassed their feelings, both physical and emotional. *This is real*, Bett thought as she moved so that they were side by side. *I've found something I never really thought existed.* Meeting Rain's eyes with certitude, she said, "Tell me the way to say it in Lakota. The way to say *forever*."

Rain did. *"Óhiŋniyaŋ."*

Bett repeated it. They fell asleep that way for the first time, facing each other, breathing in each other's breath.

Bett felt Rain's lips brush against hers very sweetly when she got up to shower the next morning. When she woke up a little more, Bett felt something in her hand. Rain's uneven writing covered a small piece of paper with the words, *There is no remedy for love but to love more. HDT.* Bett decided that Rain's admiration for Henry David Thoreau, the American naturalist and philosopher, might be justified after all.

Helen was so distracted by the events of her day that it took her some time to notice the mess around Tee's normally tidy bunk and that Tee was gone. When she'd brought the truck back to the motor pool, Lieutenant Yarborough wasn't even there. Surely she would have been, if she had some deal going with that corporal. But instead, it had been Sergeant Harris who greeted her after she parked the vehicle.

"Everything okay, Tucker?" she'd asked, peering in at the cargo.

"Yes, ma'am." Helen handed over the manifest. "Everything checks exactly as indicated."

Was there just the slightest hesitation in Sergeant Harris's hand as she reached out to take the clipboard? If so, it was gone just as quickly.

"Good," Harris said briskly. "Thank you, Private." Helen nodded and started away. "Say, Tucker. Hold up a second."

Helen turned back casually, working to keep her expression calm. "Ma'am?"

Harris came a little closer and lowered her voice. "About Lieutenant Yarborough. I hope you can just let this morning go. You'll be old news in a week or so and she'll be on to something else."

"Sure," Helen said, but that must not have been what Harris wanted to hear, because she moved closer still.

"Look, just don't do anything stupid. If there's something going on that you're not sure how to handle, you talk to me. Yarborough will come and go, but I'll be here for you, okay? Just ask Barnes or Castro." She named two other veteran drivers.

For a few wild seconds, Helen considered telling her everything, including handing over the ten dollar bill that suddenly felt hot in her pocket. But when she saw Harris's eyes drift toward the manifest again, she only nodded. "Yeah. Thanks."

Something crashed in one of the bays and Harris grimaced. "Damn. See you tomorrow, Tucker."

Helen had been so caught up in her thoughts that she'd walked back to her old barracks without thinking. She'd been about to go inside when she heard Sergeant Webber's voice going through a series of commands. When she made it back to her current lodging, she went directly to the bathroom and splashed water on her face, trying to settle her nerves. As she stared at herself in the mirror, she felt lonelier than she'd felt since joining the WAC. She wished for someone to talk to, someone who really understood her and could help her steer through this mess. She missed her brother.

They'd been close growing up, and Sinclair had always looked out for her, explained things to her, and taken the heat for her more than once. When she'd been caught trying to steal a candy bar from the local mercantile, he'd told the shopkeeper that he'd put her up to it. And during her last year of high school, when the teacher had discovered her love notes from Sally Ross, the principal's daughter, Sinclair had convinced them all they were actually for him. But more importantly, Sinclair knew what it was like for them, growing up. How scrounging and scavenging for whatever you could get could make other people's rules less important sometimes. That survival counted for much more than respectability. Helen knew there'd be no point in talking to Tee about the situation, even if she was in a better state of mind. Tee simply saw everything as either right or wrong. She'd be horrified if Helen told her about taking the money today, no matter if she explained she was doing it for them.

Helen's stomach growled, reminding her it was about time for dinner. She went back to her bunk and looked over at Tee's bed, and the shock of seeing her footlocker open and duffel half packed made everything else in her day fade away. She looked anxiously around her own bed; there was no note. Helen wondered if Casey had come by to talk, as she'd promised to. Had her visit made things better or worse?

❖

The taxi slowed and pulled over to the curb. "This church?" the driver asked, half turning in his seat. "You sure about that?"

Tee nodded, but he continued to look at her doubtfully until she added, "Yes, thank you," as firmly as she could manage. She'd made up her mind. She'd prayed all afternoon and then it had come to her that Pastor Washington and his wife were put in her path for a reason, and it wasn't just to bring her back to the base when she got lost after the party. Perhaps the Lord was sending her a message about how to reconcile the two very different versions of how her life could be and to make peace with the warring parts of herself. She would confide in them as much as possible and ask for their advice. Their answer would tip the scales.

She recalled the way the door cracked as she pulled it open. Tee hadn't really registered the music, even though it was audible from outside. But now, standing in the sanctuary, the full volume of it surrounded her and she was instantly lifted up. She closed her eyes and let it wash over her. The sound of the choir filled her with everything she wanted in her life—love, joy, and the certainty of her beliefs— and she knew she was right to come here. "Just a Closer Walk with Thee." The song was one she had sung many times, but it had never sounded like this, full of varied voices and yet so perfectly blended. She moved quickly to the back pew and slumped low, trying to make herself invisible. Nothing should interrupt the beauty, the exultation of this glorious singing.

The choir went through three more songs and each was equally magnificent. She did notice, however, that other than getting their opening notes from a terribly out-of-tune piano, all the singing was done unaccompanied. When the choir was dismissed after some reminders about Sunday's service, someone must have mentioned Tee's presence, because the director hurried out a side door as the singers congregated around, talking quietly among themselves and glancing her way occasionally. No one seemed to be leaving, and Tee was upset that they might think she wished them ill. When the director returned with Pastor Washington, she stood and extended her hand, smiling, feeling an unexpected confidence.

"Hello, Pastor. I'm sorry for dropping in on you again."

It took him a few seconds, but a smile came gradually to his face and he shook her hand very carefully. "Hello, little sister. Are you feeling better this evening?"

"Oh yes. Especially now that I've been listening to your wonderful choir. Their music was so inspiring." She nodded at the director, who was standing a bit off to the side. "I don't think I've ever enjoyed those hymns as much as I did tonight."

The woman's apprehensive expression softened. "I thank you, ma'am," she said, before glancing back at the minister.

A quick look passed between them before Pastor Washington said, "Thank you, Mrs. Peters. On your way out, could you tell my wife that we have a visitor?"

When the choir director was gone, the pastor sat in the pew ahead of Tee's, and she shifted slightly so he could see her without having to turn too awkwardly. "Is there something I can do for you, child?"

His compassionate tone and kindly expression were just as she remembered, but somehow the burst of assurance that she'd felt only a few moments before dwindled into dismay. How could she possibly tell this man of God the things that were in her heart? "I...I..." Tee swallowed hard and closed her eyes. "I'm in need of some guidance, Reverend."

"I see." His words were slow and almost cautious. "Have you considered visiting the base chaplain?"

Tee opened her eyes, grateful for a safer topic. "Oh, I have. And Reverend Culberson is very nice. But I'm confused because some of the things she says don't—well, they don't exactly match up to what I've been taught. That's why I wanted to speak to you."

"Go on." Pastor Washington put his chin on his fist, apparently ready to listen.

"I believe the Lord brought me to your door for a reason," Tee explained. "I don't...I mean...there's some things in my life right now that I just can't seem to see my way through. Inside me, it's like one of those newsreels where you see the combat overseas with explosions and buildings falling down."

"Do you know what is causing this fighting inside?"

Tee nodded, but she could already tell she wouldn't be able to say it. No matter how gently he asked or how sensitively he listened, the words would stick in her throat just as surely as they had when Mr. Gallagher was around.

The sound of heels clicking on the tile floor grew louder and Tee looked up to see Mrs. Washington approaching them. Her face had a familiar expression as well, barely disguised anger combined with apprehension. The reverend gestured toward his wife. "You remember our guest from the other night." He looked back at Tee. "Could you tell us your name, sister?"

Mrs. Washington fixed Tee with something close to a glare and she answered hastily, "Margaret," using her oldest sister's name. "But you can call me Meg."

The minister stood. "Would you mind waiting here a moment, Margaret? I'm going to get my Bible so we can refer to the Word, if needed."

Mrs. Washington watched him go before turning back to Tee, her arms crossed over her chest. "Did you not stay out of trouble like I told you?"

Tee nodded vigorously. "I did. Or I tried to. But someone, a church friend, she told me her story and it—it touched me so. I couldn't just ignore her, could I?"

Mrs. Washington sat in the pew where her husband had been. "What was her story about?"

"About how it was for her, growing up. And how she almost... she almost..." Tee hadn't cried when Casey told her, but now she felt tears starting up. Her voice became a whisper. "She almost took her own life."

Mrs. Washington sat back a bit and uncrossed her arms, her expression softening. "Did she tell you why?"

"Yes, but I already knew. It's..." *Say it*, Tee ordered herself. *Tell her it's why you're here.*

Startling as a door closed near the front of the church, Tee wiped her eyes with her hands, pushing back the tears that had gathered. *Dear God, please show me how to do this*, she prayed.

Mrs. Washington's voice was much gentler now, but she spoke firmly as she leaned forward. "My husband came to love the Lord in his teenage years. He learned the Word and he can preach it. But I lived it since I was a little girl, and I bet you did, too. And I know we both have a friend in Jesus." Tee couldn't quite manage a smile at the reference to her very favorite hymn, but she nodded. "We met in church, which is probably no surprise to you. I'd been thinking about more schooling, but before we married, we agreed he would go while I worked. He's the best man I've ever known, but he is a man. Sometimes he could look at something all day and never see it. So here's what I see right now. Your name ain't Margaret, and you're afraid that whatever troubled your friend is gonna get you, too. My husband is knowledgeable about sermonizing and other church business that I probably don't appreciate enough, but since the war I've been driving a bus for the city, and I'll tell you I've seen things that have educated me in ways he won't never know. Now you remember that even if you're talking to him, I'm gonna have to be nearby. But if you'd rather, you can just talk to me first, and then we'll see if my putting together our Savior's words and the world's ways is enough, or if we need more scriptural authority."

The reverend arrived and stood beside his wife, holding a large Bible in his hands. "Would you like to talk in my study, Margaret?"

Tee looked from him to his wife. "You," she said softly and Vondra Washington stood, holding out her hand. Tee took it, and the relief she felt in just that gesture was almost overwhelming.

"Why don't you tidy up from choir practice, dear?" Mrs. Washington's voice held just the smallest hint of triumph as she led Tee up the aisle. "Meg and I will be in the kitchen."

The soft, sliding sounds were something unusual for western Kentucky, something like a big snowfall dumping off the tree branches and onto the ground with a thump. Helen breathed in, waking to the awareness that she wasn't in Kentucky and that sound wasn't coming from a tree. She opened her eyes to see a shadow moving back and forth on the bed beside hers. "Tee?" Her voice was scratchy with sleep but Tee heard, and she turned to kneel beside her bunk.

"Hey. I'm sorry I woke you." She touched Helen's cheek with such tenderness that Helen felt a lump form in her throat. "I'm just trying to get this mess cleaned up enough that I can get in bed. I'll finish tidying in the morning."

Did that mean she wasn't thinking about leaving anymore? "I'm sure glad to see you, Tee." Helen pushed up onto her elbow, capturing

Tee's hand and bringing it to her lips. "Why don't you just leave that and come sleep over here with me?" she whispered onto Tee's fingers before realizing she might have gone too far. Tee had been so unsettled since the party. She should be careful not to push her.

Tee leaned forward and kissed the top of Helen's head, her voice even softer. "I like that I can count on you, Helen. I like that you tell me how you feel, even when you don't know how I feel." She turned away, lifting her duffel onto the floor between them. As Helen watched, Tee found her toiletry bag and headed for the bathroom. Everything in her wanted to go after Tee, to corner her in the restroom and get her to talk. Or to at least hold her and tell her how glad she was to see her. She threw back the covers and swung her legs over the bunk before having second thoughts. Maybe she needed to back off and just take whatever Tee could give. At least Tee was talking to her again. One thing she knew for certain, though. She sure couldn't tell Tee about what was going on in the motor pool.

❖

By Friday, Helen had made three more pickup runs to the train station and had spent one day delivering supplies to the mess hall and the colonel's office. On Tuesday, there was no sign of Corporal Newton and she breathed a sigh of relief. Ten dollars was ten dollars, but she wouldn't be too upset if he'd decided not to do business with her after all. Then she checked the manifest and saw she was picking up uniforms and office supplies. Helen liked her khaki, and she thought the olive dress uniform looked really sharp, but it wasn't likely that they or pens and pencils were hot black market items. Wednesday, the station hands waved her over to a closer spot when she pulled up. She had already noted that the invoice included coffee and boxes of canned milk. They were bringing in the last load when she smelled cigarette smoke and heard Newton's voice behind her.

"What's up, Tucker?"

"Oh, hi, Newton." Helen kept her voice casual as she ticked off the boxes on her fingers. Sure enough, there was one extra each of the coffee and the canned milk. She turned to face him.

He held out his hand for the clipboard and she handed it over without another word. "Two extra this time. How's fifteen?" He reached into his pocket.

"Twenty's better. If it's ten for one, it should be twenty for two."

He shrugged. "It don't necessarily work that way. More risk, less reward. See?"

Helen shook her head. "No, I don't see. What I see is two extra boxes that I could take back to the base with no risk to me. You told me last time that we could cut out the middleman, so I think some of that cut has to come to me. But if you don't like it that way, just find yourself another driver."

Newton smirked. "What makes you think you're the only one, Tucker? You think I can keep this racket going with only two pickups a week?" He stepped in a little closer. "So you didn't get no guff from that dame?"

Helen desperately wanted to ask *Which dame?* but she knew better than to spill what she didn't know. "Not last time, no. But if she gets an idea that I'm in on this with you, she might start asking questions."

His laughter wasn't pleasant. "Damn, Tucker. You stupid or something? Who you think recommended you for this little extracurricular activity? She had you pegged right off."

The feeling in her stomach was almost like being sick—a tight churning that threatened to come right up her throat. She tried to swallow the bile without being obvious. "If that's true, then you might have to make it twenty-five. I'll have to do some fast talking to keep her in the dark."

He reached into his pocket and slapped a twenty on her clipboard. "Don't get greedy, girl. There's always another driver. It'd be real easy to find someone else looking to make a little extra. You remember that." He gathered the boxes while she tried to look unconcerned in case someone else was watching. They both jumped down from the cargo area. "Same place tomorrow," Newton said. It wasn't a suggestion.

There was no sign of the sergeant or the lieutenant when Helen pulled up. She was so anxious to get out of there that she helped the others unload, which wasn't required of the drivers. She made sure to mention that the manifest matched but the corporal who took the clipboard only nodded offhandedly. "They always do," she said, before carrying it into the lieutenant's empty office.

As she walked back to the barracks, Helen's guts were churning. She needed something to steady her nerves. She turned toward the NCO club, hoping there might be someone there who she could ask to be her escort. With the twenty in her pocket, she could even offer to buy her host a drink. The guard who normally stood outside was just inside the door, his back turned while he talked to a cute corporal who was sipping on a beer. Helen took advantage of the time to peer around inside, scanning the crowd for a familiar face. She jumped when a hand landed on her shoulder.

"Tucker! Just the gal I wanted to see." It was Sergeant Harris's voice. The sick feeling in her stomach intensified. "You sure ran off quick this afternoon."

Clearing the fear from her throat before she turned, Helen put on her well-practiced innocent look. "Sergeant Harris! I don't suppose you'd be willing to let a thirsty private buy you a drink?"

Harris looked almost surprised for a few seconds before she gestured them inside. "I wouldn't have it any other way."

Three hours later, Helen waved a cheery good-bye as Ginny Harris staggered away. She hadn't expected the sergeant to be such a lightweight, drinking-wise, but she was extremely grateful to whatever God looked out for stupid privates who coveted what they didn't have to the point they let desire overrule good sense and best judgment. At least she now knew that while Harris might be the brawn, she certainly wasn't the brains behind what was going on in the motor pool. It had only taken one beer, preceded by a shot of whiskey—something Ginny called a boilermaker—to get her talking about all the ways she thought Lieutenant Yarborough was screwing her over.

"If it wasn't for my girls"—she smiled at Tucker—"like you and Barnes and Castro, I'd tell her to stick it in her ear." She'd named those drivers before, Helen remembered. They must be some of the others who were in on the deal. Harris patted her arm in a way that Helen recognized as strictly nonsexual. This was a sweet, almost motherly touch, so Helen went with that.

"Listen, Sarge, I know I'm new here, but even I can see that we'd all be lost without you. Everyone counts on you to make sure things get done and that we don't get too much guff from Yarborough." She signaled for another drink. "Anyone who just walked by that place could tell that you're the one who runs the ship. So why doesn't the top brass put you in charge?"

This question, and the second drink, led to a long harangue from Harris about how it took a college education to be an officer—something Helen had heard was not really the case—and how Yarborough and Colonel Issacson had been great buddies once upon a time and how Yarborough could probably sell off the whole fleet of trucks and Issacson wouldn't call her on it. By the third drink, Sergeant Harris was telling Helen in no uncertain terms not to ever, ever, trust a man. Especially a little shit like Corporal Newton, even if he did kiss better than her husband.

When they parted, Harris gave Helen a sloppy sideways hug, saying, "You're all right, Tucker. I knew it from the first. But you should know that Yarborough doesn't like you. Nope, not at all."

Like that was a news bulletin, Helen thought, but she gave Harris a little squeeze. "Thanks for watching out for me, Sarge. I'll see you tomorrow, okay?"

Outside the barracks, Helen stopped to collect herself. She was out almost five dollars and not really much the wiser for it. She wasn't looking forward to another trip to the station and another meeting with Newton, but she wasn't sure what other choice she had at this point. She walked quietly inside, waving at the few girls who were still up. Tee was already curled up in her blankets and Helen decided not to disturb her. But once she'd cleaned up and gotten ready for bed, she turned so she could watch Tee, sleeping innocently on her bunk. Just listening to her breathing strengthened Helen's resolve. She was doing this for them. She'd just make enough extra that they could get their own place, and then she'd figure a way out.

Chapter Nine

A fter an ineffective week, in which she had mainly moved the piles of paperwork to different positions on her desk while reading and rereading the training manuals until her head swam, Rains skipped lunch on Friday and went by the motor pool. She was surprised to see her MP friend Harold Lutz there, sitting on the floor in one of the bays, surrounded by greasy parts.

"Hey, Rains!" he greeted her, gesturing around him. "Wanna buy a motorcycle?"

Rains pointed at the pieces on the ground. "Is that it?" she asked.

"Well"—he grinned—"that's part of it." He pointed at the frame leaning against the wall. "Once I get it rebuilt, I'm gonna sell it."

Rains looked at the smooth design of the body and the flared red fenders. She thought about her run to the base every morning. It was getting colder outside. "What kind of motorcycle is it?" she asked.

Lutz got up off the ground, dusted himself, looked at Rains briefly, and then back at the bike. "Don't be mad, okay? This is a 1940 Indian brand motorcycle and the model is called a Chief."

Rains burst out laughing. She clapped Lutz on the shoulder, amused as his eyes widened even more at her rare physical gesture. "Of course it is," Rains said, shaking her head at him. "Talk to me when you get it running, will you?"

"Sure thing, Rains."

"Hey, Lutz, who's in charge here?"

"Lieutenant Yarborough, right now." He lowered his voice. "She's a total bitch, but there've been a few hints that she might be on the way out. No word on who's coming in next. Why?"

"I'm thinking about a vocational change," Rains said, looking around. She remembered the name. Yarborough was the officer who had called her Crazy Horse. The place was the same kind of mess it had been the night she and Bett had watched the big moon when it had taken her so long to return the borrowed Jeep. There were still rusty parts piled up in corners, and now two half-finished Jeeps were sitting in the bays. Except for Lutz, no one was working.

"No way! You wanna be a grease monkey?" he asked with surprise.

"Maybe. Don't say anything yet, okay?"

"You got it. You wanna talk to the lieutenant now? She's probably not here, but you might could find her at the Officers' Club."

"No, I just wanted to get a feel for the place. I need to talk to the colonel first and see if I can even get a change." Rains started away and yelled back, "Find me about that motorcycle."

Lutz grinned and saluted.

When Rains got back to her building, the stack of paperwork on her desk had doubled. She sighed, chin in hand, wondering if there was someone else in the department she could ask for help. The various instructions she'd read never seemed to apply to the piece of paper she was working on. As she breathed in, she caught a memory of Bett's scent on her fingers. For a moment she was almost dizzy, so she closed her eyes. Another breath and she smiled, remembering Bett arching beneath her, breathing hard, her eyes smoldering with desire as she clung to Rains's neck, holding on—trying to hold back. And she, almost feverish with the need to drive Bett over the edge and hear her cries of pleasure and release. Nothing in her life had prepared her for the passion of their time together.

"Sergeant Rains!" It was the colonel's voice. Rains opened her eyes just enough to see Janet Issacson standing in her doorway, looking directly at her. Wishing she had a good Lakota curse word for this occasion, Rains stood up.

"Yes, ma'am."

"In my office, now," Issacson barked.

Rains entered with as much dignity as she could muster.

"Close the door," Issacson said. When Rains had done so and turned her face back in Issacson's direction, the colonel said, "Am I correct that you are supposed to be working as a quartermaster?"

"Yes, ma'am."

"And am I also correct that the amount of work you have actually done in the last five days is somewhere in the vicinity of zero?"

Rains's head dropped slightly along with her voice. "Yes, ma'am."

Issacson sighed. "I don't know what's gotten into you, Rains, but this is not the level of excellence that I expect. Would it be better if we moved you back onto the base?"

Rains answered clearly, "No, ma'am. I honestly don't think that is the problem."

"Well, what is it, then?" the colonel asked. "Speak freely."

Rains cleared her throat. "Ma'am, I just don't think I'm cut out to be a quartermaster. I know it's an important job, but maybe it's just not for me. I don't even know why I chose this as my second option when I went through basic."

Issacson regarded her thoughtfully. "You don't remember who your instructor was on that rotation, do you, Sergeant?"

Rains considered for a moment, and recollection dawned. The lieutenant who normally did the quartermaster training had been out on leave. "Yes, ma'am. It was you."

"So did you feel pressured to sign up for this job because I was the one teaching it?"

Rains hesitated. "Not pressured, ma'am," she said, finally. "I just enjoy serving with you and I admire your management abilities and your command style. I'm sure I was thinking more about that than I was about the actual quartermaster's duties when I opted in."

Issacson narrowed her eyes. "Sergeant Rains, are you trying to bullshit me?"

"No, ma'am," Rains said sincerely. "I learn something about leadership every time I'm in here." She looked down again. "Even when I'm in trouble."

"Are you in trouble, Rains?" she asked.

"No, ma'am. I'm just having some trouble adjusting to the new job." Rains straightened and she composed herself, her voice more formal as well. "But I'll do better, ma'am. You have my word."

The colonel sighed and rubbed her eyes. "Have you thought of another department you'd feel better suited to, Sergeant Rains?" she asked tiredly.

Rains's eyes slid to her commanding officer's face for a split second. She knew Colonel Issacson well enough to believe this was not a trap, but still, the question caught her off guard. She answered deliberately, choosing her words with care.

"I think I'd like to work in the motor pool, ma'am. I'd like to work with my hands and have control over the results of my labor from start to finish. I believe that would be a better fit for me."

The colonel was still looking at her, but Rains didn't think she really saw her as her fingers drummed on the desk for what felt like an hour. The motions gradually slowed, then stopped. Everything was still for a moment until, as if returning from deep contemplation, Janet Issacson slowly raised an eyebrow.

"So you think you'd prefer working with machines to working with people?"

"I know I'd prefer working with machines to working with paper," Rains responded, trying not to sound critical of her quartermaster duties.

"This is the Army, Rains," Issacson reminded her. "There's paper everywhere."

"Yes, ma'am."

"Especially when you're a lieutenant."

Rains leaned forward slightly, not quite understanding. "Ma'am?"

Issacson sighed. "I haven't been able to get your promotion to master sergeant to go through, Rains. I've tried everything short of walking to Washington and pushing it around myself. Something was just screwy, so I tried again, this time promoting you to second lieutenant. The damn thing came through yesterday, slick as a whistle. We both know this is long overdue, so we'll consider it a field promotion. Someday, when things slow down, we'll get you through Officer Candidate School."

Rains blinked in surprise, and for a moment she thought Colonel Issacson might be fighting a smile before she continued.

"In the meantime, your timing is just about perfect. Lieutenant Yarborough is due to rotate out of the motor pool. Frankly, it's been a mess for years, but lately..." She trailed off, as if considering exactly what to say. "This isn't going to be an easy transition." The colonel's voice was pensive. "You may not want to be a quartermaster, but you'll have to work with them, especially at first. Look into procurement and possibly finance. There seem to have been some...irregularities. You'll have to find out the source before you put a stop to it, and I want the ones at the top who are involved. Report only to me on this, understand?"

Rains nodded slowly, trying to process everything her commanding officer was—or wasn't—saying.

The colonel cleared her throat in the familiar, almost brusque gesture that all her officers recognized as the end of the conversation. "So if you want to take this on, you've got it. I'm putting you in charge, starting on Monday. You have my permission to restaff both mechanics and transport as needed. Get who you want, but get that place under control." Issacson looked hard at Rains. "And I mean pronto. You've got six weeks, and if I don't see some significant improvement, then I'm busting you back to PFC and putting you to work in the mess hall. Are we clear?"

"Ma'am, I—" Rains was still stunned by the turn of events as she tried to formulate the appropriate response. Her gaze drifted to Issacson's face again and lingered there.

"Are we clear?" the colonel repeated distinctly, her words a bit more emphatic at the infraction.

Rains fixed her eyes back into the distance and straightened. "Yes, ma'am," she said, saluting sharply.

Issacson reached into the pile of paperwork on her desk and came up with some gold bars. She returned the salute and put them in Rains's hand. "Congratulations. And don't let me down, Rains."

Rains was ready to burst with excitement. "Thank you, Colonel. I'll do my very best."

"I'm counting on that. Dismissed, Lieutenant."

Rains was so excited that she couldn't wait to get to work. No one was in the motor pool when she got there, but she found an old pair of coveralls to put on over her uniform and started cleaning. It was almost dark by the time she stopped, feeling like she'd made some progress. Before she left, she attached the new insignia to her collar.

❖

Rain ran home happily, only to find Bett sound asleep on the couch. She got the blanket off the guest bed and covered her. Bett made a little sighing breath but didn't move. Rain began to make dinner as quietly as she could. She cooked some chicken and mixed it in with the noodles that Bett liked. Pasta, Bett called it. She was adding some spinach and mushrooms as she heard Bett's voice saying, "I knew I was going to like this restaurant. They have the most beautiful chef." Rain turned off the stove and walked back over to the couch. Bett stretched out her arms in welcome, and Rain slowly let herself down on top of her.

"Oh yes," Bett sighed, closing her eyes again as she ran her hands along Rain's sides. "That's what I've been missing."

Rain thought again that no matter how good a day it had been, being next to Bett made it better. "Hard day?" she asked.

"Mm," Bett murmured, adjusting herself under Rain's body. "I've looked at lines of code until I'm dizzy. I still have more to do but I just had to get back home to you."

Rain smiled. "That's exactly how I felt."

"Yes, you were late too, Beloved. Did you talk to the colonel about your job?" Bett still had her eyes closed.

"Let's eat," Rain said, "and I'll tell you all about it."

"Don't you want to change first?" Bett asked, knowing how much Rain preferred her jeans and flannel to the Army uniform.

"Not yet."

Bett opened her eyes. "Why not? What's going on, Rain? Tell me."

Rain sat up and pulled Bett into a sitting position also. Facing her, Rain put her hand to her tie, drawing Bett's attention to the new bars on her collar. Bett touched them wondrously and looked at Rain with a smile. "Your promotion?"

"And even more than I expected," Rain said, puffing her chest proudly. She could see Bett trying to remember what the different insignia represented.

"Is that…are you a lieutenant now?" Bett asked, cocking her head as she deliberately pronounced the rank like the British, *leftenant*.

"Yes, and I was hoping you'd say it like that," Rain said, kissing and nipping at Bett's neck until she began to squirm with delight. "Because I've never had a chance to tell you how lovely your accent is to my ears. From the first time I heard you speak, I've been enchanted." Bett smiled and caught Rain's mouth with her own. Their kisses deepened.

"Good," Bett said finally, her mouth close to Rain's ear as she pushed her down on the couch and began unbuttoning her uniform. "Because I need to tell you that I've just developed this mad desire to fuck a lieutenant."

Rain had heard lots of men and quite a few women say the F-word since she'd joined the Army. She had always understood it to be a curse. But as the word came out of Bett's sweet mouth in her charming, cultured intonation, it traveled down Rain's spine until it rested in her groin. She opened Bett's blouse, pushing up her bra without bothering to unclasp it so she could put her mouth on Bett's breast. Bett sat up and quickly finished removing her top before running her hands down Rain's chest, hastily opening her shirt as well. Then she pulled Rain's face to hers and kissed her almost hard enough to bruise before sliding her tongue into her mouth. As soon as Bett had undone her pants, Rain thrust against her until she felt Bett's fingers sliding in between her legs. She felt desperate to have Bett back inside her, like on their first night. She pushed herself up, even taking Bett's elbow in her hand, but Bett kept moving away, stroking her on the outside, getting her more and more aroused. Rain heard a pleading sound come from her own mouth, and Bett leaned over her, breathing hard, saying, "Tell me, Lieutenant. Tell me what you want." She kissed where Rain's uniform jacket was open and came back up to look in Rain's eyes. "Say it," Bett ordered, and the words came directly to Rain's lips without passing through her brain.

"I want you to fuck me. Fuck me now. Please fu—" Before Rain could finish, Bett slid into her, slowly but deeply. The feeling was so exactly right that Rain's arms went around Bett's back and a long deep moan came from her throat. Bett's fingers drew back and then glided back in, gently at first until she heard Rain whisper, almost in perfect time to her thrusts, "Yes…yes…more…please…" Bett was almost overcome by the deep warmth inside Rain and by her profound desire to be in it. She began to move faster, sucking harder on her breast until she felt Rain's hips pull up and her muscles tighten as her hands pulled on Bett's back and her cry was almost like pain, but Bett knew it wasn't, knew it was good, so good, as she felt another little gush of wetness come from inside Rain. Rain was still breathing little cries of pleasure as Bett lay out on her chest. Bett kissed her gently and felt a final distant spasm shudder across Rain's form as she withdrew from her body. She felt Rain's breathing slow and then Bett was waking up again, with no idea of how much time had passed. She shifted her body slightly and felt Rain stirring, felt her sighing a deep, contented breath. Rain pressed a little nearer for a moment, as if reluctant to come fully awake.

"And to think," Rain said finally, her voice slightly hoarse, "I used to like the way you said *sergeant*."

She felt Bett begin to giggle. All Rain could manage was a very relaxed smile. Then Bett began to laugh out loud, shaking until Rain shifted too much and they both fell off the couch and onto the floor. After that, they were both laughing against each other, until Bett said, "I love you, Lieutenant."

Then Rain had to put her head on Bett's shoulder for a moment, until the sharp wave of emotion passed. Bett held her close until Rain said, "I have something with you that I never expected. You are the love of my life, Bett." Then she held her closer.

After changing into her jeans, Rain told Bett the rest of the story of her promotion to the motor pool as they ate their cold chicken pasta.

"Oh, Rain, that's wonderful. And you deserve it." Bett leaned across the table to kiss Rain quickly and was gratified to see her reaction. *She's so beautiful when she smiles.* "Aren't you excited?"

"Yes, but a little nervous, too," Rain admitted. "I was thinking about everything that I want to do as I worked there this afternoon, but it's hard for me to keep my thoughts organized when there's so much."

"You should make a chart, listing the different areas you want to work on," Bett suggested. Seeing Rain's reaction, she said, "Don't make a face, Rain. Writing things down on a big project like this can be very useful. I used to do it in university all the time."

"Yes, but I don't like to write," Rain reminded her.

"But this isn't like writing sentences. You can just do words or phrases. Or you could even draw pictures."

"Hmm." Rain looked back down at her food.

"So you'll let me just show you what I mean after we eat?" Bett pretended to translate Rain's grunt.

Bett had spread several sheets of paper across the dining room table while Rain cleaned up the kitchen. Rain walked back and forth in the hall a couple of times, glancing in at Bett only briefly. *Stalling,* Bett thought.

Finally Rain came into the room, though she looked restless and didn't sit. "Just talk me through it, Rain," Bett said, taking her hand. "I'll write at first and then you'll get the hang of it. Tell me what you think needs to be done in that place."

"Equipment," Rain said after a bit.

"Do you mean equipment used to repair the vehicles or the vehicles themselves?" Bett asked, her pen poised.

"Both," Rain replied.

Bett wrote on two sheets: *Repairing Machinery* and *Equipment To Be Repaired.*

"What else?" she asked. "And don't try to organize things now. Just say whatever comes into your head and we'll sort it out later."

"Personnel," Rain said. "I need people who can operate the machinery as well as someone to organize what needs to be repaired."

"Good," Bett said, writing again. "Go on."

Rain began pacing around the table. She talked for almost half an hour, gesturing sometimes, her eyes seeing every inch of the motor pool area. Bett filled every sheet she had gotten out and two more. When Rain finished, she looked in astonishment at the tidy lists that Bett had made. She read over the columns, seeing her random ideas arranged and structured in a logical, orderly way.

Bett was looking up at her. "Okay?" she asked.

"This is…" Rain seemed at a loss for words. "You learned to do this in university?" she asked.

"Well, I used this technique there. I actually learned earlier, in prep school," Bett said. "But now that you've seen it done, I'm sure you could do it, too. It's just harder to imagine when you haven't ever put things down this way."

Rain began to gather up the papers, looking at each one again with her eyes wide. She didn't quite meet Bett's eyes as she mumbled, "I don't know what to say, Bett. But thank you."

"Oh, Rain," Bett said, standing and sliding her arms around Rain's waist, "that is all you need to say. I'm glad it was helpful." She leaned her head against Rain's warm chest.

Rain was standing very still. Bett knew something was wrong. She waited. "You must think I'm stupid," Rain said in a low voice, turning her head away.

"Rain," Bett said firmly, "look at me." She waited until Rain did, although her eyes didn't really settle. "I think nothing of the kind and I never have. Whose ideas are these? Not mine. I wouldn't have the faintest idea of what to do to get the Fort Des Moines motor pool running smoothly. I simply took your words and put them on paper, just to give you a way to remember them easily. But you are the one who thought of everything, who knows what needs to be done. And you'll be the one who does it. Don't forget, I know you, Rain. I've seen your leadership in action. You'll make that motor pool the best department on the base. I'm just like a clerk here. So if this cryptography business doesn't work out for me, I'll come work for you in the motor pool and be your secretary, okay?"

Rain's eyes went again to the papers for a time, then back to Bett's face. "I couldn't possibly work with you, Bett..." Bett wasn't sure how to take that, until Rain finished. "Because you take my breath away." She leaned over and kissed Bett, her lips lingering sweetly.

Bett loved being the one Rain spoke to in this way. "Don't ever think for one moment that I might confuse some lack of experience on your part with a lack of intelligence. You are one of the brightest, most interesting people I've ever known."

Rain smiled shyly. "Thank you for that, Bett. It means a lot, coming from you." She carried the papers away with great reverence.

An hour later, Bett was still staring at the pages of code. She knew the mistake was in there, but she just couldn't see it.

Rain tapped lightly on the door frame and came in with a cup of tea. "Bless you," Bett said, taking it gratefully. "I'm sorry this is taking so long, Rain. Maybe you should go on to bed and I'll be in as soon as I can."

Rain shook her head. "I'd rather wait up. I don't know what to do in there without you."

Bett smiled tiredly. "I'm afraid there won't be much to do with me at this rate."

"How about this?" Rain stood behind her and rubbed her neck and shoulders. Bett groaned happily and closed her eyes. Rain's touch always made her feel better. She felt the knots of tension loosening. "Can you explain this to me?" Rain asked after a few moments of massage. Bett realized she was looking over her shoulder at the pages of code.

"This is some old code that's already been translated. It's from the first year of the war, so it's declassified and I can bring it home. It's practice, to teach me what I'm looking for when I get to the real thing. The instructors have put a mistake here somewhere, and I have to find it. I feel like I've looked at every single digit at least twenty times, but I just can't see it."

She looked up at Rain to see if she understood. Rain was scanning the pages again and then she closed her eyes. Her brow furrowed for a moment. Then she opened her eyes and put her finger on a line of code, close to the beginning of the transmission. "Why is this part different?"

"Where?" Bett looked at the place Rain's finger marked, then at her decoding book. "Oh, good God, Rain, that's it! You've found it!" She made a mark on the page and then looked back at Rain. "How did you do that? Rain, in all these lines of code, how did you see that?"

Rain shook her head. "I don't know. It's just a pattern, right? So I see the pattern and then I can see where the pattern...is not."

"Rain, that is a three-rotor code. You cannot possibly see a pattern in it," Bett insisted.

Shrugging, Rain answered, "Everything in the universe has a pattern, Beloved. You just have to stand back far enough to see it."

Bett stared at her for a moment. "Well, I daresay we've settled the stupid question, if you're going to stand here talking metaphysics," she said, half to herself.

Rain was looking at the code again. "Is this actually taken from one of the soldiers in the field?" she asked, curiosity evident in her voice.

"Yes," Bett said, again making notations in her ledger. "But I don't know his name. Only his code name, Luna. He's the one I hope to start working with in a few weeks." She stopped writing and looked at Rain, who had reached out to touch one of the pages almost tenderly. As she opened her mouth to speak again, Bett cut in. "I shouldn't have told you that. That information is highly classified. I know you are not a spy and I know you won't repeat it, especially since I'm asking you not to. I trust you completely, of course, but please don't talk to me about this anymore. At least until you get a higher security clearance." She took Rain's hand. "You understand, don't you?"

Looking very solemn, Rain withdrew her hand. "Yes, Bett. I'm sorry. I won't speak of it again."

"No, it's entirely my fault," Bett said. "I'm tired and I'm not thinking clearly." She folded her papers and put them in her briefcase. "Let's go to bed."

Bett's head still hurt, but the gentle pressure of Rain's fingers on her temple was making it better. For a moment, she had almost tried to fight relaxing into Rain's touch. She wanted to understand what had happened, how Rain had seen the coding error so quickly. She almost felt threatened, like she had at Kent or at Oxford when someone else had grasped a concept first or revealed a better understanding of an idea than she had. Then she felt Rain's lips brush against her hair as their bodies drifted together, and she accepted that this wasn't a class competition, this was her life, and her beloved Rain was on her side as her lover, her friend, her partner, her protector. *Yes, Rain challenges me,* she thought, *but only to be as good a person as she thinks I am.* Sweet Rain, who was so impressed by Bett's ability to make some simple organizational lists and then so unimpressed with her own ability to read a pattern in a three-rotor code. Bett wanted to turn over and tell Rain these things, to stay up all night and talk and make love and spend every minute of the rest of her life looking into Rain's dark eyes, but all that came out was a little sigh as she fell asleep, feeling safe and happy.

Tee had never seen Helen be so quiet. In all the time she'd known her, Helen was always the one to crack jokes, make smart remarks, or tell funny stories. She'd always known how to draw others out by her own friendly chatter. But lately she was almost withdrawn, though she didn't seem angry, exactly. It was more like she was worried or even nervous, although she was trying not to show it. Tee fretted that her own behavior was the source of Helen's moodiness. She knew they needed to talk, but Helen came in late again on Friday and Tee had to work late on Saturday to make up for her missed time, so they missed each other at dinner. When she finally got back to the barracks, Helen was sitting with Jo Archer and they seemed to be in deep conversation as neither did anything but give her a quick wave. Helen had disappeared after breakfast the next day. Tee wanted to spend her time on Sunday doing the assignment that the pastor's wife had given her, but she resolved that they would take one of their nice walks that evening and catch up on things. Especially on things between them.

Tee thought Helen seemed almost reluctant to walk with her, but once they got away from the barracks, she seemed to perk up a little. She seemed happy to hear about Tee's progress at her job, but only scoffed about hers, saying everyone there was a jerk and she almost wished she'd gone into some other field.

"Why do you say that?" Tee questioned. "I thought you loved driving."

"It's not the driving. It's all the other…bullshit."

"Like what?"

Helen sighed. "You wouldn't understand."

Tee didn't think Helen had ever said anything like that to her before. She'd often been the one to explain about the subjects they had for their classes, especially when Bett Smythe wasn't around. She'd been willing, eager even, to take as much time as Tee needed to grasp ideas or memorize the facts for a particular subject. "What's wrong, Helen? Is it me? Is it because of the way I acted after the party?"

Helen looked down, almost as if she was ashamed. "No, baby. That was all my fault. I shouldn't have pushed you to go. I guess I haven't even taken the time to apologize properly. I just…I've just been real busy, you know?"

The way Helen's eyes shifted when she talked made Tee take her arm. If Helen really was upset about the party, she knew touching her would help. If it was something else, well, she didn't know what would help in that case, but she figured it wouldn't hurt. "Helen, I want you to know that I'm trying to find my way. I've missed you, but I can't…I don't want to hurt you by keeping on going back and forth about us the way I have been."

Helen looked almost surprised, as if she hadn't expected to talk about their relationship. "No, it's okay, Tee. I mean, I understand. Everyone needs time to figure things out on their own. I've got some figuring out to do myself, so…"

She trailed off and Tee waited, not even sure what they were talking about anymore. Finally she asked, "Figuring out about me?"

Helen seemed to focus differently, as if really seeing her for the first time that night. "Oh no, Tee. Nothing like that. You—" She turned and they faced each other, standing in the quiet dusk in the middle of the empty parade grounds. She reached out and pulled Tee to her, and Tee went willingly, wanting to restore that special connection she'd had with Helen from the beginning, the feeling that made her forget anything else except wanting to be with her. "You are everything to me." Helen's voice sounded almost desperate in her ear. "Sometimes you're the only thing that keeps me here, that keeps me from going off the deep end. I want things to be good for us, Tee. I want us to…to have a life together. Like my Aunt Darcy and Mrs. Murrell. Do you think you could do that much? Could you just live with me in our own place and then see what happens?"

Tee pulled back and reached for Helen's hand, tugging her along. Even in the early darkness of fall, they couldn't just stand there holding each other in the middle of Fort Des Moines. That was one of the things she needed to think about, like Vondra Washington had said about her sister. Being in the life, as they called it, meant a secretive, often frightening existence. They'd talked more about her than they had about the Bible, but somehow that was all right. The pastor's wife had told her to come back when she'd finished her assignment. "Helen, we both know what would happen if I moved in with you. Us being alone every night, I wouldn't be able to resist your charms."

Helen grinned, looking more like herself than she had all weekend. "Well, maybe you shouldn't."

"Maybe not," Tee agreed, relieved enough to give her hand a little squeeze. "But do you think you can give me a little more time to decide? I promise it won't be long."

"Take what you need, Tee." Helen squared her shoulders. "I'm just gonna make sure I've got everything ready for us when you decide."

Did Helen know that not pressuring her was exactly what she needed? Or was she just sweet that way? Tee lifted their joined hands and kissed Helen's quickly before letting go. "You're sounding pretty confident there, Private Tucker," she teased.

"I'm not just confident." Helen started running in little circles around her, waving her hands in the air as she chanted, "I'm cool, calm, and collected." She stopped in front of Tee and looked into her eyes. "And I'm so ready to be with you. I promise you will never regret a single moment with me. I swear it, Tee."

There was that little shiver, that delicious coiling in her stomach that only Helen seemed to make her feel. She needed to turn away because in a few seconds she was going to ask Helen to take her to the grove, to put her leg in that spot where her pulse was a faint beat now and kiss her until she felt breathless and senseless. She thought about Helen's breasts and how Helen's fingers had felt on hers. She knew Helen was who she wanted. It was just a matter of understanding why, and how to reconcile who she'd be with Helen with who she'd been for the other twenty-two years of her life.

Chapter Ten

When Helen Tucker reported for duty on Monday, she got the shock of her life when the only person present besides the other drivers was her former sergeant, now Lieutenant Rains. Helen joined the transport staff in toeing a line that reminded her of when she first arrived at Fort Des Moines and got just the slightest nod of acknowledgment from the new motor pool officer. No one spoke until the last of the drivers had arrived. Everyone else must have been as surprised as she was.

"For those of you who don't know me, I'm Lieutenant Rains. The motor pool is being restaffed as of now, so none of you will be driving today. I will make the pickup at the station and we'll have a new schedule posted by 0600 hours for tomorrow." She walked along the row, eyeing each of them. "I expect to be back here by ten thirty, so I'd like you to reassemble at that time, when I will begin meeting with each of you privately. Today, anything you tell me will be in strictest confidence, and there will be no repercussions for whatever you might wish to disclose." When she detected the slightest rumble of discomfort, she added, "I suggest you use the time to consider the path of our discussions."

After Rains pulled up at the station, she wasn't completely surprised when a corporal appeared at the back of the truck.

"Oh, hey," he said casually. "Is Tucker sick today?" Then he caught sight of her insignia and saluted briskly. "Sorry, ma'am."

"Private Tucker will probably be back tomorrow," Rains said, finding herself surprisingly pleased to be saluted. "If you want, I'll give her a message, Corporal…"

Newton backed off quickly. "No, no. No message. I did a ride-along with her a couple of weeks ago and just thought I'd say hi." He glanced at the men who were waiting to load the shipment. "I've got to get loaded up myself. Sorry to bother you, Lieutenant."

Rains stepped to the back of the truck and watched the corporal get into an Army Jeep. There was no cargo in it as he drove away quickly.

During her conversations with the transport crew that morning, the most frequently expressed comments were how glad they were to have someone else in charge of the motor pool. But there were also those who were less pleased, although they tried to hide it. Some of these tried to win her favor by naming people from her former squads that they knew and others by repeatedly assuring her of their support. Rains made sketchy notes as each one left, but most of her decisions were easily made. She scheduled her interview with Helen last, not only because she was the only one she already knew but also because the corporal at the station had known her name, and she wanted to see if anyone else would offer up information that could tie in to that. Certainly it could be as simple as what he'd claimed, but it might mean more. As she opened the door to call her in, she found Tucker in conversation with two other drivers with whom she'd already spoken. The other two turned quickly away and she thought she saw Tucker take in a breath. Relief or preparation for a lie?

"Private Tucker," Rains greeted her. "It's nice to see you again."

"Same here, ma'am." Tucker could hear herself as she stood before Rains's desk, and knew she sounded nervous. She went on, hoping to work the uneasiness out of her voice. "And congratulations on your promotion. It's well-deserved."

The lieutenant nodded her thanks. "Are you enjoying being a part of the transport crew?" she asked. "You're the newest member, I believe."

"Yes, ma'am."

"Yes, you're the newest, or yes, you're enjoying it?" Rains asked, and Helen thought she almost detected a smile.

Relax, she told herself, *Rains knows you. She's not trying to give you the third degree.* She managed a grin. "Both, ma'am."

"I met a friend of yours at the station this morning," Rains said, with no change in her expression. "A corporal. I didn't catch his name."

"Newton." Suddenly Helen's throat was so dry there was almost no sound. She had to clear her throat and repeat it. "Corporal Newton. He did a ride-along with me."

"Yes, that's what he said."

Rains said nothing further, and Helen wondered if she was supposed to volunteer more information. "I think he was a friend of Sergeant Harris's, ma'am."

Rains made the familiar humming sound that Helen thought meant the lieutenant had heard but wasn't going to reply. Helen couldn't think of a time she'd been more uncomfortable. She knew she was sweating, although the office wasn't particularly warm. Just when she thought she might have to start pacing if the pause went on any longer, Rains asked, "Did Sergeant Harris have many other friends?"

"He was the only one I knew, ma'am," Helen answered quickly, relieved at something she could answer honestly.

Rains stood abruptly and pointed to the chair that Helen had been standing beside. "Would you like to sit, Private? I know you've been waiting for a while."

Sitting heavily, Helen said, "Thank you, ma'am." Had the lieutenant been able to see that she'd been shaking? But then Rains came around the desk and stood in front of her, her tall frame and dark eyes as intimidating as they'd been during basic training.

"You may have already heard, Private Tucker, that I'm here because there have been irregularities in this department." Helen was able to keep her face expressionless until Rains added, "That and the fact that I'm apparently a terrible quartermaster." Rains's little joke made her want to giggle, but she was almost afraid she wouldn't be able to stop. She settled for a simple nod. "So I don't like asking you this way, but I need to know. Are there other drivers who might be aware of some other of Sergeant Harris's...friends?" When Helen hesitated, Rains leaned forward, and something in her eyes reminded Helen of the time that their drill instructor had caught Irene Dodd stealing from a couple of her squad mates during basic training. "I will find out, I assure you. But I'd like to have you on my side, Tucker."

"Ma'am, I—" Helen could see the two answers she could give and the roads they'd lead her down as clearly as if she were looking at a map. Lieutenant Rains was probably right about finding out about the motor pool end of things. The question was, how much could she learn about the transport crew? Especially if none of them talked. And she only needed two or three more scores before she'd have enough to set her and Tee up in a nice little place. *Finish answering*, her brain screamed. "I'd like to help you look into that, ma'am. Even though I'm new, I believe I've made a good impression in transport. Could you give me a day or two to ask around, see what I can find out?"

Rains studied her for another long minute. "As long as you understand that what I said about today being the only day that you can tell me something with no repercussions will still apply to you, Private. If there's anything you want to tell me about yourself, do so now."

"I understand, Sarge—uh, Lieutenant." *Stupid*, she told herself when Rains dismissed her. *That was your best chance to get out of this mess, and you blew it.* Helen tried to swallow her fear, wondering if she was allowed to pray to not get caught.

Lieutenant Rains quickly had her new staff completely up to speed. When she'd expressed surprise at the initial number of applicants she'd received, Bett had smiled and kissed her cheek. "You wouldn't be aware of this, Beloved, but you are not only well respected, you are popular. People like to work for someone who is fair and who wants to help them succeed."

Rains chose her mechanics, many of whom grew up fixing cars with brothers or uncles, from enlisted personnel she had known or who came with recommendations from those she knew. She declined to bring in a sergeant, telling her crew that she intended to promote from within, which was true. Until her investigation was over, though, she wanted motor pool paperwork to pass through as few hands as possible. That made her secretary a critical component, and she interviewed several candidates. Her choice was PFC Sharon West, a woman in her midthirties who looked to be slightly outside the physical fitness standards that WACs were required to maintain but whose background in finance and eagerness to work with people as well as numbers looked to be a perfect fit. Walking her to the door as their interview ended, Lieutenant Rains paused. "You may be aware that my assuming command of this unit is not popular on all fronts. I feel obliged to tell you that your service here may also be met with some antagonism, especially at first. But everyone on this base will know that you will have my full support. And be assured that what we will be doing is for the good of the WAC in general and Fort Des Moines in particular."

Sharon nodded seriously, adding, "My husband is stationed in Africa, doing some cleanup work in Tunis. I'll be proud to tell him that I'm doing some cleanup work here."

As each new member transferred in, they came with the understanding that their officer would expect nothing less than their best but would also provide enough flexibility to make allowances for individual needs wherever possible. After making sure it wasn't too much hardship on Sharon, Rains let them schedule their own lunchtime, only requiring that a team be present to work at all times. Consequently, there was barely a hiccup in the motor pool service, as the new mechanics worked willingly until their jobs were completed. Their lieutenant even allowed them to play the radio in the work bays, and that Thursday, after everyone had pitched in on a complex repair with a quick deadline, she let them knock off an hour early and dance. Lieutenant Rains didn't join in, of course, but she did watch a bit as she wondered what it would be like to move that way with Bett as her partner. Then, at the end of a good week, they got the terrible news that Jean Franklin's husband was reported killed in action in Italy. Rains brought Franklin into her small office to break the news and sat with her for two hours, holding her hand and just listening while Jean cried and talked about their life together.

The new motor pool staff became a tight group, and they were fiercely loyal to Rains. At the beginning of the third week of Rains's command, a fight almost broke out in the mess hall between two privates from the motor pool group and two of the latest recruits from Sergeant Moore's squad. Apparently a phrase to the effect of *redskin-loving grease monkeys* was said loudly enough for most of the hall to hear. Since no fists were actually thrown—although the grease monkeys applied a liberal dose of Army mashed potatoes to the heads of Moore's recruits—the discipline was left to the commanders of each group. Rains ran ten laps with her would-be fighters, telling them how she was always ready to fight during her younger years but how the Army had helped her learn self-control. She finished with the story of how Lieutenant Yarborough had tried to humiliate her during her rotation in the motor pool, making the point that without self-discipline she would have served time in the stockade instead of eventually becoming the lieutenant in charge of that very department. When they were finished, Rains told them, "The other things I would normally talk about would be honor and pride. But I believe you both already have a clear understanding of those." Then she saluted and dismissed them, intending to run her own extra two laps, just for spite. She finished the first, but was joined by the entire motor pool—even Sharon—for the last one. In spite of the pressure of her investigation, Rains would have been completely happy, except for being worried about Bett.

❖

Bett's security clearance came through with no problem, along with her promotion to staff sergeant, and by the end of the first week she became part of a team communicating with coders in the field. By the end of the next week, she was working one-on-one with Luna. She was very proud to be involved directly with the war effort at last, and Rain shared in her pride. Even the majors who had been working with cryptography since the beginning of the war had to admit that Bett was one of the best they had ever seen at her job. Her linguistic training made it easy for Bett to see the codes as language, and her love of puzzles and games made the job almost fun. Everything was going well, except for the headaches.

They had started during the end of her first week of coding work, usually coming on after lunch. In her desk drawer she now had a collection of every brand of aspirin available at the PX, but none of them had done any good. She had gotten to the point where it was necessary to stop at about four thirty so she could go home and close her eyes until Rain came home, usually sometime around six. Then she would wake up groggy, half ask Rain about her day, pick at her dinner, and try to finish the rest of her work at home. By the time she gave up and went to bed, the headache would be back. She knew she wasn't very good company during this time, but she seemed to be stuck in some kind of cycle. Soon nothing felt good, not even Rain's gentle touch on her temple at night. Bett found herself inexplicably reluctant to say anything about the headaches, so she would tell Rain that she was just tired.

She would make everything better on the weekend, Bett had told herself. The first Saturday, Bett slept late, waking alone in bed with a note from Rain in her hand, saying that she had gone to the market. Rain was back home by the time Bett got out of the shower, though, and they ate a late lunch together and caught up on stories of the week. Throughout their conversation, Bett felt a tension from Rain that she couldn't identify. Rain had kissed her sweetly when she came in, but Bett sensed she was holding something back.

"Beloved, is everything all right?" Bett asked coming over to sit on Rain's lap and stroke her hair.

Rain's smile was a little slow in coming. "Do you know that's the first time you've called me that this week?"

"Oh, Rain, I'm so sorry. I know I've been terrible but it's just because I'm getting used to this new job." Bett realized that she did feel better with the extra sleep and lunch. "Will you let me make it up to you?"

As she buried herself in Rain's body, she realized they hadn't had sex for days. But realizing it wasn't enough to stop it from happening again.

At first, Helen couldn't wait to get back to the barracks and tell Tee about their former sergeant now being in charge of the motor pool. For such a good girl, Tee did like to hear about the goings-on in others' lives. She would never start any gossip, but she didn't seem to mind hearing it. But then Helen realized that telling Tee about Lieutenant Rains taking over would require an explanation of why, which would require repeating Rains's comment about irregularities, which would reveal something that she wasn't quite ready to talk about.

As it turned out, Tee had already heard about the changes and had her own information to add. "Sergeant Harris is under house arrest and Lieutenant Yarborough may be resigning her commission."

Helen blinked.

"Helen? Did you hear me?"

"Yeah, yeah. I'm just…surprised."

"You didn't know?" Tee watched Helen shake her head slowly, that funny, faraway look back in her eyes. "Captain Madison went to a meeting in finance and didn't come back all day."

❖

That next weekend Bett was asked to come in on Saturday for some additional training, so she had almost no time with Rain. By the following week, her headaches had begun to affect her appetite even more, making her often feel dizzy and occasionally nauseated. She tried to conceal her reduced appetite by clearing the dishes before Rain noticed how much was left on her plate. Their evening meals had become quiet affairs. Bett didn't have the energy for much conversation. She was trying to save her strength to finish her work and Rain seemed almost as reserved as when they first met. Though she occasionally caught Rain studying her intently, Bett couldn't stand thinking that something else in her life was not going well. Her temper would fray with guilt or remorse and she would snap, "What is it?" The first time, Rain gently asked if she had done something wrong. "Of course not," Bett had answered tersely before giving Rain a quick kiss and leaving the table. The next time Bett snapped at her, Rain just looked away, not answering. Bett's only relief came when she slept. The days became a blur of less pain or more pain.

Rain pondered continually on Bett's increasingly cool distance. Did this new behavior show the person she really was? Had her enthusiasm for the physical side of their relationship already run its course? Rain had no one to talk to and no frame of reference for a relationship like this, so Bett's conduct was very confusing. Since the second week of her new job, Bett was usually sleeping on the couch each evening when Rain arrived at the house. When she awoke, Bett seemed glad to see her. She would hold Rain tightly and say all the right things, but when Rain tried to move beyond that initial contact, she felt that something was missing in Bett's response. She never said no, exactly, but she had just stopped saying yes. At night, Bett had begun falling asleep turned away from Rain with a little space between them, but at some point Rain would wake to find Bett's body wrapped around her as she had always done during their first days together. Then Rain would be flooded with yearning for sex; she wanted that close, passionate communion with Bett's body and her spirit that she had come to delight in. But recently Bett was sleeping so hard that there seemed to be no chance that she would be roused by the idea of some physical time together. Rain asked on different occasions if anything was wrong, but Bett had quickly assured her that it was nothing, that it would pass, that she was just tired. By the third week, Bett had become angry at the question, so Rain stopped asking.

Had the woman who had so joyously acquainted Rain with the pleasures of the flesh simply lost interest, now that she had Rain at her beck and call? Was the closeness that had been growing between them merely a passing thing? Considering this option made Rain angry, and sad. She couldn't stand feeling so vulnerable and conflicted, but the thought of taking herself away from Bett hurt even more. In her heart, she could not quite believe that her lovely Bett could be so callous or that what was between them could be so shallow and short-lived. So she tried thinking in another way. Was the Bett who had so willingly shared her heart and her body, the one who had given Rain every reason to believe what she had said about love, about forever—was she the real thing? And if so, then what had brought on this imposter, this false Bett who seemed drained and hurting, but would not be comforted? Why had she altered into one who acted as if they were only friends instead of lovers? And what would change her back? Rain fought to keep herself in check as she waited for Bett to confide in her or to give her some sign of what she needed, but it wasn't happening. She felt only a kind of pressure inside Bett that was like a taut wire, ready to slice into anyone who got too close.

❖

"Private Owens, report to Captain Madison's office. Private Owens, report to Captain Madison."

Tee startled as her name was announced on the PX loudspeaker. Even though she couldn't think of anything she'd done wrong, her nerves jangled as she approached the closed door. She knocked softly and waited. Nothing happened. After a minute of uneasy silence, she knocked again, a little louder, leaning closer to the door.

A muffled reply that sounded like "Come in" gave her the nerve to open the door. Captain Madison looked up from some paperwork at her desk.

"Owens. Good. Come in and close the door, please."

Tee did as she was told and stood at ease. Madison's voice hadn't sounded angry, so Tee tried to relax. After a few more seconds, the captain put her pen down and gestured at the forms. "What I'm working on are some requisitions for next month's supplies. Mostly food, but also uniforms and items for our PX here." When Tee didn't reply, the captain looked up at her for the first time. "I thought you wanted to know more about this."

"Oh—y-yes, ma'am." That sounded more like the captain's typical tone—impatient, slightly irritated, and always with that snobby attitude that said *I already know more than you'll ever learn, so don't even try.* Tee nodded eagerly, in case her answer wasn't enough. "I do."

"Well, come around here and look at this, then. I can't show you from there and I don't have all day to draw you a picture." Madison motioned her around the desk, so Tee went to stand beside her, tamping down her discomfort. This was one of her officers, and she was offering to teach her about how their PX worked with the quartermasters.

Half an hour later, she had forgotten her fears. Captain Madison was surprisingly even-tempered as Tee struggled to follow her explanations and even let her take part in some of the ordering as a means of teaching her the procedure. Tee had remembered from her classes that the same requisition that was a record of the order went to the motor pool to verify the amount that was picked up. That exact invoice then went to finance, so the supplier could be paid. Various officers, or their designees, signed off on the statement each time it was transferred to another department, so she was surprised by the large amount of paperwork that the captain was filling out. She gave up trying to keep count and simply followed the captain's increasingly hurried instruction. Once they were done, Madison's patience was apparently at an end. Abruptly, she said, "That will be all for today, Owens. Dismissed."

Tee saluted. "Thank you again for this opportunity, ma'am."

Madison returned the salute without further comment and Tee closed the door behind her.

❖

It became their routine that every third or fourth day, Tee would check in with Captain Madison. If there was time, she would spend a few minutes in her office while the captain went through different parts of the requisition process. Sometimes the captain would be in conference with someone else, in which case Tee just withdrew as quickly and quietly as she could. Once, a corporal burst in with barely a knock. Tee could tell that Captain Madison was none too pleased, but she just pointed to a big envelope on the corner of her desk and said, "I'll speak with you later, Knox."

During the third week, Tee got up the courage to ask, "Excuse me, ma'am, but would you let me know when you think I'm ready to try filling out the whole form instead of just signing it?" Helen had helped her formulate just the right way to say it, and she'd practiced her question several times over the weekend.

She was surprised to see Captain Madison smile at her. "We may need to see about getting you a PFC designation, Owens," she said. "You're doing some very good work here."

Tee was so pleased that she forgot her question. Wouldn't Helen be jealous if she made PFC first? The thought made her smile for a second, but then her mind went to the fact that Helen had seemed even more distracted lately. Tee had finally completed the course of study that Mrs. Washington had set out for her, and she and the pastor's wife had talked about the results on three different occasions. Now she kept waiting for Helen to ask how she was feeling about their relationship or to even resume the flirtatious, often provocative comments or gestures that frequently emerged when the two of them were together, but neither happened. Helen seemed to have lost her sparkle, and the dashing personality that had first drawn Tee to her had turned quiet and almost nervous at times. Even though Helen had assured her that there was nothing wrong, Tee knew there was. For one thing, Helen never seemed to want to talk about her job, only acting with false enthusiasm whenever Tee asked and assuring her that she was just working hard and once she adjusted to the new schedule, things would be better. "You know how Rains is," she'd said. "Everyone has to mind their p's and q's."

Twice Helen had gone out after dinner with only a mumbled explanation of "meeting up with some of the transport gang," but when she'd come back, there was no alcohol on her breath. What had she been doing?

❖

Helen thought back to the first meeting, when Castro and Barnes—along with two other corporals that she didn't know—had pulled her roughly into the procurement office in the deserted administration building.

"You talked, didn't you?" Barnes demanded. She turned to Castro. "Look at her. You can tell she's a snitch."

"I didn't." Helen was upset enough to make her denial completely believable as she pulled away from Barnes's grasp. "I kept my mouth shut and now my ass is on the line just like yours."

One of the corporals, whose nameplate read Knox, came up in her face. "You're a fucking liar, Tucker. You were in Rains's office for too long. It's not like you were exchanging recipes."

Helen resisted her inclination to give Knox a shove and settled for glaring at her. "Rains was my drill instructor. So we chatted a little, yeah. But think about it, Knox. If I'd talked, you'd all be in the stockade right about now instead of here in my face."

Knox glanced over at the other corporal, whose name was a series of letters that made no sense. *Some Polack*, Helen thought. The corporal tipped her head and Knox stepped back.

"So what's the plan?" Helen asked. "We gonna figure out a way around this or what?" The others looked at each other as she added, "Because I don't know about y'all, but I'm not ready to give up that little extra scratch in my pocket."

Barnes and Castro nodded in agreement. The two other corporals looked at each other.

"What do you think, Vish?" Knox asked. How she got that name out of those letters, Helen had no idea.

"We'll have to see what the boss says," Vish answered.

Gotcha, Helen thought. They couldn't be talking about Yarborough or Harris, since they were both already out of the picture. As the group parted ways, she considered her options. Maybe there was a way to use Lieutenant Rains's stay-out-of-jail offer and still pick up one or two more scores. Officially it was still today, only about 2200 hours, so she just had to talk to the lieutenant with her new information. She ran toward the officers' quarters, trying to remember what she'd heard about which of the buildings Rains lived in. She pounded up the stairs and onto the porch, only to hear an unpleasantly familiar voice ask, "What in hell's name do you want here, you stupid hillbilly?"

In the darkness, she hadn't seen Sergeant Moore sitting in one of the porch chairs, smoking. Her words slurred just enough that Helen thought she might have been drinking, too.

Helen ignored all the resentment that seeing Moore made her feel and straightened to attention.

"Excuse me, ma'am, but I'm looking for Lieutenant Rains."

"Ah, yes," Moore remarked. "Suddenly it's Lieutenant Rains. That was a neat trick, wasn't it? A field promotion, they're saying." She snorted. "What horseshit."

"Uh, I'm sorry, ma'am, but it's kind of important that I find her."

Moore took a drag of her cigarette and blew the smoke in Helen's direction. "Is it now? Well, you are just screwed then, Tucker, because she don't live here no more."

"What?" Helen tried not to think about her plan falling apart before her eyes.

Moore threw the cigarette on the ground and stood heavily, grinding it under her toe as she steadied herself with her hand on the porch railing. "Oh no. Our new lieutenant is now living off base. Surprised all of us. Been a couple of weeks now, I guess. We came in one afternoon and she was just gone. Almost thought she went AWOL, but guess I'm not that lucky. Never says a thing about it, but when did Rains ever tell anybody anything anyway?" She squinted at Helen. "My question is, was the person she had to fuck to get that promotion the same person she's fucking every night at whatever address she's at? Huh? What do you think, Tucker?"

Helen wasn't really listening to any of Moore's questions, partly because she knew they weren't to be answered and partly because she was trying to think of what to do next. When Moore swayed slightly, she replied, "I think it's time for Private Tucker to call it a night." And then, because Sergeant Moore seemed almost as defeated as she felt, she added, "And maybe it's that time for you, too, ma'am."

"Shut up, Tucker. Just get the fuck out of here."

"Yes, ma'am."

❖

Two weeks later, their meeting was a lot shorter. When they gathered again in the darkened procurement office, Knox simply said, "We start up again tomorrow." Everything had been on hold but apparently someone felt confident enough, even with the changes that Lieutenant Rains was putting in place, to resume their black market connection.

"Why now?" Helen challenged. "How do we know we'll be safe?"

Vish sneered. "You don't, Tucker. Any more than you did before. Just watch your ass and keep your mouth shut."

"But what's changed?" she pushed.

"The boss has got a fall guy. Some stupid private who asks how high whenever she says jump. Hers will be the only name on everything from now on, so any investigation should stop there."

So whoever was running this thing was making sure they wouldn't go down, no matter what. She nodded. "This lady sounds mighty smart. I'd sure like to meet her sometime."

The two corporals laughed. "As if," Knox said. "Just drive, Tucker, and leave the thinking to us."

CHAPTER ELEVEN

Rain sighed as she stood staring into the fire. It had been three weeks since she'd gotten the motor pool assignment and she wished she could talk to Bett about the situation, certain there was something just beyond her thinking that Bett would see. But as usual, Bett was in the dining room where she'd been since dinner, where she'd been every night for weeks, working on her coding. Physically, Rain felt even more agitated than she had during basic training. Her body, now well acquainted with the pleasures of Bett's touch, yearned for it almost to the point of pain, but there was no indication from Bett that she had any such longing. Such contact between them had been out of the question for this week as well. Rain took in a breath, settling herself. Something else, then. She put on a jacket and stopped in the doorway of the dining room.

"I'm going for a run. I won't be long."

"What?" Bett asked distractedly as she looked around. "It's twenty degrees and dark outside. I don't think that's a very good idea."

Rain sighed again, turning away without saying anything. In a minute, Bett heard the sound of the axe. Every chop seemed to penetrate her skull. After a minute, she went outside and asked Rain to stop. "Can't you do that another time, Rain? I just can't concentrate with all that noise."

Rain turned to Bett and stood for a moment, her breath coming in foggy puffs as she held the axe. The dim outside light made it hard for Bett to see her expression. "Then tell me what to do with myself, Bett," she finally said in a low voice, clearly struggling to find words. "You are here but so distant that I miss you almost as if you were gone. You tell me you are tired, but rest doesn't seem to help. I know something is wrong but you won't let me close enough to figure out what it is. My spirit can wait for you forever, Bett, but you've done something to my body and I…I feel this need that is only for you." She swung the axe into the chopping block. "If you don't want me to run and you don't want me to chop, what should I do with myself?"

Bett rubbed her hand over her pounding forehead and said the first thing that came into her mind. "I suppose you'll have to do what the rest of the boys do when they're in your state—take a cold shower or just jerk yourself off."

Rain reacted as if she had been slapped. She even put her hand up to her face. *The cheek I first kissed*, Bett realized, too late. Then she walked past Bett without even a glance and strode swiftly into the house.

"Rain, wait," Bett urged, stretching her hand in the direction Rain had turned. She heard the front door close before she had even moved. "Rain, I'm sorry. Please…" By the time she opened the door, the street was empty. Rain was gone.

Bett went back into the dining room and stared at all the coding papers on the table. Angrily, she shoved them onto the floor and put her head in her arms. *What a bloody awful thing to say!* She berated herself, *What the hell is wrong with me?* That was the problem, of course. She didn't know what was wrong, why these miserable headaches wouldn't go away. She was scared for herself and she was scared to talk to Rain about it. Why? Because telling Rain anything made it real, and she just wanted to pretend. To pretend it was nothing, that she was just tired, that it would all get better when she adjusted to the job, if she could just hold out a little longer. Her anger was making the pain worse, so she pulled herself together and went out into the kitchen. She looked across the room at the cheerful fire and felt tears start up. *Rain is so much like the fires she builds, beautiful and warm, and I've been nothing but a cold bitch.* She turned away and bent to the liquor cabinet. If she was going to have another goddamn headache, at least tonight she'd know why.

Two hours later, Bett was well on the way to being totally drunk, sitting in front of a dying fire. Amazingly, her head felt better, even though she had been all through her own terrible behavior at least three times and had one brief crying jag. Not saying anything about her headaches was the first offense, of course, and the one that led to all the others. Having to work at home, just wanting to sleep the rest of the time, and of course, not having sex. Now that she was relaxed by the alcohol and her head felt better, she wanted Rain so badly that her body was almost pulsing. *Oh God, Rain, please come home,* was running through her thoughts like a mantra. She wobbled to the front door again and looked out. Nothing. *Where could she be?* Bett considered getting in the car and going to look for her and then admitted to herself that she had no business driving. And where would she look? Plus, Rain might come home while she was gone. *She has to come back,* Bett tried to convince herself. *All of her things, her clothes, are here.* But in reality, Bett knew Rain didn't care about any of her things or her clothes. There was only one thing that would bring her back. Bett changed her mental message. *I love you. Please forgive me.* She fell asleep on the floor in front of the embers.

It was still dark when Bett woke up. She had a pillow under her head and a blanket covering her. She opened her eyes just enough to see Rain's folded legs next to where she was lying on the floor.

Rain's voice was like iron. "Sit up and look at me, Bett."

Considering the amount of vodka she had consumed, Bett managed to comply with a minimum of groaning. Rain had built the fire back up and the room blazed with light and heat. Bett faced Rain but her eyes weren't focusing very well. "I'm really glad to see you," Bett slurred just a little bit. "I'm so sor—"

"What is wrong with your eyes?" Rain interrupted, peering at her closely.

"I felt just terrible about what I said to you, so I had a bit to drink," Bett said, reaching for her. Rain caught her hands and held them back.

"I am aware of that, but I'm asking you, what is wrong with your eyes?" Rain repeated, staring hard, her voice still intent.

"Maybe because I was crying?" Bett asked, her hands limp, knowing it was useless to struggle against Rain's grasp.

"No, it's not that either." Rain released Bett's hands and stood up. She looked into the fire. "Call your office in the morning if you need to. But I'm taking you to the eye doctor on the base first thing tomorrow."

Bett felt a little woozy tracking Rain's movements, so she rubbed her eyes, hoping to focus them better. She kept them closed while she arched her back, stretching her neck. When she looked up, Rain was gone again. "Rain?" Bett got up and looked in every room. She lay back in front of the fire with the strangest feeling that she had been dreaming.

When she heard the kettle whistle and then stop quickly, she sat up. "Rain?"

"Your appointment is in one hour. Do you want tea first or do you want to...shower?"

Bett cringed, thinking of her words from last night. She looked over. Rain was in her dress uniform. Bett got up from the floor, still wearing her clothes from yesterday. Her head felt surprisingly steady. "I think I should clean up first," she said quietly.

Rain nodded, sipping on some tea.

Bett went into her bathroom without another word. The shower felt good, but she couldn't stop thinking about Rain and how she was going to make things right. She started dozens of speeches in her head and none of them were coming out well. She gave up and got ready, putting on her dress uniform as well.

"Do you feel like eating?" Rain was at the stove with a plate of toast and eggs.

"Yes, please."

Rain gave her the plate and started out of the kitchen. "Aren't you going to eat?" Bett asked. Rain shook her head and went into the hall bath. Bett wanted to go after her; she wanted to cry; she wanted to scream how sorry she was. Instead, she ate her breakfast and cleaned up her dishes.

Rain came back into the room. "We should go." Her tone was so formal and distant that it made Bett feel almost desperate.

"Rain, can I please—" Bett started, but Rain shook her head and stepped toward the door. Bett was so worried she was going to disappear again that she stopped talking and followed quickly, not wanting to lose sight of her.

After they were outside on the sidewalk, Rain turned to her. "We are going to solve one problem at a time. The first thing to take care of are these headaches of yours, which I think is a matter of your vision." Bett's mouth almost dropped open. Rain went to the car and got in the driver's seat. Bett was so confused that she stopped walking. Rain started the engine. Bett felt like she might still be drunk. *Rain doesn't drive my car. How did she get my keys?* Bett went to the passenger's side and got in, shaking her head. Risking a glance at Rain, she thought she saw the corners of her mouth turn up just a bit, the way they used to before Rain smiled at her regularly. Something else, she realized, that Rain hadn't done in days. The thought made her want to cry again.

"You've ridden with me before, do you remember? That night we saw the moon."

This was the first familiar-sounding thing that Rain had said since yesterday evening. "Yes, Rain, of course I remember." Bett was so relieved that she was desperate to continue the conversation. "When did you first learn to drive?" she asked, grasping at anything normal.

They pulled away from the curb and started toward the base. They were almost through downtown before Rain answered. "I would drive my father's truck when he was drinking and we needed something from town. Thomas taught me before he left."

Bett put her head in her hands. *I bloody well walked into that one, didn't I?*

Rain went on after a quick glance at her passenger. "I am driving today because I don't want you to put any strain on your eyes before your examination, not because you were drinking last night. How does your head feel right now?"

And she's letting me off the hook, even though I don't deserve it. Bett knew better than to ask anything more. "Almost normal, considering."

Rain nodded. They reached the base and the guard waved them past. Rain let her off at the eye doctor's office. "I'm going to run this car over to the motor pool while you are in there," she said. "But I'll be back before you are finished."

Bett nodded and started to open the door. Rain's hand brushed her arm for just a second, but it was so wonderful to feel her touch that Bett almost gasped. "Tell the doctor everything that you've been feeling, Bett. It won't do any good if you withhold what he needs to know in order to diagnose what is wrong."

Bett took a breath and looked Rain in the eyes. "Does that include telling him that I've been feeling like a complete and total shite because of something incredibly stupid and thoughtless that I said to the one person I love more than anything?"

Rain didn't meet her gaze for long, but Bett thought something in her look might have softened. She looked down at her lap and said, "You almost sound like someone I know."

Bett drew in a breath that was almost a sob, and Rain looked back over at her quickly. "Don't, Bett. You need to concentrate on getting better first."

First. That sounds promising. Bett looked away and nodded as Rain said again, "I'll be back soon."

❖

When Bett came out of the examining room wearing a pair of horn-rim glasses, Rain was waiting, and Bett caught the beginning of a smile before Rain covered her mouth and coughed. Bett thought that reaction alone made the entire examination almost worthwhile.

"So we'll see you in another two weeks, just for a checkup, Sergeant Smythe," the receptionist said automatically. Then, as Rain stood up, she added, "Lieutenant Rains, my husband said to tell you thanks again."

Rain touched her hat in a little salute. "My pleasure, Private Mayfield. Thank you for returning the favor."

Private Mayfield smiled so pleasantly at Rain that Bett felt a twinge of jealousy. "Will I need someone to drive me then as well?" Bett asked, just to interrupt the moment.

"No, you shouldn't, unless you're having some additional problems," Mayfield said, perhaps a bit sadly, not taking her eyes off Rain.

Rain held the door and Bett went over to the passenger's seat again. "I don't suppose I should ask what you did for Private Mayfield," Bett said, once they were under way.

"Just a tune-up, oil change, brake shoes and drums. Nothing special," Rain answered neutrally. "It was just a rush job because her husband was coming back for a two-week leave and they wanted to go visit his family."

"I'm afraid to ask how many tune-ups you've done for women before their husbands come back." Bett tried to sound like she was teasing, but her heart squeezed in her chest when Rain's serious expression persisted.

"I don't want to spar with you, Bett. Private Mayfield was the reason you got the appointment this morning. Now tell me what the doctor said."

Bett felt chastised and knew she deserved it. "Apparently I have an astigmatism, which means that my eyeballs are slightly out of shape. It primarily affects my reading vision but can be corrected with these lovely glasses." Bett put them back on, but Rain was concentrating on driving so she took them back off. "I'm to try this pair, and if the prescription isn't exactly right, we can fine-tune it in two weeks."

They pulled up in front of the house. "And your headaches?" Rain asked, not turning off the engine.

Bett bit her lip. "This should take care of it. The doctor said he wondered how I was able to work at all. But I never wore glasses poring over those texts at Oxford, though I admit it's been a while since I've done close reading like this." When Bett looked up again, she could see the relief on Rain's face. She noticed the running engine. "Aren't we going in?"

"You are," Rain answered. "I'm taking your car back to the motor pool. As I suspected, you also need an oil change and tune-up, though I think your brakes are fine."

"Are we talking about me or my car?" Bett tried to smile, but Rain didn't answer. "I'm taking the rest of the day off," Bett said, finally. "And I guess I thought you might do that, too. I'd like to…" She trailed off, trying to think how to order her list.

"To what, Bett? To continue lying to me about how you feel? To spend hours on your work after spending five minutes pretending to listen to me? To go through the motions of being with me until bedtime and then not even—" Rain looked away. Her voice lowered. "I don't know how to stop wanting to be with you."

"Oh God. Don't stop, Rain. Please don't. Please. I want us to be together, like when you first came to be with me. I'm so sorry. Sorry for all of it. I know I should have told you but I was afraid, because I didn't understand why I felt so bad. And then I kept feeling so bad that I couldn't figure a way out of it. You have every right to be angry, and all I can do is hope you'll let me try and make it up to you." She dared to put her hand on Rain's arm as it rested on the steering wheel. "I will do whatever it takes for as long as it takes."

Rain stared at Bett's hand on her arm. Quietly she said, "You hurt me, Bett."

Bett dropped her head as she felt the sting of tears again. "I know I did, Rain, I know it. Would you believe me if I said I felt worse about it than you possibly could?"

"I had my life set where that wouldn't happen," Rain continued as if Bett hadn't spoken, looking out the windshield. "I knew how to keep myself away from these emotions. Then you came along and somehow you…I gave you power over me, power to make me feel so good, and so bad."

"You have that power over me, too, Rain. Can we not get back into balance?" Bett asked.

Rain took in a breath and turned to Bett. "Tell me how. Everything in me feels shifted away from love and toward anger and hurt."

Bett looked up. Rain's voice, always so heartfelt, had an added component of genuine inquiry. *This isn't a rhetorical question*, Bett realized. *She's really asking me what to do.* "You have to forgive me, Rain. You have to believe I would never deliberately cause you pain. Know that I love you, and forgive me for being so brainless and selfish and scared." Bett knew if she could get Rain back in her arms, she could explain it all, but she could see Rain wasn't ready to let her come close yet. So she settled for a soft squeeze on Rain's arm. "You have to be strong enough to trust me once more, to let me in again. I swear I will do everything I know to take the hurt away and bring us back to how we were before. Come back to me, Rain, and let me come back to you."

During a moment of quiet, the engine shuddered. Bett thought she saw a shift in Rain's eyes. "Go inside," Rain said quietly, taking Bett's hand off her arm, looking at it in her own hand and giving it just the slightest squeeze. "The car and I will be back in a couple of hours."

Bett thought that was probably the best offer she was going to get. She cleaned the house for a while, taking a little time out to look over her coding papers with her new glasses on. The difference was astonishing. She felt the same kind of relief that she had seen on Rain's face after they left the doctor's office. Finally, she wandered into the guest room and saw Rain's knapsack there, open, with her treasured Thoreau book on top. She picked it up and sat down to read. Within a few minutes, she came upon the phrase, "To regret deeply is to live afresh." *Only if you can work some forgiveness in there, too, Mr. Thoreau.*

Then she heard the car door. Rain came in and put the keys in her hand. She didn't let go. "I want to tell you that I am still upset with you about what you did not tell me. But in thinking about it, I realize there is also something I have not been completely honest about with you," Rain began solemnly.

Please don't let it be about Private Mayfield. "All right," Bett said, keeping her voice calm. "Do you want to tell me now?"

"Yes," Rain said and led her by the hand over to the couch. *If I need to sit down, this may be worse than one Private Mayfield,* Bett thought, although she didn't truly believe that Rain would be unfaithful to her, even though their sex life had recently become infrequent. All right, nonexistent. At the moment, she was so happy Rain was touching her again that she could have almost convinced herself she didn't care if there had been someone else, as long as Rain would take her back.

Once they were seated, Rain looked away for a moment and then back at her. She took a breath. "I want to buy a motorcycle."

Anyone else but Rain, and Bett would have felt completely manipulated. But Rain was always so honest. Instead, she tried to keep from laughing out loud with relief. "I see." She worked to keep her voice level. "And how long have you felt this way?"

"Since I started working at the motor pool. Lutz and I are rebuilding his and he's teaching me about engines that way. When it's finished, he will want to sell it. I would really like to buy it, but I hadn't told you about it yet, partly because I think you might not like the idea and then we will be at odds."

"Tell me more about this motorcycle," Bett said, noticing for the first time that Rain had a half-healed scrape that was just visible under her hair. "What kind is it? Do you know how to ride it? What will you do about a gas ration card?"

Rain squirmed just a bit at all of the questions. Then words began pouring out of her. "Believe it or not, it's a brand called Indian and this model is called the Chief. She's a beautiful red color with fenders and even a sidecar, where you could sit. Lutz has been teaching me to ride on his other bike, which is a Harley-Davidson. I only fell off once. Well, twice, but that second time was on Red Cloud—which is what I call the motorcycle I want to buy—but it only happened because the throttle stuck and the brakes weren't working, but we've fixed all that already."

"You fell off? Twice?" Bett pushed the hair away from Rain's face to reveal the rest of the abrasion. "Is that where you got this?"

Rain eased away. "Yes, but Lutz says everyone falls off at least once, so now I'm done. Lutz also says I'm a natural to ride so well since I've never even ridden a bicycle." Rain's voice lowered in awe. "The engine is like eight hundred horses!"

"And why did you think I would not like the idea?" Bett asked.

Rain unbuttoned her jacket and then took off her shirt. Bett saw her wince as she pulled her arm out of the sleeve. From under the straps of her undershirt, Bett could see a deep bruise on Rain's shoulder, which had not yet started to fade, and she lifted the shirt to reveal another series of scrapes running down her torso toward her hip. "Good Lord, Rain, you could have been killed! When did this happen?"

"Three days ago," Rain said softly. "I thought you would not like the motorcycle because you would think I might get hurt. But the problem that caused this has been fixed." Her voice got a little sadder. "And then, you didn't even notice."

Bett observed that the damage on Rain's body was almost all on the side away from where she normally slept next to Bett, although on their more active nights they could end up in almost any position. "Well, I'm noticing now. And if I had noticed then, I would have been very upset with you."

"If you had noticed then, we would have talked about it then," Rain replied. "And now you tell me—why did you lie to me about your trouble with headaches?"

"I swear, Rain, I never meant to lie to you about it. At first I thought it was just a one-time thing. Do you remember the night you came home with your lieutenant's bars?"

"I'm not likely to ever forget it," Rain said, looking steadily at Bett.

"Nor am I." Bett smiled in remembrance. Then she became solemn again. "But that night I thought it was just nerves about the new job and all. And the pain had gone when I woke up. So when it happened again the next day, I thought I was just still adjusting to all the reading. After that, I got scared because it wasn't really going away anymore. And then, for the last two weeks, my head has hurt so much that I couldn't think straight. Each time, I just thought if I could make it to the weekend, I would be okay. Then last weekend when I didn't get a break it just got worse and worse. But mainly I didn't want to tell you because...because what if something was really wrong?"

Bett got up and walked over to the window, looking out into the small backyard. She spoke quietly. "You probably can't imagine what it was like growing up in my house, Rain. The demands, the expectations. In everything we attempted, we were supposed to not just do our best, but to win, to always be first, preferably while crushing someone else in the process. It wasn't enough for us simply to do something we enjoyed. We had to be more than good, we had to be perfect. And thereby prove everyone else was less." She breathed a small, bitter chuckle. "Now, I'm already so flawed in my father's view that...well, let's just say that needing to wear glasses may be a smaller fault than most of mine, but it's undoubtedly another illustration of what an inferior product I am. Not at all deserving of the name Carlton. Certainly not worthy of being...of being loved."

Rain was already up and standing behind her as Bett turned, putting her forehead against Rain's chest as she continued. "So how can I tell you, the one person who seems to think that I'm not such a colossal mess, that something's amiss? Wouldn't that just validate the lowly status that the rest of the family has already conferred on me? Maybe confirm it even, in your eyes?"

She could feel Rain shaking her head. "No, Beloved. That is not the way it is with us. You and I don't take the measure of each other's weaknesses. We measure by our strengths, because we are not afraid of finding power in each other. Believe me, if they know you at all, your family doesn't really think you are less—they know you are more. That is what they fear and why they try to diminish you to yourself, and to themselves." Bett was very still, trying to fit Rain's words into her feelings about her family. "Even not having met the rest of your people, I know this—yours is a true heart of vast courage. Those who live superficial lives are always trying to fill them with possessions, but no quantity of things from this world can match the depth of your spirit." After a minute, Rain said, "Do you hear the truth in what I am telling you?"

Bett nodded against her and her arms came up around Rain's waist. Rain's arms went around Bett's shoulders. "Then hear this, too. Even though you are strong, you are not alone. I am with you and beside you. Please don't ever hide what you are feeling from me, Bett."

Rain's body next to hers felt so good that Bett's other senses had almost stopped working. She managed to nod again. "Because part of me lives inside you now, as you are in me. Eventually I will know what you are feeling."

"How did you know, Rain, really?" Bett managed to ask. "I never said anything about headaches to you."

A small smile crossed Rain's face and her eyes twinkled. "It's not that hard to read you, Bett. And I'm sure you could read me if you tried." She took Bett's hands and put them on her heart. "Can't you tell what I am thinking?"

Bett squinted as if concentrating very hard. "You are thinking that my new glasses are very, very attractive."

Rain's mouth dropped open just a bit. "I was thinking that exact thing."

As much as she loved it when Rain played with her, particularly because she knew she'd never been like that with anyone else, Bett couldn't stand it another second. "Please take me to bed, Rain." Rain was so incredibly sexy in just her undershirt and khaki pants that Bett wanted nothing more than to get her out of them and into her arms.

"Are you sure that's what you want?" Rain asked quietly and Bett opened her mouth to object. This type of second-guessing was unlike Rain, and it worried her. She liked Rain's way of never questioning the truth of anything they said to each other. It meant everything between them was always real, was always true the first time, and Bett had become much less likely to throw out pointless or insincere remarks as a result. But when she looked into Rain's eyes, she could see some hurt still there, along with an uncertainty of what would be between them. *She's not being argumentative. She really doesn't know.*

"I've never been more certain of anything in my life." Bett kissed her gently. Slowly. Trying not to be too rough where there might be a bruise or scrape, but wanting to caress every inch. "I love you and I want you. Now and always." Rain's mouth began to respond with the same tenderness, her fingers running delicately along Bett's forehead and temples, as if checking for pain there, and then she gathered Bett lovingly in her arms. Bett had that familiar sensation of her body melting into Rain's; she had no idea how much time had passed before they were in the bedroom, and she was taking Rain's undershirt off, feeling Rain pulling off her underwear as she loosed the braid in Rain's hair. When they were naked in the bed, still deliberate, careful, Rain's mouth made its way around her body as if relearning a once-familiar path. When Bett's lips parted with soft sounds of pleasure, Rain brushed her fingers gently across Bett's most sensitive center.

"I'm certain, too." Rain's low voice was full of feeling, her long hair falling around them. "I'm certain I will always love you and always want to be with you this way."

Bett was tingling everywhere with the closeness of Rain's body and her gentle touch. She felt like she could linger there for hours, simply letting Rain love her. "You are so incredibly good to me," she breathed in Rain's ear. Everything about the way Rain moved, about the way she kissed, brought Bett to a slow boil almost before she knew what had happened. Her orgasm came in a profoundly building roll of hot delight that left her completely satisfied and smiling lazily. "So sweet," she whispered afterward, her head back as Rain kissed her neck and shoulders. "God, how you make me feel."

"Welcome back, my beloved."

"Oh, Rain. I love you so much. Does this mean you've forgiven me?"

Rain pulled Bett over on top of her. "Of course, Bett. Can't you tell? Don't you feel it?"

Bett reached down and explored between Rain's legs. "Why yes, now that you mention it, I can."

❖

"So tell me again about this motorcycle?" Bett asked when they were sitting back in front of the fire, having dinner.

"She's a great machine," Rain said. "You should see her, Bett."

"I have a feeling I will."

"Does that mean you approve?" Rain asked, wiggling a bit and clasping her hands excitedly. This was the young Rain that Bett also loved, so adorable and innocent.

Bett reached up to trace the contours of Rain's face. "It means you teach me something every day about love. It means you care for me in a way that defies my understanding. I know you could have already bought this thing without even asking me, but the fact that you want my opinion means you respect our relationship. You are devoted and forgiving in ways I could only have dreamed before I met you. You make me incredibly happy and I want to do the same for you. So no, I don't approve, but yes, I think you should bring your motorcycle home and show me my sidecar." Rain was smiling broadly. Bett added, "But you must promise me you will take good care of my most precious cargo," as she ran her hand over Rain's heart, planning all the ways she was going to make up for the time she had lost with Rain's body, all the ways she would show Rain how much she loved her.

"I promise," Rain said solemnly, putting her hand on top of Bett's. In the depths of her eyes, Bett could see a reflection of her own restored belief in their relationship.

When she arrived at work on Monday, Bett was a little self-conscious about putting her glasses on until she looked around the room and realized something she hadn't even noticed before: every single other person working in the coding department was already wearing a pair.

❖

On her run to the base that morning, Rain passed a group of youngsters who'd stopped their walk toward the local school building to play a game. They called it *monkey in the middle*. It consisted of one child in the middle of a group, trying to get a ball being thrown by the others. One girl was the monkey for so long that she started to cry in frustration. An older boy, possibly her brother, took over, saying, "Let me show you how it's done." He followed the throws carefully, and when the ball got close to where he was standing, he rushed the player who missed his catch and so became the new monkey. As Rain watched, it came to her that something very much like this was happening to her in the investigation. She was as confident as she could be that she had found only good people to work in the motor pool, and while she knew some of the transport drivers were involved in the thefts, it was also clear they were not running the operation. Gradually it dawned on her—she needed to get out of the middle by putting some pressure on one of the other departments. Purchasing was a very large operation with its arms spread wide. She needed to pick someone smaller and pressure them if she was ever going to get the ball.

Rains went first to Sharon, who confirmed that the motor pool log checked out exactly with the deliveries. Taking the ledger in hand, she went to the finance office, where a corporal scrambled to hide the magazine she'd been reading when she entered. Standing quickly behind her desk, she saluted and asked, "May I help you, Lieutenant?"

"I'd like to see your commanding officer, Corporal..." Rains studied the nameplate on her desk. Wyrzyk?

"It's easier to hear than it is to read, ma'am." The corporal nodded familiarly at Rains's confusion and pronounced her name before adding, "Lots of people call me Vish. Like *fish* but with a *V*."

"Thank you, Corporal." Rains waited.

"Oh, uh, my commanding officer is...well, we don't actually have one at this moment, ma'am. Major Jarek has been transferred, and we're awaiting his replacement. Is there something I can do for you?"

Rains hesitated, unwilling to tip her hand but hating the idea of waiting much longer to try out her idea. "Do you have any idea when your new commander might report?"

Vish smirked. "We've been told soon. But you know the Army, ma'am. *Soon* means different things, depending on which side of it you're on."

So the corporal is one of those, Rains thought. *Gripe about the Army while taking advantage of her cushy job.* Her mind made up, she shook her head. "I'll check back tomorrow."

A shrug. "Suit yourself." Rains had been turning to go, but she turned back and fixed the corporal with a hard stare. "Ma'am," Vish added quickly.

"It's Lieutenant Rains, in case you wanted to leave a note for your new commander."

"Yes, ma'am. I'd be pleased to do that." Vish was working to make amends. "What's the message?"

"Just ask him or her to contact me as soon as possible." Rains watched until the corporal finished writing.

"I'll see that the new commander gets this, first thing, ma'am." She saluted.

"Thank you, Corporal." Rains went out without waiting for a reply.

❖

Helen had turned it over and over in her mind but she still hadn't figured out how they were getting away with it. The invoices were the key, she knew. Knox and her friend Vish had procurement covered, and there had to be someone else in finance who was in on the scam. Otherwise, how could one amount be ordered and a different amount show up on the manifest she was given? And why wasn't someone in finance catching the difference between the two? Was it possible this swindle went all the way to the top? Did Colonel Issacson look the other way while her buddies padded their wallets? No, that wasn't likely since the colonel had promoted Rains and assigned her to the motor pool. If she'd been in on the deal, she'd have left things just the way they were. And judging by how jumpy everyone was the last time she met with the other drivers, it was clear Lieutenant Rains was closing in on them. What was even harder than figuring out what was going on was thinking how to get herself free and clear before that hammer came down.

Everyone else was at dinner, so Helen used the rare moment alone to count out the bills she had hidden in one of her socks. Sixty dollars. More than she'd ever had at one time in her whole life. Probably more than her daddy had ever had either. She was certain it would be enough for her to get a place with Tee, especially if she could talk Tee into sending a little less cash to her family each month.

Helen never sent anything home. If her brother Sinclair wanted to support their whoring mother, let him. Abruptly Helen shuddered, furious with herself for opening the door to the memories that came hard and fast on each other. Her father, dead at the hands of the man her mother had apparently been sleeping with for years. The town gossips, whispering how Jack Kinney, in charge of payroll at the Pearcy Coal Mine, had shot him four times with the gun he kept on the little table beside his bed, just in case. She, at age twenty-two, now taking a small cut of Mr. Hall's salary in return for actually driving him on his routes and doing most of the deliveries while he drank or napped, and so not finding out anything until many hours after it happened.

Stumbling almost blindly to the closed mortuary, she'd pounded pathetically on the locked door, her fury growing until she'd ultimately broken out their window, desperate to see the cuckolded victim, certain that it wasn't really her daddy. The local sheriff, who was deep in Pearcy's pockets anyway, had declined to even have a trial after hearing her own mother's eyewitness account that Kinney had acted in self-defense. Her brother Sinclair was fighting in the Pacific with the Army and already so susceptible to harm that Helen couldn't bring herself to be the one to write him the news. Thankfully, Aunt Darcy had taken on that task, after insisting Helen come stay with her and Mrs. Murrell while things got sorted out. For a week, Helen stayed with them while she continued helping Mr. Hall with his postal deliveries. At night she'd slip out a window and roam the town, finding ways to vandalize the Pearcy properties, imagining the repair costs coming directly out of Jack Kinney's personal pocket. When Mr. Hall died unexpectedly in his sleep the next week, Helen had carried on his work, and getting the next day's deliveries ready meant she had no time for her evening prowls. Just as she was beginning to believe the job might be hers for the duration, a man from the next county over showed up with a letter saying he was the new postman. He had a letter. She had nothing. So she began stealing. Always from Pearcy or someone she knew to be on their side. Just enough to let them know how it was to have something taken from you, to make them feel that bitterness of loss the way she did, and to send the message that she hadn't forgotten.

What she really wanted was to get something from Kinney himself. She wanted that gun. She wanted to get it and throw it in the river, after emptying all the bullets into his bed. Oddly, she didn't really fault him for being with her mama. Lena Tucker was pretty and she could be sweet, although she was never the same to her daddy after all those babies had died. Helen hadn't felt any affection from her mother for years, and when she'd learned the word estranged from something they'd read in school, she knew it described their relationship perfectly. Maybe because she simply wasn't the daughter her mother wanted. She didn't want to dress up and bring home a nice young man for supper. She was a rough-and-tumble gal, convinced she should be able to do anything her brother did, and trying most of it, much to her mother's dismay. Maybe Jack Kinney gave her mother something none of them could, and maybe she was happy with him. Probably after he'd seen them, her daddy would have been more than willing to give her up. He was easygoing that way. But because of that gun, her daddy was dead.

She was making her third pass around Kinney's house when she heard heavy footsteps behind her. It was too late to go for cover so she simply stopped, stretching like she was tired. Then she turned, just in time to see Sheriff Churney closing the distance between them. "I got word of a prowler in the area," he said, stopping too close to her for comfort.

"Really?" Helen asked. "Sounds to me like Mr. Kinney is a little skittish these days. Wonder why that is?" She knew she should say something less confrontational, but she couldn't help herself.

Ignoring her question, he asked, "You staying with your Aunt Darcy?" even though she was sure he already knew it. Everyone in town knew it, so she just nodded. "I'll walk you back there," he said. "Even a girl like you shouldn't be alone out here at this hour." She was about to make an objection when he added, "Someone might mistake you for a vandal or a thief. People have gone to jail for a lot less. And someone who thought they'd get a pass because somethin' bad happened to them would be wrong. Dead wrong."

She heard the threat and she understood the message. She was getting off this time. Next time...Aunt Darcy had covered for her, the way family was supposed to do, murmuring to the sheriff about how Helen had been unable to sleep and had begged to be allowed to take just a little walk to clear her head. She'd further rewarded the sheriff's leniency with a bag containing several pieces of her wonderful fudge and they'd said good night. Once he'd gone, she'd turned to Helen and said, "You look tired, Helen. Please get some rest."

The next night, just as she was raising the window, ready to slip out, Aunt Darcy came into her room. Helen tried to act like she was just getting some air, and they both ignored the fact that she was fully dressed at eleven thirty at night. They sat side by side on the small bed in the guest room and Aunt Darcy showed her the flyer. Helen had already seen the big poster of it in the post office. She'd always admired the picture of the women in their uniforms, but having someone always telling you what to do didn't sound like a good deal to her.

"In the Army they have those big trucks that haul people and supplies. Maybe you could get a job as a driver with them," Aunt Darcy suggested.

Helen shrugged.

"Your daddy and I talked about this once," Aunt Darcy said after a moment, and Helen felt everything inside her start to get tight. "He *surely didn't want you working in the mine, but you going on in school didn't seem likely either. He wasn't too keen on the service, mainly, I think, because he overheard some of the other men talking unfavorably about women soldiers. We disagreed on that point. I'd go myself if I was thirty years younger."*

Briefly wondering how Mrs. Murrell would feel about that statement, Helen made sure her voice was steady. "Were y'all trying to get rid of me?"

Aunt Darcy shook her head a little sadly as she brushed the hair off Helen's forehead, the way she'd done when Helen was little. "This town ain't the place for you, Helen. And the longer you stay, the more likely there'll be some trouble. Maybe big trouble. You need to get out in the world and stretch your wings. If you decide you wanna come back someday, well, that'll be fine. But you need to know what else is out there."

Helen looked away. The tightness inside was turning to trembling.

"I'm only saying this because I love you." Aunt Darcy's voice was quiet, low. Helen was horrified to realize that her eyes were filling with tears. She hadn't cried at her daddy's funeral, or at Mr. Hall's. She'd been proud she could stand there at those graves with the pain squashed so far down that no one else could see it. But the sweetness in her aunt's voice was stirring those losses so she couldn't stop feeling them. "Patty and I both do," Aunt Darcy went on, using Mrs. Murrell's first name, which was unusual. "If we thought you could be happy here, we'd be glad to have you stay on as long as you wanted. We think of you as ours, in many ways." Helen had closed her eyes to try and keep back the tears, but she could feel the bed move slightly as her aunt gestured around the room. "In fact, we got it set so this place will be yours when we're gone. Maybe by then you'll be ready to come back. If not, just sell it and do something wonderful for yourself with the money."

She thought she'd at least be able to breathe, but when she inhaled, her throat constricted and a little choking sound came out. Aunt Darcy pulled her close and Helen turned in to her, crying like the world was about to end. She wasn't sure how long it went on, only that she woke up lying on the little bed the next morning still fully dressed, except for her shoes. She'd gone and signed up for the Women's Army Corps that very day.

"Whatever are you doing?"

Helen jumped. She'd been so lost in her memories she hadn't heard some of the other girls coming in from dinner. Tee was standing there, looking at her like she might have lost her mind. Helen realized she was still holding the sock and she quickly stuffed the bills back into it.

Tee put a hand on her arm. "What is that?"

"Nothin'."

Tee's eyes narrowed in a way Helen had never seen before, and her voice dropped to a fierce whisper as she squatted in front of her. "Don't you lie to me, Helen Tucker. Now, I asked you a simple question, and I expect an answer."

Helen sighed. "It's my savings, okay? Some money I kept back since I got here."

"I know you got a PX account like everybody else. How come you don't put your savings in there?"

Helen shrugged. "It's my emergency money." She moved as if to put the sock back in her footlocker, but Tee's touch turned into a grip.

"How much you got in there?"

Helen tried to make her expression say it wasn't none of Tee's business, but Tee had beat her to it with a look that said she'd better tell it. "Enough," she said. "Enough for you and me to get our own place."

Tee's expression softened. Her hand slid down Helen's arm to the fingers that were holding the sock. "Let me see."

There was nothing for it. Helen loosed her hold and Tee took the sock. She stood, looking around casually before turning her back, making like she was getting her bed ready for the evening. When she stilled, Helen knew she was counting. It seemed to take a long time.

"Put this back wherever it goes." Tee turned back to her finally, her voice oddly flat as she extended the sock. "Then you and me are gonna take a walk."

CHAPTER TWELVE

Once she started talking, the story poured out of her. Helen was actually relieved to tell it, even though she didn't like the way Tee kept her arms crossed over herself and gave her head a little shake from time to time. As often as possible, Helen repeated, "For us or to get our own place," or some other words she hoped would prove her intentions. But Tee's expression didn't change one bit.

"So what is it exactly that you're playing at, Helen?" she'd said, when the explanation had wound down. "Why don't you go to Lieutenant Rains and tell her what you know?"

Helen felt a little rush of anger. "Didn't you hear that part about Rains giving me one chance to talk without penalty? That time has passed, Tee. What I gotta do now is figure out how to get clear of this without being caught."

Tee said nothing. She looked at Helen for a time and then cocked her head and looked at her some more, contemplating her like she was speaking Italian or something. About the time Helen was going to make a face or stick out her tongue, just to break the silence, Tee asked, "What's the most important thing to you, Helen?"

"The most important thing about this situation?"

"No," Tee clarified. "The most important thing in the world."

Helen stood a little straighter, looking past Tee into the evening. On the chill air, faint laughter was coming from one of the barracks. She pulled her coat closer. It was getting too cold for them to be walking around, talking like this. *The* most important thing? The question seemed really big, like she didn't know enough words to answer. She had no idea what to say. She looked back at Tee, her expression almost pleading, but Tee was ready.

"You don't know, do you? You can't even say what's most important to you in your whole life, can you? And do you know why? 'Cause you got no compass, Helen. Nothing inside that points you in the right direction." She sighed and then took both of Helen's hands. "I been trying to find my way to you, thinking that it was just my religion that was standing in our way. But now I see that wasn't all it was. It's also because you got no foundation for us to build on. You just go whichever way the wind blows, taking the easy way and only worrying about how to get out of the consequences." Tee's voice rose above the objections that Helen's mind was trying to provide. "Do you know how I would have answered that question until about ten minutes ago? I would have said *you*, Helen. I would have said you were the most important thing to me. But how can I change everything I ever thought about myself and give up any chance of having my family in my life for a common thief?"

She dropped Helen's hands and turned into the night, walking briskly toward the barracks. Helen didn't try to follow her or even call out. She knew there was no point. No point at all, really.

Working in the PX early that next morning, Tee was concentrating on keeping herself very busy. She'd chosen to redo the arrangement of underwear in the men's aisle, something she generally avoided, but at least it wouldn't give her a reason to think of Helen. The PX was almost deserted at this hour, so when she heard a throat being cleared beside her, she turned slowly, thinking it was some young man going to ask her about a product. Her eyes opened wide to see her former drill instructor in her lieutenant's uniform, accompanied by a woman MP.

"Private Owens, would you join us in Captain Madison's office, please?"

"Yes, ma'am." Tee had to put down the package of briefs she was holding before she could salute, wondering if perhaps the captain had taken ill.

The office was a mess, with drawers standing open and file folders and papers in haphazard piles. A male MP was removing balled-up papers from the trash can and smoothing them out before adding them to a nearby stack of wrinkled sheets. He stopped and stood at attention when the lieutenant entered. Rains led her over to the desk while the other MP took up a position in the doorway.

Rains gestured to some familiar-looking forms on Captain Madison's desk. "Private Owens, can you explain how your signature came to be on these falsified documents?"

Falsified documents? The words made no sense. For just a second, Tee had the odd sensation of falling, even though she knew she was still standing upright. As a private in Rains's squad, she'd looked her directly in the eyes only once, on her first day at Fort Des Moines when Sergeant Moore had intimidated her to the point that she almost couldn't speak. When Rains had taken over as their drill instructor, she'd calmed Tee with her gentle tone and her assurance that it was all right to look at her. When Tee had done so, she'd found something there that had made her able to find her words and to do what was asked of her from that time forward. She looked again now, wanting to find that same compassion. It wasn't there. Penetrating, intense scrutiny was all she saw.

"L-Lieutenant, I—" she started, before swallowing hard, telling herself to slow down and think clearly before she spoke. After a few seconds she began again. "Captain Madison has…has b-been training me…in p-pro-procurement and r-requisitions."

The male MP shifted restlessly while she worked to get her words out, but the lieutenant merely nodded. "Go ahead."

Tee stammered her way through the rest of her explanation while Rains listened carefully. She finished telling how the captain had walked her through the process until it had become part of their routine, that once or twice a week she'd check in and sign anywhere from four to twenty forms.

"Did you ever sign any blank forms?" Rains asked.

"I don't know," Tee answered. "I could have."

"You didn't read what was on the forms?"

"No, ma'am. I just did what the captain asked me to." Tee couldn't help that the stress was making her stutter, and she was grateful that Rains knew this about her, so she wouldn't automatically assume it was guilt. Then another thought made her face brighten and she spoke quickly. "You can ask Captain Madison. She'll tell you what I did."

The male MP snorted, but at Rains's glare he made it sound like a cough.

When Rains turned back, Tee saw something different in her expression. Pity. "Captain Madison tells us a different story, Private. She says that on numerous occasions she left you alone in her office to do some basic filing. There was no mention of any training that the two of you were doing." Tee opened her mouth but no sound came out. Rains gestured slightly and went on. "Isn't it true that you are friends with Private Helen Tucker, one of the transport drivers?"

Tee knew the color that came to her face might also mark her as guilty, but then it occurred to her that Lieutenant Rains also understood the real reason why she would blush at Helen's name. How strange it would be if this was the Lord's real plan behind why Rains had caught them together that time. Her voice was strangely steady as she said, "Yes, ma'am. We have been friends. But we're not anymore."

"I see. As of when?"

The words *last night* seemed entirely too personal. "Quite recently, ma'am."

"And what was the reason behind your…falling out?"

Tee took in a breath, feeling like it might be her last. The small office felt terribly close and she clasped her hands together in front of her, trying to hold herself together as she stared at the paperwork with her own handwriting so clearly visible. "I'd rather not say, ma'am."

Rains didn't respond for so long that Tee thought perhaps she hadn't spoken loudly enough to be heard over her thundering heartbeat. Finally, Rains must have made some signal, because the female MP took a step into the room as the lieutenant spoke. "Private Owens, there have been serious irregularities that have originated from this office. Captain Madison has already been confined to her private quarters, but due to your group living arrangements, you'll have to be placed in the stockade until we work out the discrepancies in the explanations we have so far."

Tee nodded and kept her head down as the MP took her arm. Rains followed them across the base and Tee heard her dismiss the MP after the door to the cell clanged shut. Standing before the tiny chamber, Rains's tone was a little less formal. "I want to advise you that you are entitled to counsel, Private, although I wonder if we could talk a little more first. Please understand that you are under no obligation to speak with me any further."

Tee came forward and held on to the bars the way she'd seen Helen do when she was here. Each step across the familiar sidewalks of Fort Des Moines had played a drumbeat of competing emotions inside her. Shame. Anger. Self-reproach. Indignation. Almost nauseated by the flurry of unresolved reactions, she could only nod again. As if she knew what Tee was feeling, Rains stepped away for a moment and came back with a paper cup of water. She passed it through the bars, and when Tee took it, their fingers brushed for just a second.

In all of her time with Rains, Tee had never once thought of her as anything other than an instructor, someone in command. Now, for some absurd reason, she was struck with a quick flash of awareness that Rains wasn't only a person, she was also a woman. She wasn't beautiful, like Bett Smythe, but she had a look about her that was very pleasing somehow. Right now, the strong lines of her face seemed a little softer, and Tee could almost imagine her as someone with a home and a loved one waiting for her. She sipped the water slowly, trying to bring her mind into some more rational place. She settled on the idea that whatever else, at least she could count on Rains to be fair, and that was the best she could hope for right now.

"I cannot stay long, Private Owens," Rains began. "This investigation is ongoing. Regardless of what we say here, the next person you speak to will be your lawyer."

"I didn't do it, Sar—Lieutenant Rains," Tee blurted, not waiting to be asked. "I would never do something like that."

Rains squinted slightly. "Like what?"

"Steal from the Army. Or from anyone. I'm not that kind of person."

The lieutenant nodded slowly, her voice quiet as she bent closer. "I believe you, Private. But would you be willing to tell me how you knew this investigation was about stealing?" Tee's eyelids fluttered and Rains could imagine that she was trying to think back through her remarks. "You could argue that it was a logical conclusion. But I could argue you knew what I meant by irregularities because you were already aware— though maybe only recently—of what was going on."

Even the nausea was gone now and Tee felt completely hollow.

With nothing left inside, she couldn't have explained why she still shook her head. "I can't," she whispered.

She could feel Rains's gaze on her, but she couldn't bring herself to lift her eyes. After a moment, Rains straightened. "I'll do what I can for you, Private Owens. I've left my number with the MPs here. If you want to contact me for any reason, let them know." Tee barely nodded and Rains started away. At the corner of the cell she stopped. "If you happen to see Private Tucker, let her know she needs to contact me, too. Her time in the WAC is running out."

Helen couldn't bring herself to go back to the barracks. Not after what Tee had said. Not after she'd almost felt Tee's heart shutter itself, closing her out. *You think you're so smart,* her mother's voice scolded. *But now you've gone and ruined everything, just like you always do.* Helen pressed her fingers to her forehead, rubbing harder and harder until the sound went away. Then she walked without purpose, letting the time pass until she realized she couldn't stop shivering. She needed to get somewhere warmer, like maybe Georgia. She wondered absently if the lieutenant would approve her transfer request. Helen figured that Rains would probably be glad to get rid of her, too.

Looking over, she noticed she was in front of the chapel. Would lightning strike if someone like her went in there? With the sharp outlines of the steeple softened by the night, it looked unusually inviting. And probably warm. Helen walked slowly up the steps and pulled carefully on the door handle. It opened easily, revealing a dimly lit interior of long benches divided by a center aisle. She slid down one of the benches far enough that she could stretch out on it, using her coat like a blanket, resting her head on her arm. Being out of the cold was wonderful, and feeling unexpectedly safe, she let herself rest.

When she opened her eyes, she couldn't figure out where she was for a few seconds. As soon as she identified the hard bench and unfamiliar quiet as the base chapel, her thoughts went to Tee. She was pretty sure that it really was over between them. What could she possibly say or do now to make Tee willing to give her another chance? Helen hadn't let herself think about how they'd parted, but now she could see that maybe what Tee had said about that compass thing might even be true. But how did someone like her get to have a compass without a woman like Tee in her life? And did that make Tee the most important thing in the world to her? Yes, and she was nothing but a sorry fathead to not have told her so. If nothing else, she would write Tee a letter and admit that what she'd done—no matter how she tried to justify it—was wrong.

But before she could start planning her letter, thoughts of the black market scam crept back into her head. If Knox and Vish were covering things in procurement, where was the link in finance? Was it someone higher up? She'd heard about the major in finance being transferred, although the scuttlebutt was he'd left maintaining his innocence. The boss the other girls had talked about must still be there. She wondered about the poor private who was being set up to take the fall. Someone innocent and sweet, like Tee, probably. She smiled, thinking of how excited Tee had been about getting to learn about requisitions and how they'd worked on just the right words to ask her captain if she could move to the next step, something beyond simply signing an already completed form.

Shoving aside the hurt in her heart at the thought of Tee, Helen sat up abruptly, trying to remember something Knox had said, something about how the boss had it fixed so there was only one name on the invoices, and it wasn't hers. *Oh no.* Helen scratched her head, trying to get her brain to work faster. Here she was in a church and desperately in need of some divine inspiration. Of course, just because she was in a church didn't make her a believer, and any kind of God had to know that, so there was probably no point in asking for anything. But as she finished that thought, another idea crowded in. *Hold on.* Just because she'd met Knox and Vish in the purchasing office didn't necessarily mean they worked there. She'd just taken that for granted. What if someone else had just let them use the office, and they actually worked in finance and what if—she swallowed hard—what if it was Tee being set up to take the fall?

Careful to stay a respectful distance from the cross at the front of the church, Helen paced the aisle, trying to find anything wrong with this new idea. Her first question was whether someone else knew about her and Tee. Was that why they had involved them both? Or was that just a strange coincidence? She tried thinking through it again, bringing Lieutenant Rains in as one of the bad guys, but it just didn't make sense. She went back to her new understanding and tried it again. Tee's captain running the procurement end of things and putting Tee's name on everything to hide her involvement, with Knox and Vish covering the difference in finance. But how? How would finance pay for thirteen boxes of sugar when the motor pool manifest said they only picked up twelve? Helen looked up, willing the answer to appear. After a time, she closed her eyes. She had never prayed, but she could think of one good reason to give it a try right now. *For Tee, okay? I'll accept my punishment, but she's not guilty of anything except believing in me.* When she opened her eyes, she saw a dim glow coming through one side of the stained glass windows high up on the church wall. Her heart began to beat wildly. Was this God she wasn't so sure about going to make an appearance? She turned toward the light, stumbling against the bench closest to her as her mind ran through a very, very long list of bad things she'd done. Thinking maybe she was supposed to speak first, she opened her mouth, staring at the scene where she could just make out the image she knew was Moses with the ten commandments. In each hand he held one of the two stone tablets. One of two…like one of two copies of the invoice.

"God!" she cried out as the light brightened slightly. "Thank you." Grabbing her coat, she threw open the door. Dawn had broken and the sun was rising steadily.

It didn't take much to break into the finance office, especially for someone who'd had a little practice at such things in the past. Once inside, Helen locked the door back behind her as she wondered where to start looking for the proof she'd need. One look at the nameplate on the desk made her certain she'd figured out their system, but she still needed some evidence confirming that two copies had been made of certain invoices that showed different quantities to be picked up from what was ordered and paid. She'd gone through every part of the desk and was finishing the top drawer of the file cabinet when movement on the sidewalk outside caught her eye. When the figures came into focus, she was horrified to see Lieutenant Rains and a female MP escorting Tee across the base toward the stockade. She closed the file cabinet, planning to intercept the group and tell Rains as much as she knew.

Perhaps the lieutenant would be able to find something of use here. Just as she moved toward the door, she heard keys jingling and then the knob began to turn. She hadn't yet jimmied open the door to the commander's office, so there was nowhere to hide. Sitting quickly behind the desk, she put her feet up, deciding to brazen it out.

She recognized the woman's form even before she entered, flicked on the light, and then startled at the sight of Helen in her chair. Before she could speak, Helen said, "The boss is worried about Rains getting too close. You don't have anything incriminating in here, do you?"

Corporal Wyrzyk stared at her. "What are you doing here?"

Helen sighed impatiently. "I just told you. The boss let me in so I could wait for you. She wants to make sure there's nothing here that Rains could use against us." The corporal's eyes went to the trash. *Of course*, Helen thought. *They destroy the motor pool invoice each time and substitute the fake one so the supplier gets paid the right amount.* She rose and picked up the can. "Is this all? I can get rid of it now that you're here."

"Yeah." Vish still seemed a little unsure as she went to her chair. "That's it."

Helen moved quickly toward the door. "I'll bring this back in a few."

She was reaching for the knob when Vish said, "Hey, Tucker." Helen turned back, trying to make sure her expression was only slightly irritated. "When did you talk to her?"

"She came by the motor pool early this morning. Why?"

Vish got up and came over, her hand closing around the near edge of the can. She brought her face up close and Helen saw cruelty in her eyes. "Captain Madison has been under house arrest since last night. And you are a fucking snitch, just like I thought."

Helen was grateful that Sinclair had made sure she could throw a punch with either hand. She clocked Vish on the side of her head and the corporal staggered and went down. As she fell, her hand pulled the trash can over with her and the contents spilled out. Helen cursed under her breath and tried to scoop up the balls of paper as quickly as she could. She had gotten about half of them back into the can when a hand closed around her wrist. Bent over and slightly off balance, she was easily brought down by Vish jerking hard on her arm. The corporal tried to roll onto her, but since she was outweighed by about twenty pounds, Helen was determined not to let that happen. She rolled them again and they crashed into a chair. Separated from Vish by the impact, she tried to move away, but a shoe grazed her mouth. She rolled again, getting to her feet when she saw she was clear. She dabbed at her lip, blood on her fingers. Vish was up, too, and Helen could see a growing bruise on the side of her head. They were both breathing hard.

"You're not getting out of here with that." The corporal pointed at the trash can on the floor.

"Lieutenant Rains is gonna bring you all down," Helen replied. "Why don't you let me tell her how cooperative you were?"

Vish rushed her and they were locked in a clench when the door opened behind them. "What in the Sam Hill is this?" a voice asked.

Movement ceased as the two women looked over and immediately separated as they both came to attention. Colonel Janet Issacson stood in the doorway, a slight, bespectacled woman in a captain's uniform behind her.

"Who is Corporal Wyrzyk?" the colonel asked, pronouncing the name correctly as she looked from one combatant to the other.

Vish took a step forward. "I am, ma'am."

Issacson indicated the woman behind her. "This is your new commander, Captain Sara Vernon."

Taking an extra second to smooth back her hair before she retrieved her hat from the floor, the corporal saluted. "Pleased to meet you, ma'am."

Janet Issacson looked at her new captain with an eyebrow raised. Vernon stepped through the doorway. "Can you explain to me what is going on here, Corporal?"

Vish pointed at Helen. "Private Tucker here is involved in a black market scam through her association with the motor pool. But I caught her in here this morning trying to plant evidence that would incriminate this office. She attacked me before I could call an MP."

"Bullshit," Helen snapped before her common sense kicked in and she grimaced. Turning back to Issacson she said, "Begging your pardon, ma'am. But Vish is the one who's in on that scam. And the one running it in procurement has been making false invoices for the motor pool with lesser quantities to be picked up so the extras can be diverted to her black market connection. Then the corporal here destroys them, substituting the copy so the suppliers get paid the correct amount."

She gestured at the wadded-up papers on the floor. "Those duplicates are what I was trying to get." She had to talk fast, given that it was likely she'd be back in the stockade before lunch. "I've been helping Lieutenant Rains investigate the case, and I've determined that Private Owens from procurement knew nothing about this, ma'am. She was framed by Captain Madison."

Sara Vernon looked back at Colonel Issacson with her eyes wide. "I don't even know where to start with this," she said.

The colonel looked past her at the two bleeding and bruised women. "Why don't you call an MP to come in here. Then let's see if we can't arrange a meeting with Lieutenant Rains in the stockade. I have a feeling she can help us clear this up."

"You stupid bitch," Wyrzyk growled at Helen. "Don't think you're gonna get away scot-free. You're up to your ass in the shit just like me."

"Make that two MPs," Issacson called toward Captain Vernon's rapidly departing back.

Lieutenant Rains gladly released Teresa Owens from the stockade after only a few hours, and the private was fully exonerated, but it took until the week before Thanksgiving for all the excitement around the charges, resignations, and transfers to die down. Helen's timely arrival at finance had preserved some key evidence, and the full confession Rains obtained from Captain Madison implicated several other members of the black market ring. So after much thought, she saw to it that Helen's questionable activities as a driver were somewhat glossed over in the official report. Privately, however, Lieutenant Rains made it quite clear to Private Tucker that she was on the strictest probation imaginable and the slightest waver or whiff of impropriety would result in her immediate dismissal from the WAC with a less than honorable discharge. About two hours after her conversation with Tucker, Rains had been surprised when Sharon buzzed her office to ask if she could speak to a Private Owens.

Standing at attention, Tee's expression was surprisingly firm as she asked permission to speak freely. "I wanted to tell you something, Lieutenant. I expect you know that Helen got money for those things they took off her truck." Rains nodded slightly. Everyone but Helen had admitted to the financial inducement, but Rains was quite certain that Tucker wouldn't have participated without being bribed. Tee took a breath. "Helen's no angel but she's not all bad, ma'am. She just don't always see the line between right and wrong." Rains made no response. "Anyway, I wanted you to know that money will be going somewhere it's badly needed. It's being given to a church."

One side of the lieutenant's mouth lifted slightly. "A donation to the base chapel will be put to good use, I'm sure."

Owens shifted. "Uh, we're not choosing our chapel as the recipient, ma'am. That money is going to another church in town." Tee's eyes became somewhat distant. "They have the most glorious choir, but their piano is badly in need of repair." She smiled. "Now they're going to be able to get it fixed and tuned up nice."

There was a moment of silence before Rains said, "I'm willing to trust your judgment on this matter, Private Owens. But I appreciate you letting me know."

Tee took in a breath. "I also wanted to thank you for giving Private Tucker another chance. I promise you she'll make good this time, if I have anything to say about it."

Rains had wondered about things between Tucker and Owens after they'd shared a long embrace when Owens was released. Tucker had spoken earnestly to her for a full minute before she'd been taken away for the initial debriefing and she'd seen the presence of great emotion on Tee's face. She spoke almost without thinking. "She's lucky to have someone like you in her life."

Tee blushed, and she leaned forward slightly, her posture relaxing. "We're both aware that we owe you a great deal, Lieutenant." Rains shook her head, her hand gesture mirroring the movement, but Tee pressed on. "You're one of the things I'm most thankful for. I keep you in my prayers every day, ma'am." She straightened again and saluted. "That's all I wanted to say."

Rains felt oddly touched. "Thank you, Private."

❖

On Thanksgiving Day, all nonessential departments had the day off and the rest worked with skeleton crews. As they were getting ready to go for the traditional turkey lunch on the base, Rain explained to Bett that this holiday wasn't really a celebration for members of the Indian Nations. "If the Wampanoag hadn't been so friendly and helpful, maybe we'd still have our land and you'd be the ones living on reservations."

"Hmm," Bett considered. "And here I was thinking how nice it was not to have to sit around and listen to my family complain about the service at the country club."

"I can't help but be amazed at how different our lives were and how we each ended up on the road that brought us together," Rain responded, sitting across from Bett at the breakfast table with their tea. She took Bett's hand. "I can't imagine how we would have ever met if it hadn't been for the Army."

"We were always destined to be together," Bett answered, leaning over to kiss Rain on the cheek. "I would have given up my party life and come to work in South Dakota or you would have sought your fortune in the bright lights of Los Angeles. Somehow, it would have happened."

Bett was pleased to see Rain smile warmly at her declaration. Since her headaches had been resolved, their time together had been wonderful. Her corrected vision made it easier to finish her work at the office so she rarely brought anything home anymore, and their evening conversations resumed as if they had never faltered. Bett was enormously proud of Rain's role in solving the black market scam, even though Rain hadn't spoken much about the particulars of how the case stood. But there was lots of conversation, even among the generally circumspect members of cryptography, and everyone seemed well pleased that Fort Des Moines had done some much-needed housecleaning. She was also flattered that Rain periodically consulted with her about personnel matters at the motor pool, and her lover's vivid descriptions and detailed anecdotes made Bett feel like she actually knew most of the individuals on staff. Whenever Rain sought her opinion, she made a point of answering as thoughtfully as Rain listened. She wasn't able to talk much about her own work with Luna, of course, but on the occasions when Rain asked, "How are things at your work?" Bett could feel that she was genuinely interested, and she tried to find a few details to tell her—always with the caution regarding her security clearance that made Rain lower her head and nod silently.

Beyond their work lives, Bett readily admitted to herself that Rain's commitment to her was nothing short of extraordinary. Her lover's actions had made it clear that she viewed their first week together as the starting point from which they would grow, rather than the zenith of their relationship. She had stayed, even when Bett had been at her worst, using her incredibly perceptive ability to understand and correct what was really wrong. She had found it in herself to forgive Bett for her hurtful behavior and had even used their conversation about the motorcycle to model, Bett realized later, the way people who cared about each other should talk about things that might be difficult. Bett's heart told her Rain wasn't someone just passing through her life—she was a touchstone, a center, and Bett knew she needed to start acting accordingly.

Now that their physical connection had returned and strengthened, Bett loved to envision Rain riding home each night, imagining what kind of evening it might be. Sometimes Bett would greet her sweetly and give her time to change clothes and get dinner. They would eat and talk and after the dishes were done and they settled in front of the fire, Bett would begin to kiss Rain's neck or reach over and tease her breast or casually stroke between her legs until both of them were out of their clothes and into each other's bodies. Sometimes Bett, already naked beneath a robe, would begin to undress her the moment she walked in the door, taking her urgently there in the hallway or on the dining table, sometimes getting as far as the den. Other times she would wait, letting Rain take the lead and adjusting to the pacing her lover wanted. At times Rain needed Bett immediately, wanted everything from her the moment she came through the door. Occasionally just a kiss hello would contain such joy and reassurance that Bett would be happy to lie on the couch after dinner and just be with Rain—talking, touching gently—until bedtime. Then, as Bett slipped in beside her, she would feel Rain's passion ignite and they would make love until they fell asleep. Now and then, Bett sensed that Rain only needed her presence, and would quietly hold her while they read or listened to the radio. Every night was special, and each morning when they woke there was a sense of significance to what they were becoming, together.

Now Bett ran her fingers up and down Rain's arm. "Rain, may I ask you something?"

"Of course."

"Do you believe in God?"

Rain stared at the floor. There was a long pause, and Bett thought she might not answer. But then she looked up with her eyes very bright and said, "Why do you ask me that?"

"Well, for one thing, I've just been feeling rather grateful lately, and I just don't know quite where to direct it. I was definitely an atheist in university, but now I'm just not sure. It is Thanksgiving. And you and I have never talked about it, so I was just wondering."

Rain rocked a little bit, as if trying to figure out how to say what she was thinking. "I don't think I believe in God in the same way as White people," she suggested. "But I pray every day, so maybe that counts me as religious."

"You pray every day?" Bett asked, incredulously. "When?"

"Since I've been here with you, I usually pray before I leave for the base. Before I met you, I used to pray outside my quarters, early in the morning before anyone else was up."

"And when you don't go to the base early, like today?"

A small smile crossed Rain's face. "When we don't go anywhere, I generally do my prayer in the kitchen before you get up, or outside by the woodpile if it's not too cold."

"And what do you pray for?" Bett wondered. "If you don't mind me asking."

Rain looked away and answered quietly. "I just say the prayer that my mother taught me."

Bett knew how sacred memories of her mother were to Rain. She wanted to ask more, but her heart told her not to intrude. She kissed Rain's hair and said, "Well, you are the answer to my prayer that I didn't even know enough to say. And for that, I'm grateful to whoever heard it."

Rain nodded and rocked quietly for a minute. Then she looked at Bett and said, "Aren't you going to ask me about it?"

Bett dropped her head a bit. "You know me so well. But I really was trying hard not to. I don't mean to intrude on every piece of your life, Beloved. I just think you're the most interesting person I've ever met, and sometimes I just can't seem to stop asking you questions. Please don't feel like you need to tell me anything more. It's really, really fine if you don't."

Bett could see a distance come into Rain's eyes. "I didn't really know much about our beliefs when I got back to the reservation after high school, but I had a little time to learn some before I joined the

Army. Someday, if you're really interested, we could talk more about it." Bett nodded. "My prayer, I learned it by memory because my mother wanted me to, but at that time I didn't really understand it at all. But at every age of my life, a different part of it has spoken to my heart." She focused on Bett again. "Even since I met you, I now center on it in a new way."

Rain stood, bowed her head and was very still for a moment. Lifting her face and with her eyes closed, she recited:

> *Wakȟáŋ Tȟáŋka*, Great Mystery,
> Help me know myself,
> Help me know my world.
> Let me hear the voices of those who came before,
> That I may understand my own beginning.
> Let me see the path before me and the ones to come,
> That I may know the ways of my journey.
> Teach me to trust each of my senses and the blessings of my spirit,
> So I can walk, love, and live without fear,
> Finding the balance in the gifts of each day.

Rain stood quietly for a few seconds and then looked up. Bett had tears in her eyes. "That's one of the most beautiful things I've ever heard," she whispered.

Rain knelt in front of Bett. "Loving beyond my fear is where I am now, with you. And the miraculous thing is, since I've been able to do that, my walk is much more balanced."

Bett felt her heart was so full, it might burst. She took Rain's hand and kissed it.

"I would like—" Rain started, taking Bett's other hand.

"What?" Bett asked.

Rain shook her head. "No, we must get dressed. Another time. Soon. I promise," Rain said, looking at Bett resolutely.

Chapter Thirteen

"So are you looking forward to seeing some of your old squad again, Lieutenant?" Bett asked, adjusting Rain's tie as she had started doing every morning.

"Yes, but..." Rain didn't finish. She didn't have to. Bett knew. It was all the deception that they would have to put on. They had already decided that it wasn't wise to arrive together, so Bett was taking her car and Rain would ride Red Cloud. They had even agreed that Rain would arrive ten minutes ahead.

Rain was a most unwilling liar. When asked a question that she felt she could not answer truthfully, she would simply not answer at all. Bett, on the other hand, could create extremely plausible lies on the fly and could remember them weeks later. She had no qualms about lying when it was necessary and sometimes even when it wasn't—although never to Rain. She tried to tell Rain it was like playing a game or making up stories. This made Rain frown even deeper. Still, she had apprised Rain of the vague cover story she had made up in case anyone asked.

"So, I'm living with another WAC in cryptography who transferred here from Fort McClellan. You are living with a girl who was a WAAC but opted out and is now working in the department store downtown," Bett easily improvised. "You know that one of the things I love about you is your integrity," she added, the struggle on Rain's face causing her a twinge of guilt. "I am so sorry we have to do this." Rain's moral certainty was one of the most beautiful things about her.

"Someday we won't," Rain said with conviction. "We will make a way to live an honest life together."

Bett hugged her close, letting herself take part in Rain's faith. "Yes, we will. Count on it."

❖

It was only that promise that made Rain willing to go through with it. Otherwise, she would have just stayed away.

As she was parking Red Cloud, she spotted former squad member Jo Archer going toward the mess hall.

"Archer!" Jo turned on the sidewalk and then jogged back to where Rains was standing.

"Sarge!" Archer said delightedly, her face reddening as she scanned Rains's uniform and then saluted stiffly. "Oh jeez, I'm sorry. I meant to say lieutenant. I hope it's not too late for me to say congratulations on your promotion."

"Sometimes the amount of paperwork that goes across my desk every day doesn't make it feel like a promotion, but thank you." Rains returned the salute. "And you, Archer. You'll be a sergeant yourself at the end of next week, right?" She thought Archer might be embarrassed if she knew that her former drill instructor had kept tabs on her and was quite pleased with the New Yorker's progress in NCO training.

"Yes, Lieutenant, thanks to you."

"How do you like the training? Have you picked something for your second rotation?"

"It's good," Archer said, grinning. "Like you, tough but fair. For my second, I'm thinking about becoming a quartermaster."

Rains nodded and smiled back. "I might know of an opening. Let me know if you change your mind about working with those recruits."

Jo looked at Rains for a long moment. "There's something different about you, Lieutenant, but I can't put my finger on it." She looked back at the motorcycle. "Isn't that Corporal Lutz's bike?" She started to smile. "Are you and Lutz…?" She made a gesture with her fingers.

"What?" Rains asked and then caught on. "Oh no. No. I bought that motorcycle from Lutz, yes, but that's it."

"Come on, Lieutenant, you can't kid a kidder. There's something new going on with you, isn't there?"

"Hello, Jo. Hello, Lieutenant Rains," said a lilting voice behind her. Rains knew from the rush of heat that flared up inside her that Bett had arrived.

"Queenie!" Jo cried, enveloping Bett in a hug and giving Rains time to turn and recover slightly.

Rains put out her hand for Bett to shake, but Bett was saluting instead. They switched positions, accomplishing nothing, and then all three laughed. "You're looking well, Lieutenant," Bett said, smiling sincerely.

"As are you, Sergeant Smythe. Are things going well for you in cryptography?"

Bett nodded with just enough amusement in her eyes to let Rains know she was playing the game well. "Very well, thank you."

Just then, Harold Lutz arrived on his Harley. Seeing Rains, he came toward her, asking, "Where's my beautiful girl?"

Jo nudged Bett and murmured excitedly, "Did you hear that? I think Rains and Lutz have a thing going."

Bett turned to Jo with her eyes wide. "Really!" she exclaimed, knowing that Rains had gotten the idea that her motorcycle was female from Lutz's terminology. She watched as the two of them talked excitedly about their vehicles—Rains tall, lean, and dark, Lutz just a bit shorter and a bit thicker with a shock of blond hair. "Well, they do say opposites attract."

Bett allowed Jo to walk her inside, but not until she saw Rains nod ever so slightly that she was okay talking to Lutz. Inside, Bett was genuinely pleased to find most of her old squad, sitting in their usual place. Even though she could have sat at the officers' table, Bett chose to stay and visit with her old friends. No one else from cryptography was attending. *Not the personality types to take part in something like this*, Bett decided. Instead of taking her usual place at the officers' table, Rains sat with another group in the hall, but still directly in Bett's line of sight. *That must be her staff from the motor pool*, Bett thought, anxious to get a look at them without being too obvious. But then Lutz came in and sat across from Rains, blocking Bett's view. This started Jo going again, and she began telling the whole squad about Rains and Lutz.

Barb cut in. "But I thought Lutz was married or engaged or something like that."

There were various reactions to this, most of which defended Rains's honor. From there, the conversation moved freely as each of them discussed their lives in the weeks since graduation from basic training.

Helen and Tee came in late, but the squad made room for them across from Bett as they sat together. As conversation ebbed and flowed around her, Bett was drawn to watching the two women that she had often tutored during their basic training classes. The banter had moved to families and dating when Helen got up to get something else from the drink cart. Her hand rested on Tee's for just a second as she seemed to be asking if Tee wanted anything. The look that passed between them was unmistakable. Helen's eyes glowed with a deep longing, and Tee's expression was one of great tenderness. *They are more than just friends!* Bett realized. She knew that Helen and Tee had become close during basic training but that seemed understandable, given the similarities in their backgrounds and what they wanted for themselves from their Army experiences. But this was a look that went beyond simple camaraderie, and Bett was intrigued.

"How do you like working in the PX, Tee?" Bett leaned forward to catch Tee's answer, remembering her soft-spoken ways.

"It's good, Bett," Tee replied, sounding surprisingly confident with very little trace of her previous stammer. "I'm learning a lot about ordering and stocking and display. I think I'm going to set up my own shop after the war."

"How wonderful," Bett said, sincerely. Wanting to hear more from Tee, she asked, "And how is Helen doing?"

"Well, she's driving one of those big supply trucks, bringing in our orders from the depot pretty much every day. She hopes to start picking up out of town or even delivering to other bases," Tee said, obviously proud. "So she's working hard, but that's Army life, right?"

"Indeed." Bett nodded, not sure what more to say. Then Helen returned with two glasses of milk.

"Tell Bett about Sergeant Rains." Tee nudged Helen. Bett looked at Helen with genuine interest.

"Did you know she was promoted to lieutenant and is over the motor pool now?" Helen began.

"Yes, I saw her outside and I believe she said something to that effect," Bett said neutrally.

"Did you know she was living off base?" Helen went on. Tee

looked at Helen then and Bett thought she detected a slight shake of the head.

Bett acted as if she was thinking. "I don't remember hearing anything about that."

Lowering her voice, Helen explained. "Yeah, see, one time when me and Lieutenant Rains were working on that, uh, situation in the motor pool, I went to her quarters 'cause I needed to tell her something and they said she'd moved."

"But I take it things in the motor pool are running well now," Bett asked innocently, hoping to steer the conversation away from Rain's living arrangements.

"I can tell you, it's an entirely different place since Lieutenant Rains took over." Helen nodded vigorously.

"Better, I assume, knowing our former sergeant." Bett felt safe in saying this, since they were all well aware of Rains's abilities.

"Like night and day better." Helen lowered her voice again. "The way I heard it was that Rains always liked the motor pool, but Yarborough—Do you remember that witch?—anyways, Yarborough made fun of her being an Indian so she didn't want to work there."

"Really?" Bett admitted to herself that she loved hearing people talk about Rains as if they knew her. She also admitted to herself that she was ready to have Rains back in her bed that instant.

Colonel Issacson entered the room and Bett heard Rains's voice giving the call, "Ten-hut!" The entire mess hall stood and saluted. Issacson walked to the front of the hall and returned the salute. "As you were."

The colonel talked for a bit about the holiday and led them in a prayer for those in harm's way overseas. She then announced it was time for the Department of the Month Award. It seemed to Bett that she couldn't remember anyone other than the quartermasters ever winning this prize, and everyone speculated it was because Issacson had a soft spot for them. "This month's honor goes to a first-time winner, but I'm quite sure it won't be the last. Lieutenant Rains, please come forward to accept the award for the motor pool!"

Those at Rains's table were on their feet and cheering. Bett realized she was standing, too, and was relieved to see the rest of her squad was as well. Rains saluted and took the plaque from Issacson, who said something to her as they shook hands. Bett saw Rains flash an embarrassed smile at the colonel. Then she turned and saluted her motor pool group, and then saluted her former squad. Issacson looked toward them, and Bett saw the colonel's expression turn grim as their eyes met. *She never did like me,* Bett acknowledged to herself as she looked away.

There was lots of hugging at the motor pool table as Bett watched them pass the plaque around. Bett felt like she could watch them freely, since most other people in the mess hall were looking that way, too, at least briefly. It was an interesting mix of individuals, but they seemed to enjoy each other's company, and they clearly adored their lieutenant, who was looking on like a proud mother. *I'm so happy for you. I love you so much.* As if she had heard Bett's thoughts, Rains's eyes found hers. She smiled warmly and Bett's heart leapt.

"Off base, too?" Bett heard. She turned back to Helen.

"What? I'm sorry, I was…" Bett was suddenly unsure how to explain what she was doing. Helen didn't seem to notice, but Tee turned in the direction of Rains's group.

"Aren't you living off base, too?" Helen repeated.

"Yes, with a friend from cryptography. She transferred here from Alabama."

"What's her name?" Tee asked.

For some reason, Bett hadn't thought this far in her creative lying process. She knew she had to answer quickly, but for some reason the only name that came to her brain was the one from Rains's childhood, a name Rain had been given by White people and one she didn't care for at all. "Faith Lowell."

Outside after the long lunch was over, Rains was receiving congratulations from various staff members. Bett joined the line when there were about five people ahead of her. Noting that Rains was currently shaking hands with an attractive auburn-haired captain, she remembered discussing the woman with Rains during a picnic they'd had in the grove during her basic training. Their eyes met briefly when the captain turned to go. At one time Rains often sat by the captain in the mess hall, but Bett didn't recall her ever mentioning the woman since they'd been together. Then Bett found herself taking Rains's outstretched hand. Looking up into her face she saw exactly what she wanted to see. Rains loved her. "Congratulations, Lieutenant," Bett said, shaking Rains's hand warmly, unable to look away. "I know you must be very pleased."

"This wouldn't have happened without a lot of support from some very remarkable people," Rains said, gazing into Bett's eyes. Bett's smile deepened. She wanted to say, *I love you, too.* She wanted to kiss Rains until she begged for something more. She let go of Rains's hand reluctantly, but not before slipping in the scrap of paper on which she had written, *I've just developed a mad desire to be fucked by the Department of the Month winner.*

It was early winter dusk as Bett got into her car. She saw Rain talking to Helen and Tee and showing off her motorcycle. *My only competition*, Bett sighed to herself. *It figures that she's female.*

❖

Rains's head turned to the sound of Bett's car as it drove past. Bett waved and Tee and Helen waved back. Rains's hand went to her pants pocket where she had stored Bett's note. She couldn't tell if Bett had noticed or if she was smiling at Helen and Tee.

"I always thought she was the prettiest girl on the base," Helen said, a bit wistfully. "She looks like one of those models or a movie star or something." Tee turned to her sharply and she added, "And she was always so nice to us, remember, Tee? Helping us with our lessons after class but never show-offy about it."

"Mm-hmm," Tee agreed. "You could tell that she's real smart, too."

They both turned to Rains, whose face was impassive. "She was kinda hard for you to deal with though, huh, Lieutenant?" Helen asked.

"Why do you say that?" Rains countered.

"Oh, just sometimes after you'd talk with her, it looked like you were kinda upset, like tense or something," Helen suggested.

"And it seemed like she got KP or had to run laps a lot," Tee added. "You had to have all those extra meetings with her."

They were both looking at her expectantly. Rains realized she had to say something, though her mind was thinking back through her last squad leader meeting with Bett in the conference room and that first kiss. She tried to shake off the rush of emotion. "I think Private Smythe adjusted to Army life very well, at least by the end of her basic training." She squinted a bit, as though giving the matter some consideration. "Given where she is now, I'd have to say I am pleased with her performance."

❖

Rain was home not more than fifteen minutes after Bett. "I see you got my note," Bett said, unbuttoning her shirt. Rain watched her, eyes wild and glittering like a stalking wolf, and Bett knew that Rain was indeed going to fuck her and there was nothing she could do or say to stop it. Not that she wanted to. She gave up control and felt Rain take it. She wondered if Rain sensed the want trembling in her as their mouths met. In their bed, Rain pulled Bett on top of her. Bett was surprised that Rain was giving up this power but then, as Bett rocked herself onto Rain in the way that she loved to do, Rain grabbed her hips and stopped her. Then she lowered Bett back down, but only for four or five thrusts, and then stopped her again. "Rain, please," Bett breathed, but Rain wouldn't let her finish, kept stopping her just as she began to find her rhythm. Bett's pleasure built and then stopped, built and then stopped, until she was begging. "Please, let me—"

"Wait," she heard Rain whisper fiercely. Another cycle of building and stopping.

"I can't...please—please, Rain. I can't wait—" Bett began caressing Rain's breasts, thinking this would make her unable to resist anything for long. But soft flesh and hard nipples made Bett feel her own need even more deeply and she begged again, "Let me—let me come, Rain, please..." Rain let her go then and Bett's orgasm hit her so quickly she almost missed it. Before the first wave of pleasure had completely stopped, Rain had her on her back, and for the first time, Bett felt Rain's fingers slide up inside her.

Bett had never asked Rain not to do this, even though it was not something she had ever particularly enjoyed with her past lovers. She just thought Rain's sense of what Bett wanted had told her this wasn't it. But as she heard Rain groan, Bett felt Rain's fingers gliding under the place where she had just come and into something deeper and even more sensitive. Bett gasped aloud and she pushed herself to meet Rain's movement, finding that contact again. Rain's breathing was ragged and harsh at her side and Bett was lost in Rain's strength and her own weakness for that one point, that singular desire Rain was producing over and over. Rain's motion and the sensations were the same inside her and her need was so intense that everything in her condensed to the one place that only needed Rain's stroke once more once more once more once more and—

A crest of intensity such as Bett had rarely felt peaked within her and a scream that went on and on found its way out of her throat until she ran out of air. As she tried to catch her breath, she couldn't stop moving as she felt the same incredible sensation falling away until it was just out of reach. Finally, her body seemed to be slowing of its own accord and there was something else…a ringing sound?

Rain eased her mouth to Bett's ear. "I'm so sorry, Beloved."

"Don't be sorry…for what you make me feel." Bett could barely repeat the words Rain had said to her after their first time. But it seemed right to say, because loving Rain made everything new.

"No, I'm sorry because there's someone at the door," Rain said regretfully.

"What?" Bett tried to process this.

"I think it's our neighbor. I saw his light go on. I'm afraid if I don't answer, he'll call the police." Rain pushed up, stroking very gently inside her.

"No," Bett said, not wanting Rain to leave her empty. "Why?" The doorbell rang again.

"He might think you are hurt," Rain tried to explain, moving completely out of her until Bett made a very sad and disappointed sound. "I'm so sorry," Rain said again. "Believe me." And she was gone.

When Rain returned to her arms, Bett made her tell the sequence of events twice. Rain had swiftly put on her robe, poured some milk into a saucepan, and taken it with her to the door as the bell rang for a third time. She had opened the door to Mr. Childress, their sixty-plus-year-old neighbor with his little dog Sissy on a leash. The dog yapped at her until she gave it some milk on her finger. Rain was already on speaking terms with the elderly man; she had first met him out walking with Sissy and he had mentioned his wife had passed away the previous year. Rain had twice shared vegetables with him when there had been fresh produce at the store and she had bought a little extra. Mr. Childress had said that he had just taken Sissy outside when he heard something…a scream? Rain explained her roommate had also awakened her, apparently with a very bad dream. "The war…" Rain had lowered her voice knowingly, eyes downcast, and the neighbor had nodded sympathetically.

"Warm milk's the best thing to help her get back to sleep." The man had pointed at the pan.

"That's what I thought, too," Rain had agreed. "Hopefully it won't happen again but…" The man waved as he turned away and Rain closed the door.

"I take it back," Bett said, relaxing back into Rain's body after the story was finished. "You have the makings of a very good liar."

After a few moments of absorbing the perfection of simply being held, she remembered something she'd wanted to discuss before Rain had so wonderfully distracted her. "Did you see Helen and Tee at our squad table today?"

"Yes, and I saw them after lunch also. They wanted to look at Red Cloud."

"And did you think there was anything unusual going on between them?" Bett asked.

"Unusual, like what is going on between us?" This was Rain's version of teasing.

"Yes, like that."

"That unusual thing has been going on with them since the fifth week of basic training. Or that's when I became aware of it."

"What!" Bett sat up on her elbow. "Why didn't you tell me?"

"Bett, think about what you are saying," Rain said calmly. "When would I have told you? Not while you were in training with them. Not when I first came to this house and we were getting to know each other in such a different way." She breathed out a little huff. "Should I have announced, when I finally got you into bed, oh by the way, Helen and Tee would like to be doing this, too?"

"Gale Rains! You know there have been a thousand times that you could have told me, besides the ones you have named." Bett thought the truth was Rain was just not a gossip. "And incidentally, I'm the one who gets to say *finally got you into bed*."

Rain had come to understand that when Bett used her full Army name she was not really mad. Especially if she said it while they were naked. But she spoke soberly. "Bett, it is really not a matter to be discussed lightly. They could have both been dismissed from the WAC, their reputations ruined with blue tickets. When I caught—when I found out, they were obviously both quite shaken, well aware I would have been completely justified to send them home. But, obviously, I did not. Not because of my personal feelings but because professionally I believe what was between them had nothing to do with whether or not they would become good soldiers. And I made sure they understood that. They had done good work to that point and have continued to do so since then, so I feel my decision was justified." Rain turned over on her stomach, propping her head up on her arms. There was a little space between her and Bett. She looked into the distance. "Someday you or I may find ourselves in a position where someone else has our future in their hands, as I did with Helen and Tee. It's hard to say how we might react or what might become of us then."

Bett reached out to stroke Rain's hair. "Are you worried, Beloved?"

Rain raised her head, squinting into an unseen distance. "No…not now. But you never know when the storm will come."

"Amen." Helen raised her head and waited a few seconds before she turned to look at the woman next to her on the bench—pew, she corrected herself. There was more to learn about church than there had been in all of their basic training courses combined, but she really didn't mind. The only thing she minded about church was they couldn't sit close or hold hands, and certainly not kiss. But the brilliant smile Tee favored her with made it all worthwhile.

She'd been surprised at Tee's willingness to give her another chance until she understood they would be starting all over. All over, as in just friends, which meant no touching and no teasing or suggestive comments. Once Tee had even said, "Stop looking at me like that." Helen hadn't even pretended she didn't know what Tee meant. She was working hard at seeing that line between right and wrong that Tee expected her to know, and she was certain lying was one thing people with a compass inside wouldn't do—not even pretend lying.

Bit by bit, Tee had pushed her toward talking with Reverend Culberson. When Helen finally agreed, she thought she'd shock the reverend by telling her she wasn't a believer. Driving the three hours to meet their supplier in Waterloo the next day, she found their conversation about her lack of belief in God or Jesus rattling around in her head. The pleasant-looking older woman hadn't been the least bit upset by her declaration. The issue, she'd responded, wasn't that you had to believe exactly like someone else. She said she knew many good people who had very different religious faiths or who were atheists. The important thing, she told Helen, was that you believe in something, even if that something was simply working every day on being the best person you could be. Helen had never even considered you had to work at being a good person. She thought some people just were, and the rest just weren't. Reverend Culberson gently disagreed, telling her everyone had both good and bad in them. She then asked Helen to make a list of what she thought were her five best and five worst qualities for their next talk.

Helen decided she liked this lady preacher. She was smart, but it wasn't the same kind of book smart as Bett. It seemed like the reverend was smart about people, instead of subjects, and she had a welcoming way about her—never making Helen feel like she didn't deserve to be there. Still, she put off actually writing anything for a few days, but the idea of it wasn't ever far from her thoughts. The *worst* side was pretty easy. In fact, she had more than enough there. What she needed were some good parts to balance it out. For some reason, she didn't want to tell Tee about her assignment, so asking her was out of the question. Not Lieutenant Rains either, since her commander probably wouldn't be able to come up with much good about her right now. So when she happened to catch a glimpse of Bett walking near the motor pool, she scurried to catch up with her.

After some quick initial pleasantries, Helen asked, "Could you help me with something for a minute?"

Bett smiled, and Helen was reminded of how gorgeous she was. "Of course. As long as it's nothing mechanical."

Helen couldn't stop herself from smiling back. "Nah, nothing like that. It's really kinda embarrassing, but is there anything good about me you can think of?"

"What?" Bett asked, genuinely confused.

Don't lie, Helen reminded herself, not quite meeting Bett's eyes. "So, there's this assignment I have where I have to write down five good things and five bad things about myself. I'm not having any trouble coming up with the bad stuff, but…" She looked up hopefully. "You got any suggestions for something on the other side?"

Bett stepped closer, putting her hand on Helen's arm. "Oh, Helen. I certainly do. You've been a loyal friend and you have a great sense of humor. You can be very sweet but I think inside you are also strong." She seemed to be considering her next words carefully. "I'm not quite sure how to put this, but I think you are good at figuring out what you want, and then you go after it without hesitation. Like the way you wanted to drive those big trucks since you first got here, and now you are. I guess that would be persistent or tenacious? Or strong-willed?" She smiled again. "I know because I have that trait myself, so I recognize it in you, too."

"Some people might call that stubborn," Helen suggested, before she realized Bett might be insulted. But the blonde laughed again, though she did move her hand away.

"Yes, that's true. Or even obsessive, I suppose. But I think you should say determined. How's that for a start? Did we get five, or six?"

Helen hadn't written anything down, but she was pretty sure she wouldn't forget anything Bett had said. "Yeah, thanks, Bett. Thanks a lot."

To her surprise, Bett hugged her and murmured, "I'm so proud of what you did to help Lieutenant Rains figure out the black market scam. And I'm glad you're still here."

When she stepped back, the words came out before Helen could even think about what she was saying. "Would you like to go for a drink sometime?"

Fortunately, Bett spoke at the same time. "How's Tee doing?"

"Maybe dinner out?" Helen amended quickly. "We could all go."

Bett's eyes flicked toward the motor pool building and Helen turned to see Lieutenant Rains coming toward them. *Shit.* She was supposed to have been on duty five minutes ago but she'd stopped to talk to Bett instead.

"Private Tucker, you are late for sign-in."

She didn't need to look to know what Lieutenant Rains's expression would be. Helen knew she was on the verge of a serious reprimand, but Bett spoke before the lieutenant could continue.

"That's entirely my fault, Lieutenant. Helen and I didn't get to visit much at Thanksgiving, and she was kind enough to spend a few minutes catching up." She smiled up at Rains and Helen saw something different in that smile, something more personal than the way Bett had smiled at her. "Will you forgive my distracting her?"

She looked at Rains and was amazed to see the lieutenant's face soften into a return smile. She even had a glint of humor in her eyes when she replied, "Distracting soldiers from their duty might have earned you a demerit, back in basic training."

Bett's reply was entirely playful. "Well then, I'm certainly glad I'm not in basic training anymore."

"As am I, Sergeant," Rains countered quickly, sounding serious but not looking it at all.

Helen sensed this was the perfect moment for her to slip away without punishment. "I'll just..." She pointed toward the motor pool building, but neither of them paid her the slightest attention. When she looked back before entering, the lieutenant and Bett were still standing there, having even moved a little closer together, and she caught the sound of Bett's laughter just before the door swung shut behind her.

During their second talk, after Reverend Culberson graciously pointed out ways that Helen's whole list of weaknesses could become strengths, they continued discussing the kind of person she was until Helen steered the conversation toward who she needed to be to make Tee happy. Of course, she didn't put it exactly like that, although she had a feeling the reverend knew exactly who her theoretical relationship questions were about, since her answers seemed to fit Tee perfectly.

"You have to be real, your authentic self," the reverend explained. "Putting on an act just to make the other person happy will lead to one of two outcomes, neither of which is good. One, you're so good at pretending that the person falls in love with the fake you and now you're stuck living a lie for the rest of your life, or the person finds out you've been playacting and they leave, feeling like you've played them for a fool."

Helen stored that idea away as something to think about the next time she was on the road.

Then the reverend said, "Next time I'd like to hear a little about your family, Helen. Your parents and any siblings and other relatives you'd like to talk about. Or anyone else significant in your life as a youngster."

Helen bristled. "That'll be a short story. My daddy's dead and my mother's a whore. I got one older brother who's great and my Aunt Darcy, well, she's always been real good to me, too. Mr. Hall, the town postman, he taught me to drive. That's about it. Any other questions?"

They always sat in two facing chairs, but now Reverend Culberson stood and walked over to her desk. "What time next week?" was all she asked.

But that next week her name was on the board for her first overnight excursion. Helen was thrilled to see she would be driving the biggest of the Army cargo vehicles, a GMC CCKW two-and-a-half ton truck. Helen could barely contain her excitement until she noticed she would also have company. A girl she only knew as one of the new mechanics, PFC Toomer, was assigned to share the driving, and they would also be bunking together. They would arrive late in Louisville, Kentucky, stay overnight, and then pick up a load of new synthetic tires at the B.F. Goodrich plant there and return to base. Lieutenant Rains called her into her office the day before she was to leave, gesturing for her to sit.

"This will be a long trip and an important one," the lieutenant said. "You'll be returning to your home state, I believe." Helen nodded. Rains cleared her throat. "If there is any reason, anything at all that comes to your mind, why you might prefer not to take this assignment, please tell me know. I'll respect you much more for declining than for attempting something you might not be ready to do."

Helen bounded to her feet. "I'm fine, ma'am. And I don't even need anyone with me, I promise. I could handle that whole trip by myself."

"PFC Toomer will be gathering information about upkeep and maintenance for these new tires while you handle the loading and secure the cargo. There's plenty of work to go around, I assure you."

Helen nodded, relaxing a little. Maybe this wasn't about Rains not trusting her yet. She appreciated the way the lieutenant explained things to her, even when she didn't have to. That Yarborough bitch would have just told her to shut up and get in the damn truck. "I'll hold up my end of it, ma'am. You can count on that."

Rains nodded. "Get some sleep tonight, Private Tucker. You'll have a couple of long days ahead, but then I'll make sure you get some downtime."

Helen couldn't wait to tell Tee, and when she did, Tee gave her a big hug, her first physical display of affection since the black market scam. Helen couldn't help the low moan that rose in her throat at the close press of Tee's body and she whispered, "I've missed this part of you. I've missed this part of us."

"I've missed it, too," Tee whispered back without letting go. "Maybe when you get back, we could—"

Jo Archer walked by on her way to the bathroom. "Hey, get a room, you two."

They broke apart, Tee blushing. Helen followed Jo into the bathroom, chattering on about her upcoming trip.

Tee helped her pack after dinner, but Helen was still too keyed up to sleep. She wrote a note for Reverend Culberson, explaining why she would have to miss their next appointment. It was a chilly night and Tee was sniffling a bit so Helen told her to stay behind, promising she'd only deliver the note and be right back. After slipping the note under the reverend's door, she sat on the very first pew for a moment, something she'd never done before. She looked around at the various stands and tables for the preacher, wondering if she'd ever understand all of it. There was still something scary to her about the big cross hanging from the front but she shook off the distractions and said what she'd come there to say. "This is Helen Tucker, but I guess you know that. And I guess you know I'm not all in on this yet, so I probably got no right to ask, but I'd appreciate it if you'd help me not fu—uh, mess up this trip tomorrow. Okay, thanks."

She gave it the moment of silence that the reverend always did, not really expecting an answer or anything, but just in case. Nothing happened, but she still felt pretty good about being there. Reverend Culberson had said she could pray any way that felt right to her, so that was her second prayer of all time. She gave the stained glass image of Moses a little salute on her way out.

In spite of the cold, she decided to take the long way back to the barracks, just to work off the rest of her excitement. Making her way briskly along the deserted track, she thought she smelled a whiff of smoke on the air, and then a male voice whispered, "Hey, Tucker."

Her heart sank and she looked around slowly. The dim glow of a cigarette moved up and back over near the stands. She thought about pretending she couldn't see him but decided that might not be the best course. Casually looking around to confirm they were alone, she walked to the bleachers. "Hey, Newton. I thought you were—"

"In jail?" He snorted.

"I heard AWOL," she finished.

"I like to think of it as mailing my resignation in from elsewhere. Though not too far, as you can see." He took a drag of his smoke. "You sure came out smelling like a rose, though, after turning on your friends."

Friends? Helen gave a short laugh. "Just because I didn't get mustered out doesn't mean my life is all hearts and sunshine. I'm on the strictest probation there is, with Lieutenant Rains watching my every move like a hawk."

"But she won't be watching you tomorrow or the next day, now will she?" Newton asked, and Helen pulled her coat closer, trying to hide the involuntary shiver that passed through her.

"What do you want, Newton?"

He pulled a bill out of his pocket and handed it to her. Flicking his lighter, he cupped it with his hands against the wind and held it up close so she could see the numbers. Fifty dollars. He snapped the lighter shut. "All yours for a little share of that new rubber you're picking up tomorrow."

Helen rubbed the bill between her fingers for a few seconds, letting her imagination bring up images of all it could buy. How would they do it? Fixing the invoice was out of the question since Rains had put in her new system. She sniffed, holding the bill out to him. "I can't do it, Newton. For one thing, there'll be someone else with me, a real straight arrow."

He pushed it back toward her. "Let us worry about that. People have accidents all the time. We'll make it look good."

Was he talking about the truck? Or PFC Toomer? Either way, it wasn't going to happen. "No thanks, Newton. I'm off the payroll, okay?"

"You always were a tough customer." He pulled out another bill and pressed it into her hand. She closed her eyes, not wanting to see what it was. "Now think about this, Tucker. Anything happens on this trip, or any other in the next ten years, who you think is going to take the fall? You. So you might as well get the dough for it. I could make you the richest private on the base."

She thought about how it felt to have the reverend working with her to be a better person and about Lieutenant Rains trusting her to make this trip. She thought about Tee and the promises of the future that might be ahead for them. She put the money against his chest to make sure it wouldn't blow away once she let go of it. "I'm already the richest private on the base."

He grabbed her wrist with his free hand and leaned toward her. The rank smell of old smoke on his breath made her glad she hadn't taken up the habit. "Suit yourself. But don't you even think about mentioning this little meeting, you hear? I don't want any law enforcement types coming by unannounced."

Helen jerked her arm free, her temper flaring. "If you don't want any company, then you'd better get off this base. In fact, you'd better get out of this town, Newton. I got nothin' to lose by bringing you down, just to make sure I don't get blamed for something I didn't have no part of. And you know I can do it, too." She pushed his hand that held the cigarette into his body and he jumped back, cursing and flailing at the burning embers. She ran, but not toward the barracks. She ran toward the motor pool, uttering the third prayer of her life that Lieutenant Rains would still be there.

She wasn't, but Sharon, her assistant, was just putting on her coat, keys jingling in her hand.

"I got to talk to the lieutenant," Helen panted. "It's real, real important. Do you know how to reach her?"

Sharon took one look at her and sat back down, gesturing toward the chair beside her desk. "You're lucky you caught me," she said, reaching for the phone. "I have a dentist appointment in the morning so I was just finishing up some things for tomorrow."

Helen nodded and tried to get her breathing under control while Sharon dialed. She was too nervous to sit. "Hello, this is Sharon West at the motor pool. May I speak to Lieutenant Rains, please?"

She held up a finger to Helen, but it wasn't even a minute before she spoke again.

"Lieutenant, I'm sorry to bother you but I have Helen Tucker here, and she says she must speak to you on an urgent matter." She listened for just a few seconds before holding the phone out to Helen. "Go ahead."

"I need to tell you something about that trip," Helen blurted out.

"Do you need me to come there or can you tell me on the phone?" Rains asked. Something about her low, steady voice made Helen feel like crying with relief.

"Could you—could you—" She couldn't seem to finish.

"Have Sharon make you some coffee or get you some water, Private. I'll be right there."

Helen sagged into the chair as she handed back the phone. "Thank you," she managed.

"What would you like?" Sharon asked, walking over to the coffeemaker.

How about a hundred dollars? was the answer that popped into Helen's brain, but she scrubbed her hands over her face, wiping away that thought. "Water, please."

CHAPTER FOURTEEN

Tee didn't think she'd ever been prouder. Two more members of the black market ring on base had been caught and two more were being hunted, all due to Helen's diligence in reporting the attempted bribe. Helen tried to act modest about it, but she had that little swagger back in her walk and that confident tone in her voice that Tee had always found so appealing. Lieutenant Rains had postponed the overnight trip to Louisville pending a final wrap-up of the case. The local police were called in, since all the remaining suspects were civilians, and once Helen finished with her testimony she had the rest of the day off. When she dropped by the PX unexpectedly, Tee's heart jumped and she had to force her thoughts away from returning to her old fantasy about Helen bringing a delivery to her store. Preening slightly while several of the girls who happened to be shopping gathered around her, Helen's eyes still sought out Tee's. All the feelings Tee had tamped down about the softness of Helen's lips and the way Helen's hands seemed to heat up her skin reappeared, as a surge of desire traveled from her heart to her stomach and then lower. By the time Helen made her way over, Tee knew she would need to go change her panties. Perhaps she could take her lunch now and Helen could walk back with her.

"Hey," Helen said softly. Her grin was devastating.

"Hey, yourself," Tee answered, looking down to close her inventory book. When she looked back, Helen was looking at her with such intensity her lips parted. When Helen wet her lips, Tee's mind supplied several quick images of Helen using that tongue up the side of her neck and flicking it around her earlobe before gently entering her mouth. She swayed slightly and Helen reached out a hand, her expression troubled.

"Are you okay?"

Tee gathered herself enough to look around for Major Edley. He was already looking their way, and Tee saw him start to move toward them. She took in a deep breath. "I think the major is on his way over here. If I can get lunch a little early, can you walk me home?"

"Home?" Helen grinned again. "You mean our multiple occupancy Sheraton Hotel?"

Helen could always make her laugh, even when she was in the middle of a heavy petting vision.

After watching Helen make nice with the major for much too long, Tee finally got permission to leave for her break. Once they were alone outside, she bumped Helen's shoulder. "I might get tired of sharing you pretty quick. Once your glory fades, do you think you'll be satisfied with just me?"

Helen cocked her head and looked around as if thinking, saying nothing. Tee knocked into her again and then they traded mock collisions all the way to the barracks. Helen held the door open and then tracked close on Tee's heels to their bunks, confirming as she went that no one else was around. "One, you'll never have to share me," she said, watching Tee rummage for a few seconds in her footlocker. "And two"—she turned Tee to face her—"I know I could be more than satisfied if you'd just say you'll be my girl."

"Helen, I—" Tee began, but then Helen's hands cupped her face and her mouth was on Tee's and it felt so good that she let her coat drop to the ground just so she could get a little closer. Helen let go long enough to take her coat off, too, and in that time Tee had unbuttoned her own jacket and she guided Helen's hands to her waist. She wrapped her arms around Helen's shoulders, thinking how much she would like to lie beside her with both of them naked. The possibility made her breathing hitch. She pulled away abruptly, and before Helen could protest, she took off both their hats and threw them on the beds. Pulling Helen toward the lavatory, she insisted, "Come here," and Helen obeyed without a word. Once inside, she pushed Helen against the smooth tile wall, shifting enough that her leg was between Helen's. She reached around Helen's body, letting her hands press down until they cupped her firm bottom. She pulled slightly and Helen grunted at the friction, and Tee wanted nothing more than to hear her make that sound over and over again. She leaned in and bit Helen's neck lightly, breaking off to gasp when Helen's hand trailed up the inside of her leg, climbing slowly toward the wetness that was flowing again.

The barracks door banged shut and they broke apart, breathing hard. "I need those new panties," Tee murmured, turning toward a stall. "Can you bring them to me?"

Helen nodded mutely, her eyes still heavy with desire. Waving casually to the girls who'd come in, she found Tee's underwear and got a pair of her own for good measure. After they both returned to their bunks, Tee ran her hand quickly across Helen's hair, smoothing the few strands that seemed to have a mind of their own. "I don't want to just say I'll be your girl," she whispered while they put on their hats and coats. "I want to really *be* your girl. I want to be with you. Can you make that happen for us?"

"Yes." Helen's whisper was hoarse. "God, yes. I mean, gosh, yes, Tee."

Tee smiled. "Good."

Rain woke up first as she usually did, but when she tried to slip out of Bett's grasp to take her shower, Bett murmured, "No," and pulled her closer. Rain sighed contentedly and fell back asleep. Forty-five minutes later, Bett's alarm jolted them both. Bett had to lean across Rain to reach the clock, and each time she cursed as she fumbled for the button to turn off the sound, Rain would tickle her just a little until Bett was laughing and slapping ineffectively at Rain's hands while the alarm buzzed on.

Finally she was able to make the noise stop and Bett fell panting back onto Rain's chest. "Well, I'm awake now, thank you very much."

"My pleasure," Rain said, breathing the soft fragrance of Bett's hair.

"No, I'm quite certain that's my line this morning," Bett answered, pulling Rain over so they were facing each other. She was earnest as she stroked Rain's hair and said, "Tell me how you know what I want when I don't even know it. Tell me how you find these feelings in me."

Rain kissed her as if they were in the midst of making love, making Bett almost breathless again when she said softly, "There are a thousand and one trails on your body, my beloved, and I intend to walk them all."

Bett pulled Rain as close as she could, tucking her head under Rain's chin, and asked, "Which one are we on now?"

"Six," Rain answered but Bett could feel her smile. She knew the phrase *a thousand and one* was her way of saying too many to count, and Rain was humoring her linear mind with a literal answer.

"Will you walk some of them more than once?"

"Most certainly. And I expect to lose count and have to start over many times."

"How many times?"

"At least a thousand and one times."

Suddenly, Bett couldn't play anymore. "Rain, I love you so much that I—I don't even know how to tell you."

She felt Rain nod and her arms tightened. "I know. I've searched my thoughts for the way to say what is in my heart. The first time I ever said I love you, it was to you, but I feel so far beyond that now that I…" Rain ran out of words and they simply held each other for a while, breathing and being together. After a time, Rain said, "I've never asked this of anyone before, but I want you to come with me to South Dakota and meet my people. I want you to know my family and I want them to know who you are and what you are to me."

Bett blinked against a prick of tears. She knew this request wasn't just an offer of a vacation. Rain's family was incredibly important to her, and she knew she should feel honored. But instead, she felt a rush of dismay driven by her conscience. She tried for an easy out. "Oh, Rain. You're so sweet to ask, but don't you think it's a little too soon?"

Rain shifted so she could look into Bett's eyes. "It may seem that way by the measurement of the calendar, but in my heart I've known you forever. I wanted to ask you yesterday and I have thought it other times, too." She touched Bett's face. "You needn't be nervous, Beloved, because it won't be your appearance that matters. They will see only your goodness, your faithfulness, your virtue."

Rain was saying something else, but Bett had closed her eyes and stopped listening. Her lover thought her reluctance was about being White. She had no idea that all of those qualities she'd named were tainted by the falsehood she'd let live between them all this time.

Rain seemed to be waiting on her response. Just saying no would be much too harsh, and she didn't want Rain to be hurt by— She stopped, mocking her own unfinished thought. Wasn't she really trying to spare *herself* the pain?

Rain tried again. "Bett, I am only asking you to think about—"

Bett cut her off. "I know, Rain, but I can't—I can't think about this right now. We're terribly late and there's too much else…too much else we need to talk about first." Bett, who never got up first, kissed Rain fleetingly on the lips and was in the shower in a blink. There, her tears mixed with the water and washed away. Rain was gone when Bett got out.

❖

Dinner had been a very quiet affair, so afterward, when they sat in front of the fire, Bett tried to close the distance she could see in Rain's eyes.

"I know we need to talk about this morning, Rain, but I need to ask you first about a trip I need to take," she began. "It'll be Christmas soon and we should have a few days off. I was thinking we could go to New York. You've never been, I know, and it's lovely at Christmastime. I think you'd enjoy the sights."

"I think New York is a very big city," Rain said after staring into the fire for a while, her tone almost as formal as it had been in basic training. "I'm not sure I would like it."

"I understand," Bett agreed, "but there's another matter. My mother lives in New York and I usually see her for the holiday."

"Your mother lives in New York?" Rain asked, looking directly at Bett for the first time that night. "She doesn't live with your father in Los Angeles?"

Bett laughed a bit. "No, Rain. My mother and father are divorced. Have been for years. Since I was four. I thought you might be aware of that since you've seen my records."

"Your father is listed as your first contact," Rain answered. "Besides that, there is only limited family information in your file. Explain to me about your mother."

"Well, my mother was my father's second wife. Donald is actually my half brother. My father divorced his mother to marry my mother.

Kenneth and I are her children and then my father had Gena, who is technically my half sister, with his third wife, whom he has also since divorced. Apparently the fourth Mrs. Carlton has no interest in children, and since my father never had much interest in the children he already has, that seems to be fine with him." Rain appeared shocked. "What?" Bett said finally, a little angrily. "That's not how they do it on the reservation?" Rain looked away at that, and Bett was instantly sorry. She put her hand on Rain's back. "I apologize, Rain. That was completely uncalled for. As you can tell, I'm really rather embarrassed by my convoluted family tree. I just thought you already knew." She took a breath. "My mother and I don't really get along all that well, but I guess I just want you to meet her."

Rain said nothing for a time, obviously considering what Bett had put before her. When she turned back and settled, her voice was serious. "It would be my privilege to meet your mother, Bett. And so yes, we must go to New York. You will have to be my guide."

Bett took Rain's hand. "Thank you, Rain. I know you are doing this for me. But New York really is a wonderful city. We'll talk about all the things we can do."

Rain nodded. "All right. But first, tell me about your mother. What kind of person is she?"

Bett bit her lip as she tried to imagine how to explain Ann Davenport Carlton to Gale Rains. "My mother has always been a person of wealth and she has very little idea of the lives of those who must do without. And that is the way she wants her world to be. She was very hurt by the divorce, so since I've been an adult, the one thing we have most in common is not being very fond of my father. She's a very gracious hostess, so there will be at least one big party while we are there. She loves the arts and theater, and gives money and time to those activities. She will want to take me shopping for new outfits." Pausing, Bett reflected, "She doesn't have any idea who I really am, Rain, and she doesn't want to know. She is much happier with the daughter that she has made up as opposed to the actual one. That's why I usually only see her two or three times a year. That way we can both maintain our separate realities."

Rain was looking into the fire again. "Are you trying to shock her into seeing the real you by taking me?"

Bett knew better by now than to underestimate Rain's perception of people's motives, including hers.

"That's a fair question, and my most honest answer is maybe. But the main reason I want you to go is because I'm not sure I could manage being without you for that long. Even though we won't be able to sleep together at my mother's house, at least I'll be able to see you every day and hear your voice."

"We won't be sleeping together?" Rain asked, with such an injured expression that Bett laughed in spite of herself.

"My mother's apartment has five bedrooms. Knowing her, she'll put us as far apart as possible."

"I'll bet she has no idea how quietly I can move. Especially at night."

"Hmm," Bett replied, smiling.

After many phone calls and conversations about schedules, Bett and her mother decided on dates for the New York trip. During the planning of the five-day visit, Bett had to remind her mother three times that she would be bringing a friend who would be staying there as well.

"I just don't understand why you're not bringing Phillip, darling," Ann Carlton kept saying.

Each time she answered in a tone that she hoped would end any further discussion of the topic. "Because he's in England, Mother." She'd looked casually over her shoulder each time, but Rain always gave her privacy by leaving the room while she was on the phone.

Rain's reaction to the packed schedule that they'd set out was not as dramatic as her reaction to the news they would be flying.

"Why can't we take the train?" she asked, looking anxiously skyward.

"Because it takes too long. We can't make it there and back in time by train." Bett knew Rain was nervous enough about meeting her mother. "Are you afraid of flying, Beloved?"

"I don't know," Rain mumbled. "I've never done it."

"You might actually like it, you know."

"Hmm."

❖

Things continued to go well for Bett at work. She had established a good rapport with her colleagues as well as with Luna. She was happy to send him the news that he had been promoted to captain. Bett knew she was in line for another promotion also. She wondered how Rain would feel if they ever were the same rank, then decided she wasn't going to distract Rain with anything else until the visit to New York was over.

As she drove to work one morning during the next week, the car began to make grinding sounds. Rain had already left, of course, so Bett decided to take the car directly to the motor pool and see if it could be fixed, or if Rains would give her a ride to work. She was greeted pleasantly by a dark-haired young private in coveralls who took her name and the information about the car.

"Do you think it will take long?" Bett asked.

"Hard to say until we get her up on the rack," the young woman answered. *I guess everything in here is female.* Bett smiled to herself.

"Is Lieutenant Rains here?" Bett asked. "She was my drill instructor and I thought I might say hello."

"I think she's gone over to the mess hall again," the young woman replied slowly, giving Bett a second look. "You're welcome to wait in her office, I'm sure."

"Thanks, but I think I'll just go look for her there," Bett replied, wondering why Rains would be in the mess hall—again?—at this time of day.

As she stepped into the large dining area, Bett noticed three of the smaller rectangular tables had been pushed together to make one large table. Around the large table were several elaborate place settings. Bett recognized the same attractive redheaded captain she'd last seen shaking Rains's hand after the Thanksgiving luncheon. She couldn't quite recall the woman's name, but did take note that she was sitting very close to Rains, pointing at the flatware on the table. To Rains's left was Colonel Issacson, who was demonstrating the use of different pieces on the various plates and bowls. Not quite sure what was going on, Bett tried to back out the door. She didn't feel any of the jealousy of the captain that she had before, and she knew she didn't want to run into Issacson if she could avoid it. Bett had complete faith that Rains would tell her everything at home tonight.

"Bett?" she heard Rains's voice ask and then recover with, "Uh, Sergeant Smythe?" She looked back at the table where Rains was looking at her with a startled expression.

Bett had no choice but to come back into the room. "Yes, Lieutenant Rains. I had to bring my car in to the motor pool today and they told me I'd find you here. I just wanted to say hello, but I don't mean to interrupt."

"Come on over, Sergeant," Issacson said coolly. "I'm sure you can help us with some of our flatware issues. Captain Hartley has been most helpful, but Lieutenant Rains and I seem to be stuck on the difference between the shrimp fork and the crab fork."

Captain Hartley smiled, pointing. "Actually, that's the ice cream fork."

As stunned as Rains was to see Bett, she turned back to Captain Hartley looking even more surprised. "They use a fork for ice cream?"

"In point of fact, it's for sorbet," Bett said, taking a step toward them. "To cleanse the palate between courses."

"Very good, Sergeant." Hartley nodded.

"I'm sure Sergeant Smythe has been to at least as many of these dinners as you have, Captain Hartley," Issacson said, with the merest hint of a slight in her tone.

"Wonderful! Please join us." Hartley beamed. Bett walked over reluctantly.

Issacson stood. "You can have my spot, Sergeant." Bett saluted. "I'll leave Lieutenant Rains in your capable hands." She looked hard at Bett as she returned the salute briefly and turned to go.

"Colonel, I can't thank you enough for—" Rains stood also, but Issacson waved her off.

"Let me know how it goes, Lieutenant."

"Yes, ma'am." Rains saluted.

Bett sat. She could see Rains was sweating a bit, which was unusual, especially in late November. "What are you doing with all this, Lieutenant?"

"Practicing."

"Practicing what?"

Rains didn't answer, so Captain Hartley replied for her. "Over Christmas, Lieutenant Rains is going to a formal dinner with her potential in-laws in New York City. We were talking as her fine staff was working on my car the other day, and I realized her skills in this area might need a little brushing up, so I arranged this little demonstration."

Bett could see that Rains's ears were deep red and a flush was on her neck. "Dinner with your potential in-laws?" Bett repeated. "How delightful!"

Rains didn't look at her.

"When I was a little girl, someone told me to start from the outside and work your way in. That's not always correct, but it's a good beginning," Bett said. Hartley was nodding. "Of course, you can always just watch what other people do. Especially if your intended will be there."

Rains had been staring at her plate but a small smile made its way across her face. Then she looked at Bett a little desperately. "But why do they use a fork for ice cream? Doesn't it drip through the little spaces?"

Bett and Captain Hartley both laughed.

After about twenty minutes of flatware work, the dark-haired private from the motor pool came in to talk to Rains. She got up eagerly and went outside. Captain Hartley began to gather up the silver, saying, "I think our student is finished for today, don't you, Sergeant?"

Bett nodded and began helping. "Yes, I'd say her head is about to explode as it is."

Hartley stopped and looked at Bett. "How well do you know the lieutenant, Sergeant Smythe? She clearly has no experience with any kind of formal dining."

"Well, she was my sergeant in basic and I was her squad leader. We got along fairly well in that capacity." Bett smiled, answering casually. "I've seen her several times since then, at various events. I would say she has a few good friends on the base, and I count myself as one." Hartley nodded, studying her closely. Bett went on. "I do know that Lieutenant Rains is Sioux—Lakota. I don't think our version of fine dining is a part of their culture."

"Ah, I thought there was something..." Hartley said, looking out the door where Rains was still talking to the dark-haired private. "I was also a little surprised to hear of her engagement," the captain went on, almost matter-of-factly. She looked back at Bett. "I really didn't think she was the marrying kind."

Bett tried not to react. Hartley's tone had been completely nonthreatening, but Bett knew she was on very dangerous ground. "What makes you say that, Captain?"

Hartley's green eyes assessed Bett frankly for a moment. She looked back to Rains, and seemed to make a decision. "Because I'm not the marrying kind myself, Sergeant. And based on the way Lieutenant Rains said your name when you first came in and the way she smiled when you sat down, I'd guess you're not either."

Bett cleared her throat. "You're a very keen observer, Captain," she said neutrally.

"I think you learn to be, don't you?" Hartley responded. "And please, call me Kathleen," she added, offering her hand. "I know I've seen you before. Your name is Beth?"

"Bett," she corrected, returning the handshake. She noted that Kathleen looked a little anxious at how little she had said, so she added an affirming nod. "It's very nice to meet you, too, Kathleen."

Hartley looked relieved. "I was thinking that the lieutenant could benefit from some real-life practice," she suggested. "In two weeks my...roommate and I are having a pre-Christmas dinner with four other women we know. Perhaps you could both attend?"

"What a lovely invitation!" Bett said sincerely. "But I'll have to talk to Lieutenant Rains. I don't know how she'll feel about this."

"It won't be all Army," Kathleen said, pulling a small pad from her jacket pocket. "Most, but not all. I don't know if that helps. No uniforms, though. We do like to dress up a bit."

Bett smiled. "That's another area where the lieutenant needs practice."

Rains was laughing with the motor pool private and gesturing toward the mess hall table. Bett could see she was pantomiming eating dripping ice cream with a fork. Hartley began laughing again and Bett joined in.

"We'd love to have you join us," she said to Bett, writing on a piece of paper. "Here's my phone number and address. Call me after you speak to the lieutenant. But may I ask one question?" Bett nodded. "Who is this Jesse she's supposedly engaged to?"

Bett took a deep breath and shook her head. The underlying significance of their conversation had been clear to both of them, even though nothing explicit had been said. She was about to take a revealing and potentially treacherous step. She studied Kathleen Hartley again for a few seconds and decided she liked what she saw. "There's no Jesse. Well, not like that. It's my mother we're going to see in New York."

"Perfect!" Hartley smiled broadly as she squeezed Bett's arm reassuringly. "I really hope you'll both come."

Rains came back into the room and saw them putting away the silverware. "Are we finished?"

"Yes, for now," Hartley answered. "Your sergeant and I hope to have another practice for you soon."

Rains grinned at Bett and then caught herself, sobering. "Uh, your car is ready, Sergeant."

Bett smiled back and said warmly, "That's wonderful news, Lieutenant."

Rains didn't quite know what to make of this tone, and her eyes slid toward Captain Hartley, who was packing up the plates. "May I help you carry that back to your car, Captain?" she asked.

"Yes, let me help, too," Bett said and they each picked up a box. Kathleen Hartley led them to a red Alfa Romeo sports car.

Rains's mouth was open. "This is your car? This is not the one you brought into the motor pool before."

Hartley smiled. "Actually, that car was my roommate's but she didn't have time to bring it in, so I took care of it for her. This one is not GI, obviously. Nor particularly patriotic at this time, since it is Italian. But I trust you can keep a secret, Lieutenant?"

Still admiring the magnificent lines of the Alfa, it took Rain a few seconds to process what Hartley had said. "Oh yes, ma'am." She saluted and almost dropped the plates.

"Come on, Lieutenant," Bett said a bit possessively after they secured the china boxes. "Let's go pick up my fabulous Jeep."

Hartley nodded at Bett. "That Jeep will be a classic someday. Mark my words."

"We'll be in touch, Captain," Bett replied, tugging Rains's arm to get her moving away from the car.

"Yes, uh, thank you again, Captain," Rains said, recovering slightly as she looked curiously at Bett.

Bett pulled Rains toward the motor pool, standing unusually close so they could talk in lower tones.

"Have I told you lately how wonderful I think you are?" Bett asked as they made their way across the base, her voice as affectionate as she dared make it.

"I don't feel very wonderful," Rains said, sounding unusually grouchy. "I feel stupid."

Bett knew this wasn't good. "Rains! Don't even say that. Whatever could you feel stupid about?"

Rains stopped walking and gestured at Bett, her voice rising uncharacteristically. "Eating, of all things. I feel stupid about eating at a big fancy dinner with so many forks and spoons and knives that I can't even guess what to do with them. Eating food I never heard of and can't guess what it is. *Sorbet?*" She snorted, drawing out the word. "I wouldn't have known. Why can't they just say ice cream?" Bett knew this was not the time to explain the distinction between the two frozen items. A major passed them on the sidewalk. They all saluted, and when Rains turned back to Bett, she had taken a deep breath and her voice was almost back to normal. "That's why I have to practice eating, so I won't embarrass myself in front of your mother."

She's really doing this for me, Bett thought, and she wished she could put her arms around Rains right there. She settled for putting her hand on Rains's arm and looking up into her eyes, her voice tender. "Please don't worry. You could eat your entire dinner with your brother's knife and I would still love you."

A corner of Rains's mouth lifted as she breathed out a chuckle, but then Bett saw her glancing at the back of the major who had passed them. Giving Rains's arm just the slightest caress before she let go, she added, "Anyway, I want you to hurry home tonight. I have some exciting news, but it will have to wait until we can talk privately."

"It could be a trap," Rain said firmly, once they were at home, finishing dinner at their little table. Bett had told her about Captain Hartley's invitation, but Rain's reaction wasn't what she was hoping for. "We shouldn't go."

"Rain, why do you say that?" Bett argued. "You like Captain Hartley. Isn't it possible that this is exactly what it seems—a wonderful opportunity to meet some other women like us? To make some friends here?"

"It's too big a risk," Rain insisted. "Besides, we don't need friends. We have each other."

Bett knew this was a sticking point between them. Rain was used to a very solitary life, while she was accustomed to having lots of people around for conversation and entertainment. She came over and sat sideways on Rain's lap, turning to face her.

"But that's just it, Beloved. I don't have anyone to talk to about how wonderful you are. Wouldn't it be nice to be able to share what we have with some other people who feel the same way about each other?"

"Hmm?" Rain was distracted by the nearness of Bett's breasts straining at the fabric of her blouse.

"Couldn't we go and not say anything incriminating? Just see what it's like?" When Bett undid one button on Rain's shirt and kissed where the closure had been, Rain was dimly aware of being manipulated but it didn't matter.

After two more buttons and several more long, deep kisses, Rain stifled a groan and shifted until Bett was straddling her. "If I say no, will you stop doing this?" She stroked up Bett's sides and onto her chest.

"Of course not," Bett murmured.

"Good," Rain said, almost holding her breath as she unbuttoned Bett's blouse, revealing inch by inch of Bett's perfect breasts. She was convinced there wasn't anything lovelier in the world. "Then no."

"But, Rain..." Bett objected, pulling away. Rain let accusation show in her expression until Bett relented. "All right," she said, kissing her hastily. Bett helped with the last buttons, a knowing gleam in her eye. "It would be such good practice for our trip to New York." She kissed from Rain's ear down her neck as she spoke. "Meeting new people. Wearing new clothes. Eating a fancy dinner."

"All things I don't enjoy." Rain reached under Bett's blouse and unclasped her bra. "As opposed to—"

Bett took off both garments, and Rain couldn't finish. Never willing to turn away from Bett's full, firm breasts, Rain spread her legs wider, opening Bett more as well. She put her hand onto the seat under Bett, turning it so Bett's center met the flesh where Rain's thumb joined to her wrist.

"Oh God, Rain," Bett gasped, rocking against her.

Rain sucked Bett's erect nipple, supporting her as she leaned back, offering easier access. Rain bit lightly as wetness flowed through the soft pants Bett was wearing. "Is this all right?"

Bett groaned. "Yes." She flexed her legs, pushing herself against Rain's hand, controlling the pressure, the speed of her thrusts, getting exactly what she wanted—just as she always did in Rain's arms. Almost dizzy as the pleasure built inside, she eased up. "I mean no." It was going to be over too quickly. "I mean, if you don't stop"—Bett panted—"I'm going to—"

"Going to what, Beloved?" Rain's eyes were teasing and her momentary restraint vanished.

She pushed against Rain's hand again. "I'm going to come...oh God...right here on this chair."

"Good." Rain kissed her earlobe softly. "I want you to come for me."

Rain's words made her quicken, her need urgent, her swollen flesh demanding release.

"Give yourself to me now, Bett. Let me have you. Let me keep you."

Her lover's voice was warm and low. Rain had never before talked like this during sex, and Bett grew impossibly wetter. *Oh yes.* Her heart pounded as she reached for her release, trembling and panting with the need pounding inside her. Rain sucked on her breast again, pushing the climax deep inside her.

She bowed, shuddering with pleasure, moaning as she spasmed, safe in Rain's embrace. Rain shifted Bett's body onto her thigh, rocking her slowly. No one had ever satisfied her this way, or ever loved her so well.

"I love your mouth." Bett kissed Rain intently. "I love your hands." She kissed each one. "I love your body."

Stroking Rain's breasts, Bett lowered herself to the floor. She knelt, pulling Rain's hips to the edge of the chair. She slowly unzipped Rain's pants, then slid them off in one motion. Bett breathed her in. So good. So sweet. All hers.

She lowered her mouth, tasting the sweetness of Rain's scent and the essence of her arousal. Rain groaned at the first touch of lips. Her thighs spread wider and Bett licked her way deeper, caressing Rain's taut belly and across her breasts again.

Rain strained toward her as Bett found the place that made Rain's hips jerk. Rocking in pace with each stroke of her tongue, Rain whimpered, a sound so full of desire that Bett wanted to hear it over and over. The sound that meant *there*. The sound that meant *more*. The sound that meant *now*.

❖

"Okay," Rain said later as they were lying next to each other on the kitchen floor. "We can go."

It took Bett several seconds to realize she was talking about the dinner. "You know I stopped caring about that an hour ago."

"Yes," Rain teased. "That's why I'm agreeing." Then she rolled onto her side to look at Bett, her eyes warm. "But mostly, I just want to make you happy."

"It will make me very happy if you tell me that we're not actually going to sleep here tonight."

Rain got to her feet and helped Bett up. Then she slung Bett over her shoulder and started walking toward the bedroom.

"Rain, stop! You're going to hurt your back or something," Bett protested, but she was laughing, too, so Rain didn't stop. She bounced Bett onto the bed and jumped in beside her.

"Rain, I am happy," Bett said, suddenly serious. "I'm so happy it scares me sometimes. And if we go to that dinner and one of those ladies looks at you a little too long, I'll have you out of there so fast it will make your head spin. You are mine, Wind and Rain, until the end of our days."

Rain brushed some hair away from Bett's face. "On Thanksgiving, after you left and I was talking with Tee and Helen," Rain said, "they were talking about how beautiful you are. Like a model or a movie star, they said. And all I could think was, *You don't know the half of it.* Because they have no idea how beautiful you are inside. It is that beauty which illuminates you, makes everyone look at you the moment you enter a room. That is what I will always see in you, so I will never lose it or ever have to give it up." Bett smiled. "So it is with me, too. What you know of me will always be yours. And what you know of me is yours alone, Beloved."

Bett pulled her close. "It is really okay to go, Rain?"

Rain sighed. "You spoke with Captain Hartley, so you have a better sense of this. Think again of what she said to you and search your heart when you hear her words. How does it feel to you? Use your intuition."

Bett thought. She had really been concentrating on her own responses at the time, and not taking into account how Hartley had sounded or what motive was behind her invitation. "I don't know, Rain. I'm not as good at this as you are. I felt like she was sincere, but...Why don't I call her and tell her no, and then see what she says."

"Why don't you call her and tell her we are still thinking about it, which is the truth. See if the conversation gives you a way to know who else will be there, which is something we do want to know. If this is, as you hope, a chance for us to make friends, then we don't want to start this friendship off with a lie."

Bett put her arms around Rain's neck. "You are the one with the beauty inside, Rain. Sometimes I feel humbled around you."

"Hmm." Rain sounded embarrassed.

Wanting Rain near, Bett led her to the phone and called the number Hartley had given her. A woman's voice answered brusquely, "Whitman."

Bett asked for Captain Hartley.

"Who's calling?" Whitman asked, still sounding very official.

"This is Bett Smythe. I was calling with regard to a dinner that Captain Hartley graciously invited me to yesterday."

"Oh yes, Sergeant Smythe." Whitman's voice became much warmer. "Just a moment."

Kathleen Hartley came on in a matter of seconds. "Bett, I'm so glad you called. I hope you're accepting."

"Well, we would like to but we had a question about the other participants," Bett said awkwardly.

"Yes?" Hartley waited.

Giving nothing away, Bett noted. An idea came to her. "None of them stutter, do they?"

"Excuse me?" Hartley sounded puzzled.

"You see, there were two girls in my squad who...well, let me just say that Lieutenant Rains was put in a most uncomfortable position with them, and I know it wouldn't be a good situation for her to see them socially. One of them has a bit of a stammer."

"Ah, I see." Hartley sounded a little more at ease. "No, I don't believe anyone has that particular speech impediment." She paused. "Is Lieutenant Rains there?"

"Yes," Bett said, surprised.

"May I speak with her?" Hartley asked.

Bett put Rain on the phone after quickly explaining the conversation to that point.

"Hello?" Rain asked, sounding the slightest bit awkward.

"Lieutenant, I just wanted to try and ease your mind about coming over for dinner. I know you might feel uncertain because I was speaking only with Bett when I made this invitation, but you might recall that I asked you to the house once before, and I made that offer just to you."

"After the big moon," Rain said, remembering.

"Yes, that's right." There was a smile in Hartley's tone. "I just want you to know this will be a gathering of like-minded couples I think you'll enjoy meeting. I know they'll enjoy meeting you." Rain said nothing. After a few seconds Hartley's voice strengthened. "You have nothing to fear from me, Lieutenant Rains. You have my word as an officer."

"Thank you, Captain Hartley," Rain said and handed the phone back to Bett. She nodded.

Bett confirmed the time and Kathleen gave her some more specific directions. Bett asked if there was anything they could bring.

"Wine?" Hartley suggested.

"Of course, but I should probably tell you Lieutenant Rains doesn't drink," Bett said.

"Then we should probably practice having her decline, just so she gets to feel comfortable with doing it in public," Hartley observed. "And am I right that her first name is Gail?"

Bett spelled it. She could almost hear Hartley's mind working. "How very interesting. I'm so glad you are coming."

"We're looking forward to it," Bett said.

CHAPTER FIFTEEN

Tee was so nervous she thought she might faint, so she lowered herself into a chair. Even though the Fort Des Moines Hotel lobby was nearly empty on this Thursday afternoon, it took her a few minutes to accept that no one was paying any attention to her. Once she felt slightly more composed, she took some time to look around, having never been in such a grand building before. Dark wood walls over cool tile floors led to a wide marble staircase with a brass railing. The lighting gave off a warm glow that was absorbed by the gold-colored drapes. Many famous people had stayed here, Helen had told her, including former President Woodrow Wilson. Thinking of that reminded Tee of President Roosevelt's recent reelection to a fourth term in office. She supposed most Americans were comforted by hearing his familiar voice on the radio, as she was, even though the Italian campaign seemed to have stalled due to bad weather, and there were new reports of those terrible kamikaze attacks on ships in the Pacific. In a week, it would be the third anniversary of the bombing of Pearl Harbor. It was amazing to consider how that action had resulted in the whole nation becoming engaged in the fight in one way or another, including women being allowed in the service. And that had led to her becoming a soldier and meeting Helen. She swallowed, coming back to the realization that she was about to check into a hotel room with another woman and… *Stop*, she told herself. *You asked for this. You want this.* Helen was checking them in at the desk, and gestured briefly in her direction. Tee attempted to smile at the clerk, who simply pushed a card at Helen before turning to pull a key from the rack.

Tee had been angry when she realized that Helen had kept back twenty dollars from her bribe money, donating only forty to the Living Faith Bible Church. Still, Pastor Washington had assured her that amount was more than enough to get their piano repaired, and Mrs. Washington had hugged her so tightly she'd lost her air for a moment. She supposed it was her own fault for telling Helen at an earlier time that most folks tithed 10 percent of their income. When she'd given Helen a look that afternoon at the church while the Washingtons were getting them some tea, Helen had whispered that she had given way more than 10 percent, and she was going to use what remained on something special for both of them. Now, Tee thought, Helen was keeping her word.

Helen returned with the key and they picked up their suitcases, riding the elevator to the third floor without saying a word. Helen led them to their room like she'd done this a hundred times before, opening the door and gesturing Tee inside. "After you."

In her worst dreams, Tee had imagined some seedy place with stains on the walls and a dank, musty smell, with a shared bathroom down the hall. This was nothing like that. The room was bright and comfortable with a slightly sharp, pleasantly antiseptic scent, and the muted floral wallpaper looked unsoiled. A mirror topped the wooden chest of drawers on one wall, and there was a small writing desk and a comfortable-looking chair on the other. A door by the window presumably led to their private bathroom. Tee let her eyes move slowly to the double bed that took up most of the space. Helen came over and took her suitcase, propping it up on a holder that seemed made for that purpose. Then she stood beside Tee, not touching her.

"Is this okay, baby? I asked for the nicest room they had in our price range."

A little smile lifted Tee's lips. "We have a price range?"

Helen stroked her arm very lightly. "Well, I can't afford the presidential suite just now, but…"

Her voice sounded so full of regret that Tee turned to her. "That's all right," she said, letting her fingers trail down Helen's cheek. "I'm not the president just now anyway."

Helen grinned and leaned forward to give Tee a quick, sweet kiss. Then she pulled her toward the suitcase. "Get ready. I'm taking my girl out to dinner."

❖

Once she'd checked their schedules and made her plan, Helen had told Tee to bring a civilian outfit. Tee had only the dress she'd been wearing when she first came into the service, but for the first time in her memory, she'd wanted to look really, really nice. And since she'd been wearing nothing but her Army uniform for four months now, she wanted a very different look for their special occasion. When she tried on a deep blue dress with a V-neck that highlighted her bustline and a belted waist that emphasized the curve of her hips, she knew it was the one. Spending almost ten dollars on a new dress and close to eight more on some matching shoes felt totally extravagant, and she was sure she blushed when the clerk who totaled her purchases teased, "Looks like someone's got a hot date." But when she came out of the bathroom, Helen's expression as her gaze traveled over her made it all worthwhile.

Helen was wearing a woman's dress suit with a more mannish cut, and Tee knew without asking that it was new as well. The fabric was dark with a delicate pinstripe running through both the skirt and the longer jacket. Her black shoes were almost as severe as their Army shoes, but they went perfectly with the black shirt. Helen looked amazing, and for the first time in a long time, Tee almost stuttered when she said, "Wow. You look great."

"You, too, Tee. You look like a fairy-tale princess or a real-life duchess or something." Tee couldn't stop smiling as Helen offered her arm. "Come on, beautiful. I want to show off my girl to the rest of the world."

They had a wonderful dinner. The waitress wasn't busy, and soon she was laughing and teasing with them while she patiently explained some of their menu options. She didn't bat an eye when Helen mispronounced her order of veal scaloppini, and when Tee ordered the beef stew, she leaned in and said, "I wouldn't if I were you. It's at least two days old. But we just got the fish in today. Would you like to try that?"

"I've only had catfish," Tee said. "Is trout like that?"

"Pretty much in looks. It has a delicate flavor, though you do have to watch out for the bones. But if you like fish at all, I think you'll enjoy it."

Tee agreed to try it and Helen told the waitress, "Look, we're in no hurry. In real life we gotta rush through every meal, but not tonight. Okay?"

"I understand," the waitress said, giving Helen a wink. "And my name is Susan. Just wave if you need anything."

They ate and talked for two hours. When the waitress brought Helen a glass of port and Tee a crème de menthe at the end of the meal, Helen said, "We didn't order this."

"Compliments of the house," the waitress said. "I hope you enjoy your stay."

When Tee lifted the glass to sniff it, she wrinkled up her nose. "Is this alcohol?"

Helen didn't know for sure, but she scoffed. "It's green. No alcohol I know of is green like that."

Tee took a sip. "Oh, Helen." She breathed in. "This is delicious. It almost tastes like medicine, only so much better."

Helen laughed as she lifted her glass of port. "You realize that makes no sense, right?" She took a healthy swallow. "Oh, yeah." Her voice was a bit strangled and she put the glass down a little too hard. "That's gonna do it."

When their bill came, Helen wouldn't let Tee see it. "I want to chip in," Tee urged, but Helen only smiled and said, "Maybe next time." Studying the bill, she frowned, remembering something she'd meant to ask someone before now. She'd appreciated everything about the service but she knew nothing about tipping. In the end she decided if 10 percent was good enough for God the Almighty, it was good enough for Susan the waitress. When she told Tee this, Tee giggled all the way to the elevator.

But once they were back in the room, there was a moment of awkward silence. "Let's get comfortable," Helen said when it was obvious Tee wasn't going to speak. She let Tee change in the bathroom again and when Tee came out in her WAC pajamas, Helen grinned, gesturing at her own set. "Well, that's a familiar sight, at least."

Tee ducked her head a little. "I wanted to get something nicer, but I spent all my money on my dress and shoes."

"Maybe next time?" Helen suggested, moving a little closer. "I'd like to see you in one of those sheer nightgowns."

Helen was like a magnet, Tee decided, which must make her those iron filings they'd shown in that munitions class. She was attracted to Helen without really having any say in the matter, like it was her nature. She was trying to figure out a way to say that to Helen without making it sound overly scientific when something shifted in Helen's expression. Worried that Helen must be misreading her silence, she reached out her hand and Helen took it. Tee was about to tell her how good it felt when Helen said, "Let's sit on the bed for a minute and talk."

They both sat with their legs stretched out, propped up by pillows on the headboard behind them, Tee automatically taking the position on Helen's left, the way they were in the barracks. "There's something I need to tell you," Helen said, and before Tee could come up with something terrible, like *I've decided I don't want to do this with you*, Helen added, "It's about me. And about my family."

"Okay," Tee said, watching as Helen took in a deep breath.

"When I tell people my daddy was a miner and that he got killed, everybody thinks he died in some mine accident. But that wasn't the way it was."

Tee shifted slightly. She'd certainly thought that. Helen went on, talking fast like she wanted to get it all out about her mother committing adultery and her father being shot over it. Helen looked drained when she finished, her eyes dull and her skin paler than usual. Tee took her hand, rubbing her thumb lightly over the top of it. "Why did you want to tell me this now?"

"Because I've come to understand that some of what it takes to be a good person is to admit who you are, so you can see what you need to work on. And because you, Teresa Owens, deserve to know exactly who it is you've been mixed up with."

Tee thought she recognized some of Reverend Culberson's work here, although it was obvious Helen was taking it to heart and making it her own, the way she always did. She wondered if maybe she should tell Helen about Mr. Gallagher but pushed that thought aside, knowing she didn't want those memories in her head right now. Instead she feathered her fingers through Helen's hair and brushed lightly down her cheek. "There's something I need to tell you, too. Something I've been putting off saying for a couple of weeks."

Helen had been relaxing under her touch, but Tee felt her tighten up again and she looked away. "Okay," she said, in a tone that suggested she was bracing herself for the worst.

"I love you." When Helen turned back to her with her mouth open slightly, Tee went on. "It's probably been more than a couple of weeks, honestly, but I can't say exactly. I just know that once I had that feeling, I couldn't shake it. Not even after I prayed and prayed to God to take it away. Other sins I've committed—times I've willingly heard gossip or coveted a new dress that my sister got—I've always been able to see the error of my ways and been able to seek forgiveness. But this...I never seemed to be genuinely able to repent, even though there were passages in the Bible that said it was wrong. But that pastor's wife, Mrs. Washington? She told me to look for what Jesus said about it. She said to remember we're called Christians because we model our beliefs on Christ's teachings, and what he taught should be over any prophet or old law. So I looked. I reread all the Gospels. And do you know what Jesus said about people like us?" Helen shook her head. "He didn't say nothing. Not one thing. If this is so terrible"—Tee gestured between them—"why wouldn't he? He mostly talked about loving God and about taking care of your neighbor. So I figure if I can love you and still do those things, I'll be all right."

Helen bit her lip and Tee swallowed hard, trying not to worry that she might have seen tears in Helen's eyes. "In some ways, I can't understand why I'm here, in this place, with you. But the fact is I'm exactly where my heart wants me to be. And apparently the rest of me kinda follows along." She didn't want to mention she was almost aching for Helen to touch her, that she'd already imagined their WAC pajamas in a pile on the floor and their naked bodies rubbing together, creating that delicious need inside her. She knew her voice would be shaky, but she added, "I hope that's all right with you."

She wasn't prepared for Helen's quick move. In what seemed like less than a second, Helen was on her knees, straddling Tee's hips, arms around her shoulders, pulling her close to kiss her forehead, her hair, bending to kiss her neck. "Oh God, Tee," she said, pushing back to look into her eyes. "I love you, too. I think I've been in love with you since the first week of basic training." She squeezed her eyes tightly. "I meant to say *gosh*, Tee. I'm sorry. I'm really trying to break that habit."

Tee laughed, even as her heart swelled. She appreciated the things Helen had begun trying to change for her, for them. "There's just one more habit I want you to break right now."

"What? I'll do anything, Tee. I mean, I'll try really hard."

Tee pulled her back down, whispering against Helen's ear. "I want to try kissing you without any clothes on. I think we've been overly dressed for way too long."

When she looked into Helen's face, the worry had been replaced by the expression Tee had seen in the grove and at the house party. The wanting in her eyes immediately transferred itself to Tee's skin, heating her everywhere. While Helen's fingers loosened one button after the other, Tee caressed up the sides of Helen's shirt before realizing she could touch her under her clothing now. There would be no interruptions this time. The only thing that could stop what was happening between them was a word from her. *Wait*, she'd told Helen once before, and she had. There would be no more waiting now unless she let some fear stop her. But that little tingle of uncertainty vanished the moment her hands found Helen's tight breasts, their nipples already hard. Helen gasped when Tee squeezed lightly.

"Does that hurt?" Tee asked, lowering her hands. "I don't want to—"

"No," Helen urged, taking Tee's hands and pushing them back up. "It feels wonderful. You feel wonderful." She slid Tee's pajama shirt off Tee's shoulders, then fumbled hastily with her buttons.

"Helen." Tee's voice was huskier than usual and Helen stopped moving. "You don't have to rush," she said. "We have all night."

Helen hesitated for a second and then rolled off her, onto her side. "You're right, baby. I didn't mean to hurry y—" She cut off when Tee stood and pulled off the rest of her clothing, sliding quickly under the top sheet.

Grinning, Helen did the same. Tee turned toward her as she climbed under the light covering and for a moment, only their lips touched, sweet, soft kisses that gradually lengthened and deepened until they were holding tight to each other, both moaning quietly. Tee wanted to explore every inch of Helen's body, but she also wanted Helen to do something about the terrible pressure she felt in her stomach and especially between her legs. When Helen's mouth kissed down onto her breast, her body began to move of its own accord, and when Helen gently sucked her taut nipple between her lips, a wild urge made Tee cry out with a sound unlike anything she'd ever heard herself make before. Helen seemed to know what it meant, though, because she let her tongue swirl around before sucking a little harder, even as her hand moved between them and her fingers lightly brushed the hair between Tee's legs.

She kissed her way toward Tee's other breast as she murmured, "Can I touch you, baby? Can I touch you there?" Her fingers dipped a little lower. Tee thrust against her, giving over to her body's need as she grunted her assent. When Helen's finger pressed against her swollen flesh, she understood the reason for the wetness she'd been feeling for all these weeks. It was almost unbearably right, the way she could slide against Helen's firmness, each movement revealing places that made her pulse and tingle inside. When Helen rose up slightly onto her elbow, Tee went onto her back, her legs parting automatically, needing to have more, wanting Helen to move with her, just a little faster. Helen followed exactly the way she moved, even pressing a little harder, which made Tee moan with delight. She'd never imagined it would feel so good, that the sound of Helen's hoarse breathing near her ear would make her feel so wildly desperate. Something was building in her, growing like a fire, threatening to consume her. She would have been worried if it hadn't been for Helen's voice urging her on.

"That's right, baby. Keep going. Give it to me now."

"Oh!" Tee called, wanting to do just that. To give Helen all of herself, all of this incredible pleasure, this hot tightening inside. Helen moved to take her breast into her mouth again, and when her teeth grazed Tee's nipple, a streak of lightning ignited her and she burst, her back arching and her neck straining, her mouth crying *Oh* over and over in time with sensation after sensation that fired through her body. Time seemed to stretch out like the taffy they used to pull at the church socials, dripping and drooping between them until she was covered with the sweet stickiness and so heavy she could only lie there, breathing. Helen moved her though, pulling Tee onto her side as she lay back. "Oh," Tee said again but very softly this time, as if that would disguise the fact that it seemed to be the only word left in her vocabulary.

Helen's hands ran through Tee's hair and down her back, coming back up her sides, which made Tee shiver, her body echoing the remnants of the most amazing thing she had ever felt. After a few minutes Helen said, "I love you," stirring Tee with a wave of tenderness so profound she wanted to cry.

Tee swallowed, trying to find her voice. "I never knew...I never even let myself dream...oh, Helen." She burrowed her face into Helen's body, feeling embarrassed, like the way she used to when her stutter was so bad. But now, it wasn't that she couldn't say the words, it was that she had no idea what they would be. She tried the only thing that came close. "I love you, too."

"I'm really glad," Helen said, holding her close. Tee could hear the smile in her voice.

"So am I," she answered, savoring the moment. They were alone, lying naked together on this big bed, safe from intrusions or anyone's misunderstandings. Everything was perfect. She took in a deep breath, about to sigh contentedly when she realized something. What about Helen? She wanted to make Helen feel as good as she did. But how? All Helen had done was touch her. She didn't even know what else there was to do. Would that be enough for Helen, too? Tee reached her hand across Helen's body, her left hand feeling a little awkward as she took Helen's breast softly in her palm. "I want to do something nice for you."

"Mm. You are doing something nice for me."

"I mean, I want to do for you like you just did to me."

"I'd like that." Helen shifted a little, pulling back so Tee could see her face. "But you don't have to. I don't want you to feel that it's, like, required or something."

Tee shook her head. "It doesn't feel like that. It feels like I want to. I just—I'm not sure…"

"Come over here." Helen moved them so her body was on Tee's left side. "Since you're right-handed, you might find this a little easier."

Tee propped herself up, the way Helen had done. Starting at her mouth, she ran her fingers slowly down the center of Helen's body, between her breasts, past her navel, stopping at the mass of short dark hair. She liked it that Helen squirmed just a little. "I think you're the most beautiful woman I've ever seen."

"I bet I'm the only woman you've ever seen naked like this."

Tee sat up a little, indignant. "I've seen my sisters naked."

"Okay, okay." Helen waved her hands in surrender. "You are indeed a woman of the world."

Tee swatted as close to her behind as she could get. "And you are a smart aleck, Helen Tucker." Then something else crossed Tee's mind and her face grew solemn. "You've done this before, haven't you?"

Helen wondered if this was a time that *Don't lie* wasn't a good policy. In the time it took her to think about that, Tee lay back, very still, beside her.

"Never mind," Tee said, her voice flat. "I don't want to know."

"But I want to tell you," Helen said quickly, and suddenly she really did. "I've never done it quite this way. I mean, not in a nice place with a nice girl like you. That's why I kept putting it off with us. 'Cause I wanted it to be different."

Tee turned back to her side, looking at Helen thoughtfully. "All right," she said after a few seconds. "Tell me."

Helen sighed. "The first time was in an abandoned mine shaft. Carole Anne, one of the other miners' daughter, and me, we were young, just playing around really, trying to figure our bodies out, you know? Then I did it once in the bushes behind the school playground with Sally Ross, a girl who really wanted to be with my brother, but I'd convinced her I might be the next best thing." That wasn't exactly true, but it sounded better than the other way.

"Oh, Helen," Tee said, but Helen wasn't sure if she was feeling sorry or angry.

"The last time was before I got in the Army. That girl was just passing through, and she'd been begging outside the mine. She was a big tough gal, kinda like Casey, you know?" Tee nodded against her shoulder. "But my daddy felt sorry for her and brought her home for supper. She was out on the porch for a while, cleaning herself up, and I saw enough of her body that I…well, I got interested, you know? Then while we were eating it started to rain, so I told them she could stay in my room just till the rain let up. She wouldn't let me touch her, really, but that was the first time I…you know." Tee shook her head. Helen sighed. "The first time it felt for me like it just did for you."

Tee was quiet for a moment. "What was her name?"

"She told us she went by Dutch. I don't know anything else about her. She was gone when I woke up."

"Did you love her?" Tee's voice was small.

"God, no. I mean—"

Tee covered Helen's mouth with hers, stretching out on top of her and kissing her until they were both breathless. "You better not say yes. And you better not say that about anyone else but me, ever again."

Helen's eyes went wide. "Ever?"

"Ever," Tee confirmed with great finality. "I might not be tough like that Dutch girl or Casey, but you don't want to get on my bad side."

"No, ma'am," Helen agreed, "I do not."

Tee stayed where she was. When she had time to think about the girls she'd grown up with, she wondered how many of them she'd come to realize she'd actually been attracted to. She felt Helen's body twitch slightly beneath her. "Am I too heavy?"

"No."

She kissed Helen's neck and then her chest. Another twitch.

"Are you getting sleepy?" she asked.

"Negative."

Tee giggled. They'd learned that word in the radio class but they hadn't used it for a while. The slight shaking of her body as she laughed made Helen groan. She knew then that she was being a bit cruel, but she couldn't seem to help wanting to tease Helen some more. Sliding down until her center was between Helen's legs, she said, "Are you sure?"

"Uh-huh." Helen's voice had a slightly strained quality to it now.

Tee pushed herself against Helen. It felt so enjoyable that she did it again.

"Tee…" Helen pushed back, rubbing herself against Tee's body.

"Yes, baby?"

Helen caught her breath. Tee knew why. She'd never said that to Helen before, never called her by anything other than her name. But she liked saying it. She really liked saying it while she was between Helen's legs and Helen had that half-desperate tone in her voice. *Fully desperate*, she decided. That was what she wanted.

She put her fingers on Helen's nipples, squeezing as hard as she dared. She genuinely didn't want to hurt her. Just enough to get that response—the way Helen lifted her hips and tried again to rub against her and the way she moaned when Tee pushed back, just once. Tee stretched herself until she could take one nipple into her mouth, keeping her fingers on the other. Because Helen tasted so good and because she kept making that sound and rocking her hips, Tee put her leg there, letting Helen have some gratification.

"Did Dutch do this to you?" Tee demanded when she felt Helen's wetness on her skin.

"Who?"

Tee wasn't sure if Helen hadn't actually heard her or if she just knew that was the right answer. In one motion she moved her leg and slipped her hand through the fine hairs and into a slick heat so inviting that she cried out along with Helen. For a minute, she couldn't move. Eyes closed, mouth open, she breathed quickly, wanting to memorize everything about Helen's sex. The soft folds and the hard ridge of a delicate prominence that almost begged to be touched again. When she touched it, Helen jerked against her.

"*That*," Helen gasped.

Tee touched it again and then she didn't. She let her fingers glide along other parts, finding an opening that made Helen whimper in a different way. She remembered how sweetly Helen had asked, so she did the same. "Can I touch you there?"

"Anything," Helen said through gritted teeth. "Do anything you want. Just do it now. Please, Tee."

Please. That was desperate enough, Tee decided. She pushed in and found herself enclosed in a deeper, warmer place. Inside. She was inside Helen. Her head swam. "Oh God, Tee," Helen moaned. There was no apology this time and Tee didn't want one. She followed the movement of Helen's hips, the way Helen had followed her, moving a little and then a little more. Never all the way out, but finding the rhythm from her pounding heart and the panting sound of Helen's breathing. When she turned her hand just a little, she found she could move her thumb, too, and it touched that hard place where she'd been before and when she did Helen said *yes* in a way that let her know she was making Helen feel like what Helen had done to her. That knowledge made her almost mad with power, and she moved faster, fighting the urge to push harder, some tiny part of her mind cautioning her not to hurt this wonderful, beautiful woman who she loved so much. But Helen matched her, arms tightening around her, saying *yes* again, making Tee need to push, her thumb skating back and forth until Helen's back came up off the bed, her mouth pressing into Tee's neck, only partly muffling the long high cry that made something inside Tee certain, absolutely certain for the first time in her life, about exactly who she was. She was Helen Tucker's girl.

❖

If this is what being in love feels like, Helen thought, *I'll take it.* The morning sun was streaming in through the curtains they'd neglected to close and Teresa Owens was sleeping naked in her arms. Helen was admittedly a little sore in places, but the best kind of sore. Tee had proven to be exactly as she'd expected—passionate, a little wild, even, and oh so willing to be taken, and to take. Helen's stomach growled and Tee stirred.

"Did we sleep through reveille?" she mumbled.

Helen suppressed her laugh, kissing the top of Tee's head instead. "Not sure, baby. But I am sure I don't want to find out just yet."

"Mm." Tee's breathing evened out for a moment, before her head popped up. "Helen!" There was more than a hint of panic in her tone.

Helen made sure her voice was soothing. "Yeah, baby?"

Tee sat up and looked around for few seconds before she fell back, covering herself again with the sheet. Helen felt her relax and assumed she was remembering where they were.

"I don't think I ever want to leave here," Tee said. "Could we manage that?"

"Not if you want me walking the straight and narrow." *That hundred dollars would have bought us a lot more nights like this,* Helen thought, a little sullenly. She sighed. It wouldn't have bought her Tee, though. "But I can offer you breakfast."

"No," Tee said, wiggling in a little closer. "I'm buying this time."

"Careful, Miss Moneybags," Helen teased, running her hands down Tee's back. "I could be easily swayed by an offer like that."

When Tee's tongue teased around her ear, she jumped slightly, surprised at how quickly her body responded. "Do we have to go right now?" Tee asked, her voice a little raspy.

"That depends." Helen tried to be coy. "If you're willing to skip a shower and just grab something at that diner, I think we could sleep a little more and still make it for work."

"Sleep?" Tee asked, and the indignation in her voice made Helen laugh.

❖

It would have been more fitting, Bett thought in a rare moment of rationality, if this bombshell had hit a week later so it could coincide with Pearl Harbor Day. Rain was late as she often was toward the end of the week, finishing up accumulated paperwork. Bett had been sitting for so long that the early winter dusk had turned almost dark, but she hadn't gotten up to turn on any lights yet. The door opened and Rain moved quickly through the house, clearly assuming Bett wasn't home yet, turning on a few lights on her way back to her bedroom to change clothes. Coming back into the kitchen a few moments later, she must have seen the empty yellow telegram envelope sitting on the breakfast table, because she called Bett's name then, walking back up the hall. Bett sat at the dining table with her head in her arms, that phrase about chickens coming home to roost swirling around with the rest of her dreadful thoughts.

Turning on the light, Rain embraced her from behind. "Beloved, what's wrong? What's happened?"

Bett didn't want to lift her head, because she knew the evidence of her tears would be visible. Her words were muffled by her arms, but she knew Rain would still hear them. "Rain, you really do love me, don't you?"

"Yes, Bett. I love you, regardless of anything else. What is it?"

"Can you kiss me one time now so I can make sure it's the same later?" She hiccuped a little.

Rain's fingers lifted her chin gently and after only a quick glance, she enfolded her. "I'll kiss you before, during, and after. Just please tell me what's going on."

Bett took Rain's arm from around her and pressed the telegram into her hand. Then she pulled Rain into a chair beside her so she could watch her read the message. *How now, wife? Passage money arrived from Mummy today. Will be at your new Iowa digs on 20 Dec. for wedded travel to NYC X-mas. Love, as always, Phillip.*

Rain looked so confused that Bett put her head back in her hands. "I don't understand," Rain said. "Who was this written to? Who is Phillip?"

Bett steeled herself with a deep breath. She knew she had to look at Rain's face when she answered, even though she was afraid of what she would see. "It was written to me. Phillip is my husband. Smythe is his last name and my legal last name. We're married."

Rain didn't move at first. Her face didn't change. Bett watched her read the message again. Then she looked at Bett with an expression that made Bett close her eyes.

"Please let me explain," Bett began very quietly. She felt the air move and opened her eyes. Rain was gone.

Bett ran into the hall. The front door was still closed. She looked back to see Rain's form going into her bedroom. She came back out quickly and they met at the kitchen. Rain had her knapsack on her shoulder.

"Where are you going?" Bett asked, panic making her words almost clipped. "Rain, you have to listen—"

"Listen to what, Bett? To another lie about who you are? To another lie about what we are to each other?"

Rain's voice was so low and dark that Bett felt a chill, but she locked her arms around Rain's waist and spoke bravely. "You just said you loved me, regardless of anything else. Was that a lie, too?"

Rain broke her grasp easily and held her wrists so tightly that Bett had to clench her jaw to keep from crying out.

"Don't you dare talk to me about love." Rising anger emphasized each word. Then Rain dropped Bett's wrists abruptly. "I will love the memory of you until the day I die, but I am not staying here with a married woman as her husband comes home to—" Rain's jaw clamped down tightly as she turned toward the front door.

Desperately, Bett put her arms around her from the back, holding on for all she was worth.

"Rain, if you would truly honor our time together, you will hear me out. Then if you still want to go, I won't try to stop you." Bett closed her eyes, knowing those stakes were way too high, but knowing there was no other way to make Rain listen. She could feel Rain's shallow breathing, and knew she was struggling with her answer.

"Take your hands off me," Rain said tightly. Bett fought back a sob, fearing Rain would leave then, but she let go.

To her surprise, Rain turned to face her, but her tone was so vicious Bett almost wished she hadn't asked her to stay. "Tell me your story. Let me find a place for it in my memory of you."

Bett took in a shuddering breath, her knees wobbly. "I have to sit down." She moved to the couch. "Would you please sit, too?" Rain pulled a chair from the kitchen table over and turned it so the back was facing Bett, like some kind of fence between them. She straddled the seat and kept her knapsack on her shoulder.

Bett mentally replayed the conversation she'd had with her best friend, Suzanne Mynor, who she'd frantically called long-distance not long after the telegram arrived. Suzanne was the only person in her life who knew all about Phillip and all about Rain. They had talked the morning after Rain had first spent the night, and twice since then. During their other chats, Suzanne had pretended to be shocked when it became increasingly clear that her wild friend Bett was on the verge of settling down. Today she'd been unperturbed when a fearful Bett explained, "I didn't tell her at first because, well, it just wasn't important and I can't tell her now because…because now it's too important."

"You have to tell her the truth, Bett," Suzanne said calmly, as if it was the easiest, most obvious thing in the world. "If she really loves you, she'll understand. Tell her everything."

Tell her everything. It was too late to do anything else.

"I told you about Emma," Bett began, hoping the mention of her first love lost would stir some hint of compassion in Rain's expression. But Rain didn't even nod, she only blinked. There was no other motion, or emotion. "Well, when I got to Oxford, I was still aching for her, and even though I was relieved to find there were other women like me, I was afraid—I didn't want to feel pain like that again. And I thought what I wanted was wrong, perverted. That would explain why I felt so bad, why Emma breaking it off with me had hurt so much. I hated that I still had this need. So I just…I just went to bed with women, but I never stayed. I didn't want to get involved. I didn't believe there would ever be any chance for an actual relationship. I just wanted…I just wanted…"

"To fuck someone?" Rain filled in with the same terrible voice.

Knowing what she was thinking, Bett's tears started up again. "Rain, I know you don't believe me or you don't care, but I'm telling you it wasn't the same thing at all. I can't explain now—" Bett shook her head, trying to get herself together, knowing she had to go on. She gazed at her hands folded in her lap and took a breath.

"In the second term I attended lectures given by a woman who was to become my favorite tutor, Professor Cassidy Spencer. I was getting more serious about school, but I went with a group of friends to London for a weekend and I met this girl, Lois. She was nothing to me, but I bought her some things. We were only together two or three times before I ended it, but then she wouldn't leave me alone. She came to the college. She broke into my room. She waited outside the lecture halls. She wouldn't stop trying to see me. The situation was becoming intolerable, really, until one day when I was lingering in the hall, hoping Lois would give up and go away, and Professor Spencer asked me what was wrong. I tried to play it off, but she was so kind…I just broke down and told her everything. I was sure she'd be shocked or probably disgusted, but to my surprise she offered me a room at her place, somewhere Lois wouldn't know to find me. I ended up living there for a few months. She—Cassidy—she helped me, Rain. She helped me see my feelings weren't really wrong, they were just different from societal norms. She showed me studies of animals and plants, and explained how homosexuality existed everywhere she had ever worked or studied. Those whose hearts are the same as ours, Rain. It is a natural thing. It made me feel better, just to think that perhaps I was okay, that I was meant to be this way."

Bett dared to look at Rain. Her eyes were focused but Bett couldn't read her expression. "Cassidy and I became lovers, briefly, during this time, even though I didn't really feel that way about her. I thought she might be in love with me and I cared for her deeply but not…not like that. I know you would never do such a thing, Rain, but I was coming out of a very difficult time and she helped me so much, and I just let it happen."

Rain sighed. Surprised, Bett watched as Rain got up and went into the kitchen, filling two glasses with water. She came back and handed one to Bett without a word, sitting back down and drinking from her own glass. Bett was almost too emotional to drink, but she managed a small sip. It made her feel better. Encouraged, she went on.

"What I didn't know was Lois had somehow managed to get a letter to my father. It wasn't blackmail exactly—she was just desperate to find me. Or so she said. But the letter was full of incriminating details and language that disgusted my father, to the point that he sent some business associates over to handle the situation. Apparently, they first threatened Lois and then offered her enough money that she decided to get over me. Then they started in on Professor Spencer. Of course she wouldn't be bought. She also refused to tell me what was going on at first. I never actually saw these men, but I began to suspect something was wrong after she was becoming increasingly upset and anxious after a series of phone calls. Finally, I listened in on one of their conversations." Bett's head dropped. "It was terrible, the things they said. Her position, her livelihood, her reputation—they were going to take it all. Because of me."

"So I called my father and he offered me a deal. Find a suitable man, get married, and he would drop his vendetta against Cassidy." Bett lifted her head, no longer trying to hide her tears. "As much as I tried, I couldn't think of another way out. My father, as usual, had covered every angle. I asked him if I could finish school first. He told me I would need to get married within that year, but I could continue with school after that. I wanted a guarantee in writing that he would not touch Professor Spencer if I complied with his terms. He sent over a courier with a packet of evidence regarding the two of us, plus some material on another woman Cassidy had been with three years before. This woman was in government, making her way up through the ranks. I knew about them. I had met her. I liked her. So the damage my father would have been able to do would have been even more widespread than just Cassidy. This was a bonus, you see? Just to sweeten the deal. In the packet was a sworn affidavit that he had not made copies of anything."

Bett chanced another looked at Rain, but her face was still unreadable. "So I agreed, though I had in mind an angle of my own. I would find a suitable man, but one with whom I could strike a bargain. I was sure it would work if I could find someone who needed something from me—perhaps someone who was also homosexual or whose family could benefit in some way from the Carlton name, or the Carlton money. I'd offer him a marriage in name only, and after the ceremony we could each go on with our lives. Surely in the next year I could find someone who would fit the bill: a good family name, a decent reputation, and the slightest bit desperate. But I was also working very hard in school, and the time passed quickly. Then I met Phillip on a trip to Swanage at the end of the school term. He was handsome, funny, and charming—at the time. I didn't want my father involved at this stage, so I hired my own private investigator to look into his background. Most of it was routine. Phillip's father came from humble stock but had made good money in shipping in World War One. His mother had been a teacher, but she was able to quit once the family's fortunes improved. Phillip was the youngest of four boys, the rest of whom were gainfully employed. He had gone to a boys' prep school and was now at Cambridge. But my investigator also discovered that the business had fallen on hard times during the Depression and Phillip's parents were now living on much less than they'd become accustomed to. It was only with the financial help of his brothers that Phillip had been able to continue his education.

"We went out a few times. Trying not to let on what I knew about his finances, I would suggest we go someplace modest, but he'd insist on lavish dinners at the best restaurants. I noticed he could be sharp with the people serving him, but that's often the case with new money. Or that's what my mother used to tell me. Perhaps he thought his ability to dominate others would impress me. On one of our last dates, he drank more and his mood seemed to swing from ill-humored to depressed. I assumed he was feeling guilty for these expenditures, something that would be remedied if he accepted my proposition. In any case, I was running out of time."

After sipping her water again, Bett went on. "So I made my pitch to him, telling him I intended to remain an independent woman and that he was free to explore whatever interested him. I never specifically spelled out anything more because I didn't want to even hint at a discussion of sex, but I did say that our marriage would be in name only. He agreed. Needless to say, I didn't plan on having any friends at our ceremony. It would just be a few words at the register office anyway, but one night I was having doubts about my decision and I called Suzanne. After our conversation, I wasn't surprised that she came, offering what she referred to as immoral support. My mother was there, not my father. Afterward, we all had a lot to drink. A lot. When Phillip and I got back to our hotel room, we just collapsed on the bed. But then he started kissing me. I hated the way he kissed, but he was also running his hands on my body. I hadn't been with anyone in almost a year. I was drunk. I thought, *What the hell? Let's see what this is about.* In spite of everything I believed to be true about myself, I'd had enough alcohol to think perhaps I should at least try sex with a man. Maybe marriage would change me."

A long breath, almost like a sigh, came out of Bett's mouth. When she spoke again, her voice shook slightly. "We were half undressed and sloppy drunk. Whatever the cause, he couldn't manage. I don't remember what I said as he raised himself off me, but I started laughing.

It was the absurdity of the whole situation that set me off, not anything about Phillip personally, but he clearly took it that way. I didn't see his hand move, and it was several seconds before I figured out that the stinging sensation on my face was because he had slapped me. I had no control over the last of my laughter that was bubbling up out of my throat, even as I automatically pressed my fingers to the painful spot on my cheek. Apparently he couldn't tell that my amusement was dying down because he brought his hand back across, striking the other side of my face even harder. Involuntarily, I cried out, hurt and shocked in equal measure, and I slapped him back.

"Phillip's whole expression, especially his eyes, changed in such a way that I grew very frightened. I've often wondered if it would have made any difference if I'd tried to reason with him, or spoken in a gentle tone, reassuring him that it was all right. Or apologized, even. But I did none of those things. I did what I always do when I feel threatened. I fought back. Ineffectively, as it turned out. I was on my back, still slow and awkward with drink, while whatever inebriation Phillip felt had transformed into a level of fury unlike anything I had ever seen. My struggles only seemed to incite him to further violence, and his hands turned to fists as he loomed over me. He easily warded off my attempts to grasp his arms, and when I tried to protect myself by turning my shoulder, he punched me there as well.

"He was grunting with what I thought was the exertion of hitting me, but I began to feel that it was…exciting him. That's when it finally occurred to me to scream. He grabbed the edge of my blouse and stuffed it into my mouth. I tried to spit it out, but the next blow broke my nose." Bett shivered, hearing echoes of that awful crunching sound. "My eyes were watering so much I'm sure he thought I was crying. Maybe I was. The pain was so intense that I passed out for a while, I'm not sure how long. When I came to, there was blood everywhere. I had just managed to stand when Phillip came out of the bathroom with a towel. I could see that it had been white, but he'd obviously been trying to rinse it out, because it was an odd shade of pink. He held it out to me and told me to sit back down. I should have lied and said I'd heard someone in the hallway or some such. But instead, with all the strength I could muster, I told him I was leaving right then and he'd best get out of my way if he knew what was good for him. My voice sounded odd, rusty and feeble, even to my own ears, so I'm sure he felt no threat. With an expression that was almost sweet, he reached for my arm but I jerked away. The rush of pain caused by the sudden movement made me dizzy and nauseous and I hesitated, half closing my eyes. His punch to my stomach would have made me vomit, except I didn't have any air left to exhale. I fell back to the bed, trying to catch my breath, as he informed me I wasn't going anywhere until he taught me how a good wife should act. I was in too much pain to respond, and he seemed satisfied with my silence. But in the night, I tried twice more to get away, and as far as I can recall, it was after the second attempt that he cracked two of my ribs."

Bett looked away for a moment, breathing shallowly, and when she looked back she could see Rain's eyes were closed, though the knuckles on her hands gripping the chair were almost white. Somehow, that made it easier to go on. "Suzanne thought we must be having room service when we didn't show up for breakfast. She knocked on the door, pretending to be housekeeping. Just a joke, you know? My new husband asked for more towels, and when he opened the door, she could see the blood."

Bett's tone became bitter. "But it's amazing what money can clean up, isn't it? I went to hospital for three and a half weeks while Phillip went back to school. Apparently my father's faithful business associates paid him a visit to explain he was not to further damage the Carlton merchandise. When they were satisfied he would indeed keep silent about the whole matter, a monthly income was arranged, one he still receives. I have no idea what they told my father after that conversation. He didn't come, of course. My mother had already gone on to Paris to do some shopping, and I couldn't reach her. None of my other friends knew the truth. When I got back to Oxford, there was still so much bruising on my face that I had to wait another week before I could leave my rooms. I stayed with Cassidy again but, obviously, just as a friend. She was horrified by my appearance, but I told her I was mugged. Only Suzanne knew everything."

Rain's eyes opened again. They were brimming with tears, though her jaw remained tightly set. Bett just wanted to be through. "When I was able, I got my own place, but Cassidy and I remained good friends. I finished my degree. For the first year after the assault I did nothing but schoolwork, and some volunteer tutoring in one of the local schools during the summers. The next year, I went out a few times for dinner, always in a group, and never anything more. I didn't know if I could ever be with anyone again, and I wasn't sure if I even cared one way or the other. I wanted to stay on in England after graduation, but it was obvious war was coming, so I went back to California. I did encounter Phillip one time before I left. He came up to my table at a restaurant where I was eating with some friends. He apologized for his ungentlemanly behavior on our last encounter and said he hoped very much we might resume our relationship. He seemed almost pleased that I was shaking so hard I couldn't answer. After my friends suggested he should leave, I went to the bathroom and threw up. The thought that I would never run into him again was one thing that made it easier to leave England.

"Not quite sure what else to do, I went back to my father's house in California where I'd grown up. I don't know if it was my name or my education, but I got a job teaching English at a women's junior college. I worked hard at becoming a good teacher and the girls were sweet, but sometimes at night, I would feel so empty, so lonely, and I wondered if my life would ever be anything more, if I would ever feel anything more. Then the war started and I was let go. I had nothing else to do, so just out of boredom I went to some dinners and then parties, some of which were by invitations sent to my father and some I'd just heard about through friends. The women there were much more forward than I was accustomed to. There was lots of flirting, and I began to remember how much fun that could be. I began to feel almost like my old self again. Once I was accosted in the wine cellar of someone's home by a woman who kissed me very passionately for about ten minutes, then disappeared when a man's voice called. I was amazed at how my body responded to her. A few months later at the USO where I did some volunteering, some of us were dancing together, and when this woman put her arms around me and pulled me close, it felt like heaven. A month or so after that, at a dinner, I was seated next to a woman who was in the Navy—the WAVES, I believe it is. All through dinner, she touched my arm, she whispered in my ear, she had her hand on my leg under the table. By dessert, I could barely control my breathing. I excused myself to go to the bathroom. She was in the door behind me before I could even turn around. We had sex twice before someone else knocked at the door. It felt so good to feel normal. It felt so good to feel good."

Bett paused for a few seconds. "I was involved with two other women before I joined up. In both cases I enjoyed the sex but in neither case did I ever stay over for more than a little while afterward. I couldn't see myself ever doing that. I thought it just wasn't in me to be with someone like that, until…until it became the only thing I could see myself doing." She extended a trembling hand in Rain's direction. "The only thing I ever want to do."

Rain made no response and Bett went on, the rise and fall of her chest feeling increasingly heavy. "I know I should have told you all this, Rain. I know I should have told you before. You know what it's like when your story isn't an easy one to tell, but I know that's no excuse. But this is why, when you started talking that morning after Thanksgiving, I knew I had to tell you this first, before I could agree to meet your family. I couldn't say it then, because I was too afraid. Afraid I would ruin everything. Because you, Rain, you mean everything to me. I also want to say that in my heart, you and I are already family. But if you don't want…if hearing all this has changed the way you feel about me, I—" Bett fought to finish. "I'll understand."

Rain said nothing. The room was too dark for Bett to see her expression. The house had gotten colder. *I wish we were lying in front of the fire*, Bett thought, absently, her heart heavy. "I think I need to lie down now," she said, getting up. Rain said nothing. As she walked by, Bett stopped next to her lover. She hadn't moved and she didn't look over now. "You must understand, Rain, I did what I thought I had to do to save a dear friend. I never loved him. I never even liked him, really. Now I hate the very thought of him." She swallowed hard. Then she reached hesitantly and brushed her hand across Rain's cheek. When Rain didn't withdraw from her touch, Bett found the courage to say, "I learned about love from you." Feeling completely drained, she went into the bedroom and lay on the bed with her clothes still on. When she heard the front door open and, after a long moment, close, she turned into the pillow and began to cry once more, knowing she would never see Rain again.

Then a hand touched her hair and she felt the weight of Rain's body settling in beside her. Bett turned into Rain's chest, still crying. Rain had all her clothes on, too. When she put her arms around Bett, Bett began to cry harder. She said Rain's name once, her hand fisted in Rain's shirt, and Rain stated, "That man is not coming into this house."

"Okay." Bett sniffled, trying to stop crying.

"And he is not going with you to New York. I am."

"Okay." Her voice felt weak, but she knew Rain heard.

"You will divorce him." Rain's voice was very firm.

"All right, yes, I will." Bett nodded into Rain's chest.

"And then you will come with me to the reservation," Rain finished. "And we will find you another name. One that is not his."

"Okay," Bett said, crying again.

"And you must promise me this, Beloved. I need to know you will always fight, as you did with"—she swallowed—"that man. That is who and what you are and one of the reasons I love you. You did nothing wrong then, and if you will make me this promise, everything will be all right now." Rain kissed softly along Bett's hairline and began to hum her mother's song. Bett was still crying a little, but Rain sang some more and they rocked very gently. She lightly stroked Bett's back until Bett's breathing became softer and slower. When Rain whispered something to her in Lakota, a little smile crossed Bett's face. She liked to hear Rain speak her language, and even though she didn't know what the words meant, she could tell from the tone that she had said something very sweet.

"Thank you," she said, pleased that her voice was steady despite the hoarseness.

Rain breathed out a little chuckle. "You understand Lakota now?"

Bett snuggled a little closer, feeling wonderfully relieved when Rain's arms tightened around her in response. "Maybe I'm thanking you for something else," she suggested, intending to only let her eyes close for a moment. If Rain answered, she didn't hear it.

Chapter Sixteen

They woke feeling rumpled and very hungry. Rain turned onto her back, shifting uncomfortably. "I don't like sleeping in clothes," she said, trying to smooth out the wrinkles in her shirt. "I had to do it for almost two years once and I never got used to it."

"Let's change quickly and go to that diner in town for breakfast," Bett said, moving to her back also. "It's early enough. We can have a nice meal before we go to work."

"Okay," Rain said agreeably, starting to get up. Then she turned back to Bett, gathered her in her arms, and kissed her softly, looking into her eyes. "Are you feeling better, my beloved?"

Bett smiled, suddenly shy. "I am now."

Rain smiled back. "Good." She touched Bett's face. "Good." The second time it sounded more like a description.

Bett put her hand on Rain's arm. "I heard the front door last night after I came in here. Were you going to leave?"

Bett watched Rain's face working. "No," she said finally. "But I had to let my anger out before I could come to you."

"So you let it out the front door?" Bett asked. Rain nodded. "Where will it go?" Bett was so relieved that she had to giggle just a little bit.

"I don't know," Rain said, pretending to be annoyed at such a disrespectful question. "But you can bet someone will find it."

"I do hope it's not that little dog next door," Bett said, giggling some more. Rain started kissing her everywhere until she got to her toes, which always made Bett scream. It wasn't as much fun with their clothes on.

Bett felt a lightness in her spirit and fullness in her heart. *Everything is all right*, she said silently to her reflection in the mirror as she changed. *Rain really does love you.*

❖

There was only one open table at the diner, a four-top, but the hostess waved them over. After they got their tea and ordered, Bett looked up to see her lover's gaze on her, her eyes tender.

"You are looking at me more than usual," Bett observed.

"I am seeing you more than usual," Rains replied.

"More what?" Bett asked, a bit guardedly.

"More beautiful. More brave. More strong. More beloved."

Bett smiled deeply, thinking she might just reach for her hand. *Who would notice?*

"Hello, Lieutenant Rains. Hello, Sergeant Smythe." They looked up to see Helen and Tee standing at their table. Helen was smiling a bit shyly and Tee's eyes were wide with surprise.

Rains had been so absorbed in Bett she was taken completely off guard. She stood up to salute and then realized they should be saluting her. Instead, they just looked back and forth at each other.

"We were on our way to sit at the counter and then we saw you," Tee said.

"Yes, we ran into each other in line and decided to eat together," Bett said, without missing a beat. "Won't you join us?"

Helen glanced at Tee for the briefest second before she said, "Great!" and motioned Tee into the chair on the aisle before sitting in the one closer to the window. Rains sat back down, trying to identify the scent she'd picked up when Helen walked by her.

"We've already ordered, I'm afraid, but I'm sure the waitress will be by in a minute," Bett said smoothly, picking up her cup.

"So you both drink tea," Helen observed.

"Yes, we were just commenting on that when you came up," Bett smiled, shooting Rains a quick glance.

"We both drink coffee," Tee said. There was an awkward few seconds and then the waitress came up and they gave their orders.

"Didn't see that great-looking motorcycle of yours, Lieutenant. She parked around back?" Helen asked.

"No, I'm running today," Rains answered, trying to speak the falsehood in a normal tone of voice. They had ridden together in Bett's car and she was going to drop Rains at the base before going to her building. "I must do something to stay in shape somehow since I'm not working out with recruits anymore."

Bett gave her just the briefest nod and then smiled at Helen and Tee as she said, "Well, I for one don't miss those workouts, how about you two?" A general discussion on the ups and downs of basic training followed. Rains stayed out of it.

Their food came out together and as they ate, there was more discussion about Army food. When they were almost done, Helen said, "So you must live pretty close to here, Lieutenant."

Rains had her mouth full, so she just nodded and pointed vaguely back up the street.

"What about you, Sergeant?" Helen asked. "Do you and Faith live near here?"

Rains had swallowed and was just taking a drink of her tea. Trying not to spit it out, she began to choke. "Are you okay, Lieutenant?" Tee asked. Rains nodded, her eyes watering.

"Do you two live nearby also?" Bett said, not having answered the question, but giving the impression that she had. "Is that why you're here for breakfast?"

Tee's eyes cut quickly to Helen, who shook her head slowly. "Nah, we both still live on the base. We just, uh, we both had yesterday off so we…we decided to go for a drive. I borrowed a car and it broke down. It wasn't one from the motor pool, though," she added quickly, obviously not wanting to insult Rains.

"Most mechanics are so busy these days," Bett noted, "what with everyone trying to make do with what they have. Did you have to wait long?"

Tee nodded quickly. "Uh-huh. All night." Then she looked down and blushed.

"Yeah, that's right," Helen confirmed, not acknowledging Tee's expression. "We had to stay over in—What was the name of that town, Tee?" When Tee looked at her in a panic, Helen inclined her head a bit, adding, "You know. The one north of here? Where we had to stay over?"

Tee opened her mouth and then closed it. The motion made Rains look at her more closely, and she noticed Tee's lips were puffy, slightly bruised looking. Just then, her mind identified the scent she'd smelled on Helen. Sex. Definitely female. Biting back a smile, she came to Teresa Owens's assistance. "Ames?" she suggested, having seen the name on a map. It seemed feasible, and besides, she hated seeing that anxious expression on Private Owens's face. She was fairly certain that Tee was responsible for helping Helen Tucker get her head on straight, and she felt like she was still in Tee's debt for the false arrest. As much as she hated lying, she'd already done it herself, so it didn't seem fair for these two young women—who had already been through so much together—to be under such strain first thing in the morning. Especially on what appeared to be a significant morning.

Helen turned to her, gratitude obvious in her expression. "Yeah, that's it. Ames. So we finally got the car fixed this morning and then we…well, we thought we were too late to get back to the base for breakfast, so we stopped here to eat." She nodded with great conviction.

Everyone breathed out, relieved the story was finished. Bett glanced out the window. Just up the street was the Hotel Fort Des Moines. Word among the girls was they accepted WAC guests with no questions asked. Tee followed her gaze and her blush deepened. Bett knew better than to ask how or even where the car was. She felt deeply grateful that she and Rains didn't have to scrounge for a place to be on a rare day off together. She smiled at Tee and said, "I'm sure you had a nice evening, at least. Sometimes adventures like that are things we remember fondly, after the fact."

Tee smiled back, clearly relieved, and nodded. "I'm sure I'll remember this one."

Helen's tone was a bit dejected as she returned to the earlier topic. "It's so hard to find a decent place in town on our Army pay. What's your rent, Lieutenant?"

"My rent? Well, I don't know exactly." She cleared her throat. "I mean, Emma pays the rent and I pay for food and utilities. It seems to work out okay."

Bett was putting down her teacup, giving a little cough as if suddenly congested. "Bett?" Tee said. Bett gestured that she was all right. "Man, that tea must be strong stuff."

Bett nodded, swallowing again. "So I take it you two would like to move off base together?" When Rains gave her a look, frowning, she persisted. "What? That's clearly what we're discussing, isn't it?"

Helen jumped in. "Yeah, but we don't really know. I mean, we haven't made plans or anything. We're just…"

Tee finished, "Talking."

Suddenly remembering Rains's history with Tucker and Owens, Bett looked abruptly at her watch. She wouldn't get any more details from these two with Lieutenant Rains here. Plus, she knew how her lover hated lies, and the morning was already rife with them. "Oh, I really must be going." This would be the earliest she had been at work since the first day. She dropped a five on the table. "Please let me treat."

"Thanks, Sergeant Smythe!" Helen said, grinning.

"Nice to see you again, Lieutenant," Bett said, trying not to acknowledge Rains's glare.

"Sergeant." Rains's voice was a bit chilly. "Thank you for breakfast."

"'Bye," Tee said. "Maybe we'll see you here again sometime."

"Yes, that would be nice." Bett smiled and left.

Helen indicated the bill lying on the table and lowered her voice knowingly. "She's really rich, isn't she, Lieutenant?"

Rains sat up a bit straighter. "I wouldn't know, Private."

"Yes, you do. You must have seen her file when we were in basic. Come on, Lieutenant. Her daddy's somebody real important, isn't he?"

"Private Tucker, you are out of line," Rains said firmly.

"Okay, okay, but you gotta admit—she's living off base, she's got a car. You can't afford those extras on a private's pay."

"Maybe not even on two privates' pay," Tee agreed.

Rains stood. "Ladies, I'll leave you to finish up here."

"Lieutenant, wait." Helen looked across the table, and when Tee met her eyes they remained focused on each other for several seconds. From their expressions, it was obvious something very profound had happened in their relationship. Then Helen took a breath. "Tee and I, we wanted to thank you again for, you know, for not—"

"For everything you've done for us," Tee finished.

Rains liked seeing that Owens wasn't afraid to speak up for herself these days. She would have to tell Reverend Culberson about her observation. "Private Owens, Private Tucker, I told you then and

I'll tell you again. The most important thing to me is that you do your jobs to the best of your abilities and honor your country with your service—both of you. Do that, and I'll be satisfied my decision was the right one."

Rains walked out. As soon as she hit the sidewalk, she started to run toward the base. A few hours later, Sharon had gone to lunch, so she answered herself when the phone rang.

"Rains," she said. She heard a little giggle on the other end.

"Emma?"

Rains knew exactly who it was. Sharpening her tone, she said, "Faith?" drawing out the name questioningly.

The line disconnected. Rains went through the rest of the workday chuckling at odd times for no apparent reason.

On her way back home that night, Bett stopped at Western Union. She pulled Phillip's wrinkled telegram out of her purse and put it on the counter.

"I need to send a reply to this right away."

The young woman behind the counter handed her a form to print in her response. Bett wrote, *Keep the money. Do not come. You are not welcome here or in NY.* She thought for a moment and added, *I am not your wife.*

The clerk popped her gum and raised her eyebrows, looking at Bett across the counter as she read the reply. "That's tellin' him, honey."

Damn right, Bett thought. *To hell with my father. Next time, I'm marrying for love.*

"Bett's money not only paid that bill and the tip, but look." Helen held out her hand excitedly, showing off the remaining change. Then she grabbed Tee's hand and pushed one of the bills into it, closing her fingers gently into a fist. Her eyes focused on Tee's. "That's for you to buy that nightie we were talking about."

"No, Helen," Tee protested, blushing as she tried to hand it back. Helen put her hands in her pockets and started walking faster, whistling.

"Wait." She scurried to catch up. "All right," she whispered. "But don't say something like that out on the street like this."

"Why not? You afraid Lieutenant Rains got supersonic hearing or something?"

"No." Tee gave a little glance around her, just in case. "But who would have thought we'd run into her at a diner in town?"

"Eating breakfast with Bett Smythe?" Helen agreed. "I guess it's true that wonders never cease."

Tee stopped walking for a second, her expression contemplative. "Helen, when we first saw them…"

Helen had gone on for a few steps but she came back. "Yeah?"

"I just…I had the feeling their conversation was very personal, you know? Like maybe we shouldn't have intruded."

Helen frowned, as if trying to remember. All she was thinking at the time was how she hoped Bett wouldn't mention that she'd asked her out. Flirting that way was just a reflex, something being around a beautiful woman seemed to bring out in her, like throwing a line in a pond where you didn't even know if there were any fish. That was another habit she needed to reel in right quick. Tee had made it clear last night that she wouldn't tolerate that kind of fishing for one second. *Not like I'd have a chance with Bett anyway.* But in recalling that moment outside the motor pool, she considered how Bett's tone had turned warm and playful when Lieutenant Rains appeared and how the lieutenant had smiled and the way they'd moved closer to each other once she'd left. "You think there's something going on with those two?"

On the surface it seemed ridiculous. The two women had clashed repeatedly during basic training in what was clearly a battle of wills. Overall, she was of the opinion that Lieutenant—then, Sergeant— Rains had won, although Bett had clearly gotten in her shots. At times, everyone in the squad could see evidence of some real tension there.

"I don't know," Tee said, smiling at Helen, waiting so patiently for her answer the way she always had. Today, when they'd noticed the lieutenant and then realized Bett Smythe was sitting with her, for just an instant she thought she'd seen something sweet passing between them. She shook her head. Whatever the case, it wasn't her business. Her thoughts turned serious. "But do you think Bett figured out about us?"

Helen jerked her head a little and they started walking again. "Bett knows we're best friends. That's all."

Tee decided not to mention the way Bett had looked at the hotel before she'd made that comment about remembering certain evenings fondly. *Fondly* didn't begin to describe the way she remembered last night. She leaned into Helen a little, letting their hands brush a few times as they walked. "Do you still love me even if we don't have a place of our own right now or a car or five dollars to throw around first thing in the morning?"

Helen stopped and faced her. "Baby, I'd love you if we lived in a shoebox and had to eat worms. No car? Heck, I'll drive you in the finest vehicle Uncle Sam has to offer." She stepped closer and put her hands on Tee's arms, making Tee's heart beat faster. "And I'll love you even if we don't have two nickels to rub together." She glanced at the sky. "Which might happen soon if I don't get to work on time. 'Cause I can tell you, whatever it is that Rains gets up to at night, she's still hard as nails in the morning."

Tee hugged her, right there on the street. She couldn't help it. "I love you, too," she whispered in Helen's ear.

"Thank God," Helen said.

About the Author

Jaycie Morrison is a second-generation native Dallasite who is also in love with Colorado and now splits her time between the two. She lives with her wife of over two decades and their spoiled dog. As youngsters, she and her friends entertained themselves making up and acting out stories featuring characters from popular TV shows or favorite bands—lots of action and a little romance even then! A voracious reader, she always wondered what it would be like to write a book and found that once she started, it was almost impossible to stop. Her Love and Courage series combines her appreciation of the written word and her interest in history.

Catch up with Jaycie's latest at www.jayciemorrison.com or reach her at jaycie.morrison@yahoo.com.

Books Available From Bold Strokes Books

A Date to Die by Anne Laughlin. Someone is killing people close to Detective Kay Adler, who must look to her own troubled past for a suspect. There she finds more than one person seeking revenge against her. (978-163555-023-8)

Captured Soul by Laydin Michaels. Can Kadence Munroe save the woman she loves from a twisted killer, or will she lose her to a collector of souls? (978-162639-915-0)

Dawn's New Day by TJ Thomas. Can Dawn Oliver and Cam Cooper, two women who have loved and lost, open their hearts to love again? (978-163555-072-6)

Definite Possibility by Maggie Cummings. Sam Miller is just out for good times, but Lucy Weston makes her realize happily ever after is a definite possibility. (978-162639-909-9)

Eyes Like Those by Melissa Brayden. Isabel Chase and Taylor Andrews struggle between love and ambition from the writers' room on one of Hollywood's hottest TV shows. (978-163555-012-2)

Heart's Orders by Jaycie Morrison. Helen Tucker and Tee Owens escape hardscrabble lives to careers in the Women's Army Corps, but more than their hearts are at risk as friendship blossoms into love. (978-163555-073-3)

Hiding Out by Kay Bigelow. Treat Dandridge is unaware that her life is in danger from the murderer who is hunting the woman she's falling in love with, Mickey Heiden. (978-162639-983-9)

Omnipotence Enough by Sophia Kell Hagin. Can the tiny tool that abducted war veteran Jamie Gwynmorgan accidentally acquires help her escape an unknown enemy to reclaim her stolen life and the woman she deeply loves? (978-163555-037-5)

Summer's Cove by Aurora Rey. Emerson Lange moved to Provincetown to live in the moment, but when she meets Darcy Belo and her son Liam, her quest for summer romance becomes a family affair. (978-162639-971-6)

The Road to Wings by Julie Tizard. Lieutenant Casey Tompkins, Air Force student pilot, has to fly with the toughest instructor, Captain Kathryn "Hard Ass" Hardesty, fly a supersonic jet, and deal with a growing forbidden attraction. (978-162639-988-4)

Beauty and the Boss by Ali Vali. Ellis Renois is at the top of the fashion world, but she never expects her summer assistant Charlotte Hamner to tear her heart and her business apart like sharp scissors through cheap material. (978-162639-919-8)

Fury's Choice by Brey Willows. When gods walk amongst humans, can two women find a balance between love and faith? (978-162639-869-6)

Lessons in Desire by MJ Williamz. Can a summer love stand a four-month hiatus and still burn hot? (978-163555-019-1)

Lightning Chasers by Cass Sellars. For Sydney and Parker, being a couple was never what they had planned. Now they have to fight corruption, murder, and enemies hiding in plain sight just to hold on to each other. Lightning Series, Book Two. (978-162639-965-5)

Summer Fling by Jean Copeland. Still jaded from a breakup years earlier, Kate struggles to trust falling in love again when a summer fling with sexy young singer Jordan rocks her off her feet. (978-162639-981-5)

Take Me There by Julie Cannon. Adrienne and Sloan know it would be career suicide to mix business with pleasure, however tempting it is. But what's the harm? They're both consenting adults. Who would know? (978-162639-917-4)

Unchained Memories by Dena Blake. Can a woman give herself completely when she's left a piece of herself behind? (978-162639-993-8)

Walking Through Shadows by Sheri Lewis Wohl. All Molly wanted to do was go backpacking...in her own century. (978-162639-968-6)

Freedom to Love by Ronica Black. What happens when the woman who spent her life worrying about caring for her family finally finds the freedom to love without borders? (978-1-63555-001-6)

A Lamentation of Swans by Valerie Bronwen. Ariel Montgomery returns to Sea Oats to try to save her broken marriage but soon finds herself also fighting to save her own life and catch a murderer. (978-1-62639-828-3)

House of Fate by Barbara Ann Wright. Two women must throw off the lives they've known as a guardian and an assassin and save two rival houses before their secrets tear the galaxy apart. (978-1-62639-780-4)

Planning for Love by Erin Dutton. Could true love be the one thing that wedding coordinator Faith McKenna didn't plan for? (978-1-62639-954-9)

Sidebar by Carsen Taite. Judge Camille Avery and her clerk, attorney West Fallon, agree on little except their mutual attraction, but can their relationship and their careers survive a headline-grabbing case? (978-1-62639-752-1)

Sweet Boy and Wild One by T. L. Hayes. When Rachel Cole meets soulful singer Bobby Layton at an open mic, she is immediately in thrall. What she soon discovers will rock her world in ways she never imagined. (978-1-62639-963-1)

To Be Determined by Mardi Alexander and Laurie Eichler. Charlie Dickerson escapes her life in the US to rescue Australian wildlife with Pip Atkins, but can they save each other? (978-1-62639-946-4)

True Colors by Yolanda Wallace. Blogger Robby Rawlins plans to use First Daughter Taylor Crenshaw to get ahead, but she never planned on falling in love with her in the process. (978-1-62639-927-3)

Heart Stop by Radclyffe. Two women, one with a damaged body, the other a damaged spirit, challenge each other to dare to live again. (978-1-62639-899-3)

Undercover Affairs by Julie Blair. Searching for stolen documents crucial to U.S. security, CIA agent Rett Spenser confronts lies, deceit, and unexpected romance as she investigates art gallery owner Shannon Kent. (978-1-62639-905-1)

Taking Sides by Kathleen Knowles. When passion and politics collide, can love survive? (978-1-62639-876-4)

Unexpected by Jenny Frame. When Dale McGuire falls for Rebecca Harper, the mother of the son she never knew she had, will Rebecca's troubled past stop them from making the family they both truly crave? (978-1-62639-942-6)

Canvas for Love by Charlotte Greene. When ghosts from Amelia's past threaten to undermine their relationship, Chloé must navigate the greatest romance of her life without losing sight of who she is. (978-1-62639-944-0)

Repercussions by Jessica L. Webb. Someone planted information in Edie Black's brain and now they want it back, but with the protection of shy former soldier Skye Kenny, Edie has a chance at life and love. (978-1-62639-925-9)

Spark by Catherine Friend. Jamie's life is turned upside down when her consciousness travels back to 1560 and lands in the body of one of Queen Elizabeth I's ladies-in-waiting...or has she totally lost her grip on reality? (978-1-62639-930-3)

Thorns of the Past by Gun Brooke. Former cop Darcy Flynn's heart broke when her career on the force ended in disgrace, but perhaps saving Sabrina Hawk's life will mend it in more ways than one. (978-1-62639-857-3)

You Make Me Tremble by Karis Walsh. Seismologist Casey Radnor comes to the San Juan Islands to study an earthquake but finds her heart shaken by passion when she meets animal rescuer Iris Mallery. (978-1-62639-901-3)

Girls Next Door, edited by Sandy Lowe and Stacia Seaman. Bestselling romance authors tell it from the heart—sexy, romantic stories of falling for the girls next door. (978-1-62639-916-7)

Complications by MJ Williamz. Two women battle for the heart of one. (978-1-62639-769-9)

Crossing the Wide Forever by Missouri Vaun. As Cody Walsh and Lillie Ellis face the perils of the untamed West, they discover that love's uncharted frontier isn't for the weak in spirit or the faint of heart. (978-1-62639-851-1)